A Precarious Man

ATOPON BOOKS

Atopon Books
907 15th Street
Santa Monica, California 90403
United States

This is a work of fiction. Names, places, characters, and incidents either are the product of the author's imagination or are used fictitiously. Any resemblance to actual persons, living or dead, events, or locales is entirely coincidental.

Library of Congress Cataloguing-in-Publication data
Names: Mattessich, Stefan, author.
Title: A precarious man / Stefan Mattessich.
Description: Santa Monica, CA: Atopon Books, 2023.
Identifiers: LCCN: 2022943335 | ISBN: 979-8-9862104-6-9 (hardcover) | 978-1-64713-035-0 (paperback) | 979-8-9866109-5-5 (ebook)
Subjects: LCSH Psychological fiction. | Cosmopolitanism in literature. | Precarious employment—Fiction. | Neoliberalism in popular culture—Fiction. | Academia—Fiction | Los Angeles (Calif)—Fiction. | Paris (France)—Fiction. | New York (NY)—Fiction. | BISAC FICTION / General | FICTION / City Life | FICTION / Romance / Polyamory
Classification: LCC PS3613.A8438 P74 2023 | DDC 813.6—dc23

Cover design: Nataša Prosenc Stearns

Cover images: Blue background © Adobe Stock / Arlenta Apostrophe. Panoramic view of Manhattan @ Adobe Stock / sborisov

Printed in the United States of America

Lost are we and only so far punished
That without hope we live in desire.
—Dante, *Inferno*, Canto IV

Amor Fati

1

Nick Moran met his agent Lou Perkins one day at the office of a studio executive in Culver City. They came to discuss a screenplay he'd been hired to write and submitted the week before, an adaptation of Cuban novelist Alejo Carpentier's 1953 masterpiece *The Lost Steps,* about a disillusioned composer who leaves New York in vain pursuit of an authentic life on the Orinoco River. Nick knew little about Latin America, or little more than any reasonably curious outsider, and his Spanish was only passable, but he'd tried his best to express the tragic story in three acts, setting scenes, updating dialogue, and finessing at least some of its baroque symbolism onto the page. He hoped he'd done it justice, though what that might be given the nature of the task was hard to say.

He took his seat at a conference table in the office, on the top floor of the studio's ziggurat-shaped headquarters, and waited while Lou got the preliminaries out of the way. Through banded windows he had a view of the Baldwin Hills, dotted with the pump jacks and storage tanks of what must have been LA's last oil field. The walls were decorated with framed cells of cartoon characters—Bugs Bunny, Tom and Jerry, Mickey Mouse—all frozen in the midst of some calamity or other. Animation was a personal interest of the executive, Don Torrance. The first time Nick had met him, he'd proclaimed SpongeBob SquarePants the equal of silent film star Buster Keaton, that other paragon of artless ingenuity. Nick hadn't thought much of the comparison—Buster Keaton might appeal to children without SpongeBob being a modernist icon—but he'd held his tongue, hoping what Don lacked in judgment he compensated for in the cunning it took to get things done in Hollywood. Nick needed his help more than an argument. He'd made no decent money as a screenwriter in over a year, and relying on credit cards to pick up the slack had set him back rather badly. Something had to break for him soon.

When conversation turned to the matter at hand, Don's chatty tone changed. "What is this, Lou?" he asked, opening the script where it sat on the table. "Is this a screenplay or another novel?" He seemed to want an answer, yet he studiously avoided looking Nick in the eye. It was all about Lou. His credibility was also on the line. Nick had only gotten the job thanks to Lou's persuasion.

"I don't see the story," Don said. "I see it in the book. Very simple. The guy leaves the city with his mistress. He dumps her for another girl in the forest. It's bliss. But he can't commit and goes back to his wife, who hates him. Another guy gets the girl instead, and he has nothing."

"It's a draft, Donnie. We can work on it."

"There's too many words. Look." He held up the opened screenplay, where, indeed, there were many words. At last he shifted his gaze to Nick, more glued to his chair than he was before. "If you want to write a novel, go ahead. Write your own novel. But don't waste my time. I don't want to know what you think. I don't want to be impressed by your words. What I want is something I can use."

"Give us your notes," said Lou, "and we'll work up another draft."

"I don't know where to start." He flipped derisively through the pages. "What's all this about circles? Everything's round. Moons, drums, rotundas, Ferris wheels, waterwheels, planispheres. What *is* a planisphere anyway?"

"A map," said Nick.

"Then just say 'map' and move on."

Nick braced himself for a fight he already felt pretty sure he was going to lose. Don had seized the high ground. "The story has a circular design," he explained, forging ahead. "It's not linear. The end is in the beginning. The protagonist is caught in a loop. He keeps making the same mistakes. The more things change, the more they stay the same. The author suggests this paradox in those details."

Don and Lou gaped at him.

"The story's there," he said, disconcerted. "I stuck as close as I could to the plot. If anything, I was too literal about it."

"It has no heart," Don said, agreeing, Nick supposed. "I don't know who this character is. I don't know what he wants."

"He doesn't want what he wants. That's the whole problem. He's alienated from himself, and not in the sense of being out of touch with his feelings. It's when he gets in touch, when he gets a hold of his own nature and finds his own voice on the river, that he feels the pull back to a decadent life he hates. Nothing about this character makes sense if not that breaking with his past connects him to it. Escaping his own time and history synchronizes with the deepest tendencies of both. The truth he's after is an illusion. The real Orinoco's in his mind."

Even Nick heard how this perfect disaster of a speech sounded in that room. He could only wonder what he was thinking. Not about tactics, that's for sure. Certainly not about breaks and debt traps. He had to remind himself that it was his job to get the idea across in terms Don would understand.

"Take Buster Keaton," he said, in a kind of flanking maneuver. "He's always at odds with authorities, rules, forces, right? He can't stop being a misfit even when he tries. He goes through a revolving door for a job, and it shoots him out again. He steals a man's wallet by continually returning it. He follows the steps to be a good detective and promptly fingers himself. Each time this happens he's perplexed, but not just because the world is against him. The world is a reflection of his mental state. His perplexity is about his own motives, his own desires."

"He's caught in a loop," Lou said helpfully.

"Or he doesn't want what he wants. He's ambivalent, like the guy in *The Lost Steps*."

"Only the other way around."

"What?" Nick said, not following.

"Keaton doesn't really want in," Lou said. "Your guy doesn't really want out."

"Right." Nick felt the strain this nice distinction gave to his analogy. It might not have been as apt as he thought. "But the idea's the same."

"That's why the guy won't fuck the mistress at the bar?" Don asked.

"Well, sure. He doesn't respect her."

"Or his wife in the bedroom?"

"They're estranged."

"Does he want to fuck the girl in the forest or not?"

"He loves her, yes. The question is why he sabotages that."

"Because he's got his head up his ass, that's why," Don said, obviously not meaning the character anymore. The room went quiet. He threw the screenplay down with the air of someone whose patience had run out.

"We can't use this script," he declared. "It's too 'ambivalent.' We'll have to start over."

"Come on, Donnie."

"No." He jerked a thumb at Nick. "I don't think he's got a heart either. We'll have to find another writer. Someone I can trust. We're talking to Mark Peploe."

"Give us another chance," Lou said.

Ignoring this, he asked Nick, "Do you know Mark Peploe?"

"I've heard of him."

"Do you think you could do as good a job?"

"It would be a less expensive job anyway."

"Do you think he'd give a shit about planispheres?"

"He might."

"No way!" Don cried. "He's a professional. He finds the heart of the story and he cuts it out, like an Aztec. He holds it up"—here he raised an upturned hand to heft its weight—"and lets the blood drip onto the floor."

Nick lost his composure at this point, and not simply because he was being insulted. Don had touched with his ghastly simile on another of the novel's main themes. The protagonist often compared himself and those he met on the river to conquistadors looking for El Dorado. It was a way for the author to associate possessive desires for escape into the primitive with a civilizing mission, the true object of reproach. Myths of the natural man were the last things Carpentier wanted to tell. That Don wanted Nick to tell one he might have been able to understand. The aim was to make an entertaining movie, not do the novel justice. That Don wanted him to *be* in one was, however, more than he could take. His job description didn't extend quite that far.

Rising to his feet, he feared in the surge of heat and hurt pride that he might lose his balance. "Can I at least have the money you owe me?" he stammered out. Another reason to be there was to collect the second half of his fee. "I don't care what you do with the script, but I need that money."

"Why should I give it to you?" Don demanded, rising in turn. He was a pit bull of a man, short and compact with a spatulate face, and not used to being crossed. "What do I get for it? I'm not in the habit of giving away my money."

"It's not your money."

"Donnie, let's work this out between us, okay?" interjected Lou, easing Nick toward the door. "Come on. You won't get what you want like this."

"He owes me, Lou," he said, pushing back.

"I know."

"There's a contract."

"Not for garbage," said Don.

"*Even* for garbage," Nick shot back. "How would you know anyway? Everything that comes out of your mouth is garbage."

"Get out of my office."

"It's a good draft." Nick heard in the remoteness of his voice just how little trust in himself he really had. That was the true failure here. "As good as anything Mark Peploe might write."

"Fuck you and Mark Peploe!" Don bellowed, charging around the table imbued suddenly with the force of a predator about to strike. "You can't hold Mark Peploe's jock, you cunt, you fucking pussy. Get out of my office! Get out of my life! I don't want to see your face around here ever again."

Lou opened the door and shunted Nick out before him. They rode the crowded elevator in a state of shock that continued through the atrium under its slanted glass canopy to the sidewalk out front. There Nick headed for a corner of Washington Boulevard, away from the entrance to the building, as monumental as it was tacky in its nod to the vernacular of ancient Mesopotamia, and shakily lit a cigarette. It was a bright autumn afternoon on a commercial strip. Cars came to a halt at the intersection, their chrome and glass glinting, a febrile heat emanating from under their hoods. An old Japanese man with a cane and an eye patch had started into a crosswalk, his progress slow.

"Got another one of those?" Lou asked. Nick pulled a cigarette from the pack, gave it to him, and offered him a light. "I'll go back up there in a minute."

"I'm sorry, Lou."

"Forget about it." He took a drag and squeezed the smoke out the side of his mouth. "The guy's a hothead. You'll get your money. He doesn't want any trouble."

"I thought I gave him a solid script."

"You did."

"I didn't think it was that bad."

"It's not. It needs work, that's all. He didn't like it because it's smart. It reminds him how much of a moron he is."

That might not have been sincere. The two men had known each other a long time. They had the same appetites if not the same tolerance for nicety. But it hardly mattered now. A part of Nick's spirit had broken past caring. "I think it's the end for me," he said, in the hushed tones of revelation. "I can't do this anymore."

"It's a rough business," Lou observed. "It beats you up."

Nick noticed that the Japanese man had failed to reach the other corner before the light turned green again for the cars. They slid impatiently around him, and he waved his cane as if to fend them off. It was a familiar sight. LA showed no mercy if you couldn't keep up.

"I've been thinking it's time to make a change," Lou said then. Nick waited, fearing another disappointment. But Lou surprised him by what he came out with next. "I mean for myself. I need a break. Maybe I need a long break."

"Tired of being an agent, eh?"

"It becomes routine. I've been signing anything that moves for thirty-five years now. That gets under the skin."

"I bet."

"Lately I've been itching to travel. I haven't been to Asia in a long time. Thailand, Vietnam, places like that. Hell, maybe I'll take a trip around the world—buy a ticket on the Trans-Siberian Railroad. I hear that's a fun thing to do. What do you think?"

"Sounds like a good idea."

"Yeah," he said, nodding with more vigor as the plan solidified in his mind. "I could end up in Europe—maybe stop by and see Evan."

Evan was Nick's father, an actor. Lou had been his agent, too, before a diagnosis of Parkinson's had him retiring to Paris with his French wife and infant daughter. No one missed him in LA more than Lou. Their friendship meant a lot to him. Nick suspected, in fact, that his father was the reason Lou had stuck with him as long as he had. Without that connection, in all likelihood, he wouldn't have thought much more of him than Don did.

Lou coughed significantly. He had something else on his mind. "I was hoping for a better time to bring this up," he said, "but, well . . .I've been talking to this guy about renting him my house."

Nick was also Lou's tenant. He lived in a small apartment that took up the bottom floor of his hillside home in Castellammare, a well-heeled neighborhood near the juncture of Sunset Boulevard and the Pacific Coast Highway, not far from the Malibu border.

"He wants to move in as soon as possible."

"Uh-huh."

"And he wants the downstairs for his office. He runs his own home security business."

"I see."

"The thing is, he'd be paying a lot of money: fifteen grand a month, can you believe that? I bought the place for $45,000 back in the day. But it doesn't make sense me asking him to take on a tenant."

"No."

"I said I'd ask how soon you might be able to find a new place to live."

"I'm broke, Lou."

"Right." He rubbed an overtanned cheek with his free hand. Past sixty, Lou stayed in preternaturally good shape by riding his bike most weekends in the Santa Monica Mountains. "Like I said, Donnie'll cough up the money sooner or later. I'll make sure of it."

"That's not going to help for long."

"I know."

"I guess I have to find a job. A real job."

"Funny you should say that." Lou flicked his half-finished cigarette to the curb. "I was talking to a producer friend of mine, Marty Siegel. He has his own company. He tells me he can't find a good assistant."

"An assistant?"

"Yeah."

Nick stared. "You think I should try that?"

"Why not? Marty's a smart guy. You'd like him. And the company's small. He runs it out of his backyard. He's looking to do the tasteful small movie. Nothing too big. Five to ten-million-dollar deals tops. The kind you're good at."

"I don't know."

"I could talk to him," Lou said, averting his gaze in what for him seemed an unusually civil gesture, "if you want me to."

Nick didn't want him to, but it was clear he had little choice. Whatever else he decided to do, he'd have to start earning the rent on a new apartment right away. Tasting the filter on his cigarette after one final drag, he thought, with Buster Keaton more than Alejo Carpentier it appeared, that there really was no escaping your own time and history.

2

Don was right in his fashion. Nick wasn't a natural at screenwriting. He hadn't come to the profession with the same feeling and ambition most people did. He'd come much more divided of mind, a typical enough state for him but acute this time on account of his father, with whose success Nick had a complicated relation. He would have preferred almost anything to entering his father's sphere of influence when he did just that six years ago. He'd always headed in other directions, in search of other arenas where he might distinguish himself without invidious comparisons.

That, sadly, had led at an earlier stage of his life to a dead end. He'd spent the better part of his twenties getting a PhD in comparative literature at NYU (with modernism his field of specialization), and a good three years on top of that trying for a career as an academic somewhere, anywhere he could find it, to no avail. The job market had collapsed on him. Nothing he did—no commitment made, no competence acquired, no distinction won—set him apart from the competition.

It was broken on this wheel of futile effort that he finally took his father's advice and tried his hand at a screenplay. In a defiant mood one Christmas break between semesters spent working as an adjunct writing teacher at various New York colleges, he hammered out a story about two brothers—one an idealistic journalist who investigates the other, a hotshot bond trader involved in a Ponzi scheme—loosely based on the rivalry between Cain and Abel. He sent it to his father, who passed it on to Lou, and within a month it sold for $150,000. It took him two weeks to write.

Nick moved to LA after that, hoping his advantage as a successful actor's son might also make for a life he could call his own. For a while that seemed a fair bet, although the truth was his luck turned almost as soon as he arrived. The script never made it to the screen, and nothing he wrote afterward attracted as much attention. The more care and craft he put into his stories, the less relevant he became, gaining little by little the reputation of a writer who preferred "character" over plot, which was a polite way of saying he lacked a talent for commercial material.

He tried to compromise. He never claimed to know what a good screenplay was better than producers with one eye on the market. He wrote what he thought they wanted. When this went nowhere, he set aside his own ideas and worked for other people on theirs. He even did punch-ups of other people's work. Still that downward slide continued, wearing the realism out in him. Well before *The Lost Steps* came along he'd been asking himself not if any compromise was enough but if it was even the point. Compromise involved a negotiation, after all. He had to have *some* position in it. If not, it became something else, surrender and defeat, a beatdown, a sacrifice—Don's Aztec at his altar, extracting the heart itself.

He would have dismissed such conjecture as fatalism were it not for the suspicion that his true problem was an insufficient drive for which fatalism strangely provided the crucial ingredient. As his father liked to put it, with his standard condescension, Nick wasn't "hell-bent" enough. He had none of that quixotic faith in the impossible on which success in the movie business depended. What held him back, then, may well have been his idea of compromise. However naive or presumptuous it might be, he still believed in the world negotiation implied; he still needed its ethical horizon to orient and guide him. Without it, he pretty quickly lost his bearings. What remained were misplaced desires for justice and a too easily offended sense of fair play.

In any case he'd reached yet another dead end. He couldn't go on writing screenplays that never went anywhere, like a fly banging its head at the window because it sees that world on the other side. Either he had to change his whole approach and acquire the shrewdness he needed in the face of adversity, or he had to stop pretending he could and get out while he still had his self-respect, not to mention his sanity. Hollywood was killing him in more ways than one.

19

ℵ

The next day he spoke by phone with Marty Siegel's wife, Laura, who was also his business partner in the company Harvest Moon Productions. She had to be convinced of his fit for the job, citing the need for office skills he confessed he'd have to pick up along the way. She also worried, in so many words, about his age—thirty-nine. It was work you usually gave a younger person, someone you could push around without feeling guilty when you did. He tried his best to put her at ease, or hide his unease, without much effect but sensing she was sufficiently in a bind to overlook her qualms. In the end she gave him a chance, provided he could start right away. He told her he'd be there the next morning.

The Siegels lived in a neighborhood that stretched south from the Santa Monica Canyon to Montana Avenue, a strip of upscale restaurants and boutiques situated at a right angle to the beach. Nick thought, parking his car on their block, that his destination would be a large home built to the edges of its lot, with a couple of elephantine Greek columns flanking a semicircular entranceway. To his surprise, though, Marty and Laura lived next door, in a simple ranch house with tacky carriage lanterns in the front yard. Taking this hint of modesty as a good sign, he resolved to concentrate on the work as best he could, with a minimum of attitude.

A slim blond woman in her forties opened the door for him. Just on the far side of magazine quality beautiful in a sleeveless tunic and bell-bottom slacks, she had tense blue eyes punctuated by the faint beginnings of crow's feet. It seemed from her blank expression that she had forgotten he was coming.

"I'm Nick," he reminded her.

"Yes." With a slight bow suggesting his assumption annoyed her, she took a crisp step back. "I'm Laura."

They spent a few minutes exchanging pleasantries in the vestibule. Then she led him to the office, located in a detached garage out back. As they passed through the house he glimpsed a boy tying his shoes on the floor of a bedroom. He wore the uniform of an elite private school called Carlthorp Academy. Nick knew because the woman he'd been seeing until recently, Bojena, also sent her kids there.

In the office Laura went over his duties, trying to remember what they were in the vexed manner of someone with a lot on her mind. Roughly they consisted of sitting at a desk and managing five phone lines, a fax machine, and a yellow Labrador retriever that had the run of the backyard.

"You log each call in a spreadsheet," she explained, opening up an icon on a computer and taking him through the fields for name, time, message, and return number. "It's essential you stay on top of this. There are people we keep in contact with, important people who expect prompt callbacks. Is that clear?"

"As a bell." The dog had entered through the open door and hurried to her side, happily wagging its tail.

"When there's nothing else to do," she went on, fiddling abstractly with the dog's ear, "we'll need you to research something for us online." One of their development projects, still at the concept stage, was a drama about teenage girls with anorexia. She wanted him to find out as much as he could on the subject, creating a database of articles to be consulted down the line.

"Sure thing," he said.

They heard the boy calling for his mother from the yard. He was going to be late for school. Marty must have already left.

"We'll be in and out most of the day," she said.

"Okay."

The phone rang. They both looked at it. "Guess it's time for me to start," he said, sitting in a swivel chair. He picked up the receiver and hit the button with the red light. "Harvest Moon Productions!"

ᚷ

The idea that he'd have time to research teenage anorexia quickly proved ridiculous, as it was all he could do to field the calls that started coming in one after the other, sometimes two and three at once. Keeping the spreadsheet current proved a next to impossible task. Often he found himself listening to one message while recording another.

The people he spoke to were quick to anger. He made them wait, and they didn't like that. They weren't used to it. Several asked who he was as if they intended to report on his incompetence later. When he told one woman he was new and still learning the ropes, she cut him off with a demand for a direct number, which Laura hadn't provided. More than once someone hung up on him.

Things got worse when the messengers started arriving. The first time this happened he heard a bell ring out from somewhere in the office. He had no idea what it was. When it rang again, he had to abandon the phones to figure out the source. The dog helped because it barked, which led him into the yard and down a paved driveway that skirted the house to a door, framed in a tall wooden fence. There he found the dog and a man with a package that Nick had to sign for. He could tell it was a script.

Such interruptions came every half hour from then on, and they so distracted him from the phones that he fell several entries back in the spreadsheet. Soon he had to stop trying and write down the information on a notepad for later.

Around noon husband and wife appeared. Marty, another sixty-year-old man in excellent shape, shook his hand and proceeded in a businesslike manner to act as if Nick wasn't there. Whatever civility he might warrant, if only on Lou's account, would be more than he was going to get. Not for the first time Nick was reminded that in LA the friend of your friend is not your friend.

They stayed only long enough to ascertain who on the list of petitioners they needed to call back first, taking off again for a business lunch at Spago. Nick himself had no time to eat. If he broke away from the phones for even ten minutes the onslaught would become a rout, sweeping him away altogether.

The bell rang again. He jogged out with the dog, expecting yet another messenger and another screenplay. Instead he opened the door on a young man dressed in a tailored blue velvet jacket a size too small, tight black jeans, and pointy boots—he looked like a leprechaun. Nick took him for a writer.

"Hello!" said the young man cheerily. "I have a two o'clock meeting with the Siegels."

Nick wedged himself in the doorway to keep the dog back. "They're not here."

"I'm early."

"They didn't mention a meeting to me."

The leprechaun fixed on him a look that said the oversight didn't mean there wasn't a meeting. Nick felt the dog press against his pant leg. "I'm not sure what to do," he said. "You can come in and wait, but I have a feeling they forgot."

"If it's all right I'd like to wait."

"Sure." Nick swung back down the driveway, intent on those phones.

The leprechaun stood in the entrance to the office as he returned to the desk. "Where should I sit?" They both looked at a sofa that was covered with screenplays. In a corner stood another desk, cluttered with various papers, and a free chair. Nick pointed to it.

For the next half hour he fielded calls, talking to one asshole after another. Each time he grew brusquer. He grew more like them.

On one occasion a woman called asking for Marty. "Not here," he snapped. "Can I take a message?"

"Tell him it's Lynn."

"Lynn."

"His daughter."

From another marriage, he guessed. She was closer to his age. She was also different from the other callers. Deference welled up in her voice, thoughtful, shy deference he attributed to a lifetime spent around aggressive Hollywood people on whom she emotionally depended. He liked her at once. They had things in common.

"Do you know when he'll be back?" she asked.

Nick glanced at the leprechaun, who was staring at the desk beside him, thinking it might finally be time to go.

"I'm afraid not. Don't you have his mobile number?"

"No." She didn't say why.

"I'll mention it to him when he gets here, then. . .if I can remember."

"You must be swamped."

"I am."

"I know how hard that job is."

"I'm not very good at it."

"Be glad you're not," she joked. "You don't want to be good at it. The worst that could happen is that you get good at it."

Just then Laura entered, and it was immediately clear that she'd not only forgotten about the screenwriter but had no idea who he was. She went straight for Nick assuming he must be a friend of his.

He put his hand over the receiver and said: "He told me he had a meeting at two."

"He's sitting at my desk," she hissed.

Nick blinked. "So?"

"There are trade secrets there, contracts, memos, letters no one is supposed to see, and a strange person is looking at them."

Before he could answer she pivoted to the strange person, apologizing for the confusion and herding him out the door. As Nick hung up on Lynn, Laura turned back around, still upset.

"Why didn't you put him in the house?" she demanded.

"The house?!" he exclaimed, wondering how on earth that would be a preferable option for anybody. "You didn't tell me to put him in the house. You didn't even tell me he was coming."

"You could have looked at the schedule."

"What schedule?"

She didn't acknowledge this *third* omission on her part so much as subdue it with her iron will. She walked to a table that stood by the door and grabbed a large diary with an El Greco portrait of a towheaded man on the cover. She opened it and, returning to his desk, pointed to the schedule. Her phone rang at the same time. She stared at the number before answering it.

"Yes?" Nick saw her tightening eyes dart everywhere but at him. "I see. I'm sorry for the trouble. Of course, officer. I'll come and get her as soon as I can."

She was referring to the dog. The police had found her wandering into traffic on Montana Avenue. She must have escaped when Nick let the young man in.

ϰ

Laura went to dispense with the screenwriter and retrieve the dog. Fortunately, she had survived her little misadventure unharmed. Nick, however, felt the day getting the better of him. The Siegels' lack of communication didn't matter any more than his good intentions; it was his job to know ahead of time, to predict and preempt, to divine the inscrutable needs of his employers even before they did if it came to that. Unless he met the challenge of working for them on this oracular level, he wasn't going to cut it.

Within the hour Marty appeared again, more irked in his studied indifference than before. He pushed some of the scripts off the sofa and sat down, talking on his phone about a deal. "Don't say a number," Nick heard him say. "As soon as you say a number he'll come down on you. I know. He's a producer. . ."

Nick caught sight of the son through a window, standing in the yard outside. He'd changed into a baseball uniform and was waiting for his father to finish.

Marty lingered in the details of that deal. The boy poked his head in the door, forcing an acknowledgement. "I gotta go," his father said to his interlocutor. "I really gotta go. We have to talk about this tomorrow. My son's asking for me. As soon as I hang up this phone, it's all about my son. Nothing else matters but my son and his game. I'm one hundred percent a dad. . ."

Nick winced at the obvious insincerity of this remark. It wasn't lost on the boy either, who flashed his father a look of dark reproach when at last he did shuffle past him into the yard.

The phones went on ringing with as much urgency as ever. Nick answered them until about seven o'clock, when he heard Laura in the house again. She was in the kitchen preparing dinner. This lasted too long for comfort. She was plainly ignoring him. Just as he decided to go in and announce he was leaving, and probably not coming back the next day either, he answered one last call. It was Marty. He wanted to know who'd called for him since he left.

Nick ran down the list. When he came to the name Dave Thalberg, Marty stopped him. "Did he give a number?"

"No."

"Shit."

Nick heard a cheering crowd in the background. Marty must have been sitting in the bleachers at some ballpark.

"You're supposed to ask for a number."

"Right."

"Especially when it's a guy like Thalberg!"

Nick evidently should have known who that was. Marty said, "The next time he calls I hear about it, understand? Any time, whatever's happening, even if I have an audience with the goddamn president, I hear about it."

"You didn't tell me." Nick closed his eyes, trying to stay calm. "I'm not a mind-reader." All at once his resolve collapsed, hard, like an avalanche. "I couldn't have called anyway," he went on, flung this way and that in roaring darkness, "because I didn't have *your* number. And I wouldn't have even if you'd bothered to give me your number, because I thought you didn't want to be disturbed at your son's fucking game."

Marty's answer to that was prompt: "You're fired."

"And you're a dick."

He slammed the phone in its cradle and sat watching the red lights blink, amazed at how fast events could turn around, or turn over, repeat themselves, in a kind of fatal pattern. Moments later he rose from his seat, collected what things he'd brought with him, and walked in a daze down the driveway to the door.

At his car he lit a cigarette, only his third of the day. A small miracle. Evening had set in by then. The light had gone all circumambient. It glowed in high swaying palm trees, warmed a stucco wall draped in bougainvillea, and blanked out picture windows. The street was eerily deserted. It made him think of a detonated neutron bomb, the kind that killed people but left the property intact.

X

He didn't know what to do with himself afterward. His friend Carson had invited him to a party he had no interest in attending, but he also didn't want to return home and brood over what had just happened. Caught in a deadlock, he drove aimlessly around Santa Monica for a while, until the stupidity of that forced a decision. There would be food at the party anyway, and he was starving.

He found it in the backyard of a Jamaican man named Big John, who lived on the mesa in Playa Del Rey, next to the flight path of the planes that took off from the airport. A Rastafarian woman seated by the side gate informed him he had to pay twelve dollars to get in—a first sign he'd made a mistake in coming.

Gas torches illuminated the yard, and a sizable crowd sat or stood around tables that had been arranged under umbrellas. Toward a back fence he glimpsed a bonfire burning in a pit. The food, sumptuous quantities of it, had been laid out in heating trays, cafeteria style. The atmosphere was convivial. People seemed to be having a good time.

He noticed Carson behind a makeshift bar, pouring gin and cranberry juice into cups and selling them to prospective buyers. She must have volunteered her services—why he couldn't say. A plastic water jug on the table was stuffed halfway up with money.

He met her eyes as she spoke with a man clearly hoping he could get to know her better. He had no chance. Carson, tall and athletic, with a strong symmetrical face, bronze complexion, and straight blond hair pulled back in a braid, was at the moment involved with a Nigerian man named Cedric, an experimental dancer like she was, or tried to be, when not teaching yoga at different studios around LA. Nick had noticed Cedric, a good-looking twenty-five-year-old kid really, in the crowd on his way in, and guessed he was Carson's connection to Big John.

The other man, who wore a plaid shirt and a billed hat, proclaimed himself a poet, citing a book he'd recently published. Carson also wrote poetry: meditations on the deep unity of nature, chi, yin and yang, mystical flows of energy as vague and sweet as she was. Nick had read some of it on her blog.

"Poetry is a lifeline for me," she was saying. "I don't know what I'd do without it."

"Don't give up," the man urged. "Keep trying." He meant keep trying to make it as an artist. "Tenacity is everything."

"It really opens up my dance," she went on. "The words are fingers and tongues and hips. They move and twist and turn, like bodies."

"Poetry is food, like jerk chicken." The man eyed the thigh he held up on a paper plate.

"It's powerful," Carson said, thrown without knowing why by the hint of sarcasm in this remark. She poured drinks, handed them out, took the money.

"Absolutely." He tore into that thigh, finding it a bit chewy. With his mouth full he said, "I don't like reading poetry, though."

Carson nodded. She didn't read much herself. She was severely dyslexic. Nick understood that coping with the tricks her eyes played on her had been a struggle all her life.

"And I don't like readers either," the man declared. "I don't like talking to them."

"No?" Carson did like that, to her credit.

"Did you ever notice people who read a lot always end up talking about third things? You're standing there trying to relate to this person, and he's busy relating to something else: a third thing. Jane Austen or Tolstoy. I hate that. Third things just get in the way."

Cedric sashayed up with Big John, a broad-shouldered black man with long dreadlocks. He cut in the line and demanded a drink from Carson. Cedric, meanwhile, squeezed between two tables into the bar area and slipped a sinewy arm around her waist. She planted a hard kiss on his lips. The poet's face fell. They were thrilling to look at, no doubt about it.

Carson introduced Nick to Big John. "How you doing?" the man asked, shaking his hand.

"I'm between zero and a million."

Big John laughed. "Aren't we all, mon. Aren't we all."

He had a special reason for celebrating that night: he'd been chosen as a contestant on a reality TV cooking show. After grueling rounds of interviews and tests he now had his big chance. Were he to win, or even place second, he'd be able to open his own restaurant with the reputation it brought him. He'd always wanted to do that: open his own restaurant. He was tired of working for a boss. Presently, of course, he was unemployed. His backyard was his restaurant.

"It's all part of the plan," he said, making everyone think he had in mind a "cosmic" plan. "If I invite Cedric, and Cedric invites Carson, and Carson invites—"

"Nick!' she cried, drawing him further into the conversation.

Big John placed his hand on Nick's shoulder and smiled. It was a warm smile, a welcoming smile. "Before long there'll be dozens, even hundreds of people who know my cooking, and I'll have a built-in customer base for the time I do own my own restaurant. . ."

He seemed about to launch into a pitch, and people around that bar did what people do in such a circumstance. They fell silent and listened. Nick thought it was pretty good. He'd go to Big John's restaurant. But he also wanted to leave now, even though he'd only just arrived. Too much news was accumulating about the city where he lived, with its relentless pressure to compete and promote oneself. He couldn't take more. Stepping away from the bar, he headed for the food trays, wolfed down his own piece of jerk chicken, and quit the scene without saying goodbye to Carson.

3

Back at his apartment under Lou's house Nick sat on the sofa with the lights off, worried he really was losing his grip. Events were testing his credulity, that's for sure. He thought he knew how things worked in LA. He'd been there long enough, too long to be this hapless. It suggested an increase of nervous tension that had him making poor decisions, missing cues. The problem was he couldn't tell which decisions were poor, which cues he should be taking. Definitely at Harvest Moon Productions, but even in Don's office when it came down to it, he couldn't separate the right thing to do from the wrong, good faith from bad, decency from indecency. They seemed inseparable, like signals fed back into themselves, producing not moral complexity or the chance at moral correction but static, noise.

He listened, through his open window, to the intermittent roar of passing cars from the Pacific Coast Highway, which dropped unseen behind a welter of terra-cotta rooftops, and the dull thud of crashing surf on the beach beyond. The sounds, regular yet meaningless, and even more plangent in a thick fog that hugged the shoreline, struck him as only more evidence that the problem was not his alone, not personal. It was out there, objective, a feature of the situation in which he found himself. The world was crazy. And it made no difference that he was crazy to think so, confusing what he sensed with what he merely imagined. The world was crazy not because he knew it was crazy but, more subtly, because he couldn't know with any confidence. In what came as a revelation to him, his uncertainty was just more noise. Doubting his intuitions just confirmed them all over again. Even to forget and move on—the practical thing to do—would be a kind of proof, he surmised, since then he had to stop thinking altogether, and what was that but another way to harmonize with those monotonous sounds in the night air?

It took him just a moment, of course, to realize that all he had with this discovery, if he could call it that, was another reason to do the practical thing. Like everyone he had to cope anyway, crazy as the world was. He had to operate on the blurred borders of backyard and business, private and public life, inside and outside, even as he, too, lost any sense of the differences between them. So what if an empty house was no place to leave a leprechaun alone and an overwhelmed secretary shouldn't also have to mind the bosses' pet? So what if Marty was a dick? And so what if Big John's calculation did strain the sympathy rightly owed someone's desire to be his own boss? He still had to resist letting the dissonances get the better of judgment. And he had to do whatever that took—even stop criticizing or blaming other people for what could only be, in a crazy world, his mistakes. The feeling that the shame was on their side, in their attitudes and their callousness, in their way of life, simply had no bearing on the need to keep an even keel.

The *clop* of a high-heeled shoe through the ceiling interrupted this more salutary train of thought. The sound, after a pause, traveled in uneven rhythm across Lou's wood floor out onto the deck above Nick's bedroom, where he heard voices and laughter. His heart sank. Lou had brought home another of his modelly nineteen-year-old sexual conquests.

This happened a lot, and when it did Nick had to listen for how much time it would take, how much small talk on the deck, how many drinks, before Lou had those high heel shoes off. Then there were the sex noises, the loud staging of passions neither could have felt, in Nick's view, since Lou was old enough to be her grandfather, and he just couldn't believe the girl wanted more than what else Lou had, which was power, and power wasn't sexy, whatever it might also offer.

Clop clop clopclopclop cloooopppp clop. . .

Almost no one Nick knew agreed with him here, of course. They thought power was sexy because sex involved power, looking at him askance when he observed that the one didn't necessarily follow from the other. They'd allege his monkish tendencies, mortification of the flesh, a wish that power not be sexy. He might concede his moralism but not the point, telling them about his libidinally obsessed landlord with special emphasis on the carton of Viagra Nick once opened by mistake and noticed every month or so thereafter in the mailbox they shared out on Castellammare Drive. He'd let its hint of a compulsion, a mechanism, hang in the air between them, troubling the freedom allegedly consummated in Lou's bedroom. For the most part his interlocutors laughed the implication away, and the matter ended there. But Nick at least saw no reason why their euphemism would be less wishful than his prudishness.

The phone rang. He groaned. It was his father. He liked to call late at night, or early in the morning for him. Nick thought, as he answered, that it couldn't have provided a better stopper to his rotten day.

"How's it going, Dad?"

"Terrible!" he barked. "I hate this place."

"You hate Paris."

"All it does is rain. There's never any sun. Never. I feel like I'm living in a cloud."

"I wish I was there."

"No, you don't. You think you do, but you don't. Never forget how lucky you are, Nick. I bet you see stars right now. I bet there's moonlight on the water. Am I right?" The absence of a response made him impatient. "What are you doing?"

"I'm listening to Lou seduce a nineteen-year-old girl."

"Oh." Lou and his father had a lot in common. In fact, his father had probably taught Lou a few tricks.

"What do you want?" Nick asked.

"Nothing. Just to talk. I want to hear plain English for once. I can't stand figuring out what French people are saying all the time. I don't know how they understand one another. The words all flow together."

"I've had a long day."

Conversations with his father lasted for hours if he let them, and they were a chore because his father didn't want to talk. He wanted to hear himself talk. Nick hated that, but he'd had to accept it, or see it in a more forgiving light, with the Parkinson's. As time passed his father was finding it more difficult to manage his fluctuating emotions.

"Just for a while," he pleaded. "Julie won't be back all morning, and I'm alone. I'm starting to unravel. I can't help it. I don't know what to do with myself if somebody's not there."

"All right."

"I don't know how you do it—spend so much time by yourself. You could always do it."

"I had a lot of practice."

"Yeah, yeah, go ahead and blame me. But you know I'm right. You liked it. You were good at it."

"I didn't like it, Dad."

His father ignored this, or maybe he didn't hear. His tone turned spiteful. "You felt superior, admit it. Standing to the side watching other people fuck up their lives—"

"Maybe I was watching *you* fuck up my life."

"What life? Do you have a life? A life is made of mistakes, Nick, and you don't make mistakes. Except one. Not making mistakes is a mistake. Nothing good ever happens unless you're willing to get dirty."

"I'm going to hang up now."

"Okay! I'm sorry." Nick could hear the fear in his father's voice, made sharper by its tinny disembodiment on the line. "I don't know what happens to me. My mind starts spinning. Things come back at me with a vengeance. I'm a pathetic old man who feels guilty as shit. . ."

Nick didn't believe that for a second, and a part of him didn't care even if it was true. His father *should* feel guilty. But sensing the petulance in this, he decided against starting a fight over it. "Maybe I am too cautious," he said instead. "It's not because I like that about myself, though, okay? I don't. I wish I had more courage. I wish I knew how to take things as they are."

"You don't have enough fun—like Lou upstairs. I bet he's having fun."

"Maybe there's not enough of that to go around."

"What?"

"Fun."

The line seemed to go dead.

"Somebody's been stealing all the pleasure," Nick said.

This had more than its fair share of grievance behind it, but it struck an undeniable nerve, too. His father was no fool. He understood why all his notions came back at him with a vengeance, because he wouldn't believe a word he said if he were anyone else, certainly anyone who had to rely on him for love or support. His father had the mind of a hustler, and no hustler believes a hustler.

"You know what your problem is?" he said then. "You think you're smarter than other people. You think you have it all figured out. But there's one thing you don't know: there's no such thing as pleasure. It doesn't exist. There's nothing to steal. There never was anything to steal."

Nick sensed his father trying to get at something more interesting than the idea that pleasure didn't exist for him, at least not anymore. It led Nick to think they might talk past their differences to a place of emotional candor they almost never found with each other. Alert to this chance he said, "Maybe that's why I'm so cautious."

His father ignored him here, too, caught now in a retrospective mood so out of character he broke it with the declaration, "I'm going to kill myself!"

Nick sighed. The moment passed, the chance evaporated. "No, you're not."

"I'll throw myself off the balcony." He lived on the top floor of an apartment building on the slopes leading up to Ménilmontant. From the wrought-iron rail it was a precipitous drop of five stories to the curving rue des Couronnes.

"Why?"

"Why not?!" his father cried. "I have no life. I have no fucking future. All I do is potter around the house like an imbecile. Sometimes I can't even remember my own name. . ."

Nick rose from the sofa and went to lie on his bed. It would take a lot out of him reminding Evan Moran that he was Evan Moran.

ϗ

It would take all of him, going back to his childhood in the New York of the 1970s, when he lived with his parents in a ground-floor brownstone apartment near Morningside Park. It had tall ceilings, a scuffed fir floor, and access to an inner courtyard that no one else used, with a mulberry tree in it. Every wall had floor-to-ceiling bookshelves packed with jazz records. His father loved jazz. When Nick was very young, he'd worked as a deejay for a radio station that broadcast from the basement of Riverside Church. He had a husky slow voice that made people think he'd been places. Nick used to listen to him with a fascination born of the difference between that voice and the man he lived with every day. It had depths he couldn't hear otherwise.

His father gave the strong impression that he knew what he liked. His enthusiasms were larger than life. They made people want to be around him. Even as a child, though, Nick sensed this wasn't genuine. His father really knew what other people liked, only he was better than they were at showing it. He took over an interest and owned it with a flair that left the one who's interest it was feeling dispossessed. That may even have been the interest for his father. He was covetous without admitting it, and he could disarm suspicion with just a smile. The only proof would come later, when he dropped the interest as quickly as he'd picked it up. He didn't really love jazz at all.

Nick had to look past that smile to the man he did know, a careless, impulsive, self-obsessed man. He didn't see what was right in front of his eyes. To be a kid around him meant you had to watch out. He might lose you. That happened once, on a hot summer day in Central Park. Nick was four. His father had taken him to the carousel, they'd climbed rocks together, eaten hot dogs, kicked around a soccer ball on the Great Lawn. But then Nick made the mistake of absorbing himself in the distractions of a playground, and when he looked up again he discovered that his father was gone—lured away, it would turn out, by a couple of teenagers to a drum circle, where he got high, danced, and lost all track of time.

Nick, meanwhile, went in search of him, growing more and more frightened. Giving up finally, he crept into a cordoned off area of hawthorn bushes and sat in the underbrush. It was an impulse that even at the time made no sense to him, but oddly in its grip he remained there a long while, praying for his father to appear in the masses of people on the nearby walkway. At one point he heard a stir beside him, and turning round he glimpsed the switch of a rat's tail. A big rat, he thought, as big as a cat. It came flooding in on him then, with a vivid and petrifying detail, that it wasn't the only one. Those hawthorn bushes were full of rats.

The shudder that passed through him was so intense he must have blacked out for an instant. At least he didn't hear the end of his own bloodcurdling scream, which alerted passersby to a problem. Shaken to a core no child should know quite so well, he had to be escorted by strangers to the police precinct in the park and driven home to his mother, feeling guilty in the back of the squad car. Later he developed a fever and rash that doctors diagnosed as Murine typhus–transmitted, they said, by the fleas that infested rats.

Experiences like this one taught Nick he could never trust his father. He'd have to provide on his own the support he missed from him. His mother, Meredith, was an ally, of course, but she had the same problem he did. They were both captive to Evan's fake insouciance. In the aid or comfort she offered, Nick felt her own needs going unmet, and the anchor she gave him tended for this reason to float, leaving them both a little adrift.

His parents came from the same small town in Nebraska, growing up in farm country, and they married right after high school, before either had the chance to find out who they were. All they really had in common was a desire to get out. Not surprisingly, the relationship deteriorated in the years after they moved to New York and Nick was born. His father thrived, having the sort of animal spirits that connected him effortlessly with the life of the city. For his mother it was more difficult. She had her center inside herself, which made for an underlying reticence that held her back right where his father sought to break free. They tried to work around this difference, or minimize its significance, but sooner or later the reminders would come, undoing their efforts at compromise and driving them further into separate spheres.

Evan made next to no money at that time, and his mother felt the need to secure for herself an independent existence. School suited her temperament, so she enrolled at City College and worked as steadily as she could toward a degree in English. Nick tried his best to help. He accompanied her to the uptown campus without complaint and sat in the classrooms or waited with student babysitters until she was done. At home he kept himself occupied and quiet while she read books or wrote her papers. No one felt the sense of accomplishment more than he did when she finally graduated, although it also marked another milestone on the path to being his own master.

Meanwhile his mother suffered with his father, who felt caged in their marriage and less disposed over time to hide it. The rift between them opened further once Evan gained traction as an actor. That was one thing he wanted badly enough to stick with. After years spent taking classes at various studios, working in local theater, and chasing auditions, his effort paid off. He landed a couple of roles in off-Broadway plays, performing to accolades that transformed his native attraction into outright glamour. His forgetfulness became chronic then. He stopped telling Meredith of his plans or even simply his whereabouts. There were nights when he didn't come home and afterward bitter arguments filled with lies and promises he had no intention of keeping. At first Nick didn't understand just what they meant: that his father was sleeping with other women. Later, though, it became obvious. Even minimal efforts at deception proved too much of a bother for him in the end. His success had its own momentum—its own sense of justice, too—and he started living without apology by its lights.

His big break came with the role of Jamie Tyrone in a 1980 Broadway reprise of Eugene O'Neill's *Long Day's Journey into Night*. The critics admired the gritty realism of his performance, inviting comparisons with Richard Burton, whom he resembled, and before long he caught the attention of Hollywood, landing parts in films. It soon became apparent that he'd have to move there permanently for the sake of his career. As it made little sense for him and Meredith to pretend they loved each other, and she had no desire to go on feeling the sting of his infidelities or live in LA, she agreed to a divorce. The process pushed her right to an edge of nervous exhaustion, though, and there was no question of her staying in New York by herself, at least not for a while. When the divorce went through, she took Nick, eleven at the time, home with her to Nebraska while his father headed for California and his new life as a movie star.

ጰ

It came as no surprise to those who knew Nick that he'd hate LA. It belonged to his father, who embraced the status and freedom he found there with an all-consuming intensity and next to no restraint. His fame was more than Nick knew how to handle on the holidays he first spent visiting as a teenager. He felt awkward and left out, shunted still further onto the peripheries of his father's attention, care, and even simple respect. He also resented the way everyone around his father confirmed and rewarded his egoism. It felt as if the world itself were colluding in Nick's sense of his own insignificance. Nothing much had changed on this front either, truth be told, and he'd be the first to admit that an adolescent pain still inflamed his allergies to life in LA. As that phone call with his father only served to remind him once it had ended, everything he was doing or going through now he'd done or gone through before, many times before, in a coalescence of love with fate that at some point he was going to have to sort out better than he had.

4

The next night Nick went to hear the poet William Bryce at the Hammer Museum in Westwood. There was a crowd and he arrived late, so he had to stand at the back of the auditorium all through the reading. His neck hurt from the drive, in chaotic traffic. More than once he'd almost turned around in exasperation. He wondered why anyone would ever venture out in LA if they didn't have to. Not to relax, that's for sure.

He did have another reason to go. He'd met Bryce once, years before, at a dinner organized by a professor at Brown, where he went to college. He was lucky enough to sit next to the man, and they had a conversation—not about anything special, but still it meant a great deal to Nick. His mother had died a few months before, after a protracted battle with leukemia, and needing solace in his loneliness rather desperately, he found it in Bryce's lyric poems. He read them over and over in the hothouse of his freshman dorm room, to the point of incantation. They seemed to address him in the most inward and sequestered part of himself, like words in a dream, stirring depths he hardly knew were there. The effect was not so much intimate as absolute; it gave him a feeling for that ideal or transcendental dimension of life he was learning about in his first college courses from the likes of Saint Augustine and Rousseau, Wordsworth and Shelley. Nick might not have called that dimension God, or Nature, or Spirit, but it felt profound just the same. Bryce was a poet of intellectual vision. He saw with the eyes of the soul.

He might have been too convincing this way, and later Nick would question the authority he gave him. He had to, if he wanted to move on from that stage of mourning for his mother. Fervent communion with another mind, even a universal mind, became the reluctance to let go of a ghost. Inner being shrank to a point, or a private language, and so vanished into a social world where he had to make his way without her, and nothing was ever quite what it seemed. Philosophy helped here. It taught him to look for his own center outside himself, or in others, and at a remove from metaphysical desires for substance, presence, truth. This sort of skepticism came naturally enough to him. By temperament he was reflective more than spontaneous, hesitant more than categorical. He had little faith, when it came down to it, in things unseen. But if, for that reason, he finally left Bryce's romanticism behind, he also never forgot the passion it had once been for him, however distant a memory now.

Nick felt that passion again, in its knot of old sadness, as he listened to Bryce read from his latest book—poems about an island in the Adriatic Sea where he'd been living for the last ten years, and also homages to classical poets he admired. Nick remembered, too, how much it had to do with Bryce's personal qualities. He was a beautiful man, even more so now at his advanced age. Broad shouldered, with curly white hair, limpid sea-green eyes, and a baritone voice, he stepped right out of a bygone pastoral era like the shepherds he sometimes evoked from his lectern, watching over their flocks, seeking out the good pastures, knowing the season's laws. In fact, Bryce radiated substance, presence, and truth with all the assurance Nick had lost in the meantime, pushing back against his skepticism, insinuating less of a gain in honesty than he had imagined. And Nick had to admit, honesty wasn't the right word for what he ended up with. It was more an aware dishonesty, an inner problematizing of his actions and reasons that could at times verge on the morbid. He might attribute this difference to his character flaws, and concede everything to Bryce's nobility, if he didn't have to keep rubbing his neck in that auditorium and go on living in LA, where pretense was so much the rule. There, self-consciousness still seemed like a survival skill.

So Nick couldn't but feel annoyed with the poet from his spot at the back. The wind, rain, and birdsong to which Bryce paid such close attention on that island so sharply contrasted with anything in his experience as to ring a little hollow. The thing was Bryce had nothing to say about that experience. He might have presented a persuasive example of another way to live, a more authentic connection, but he offered no account of disconnection, no exploration of the inauthentic conditions that held so completely in the audience and outside the museum as to boggle Nick's mind. This lapse struck him finally as remiss for an artist of Bryce's caliber, if only because it lent that example all the more as an alibi for people otherwise committed to their pretenses.

It may even have been *the* alibi they required. A kind of pastoral machinery ran in the background of LA when Nick thought about it. He had felt it often enough in the nature people liked to praise, and consume, in yoga and organic food. It was there in the need they had for personal assistants, life coaches, and trainers. People were obsessed, really, with guidance and supervision. It made even that attention in Bryce—understood, again, as the attribute of a shepherd—just too familiar to him. Bryce might not have cared to think of himself as an expert, or a guru, but little in what he said disturbed the desire for one that was such an obvious subtext of his reception in that auditorium. Nick could feel it arousing the crowd spread out before him, and without appreciable contradiction. People didn't seek relief from the tense negotiation of freeway and boulevard that it took to get there. They sought an end to justify their means.

Afterward the poet sat at a desk in the lobby and signed copies of his book. Nick deliberated over whether to wait in the long line that had formed, thinking he might remind Bryce of that dinner at Brown. But before he came to a decision he saw Bojena, his erstwhile lover, in the crowd, standing beside a man he realized with a start must be her husband. All at once his wits deserted him.

He withdrew to an adjacent terrace that looked over the museum's central courtyard, intent on avoiding an encounter. He thought to leave, but once outside he paused, unable to resist, from the darkness, the surreptitious view he had of Bojena through a floor-to-ceiling glass wall. It was like watching someone he knew in a movie. A striking woman with fine features, brown eyes, and chestnut-colored hair that fell below her shoulders, she was sipping wine from a red plastic cup, pleasantly engaged in conversation with her husband. Nick saw her lift her heels slightly when she made a point. He saw her worry the edge of her mouth with her tongue as she listened intently to a reply. All the warmth and intelligence he knew so well showed in her expression. The reading had pleased her. She, too, wrote poetry, in a similar lyrical style to Bryce, for all the trouble she had finding the time for it in her busy life. Nick should have guessed he'd see her there. At some level, maybe he had.

A mutual friend on the east coast first introduced them. They seemed a good match. Both were New Yorkers, both were avid readers, and both lived in the Pacific Palisades. Both also felt like misfits in LA. From the beginning a principal pleasure, shared over coffee or lunch, had been corroborating their frustrations with the place. Bojena, even more than Nick, felt alone with them. She lived in a wealthy enclave way up in the hills, surrounded by buttoned-down people she didn't much like. Her husband, a successful businessman, offered little support. He considered her judgmental attitude to be the problem. It not only savored of its own snobbery but offended an optimism he thought the right way in general to face the world. She found this criticism more than a little condescending, but it also put her in a bind. From what Nick understood, she'd married her husband because she took for granted the same affluence she knew growing up. But that affluence meant culture—her father was an executive at the New York Philharmonic—and she hadn't anticipated just how at odds the capacities for one could be with the dispositions of the other. Life had since taught her better, but not before choices that locked her into an affluence without culture. It made for an intellectual solitude that was no less acute because she had no one but herself to blame.

They grew closer with the sympathy Nick offered. He, too, had experience with that condescension. He knew all too well, in fact, the trap it laid for people too sensitive either to buy the positive thinking her husband professed or stay with the truth of their alienation. They ended up ashamed on both fronts, unable to withstand criticism on the first in the consciousness of their failure on the second, and ever more prone to resignation. The self went silent, or underground, losing the feeling of its own existence. Nick had seen this happen before. He certainly felt the risk to himself.

The affair, once it started, became a way for both of them to wrest themselves from this trap, to be what LA so relentlessly reduced to caricature: engaged, serious people whose inner aspirations mattered. It might have been the only way. No space existed for the acknowledgement they gave each other unless it was taken, or stolen, in some form or other, and even then it had to be braced against the pressure of anachronism, of isolation from duty and habit. It bothered them that this space had to be one of exception. They didn't like to think of that mutual support as a fantasy, or themselves as fantasists. It wasn't escape they sought. In the time they spent together—usually at his place having a meal, drinking too much wine, smoking too many cigarettes—the aim rather was candor in the encounter with another, the ordinary returned to itself in the admission of just how hostile an element it had become.

But they underestimated what they were up against. Candor turned out harder to separate from deception, the ordinary from the conventional. LA closed in on them. Bojena felt it every time she had to lie to her husband or her children to be with him. It struck Nick every time she had to leave, every time he had to equate in his mind the singularity of their love with its occasional character. Bojena saw it wasn't working sooner than he did. She started limiting her visits, not calling, making excuses, introducing the idea that they would have to go back to being friends. He held out longer, clinging to the hope that they might learn how to live with the dissonances of infidelity. The effort gave him an edge, a desperation that sometimes confused Bojena. It may even have broken the erotic spell that had bound them so tightly together; in any case, the times they saw each other, even as friends, grew less and less frequent. Things stood this way now. There'd been no definite end. They still very much cared for each other. But as much as he might wish it wasn't true, he knew in his heart that the affair was over.

Her husband managed a private equity fund—a nasty business from what Nick could tell. It involved buying up different companies and sweating them for profit by firing employees, stripping assets, increasing debt, and selling what remained at inflated prices. It seemed not only predatory but antisocial, like so much else coming from Wall Street these days. According to Bojena, the cost for her husband was a lack of emotional depth, and Nick had always taken the comfort of a rival in believing this to be true. It suggested in the contrast, or the confidence, that Nick offered what he didn't and that their feelings were more genuine because of it.

To his surprise, though, he saw nothing in her husband to corroborate this view of him. He seemed through that window, on the contrary, charming and intelligent, not the vulpine corporate raider Nick had imagined. Indeed, from his spot on that terrace they appeared a fine match: attractive, self-assured, attuned to each other on levels he was never able to reach with her.

The force of this impression flattened him. It also put the focus squarely on his desire. For a moment he saw his whole life in the shame he felt hiding there in the dark, looking on like a voyeur and deluded as any interloper, trying to fit where he didn't belong. Worse still, he caught in himself an equivocation, touching on the assumption that awareness offered immunity from the pretense he so disliked. Had he been mistaken? Was he deceiving himself about where he stood even on this sideline, this margin? Could it be just the proper place of a "bounder"—as recognizable a type in LA as any other—hovering enviously on the edges of other people's lives because he had no life of his own, or wanted one he hadn't earned?

He liked to think that questioning himself in this manner added nuance to the picture. He might not *only* be a bounder. He might still redeem his dishonesty. It hurt to know he was mistaken even in this. It hurt that Bojena knew it, too. That was why she stood in the lobby with her husband and not out there with him. She'd come to accept what he couldn't: that the only choice for anybody in this conventional world was between different lifestyles, none of which felt conventional from the inside. Exception, in other words, *was* the rule. It indicated just how casually people trimmed their desires to circumstances.

Bojena's choice he had to say looked pretty stylish right then. It had Bryce's elegance on its side, for one thing. Nick could see it tint her shining eyes. She might be walking still through the vineyards and lavender fields of that Mediterranean island—on the way to some villa her husband had rented for her. Or bought. They were that rich.

On this note he did at last quit the scene. He withdrew farther down the terrace, the long way around the courtyard, and took the flights of stairs to the first floor almost at a run, not stopping until he reached his car in the underground parking garage. There, bent in the driver's seat with his hands furiously gripping the wheel, he burst into tears.

5

Not long after he called his friend Haley Dunne, hoping for a consolation she would be uniquely able to provide. They'd known each other a long time, since the days at Brown, where she, too, had gone to school. No one understood him better, or more critically, in part because he'd fallen hopelessly in love with her when they first met, and she didn't return his feelings at all. To say he took her rejection hard would have been an understatement. He burned for her like a man at the stake. He'd never felt so anguished, not even after his mother's death—though emotions pent up over the year or so that had passed since she died certainly added fuel to the fire. It tried Haley's patience to watch, especially over the months that the infatuation went on, but she cared enough to coax him from the flames and help break the sacrificial spell.

It broke, finally, and though he never quite shook his disappointment and longing, the closeness they later developed went interestingly beyond the mystifications of romance and sex. They could discuss their differences, search their feelings, and compare their experiences with a frankness that was rare between a man and a woman. This advantage wasn't lost on either of them. Both had come very much to depend on it.

They did have similar interests. Haley graduated the year after him in the same comparative literature major, and she joined the graduate program he'd started at NYU. Both had a taste for French culture. They spent a year together in Paris as exchange students, living in an airy apartment on the quai de Valmy, across from the Canal Saint-Martin. They took the same classes, read the same books, saw the same films, and cultivated the same circle of friends. At night they either cooked dinner or went out, like two lovers. It would have been better for Nick had they been lovers, of course, but the time still counted as one of the happiest in his life. He'd never felt more like an engaged, serious person whose inner aspirations mattered.

For Haley the year proved a sea change, as she chose not to leave. He returned to New York and she dropped out of school with the express aim of becoming French, or a different person anyway, far from her humbler origins as the daughter of a commercial real estate broker in Atlanta. She still lived in the apartment now, more than a decade later, and her cosmopolitan transformation seemed complete.

Nick Skyped her one morning from his sofa. She appeared on his laptop sitting before a table by opened French windows, through which a restless Paris traffic could be heard, punctuated by the two-tone siren of a passing police car. A lace curtain ballooned gently at her shoulder. The scattered light it cast shone in her auburn hair, bringing out the luster in her eyes and accentuating her high cheekbones.

"Why aren't you out skipping stones in the canal?" he gruffly demanded, thinking of the heroine in the movie *Amélie*, who did just that. Parts of it were filmed in Haley's quartier, showing to advantage the locks, tunnels, and peaked iron footbridges for which it was well known.

"Don't mock me!" she cried.

He'd caught her translating a software manual from English to French, how she made her living in Paris. A New York company had hired her on a freelance basis when she was still in school, and since the work could be done handily over the internet, she took the job with her when she moved.

"I'm a drudge," she said. "A toiler. I hate computers. It's time to change my life. On the Format menu, I click Default."

Haley was sardonic by nature. When she spoke an eyebrow was always lifting somewhere. She liked to think of herself in this as intolerant of cant, but Nick knew she could be as good at it as the next person. The real function of her dry and elliptic style was to protect a deeper delicacy of soul. She might have been too good at that.

"Should we Default together?" he asked.

"I really am ready to quit."

"So am I."

"I'd rather do anything than sit at my desk," she said. "Just the thought of it gives me a migraine."

She wasn't kidding. For years she'd been plagued by them. She'd tried all manner of remedies, each more drastic than the last. The most recent had been experimental Botox injections at different pressure points on her skull, and even these hadn't helped much.

"You don't want to write screenplays anymore?" she inquired, catching finally the serious note in his last remark.

"I'm washed up. Finished." He lit a cigarette. "Three days ago a studio executive called me a 'cunt' in his office and a producer fired me as his assistant. I can't take it anymore."

She looked harder at him, tilting her head quizzically.

"Hold on," she said, flitting into her *séjour* and returning a minute later with her own cigarette. She waved it at a cloud of smoke. "You've picked a fine time to tell me that."

"Why?"

"I've decided to write a screenplay."

"No!"

"It's about an American woman in Paris," she said, bracketing this querulous response. "She starts experiencing strange coincidences, strange little chance events that don't seem accidental. They're more signs, or signals. It's like the city is trying to tell her something."

"The city?"

"Yeah."

"What's it trying to tell her?"

"I'm not sure." He noted a vein running down the middle of her forehead. It tended to appear in moments of intense reflection. "Or, maybe, I don't want to say. Sometimes it's like *Invasion of the Body Snatchers* in my mind, but there are no aliens. It's more psychological than that. Another movie I like is *Mulholland Drive*. Its ambiguity is pitch perfect to me."

Nick hesitated a moment too long.

"You don't like the idea?"

"I do," he assured her. "I just don't think *Mulholland Drive*'s all that ambiguous. It seems pretty straightforward to me."

"How can you say that?!"

"It's one of the best, most truthful movies I've ever seen about Hollywood," he declared with just too sententious a ring. "A girl comes to LA—from Atlanta or somewhere—and commits suicide. No, she's already committed suicide by coming to LA, and the audience just has to figure that out."

"She's not from Atlanta."

"Hollywood is suicide, Haley. That's my point."

"David Lynch made *Mulholland Drive* in Hollywood." That shut him up with an alacrity she very much enjoyed. "Poor Nick," she said, in a teasing voice. "Always forgetting things are never what you think they are. You idealize everything. You go looking for noon at two o'clock, and when you don't find it, you blame the world instead of yourself."

"Don't mock me," he returned, sensing how effectively aspersions cast on self-pity preempted any defense. The truth in what she alleged, however, kept him from pointing this out. He had no idea how David Lynch, with his dark antinaturalism, could be so successful in the business he knew, run by Aztecs like Don Torrance. It suggested capabilities far beyond his reach.

"Besides," Haley said, "Hollywood isn't Paris, and they make movies in Paris, too, if you hadn't noticed. I've started taking a class with a director, Jean-Claude. He runs a school in Belleville. It's more an atelier really. People collaborate on all these different levels, designing projects for themselves to work on when they're made."

"Are they made?"

"Jean-Claude hasn't landed a feature yet."

Just then Nick noticed two middle-aged women in his terraced yard. They were going on about the garden Lou's old Mexican handyman kept in a generally flourishing condition. Nick had never seen either of them before.

"They like my idea," Haley said. "They want me to keep going with it."

"Great."

"In fact they're inviting me into their group, and it's pretty tight-knit. They don't accept just anybody. It's kind of an honor."

The two women, engrossed in the flowerbeds on the top terrace, had come not five feet from Nick's window, close enough to hear him. He threw the window open. "Excuse me," he called out. "What are you doing here?"

One of the women, lanky with narrow set eyes, in loose-fitting pants and a striped shirt that made Nick think of a harlequin in a chain gang, introduced herself with affected breeziness as the wife of Bob Kirschner, the man taking over the house in a month's time. "I wanted to show my friend the roses. There's so many wonderful varieties."

Haley took a drag on her cigarette and waited.

"I wish Lou had told me," he said crossly. "I'm talking to a friend here, and you're interrupting."

The woman promised they wouldn't be long, but she also conspicuously stood her ground. This hint of defiance irked Nick still more. He had half a mind to kick them out.

"What's going on?" Haley asked.

"Nothing," he grumbled. "I have to move. Lou is renting the house."

"Really?"

He nodded.

"That's terrible! It's such a lovely spot."

"In a sordid way, yeah."

She gave another quizzical tilt to her head.

"You really can't take LA?"

"I don't know what I'm going to do," he said. "I'm broke on top of everything. I don't even have the money for a new apartment."

"Maybe you should try something else for a while."

"What?"

"Technical writing. I have contacts in New York—"

"You were just telling me you hated it! You're about to quit!"

"It's awful work," she admitted. "You can forget doing anything imaginative when it hangs over you every day."

"I couldn't stand that."

"Maybe apply for professor jobs?"

He heard the lanky woman effuse, "This one's called a Wild Blue Yonder Grandiflora. It won a gold medal at the American Florist

Society's national competition in Orlando. A single stem costs thirty-five dollars."

It took him a moment to contain his indignation.

"I saw your father the other day," Haley said, seeing a change of subject was in order.

"Yeah?"

"On the rue Oberkampf. He didn't look well, Nick. He'd let his hair grow out, and his clothes were shabby. He walked in an odd way, too—a shuffle, really, with his arms kept rigid beside him. I almost took him for a clochard."

"The Parkinson's is getting to him."

"It was a bit of a shock."

"Did you say hello?" he said with a tinge of sarcasm. Her solicitude for his father annoyed him. It touched on sore points between them.

She shook her head. "He was too wrapped up in himself. I didn't know how to break into that."

Nick sighed. He wasn't getting what he wanted from this conversation. The boundaries were not set, not clear. The world was always trespassing. He asked again about Jean-Claude and his atelier, leading Haley back to her own preoccupations. They would have to afford the relief he was beginning to suspect existed nowhere in himself.

⁂

Haley's mention of academic jobs stayed with him after they spoke. By coincidence, the season for sending out applications was under way, ahead of a national conference put on by the Modern Language Association, where interviews were typically conducted. As he had no better ideas, he went online and searched the listings. He was quickly discouraged. The only positions he fit were in Wyoming and Tennessee, and he couldn't easily see himself living in such places, so remote from anything or anyone he knew, with only the work to interest him. The time had passed when he was resilient enough for that kind of sacrifice.

He applied anyway. Some jobs that he might stretch to fit didn't strike him as quite so bad: one in Milwaukee and two abroad, in Auckland and Vancouver. He had a letter, a CV that highlighted the book he'd made of his dissertation and published at an academic press, and a dossier of recommendations from former advisors at NYU—one of whom, Pierre-Yves Ozouf, he still considered a friend. All he had to do was change a few dates or request that it be done, assemble the materials, and send them off. The whole process took a couple of days. Then he forgot about it, having no reason to think anything would come of the effort. It was more or less like playing the lottery.

Meanwhile he put off looking for a new apartment. That he had no money was a reason to wait, but the excuses ran deeper, too. He foresaw having to settle for some featureless neighborhood in the vast flatlands of LA, where blocks stretched like taffy to accommodate walk-ups that looked like motor motels and bigger complexes resembling beehives. He'd never had to compromise that much with the city's suburban character before, and the thought of doing so now frankly scared him.

He did sign up for temp work at an agency. He'd done this in the past, making coffee for downtown stockbrokers who took a faintly sadistic pleasure in treating him as the loser he was in their eyes. The thought repelled him even though he had no choice, at least in the short term. He could ask his father for help, but he'd rather suffer the contempt of stockbrokers. Favors came at the cost of fresh humiliations. His father could be very cutting in his judgments. Even when he wasn't, Nick felt the sting of a comparison neither could help making. That was why he hadn't taken advantage of his father's connections in Hollywood as much as he should have. Friends considered this a criminal form of self-sabotage, but he had his reasons. He needed what success he did have to be his own. Otherwise, he never came out of the shadow where his father's fame put him.

And besides, Evan didn't have the resources he once did. His all-consuming freedom became self-consuming in the end, catching up with him as addictions to cocaine and other painkillers, which had him falling apart in a serious way. The result was a spectacular bankruptcy that garnered a lot of attention in the press. He checked himself into a rehab center in Malibu and lost almost everything he had, including his palatial house in Benedict Canyon. He might not have survived the ordeal at all if he hadn't met his future wife Julie. She taught yoga and cooked health food for the patients in the rehab center. Her moderating influence and care pulled him back from the brink.

Nick badly needed Don Torrance to cut the check the studio owed him. That would at least get him into an apartment and allow for some time to plan out his next steps. Lou promised to work on that for him, but as the days passed Nick feared it wasn't going to happen soon enough for his needs. . .if it ever did.

ẋ

In this stretch he met Carson—a friend of Julie's, actually—for a drink in Venice. He drove one afternoon to an exercise studio and waited while she finished a spinning class. Through an open roll-up door he watched the exhausted cyclers on the last leg of a mountain tour, conjured into a microphone by their instructor, who must have been an aspiring actress. She had a knack for describing dips in tree-lined roads and sudden vistas.

Afterward the two of them went to a bar on Abbot Kinney Boulevard. The place had big bay windows, and they sat with their backs to a brick wall, watching the steady stream of rush hour traffic. A viscous light charged the street outside with the oncoming drama of another spectacular sunset.

It had Carson, flush from her recent exertions and still in her Lululemon outfit, overcome with a sense of wellbeing. "We're so lucky," she declared.

"We are?"

"It's such a perfect moment. Happiness surrounds us, encloses us. Love flows through the universe. Don't you think?"

"No."

"Come on!" She dug at him with an elbow. "Don't be such a grump. Love is everywhere. It holds everything together. Or it holds everything up. . .like an elephant with the planet on its back."

"What holds the elephant up?"

"A turtle, I think."

"Right."

Nick braced himself for more of Carson's standard New Age pantheism. An ersatz hippie from Phoenix, she thought for the most part in cloudy generalities, borrowing her truths from Indian men with doe eyes and wavy hair. Her vocabulary was peppered with transliterated Sanskrit words. It pained him to hear how much she believed in them.

"How's Cedric?" he asked.

She burst out laughing. This went on for too long, and when it seemed she was about to recover, a strange inquiring glance brought it all back again.

"That good, eh?"

"Cedric," she said, on at last catching her breath. "God, Cedric is incredible. Sex is an art with him. I've never been so turned on in my life."

"Uh-huh."

"But Cedric's tricky, too."

"He is?"

"The other day," she said, fighting past a reluctance to confide in him, "I showed up at his place, and I thought we'd, you know, do the usual. Out of the blue he said he wanted a hundred dollars. I laughed at first. I thought it was a joke. It had to be a joke, right? But no, it wasn't. He was serious."

"He wanted you to *pay* for sex?!"

"He told me he was going to charge a hundred dollars when we did it at his house and two hundred when we did it at mine."

"You're kidding?"

"Can you believe it?"

Her embarrassment was clear now. Cedric had blindsided her more than she let on. He raised questions about her judgment that she didn't know how to plumb in much depth. Carson could be a little guileless. It was off-putting in someone so physically self-assured, but also a reason to like her. She was, at heart, a decent person . . .too decent, it may be, for a place like LA.

Nick shifted his position on the bench. It wasn't comfortable. He said, "I guess the question is can you afford *not* to believe it."

She mulled this over, confounded by that negative. A desire to understand herself better struggled with the stronger instinct for evasive action, for escape. "The thing is, I thought about it. I couldn't help myself. I wanted to fuck him so bad I didn't care what I had to do. Nothing else mattered. I even checked to see how much money I had."

"Did you fuck him?"

"I didn't have enough."

"What if you had?"

"I wouldn't have even then," she assured him. "But I was tempted."

"I think I feel love flowing through the universe now."

"Oh, come on!"

"What?"

"It's not the same thing."

"Why not?"

She picked her next words with care, summoning up notions she felt obscurely imperiled. "Love is expansive," she said, sounding vaguely as if she were quoting from a self-help book. "It fills, it spreads. It's not about closing down, or shutting out. It's about staying open to the moment. It's about being available for what happens in the moment."

"Why do I have the feeling you've got it backward?" He often had this feeling with Carson. "To be open means to shut out what's happening. To see what's happening, on the other hand, is to close down, to be emotionally unavailable. That makes no sense to me."

"It doesn't?"

"No." He frowned. It frustrated him, talking to her. Often he ended up as confused as she was confusing. He tried to pin down just what it was he did think. "Love and understanding can't just be opposites," he said. "To believe they are is the real abstraction. Both end up rationalized. All you have is love without mind and mind without love."

"I'm all for mindful love," she said, faintly offended. "Mindful love is a beautiful thing. But the mind goes all over the place. It doesn't stay. It leaves the body behind. It's not available for what happens in the moment."

"And what happens in the moment is always beautiful and perfect and benign?"

"It's a happy planet, Nick. We're the ones who are unhappy."

"Nothing out there," he said, pointing through the bay windows to the traffic congesting Abbot Kinney, "makes you unhappy?"

"Not unless you let it."

"And you don't see that as a kind of shutting out, or closing down?"

"Now you're the one who's got it backward!"

Nick took an exasperated sip of his Hefeweizen. "Everything's a tautology with you, Carson."

"What's that?"

"A tautology is a tautology."

"Oh."

"'It's all good,'" he said, mimicking her.

"That's right!"

"What if it's not? What about Cedric? Is he good, too?"

"He's very good."

Nick's staring eyes melted the slyness from her face. They were a shocking gray and, together with a long straight nose and sharp jaw, known to disarm when looked at too closely. While not what anyone would consider all that forceful in his demeanor, he had an inner confidence, and a quiet reliance on intrinsic qualities, that could on occasion make for manly virtue.

Carson laughed again, less sure of herself this time. "I'm such an idiot," she confessed. "How could I have been so wrong about him? I thought we had things in common. I trusted him."

Nick appreciated this more honest note. It allowed them to get at what was actually happening, and with less judgment. What bothered him wasn't how Carson opened herself to experience. He saw, in fact, a lot to admire in that. "I guess it shouldn't come as a surprise," he said, with a softer inflection. "Everything's transactional in LA. Cedric's just getting with the program."

"Sex is so powerful."

He tensed up on hearing the familiar chord this very Carson-like sentence struck. "Is power sexy?" he asked her.

The shift of emphasis hung between them. "What do you mean?"

"Are people attractive because of their wealth, their status, their friends? Is it exciting to use sex as a means to get ahead?"

"I wouldn't say exciting," she said. "It's just that there doesn't seem to be a way around it. Everybody has to play the game."

"Why does everybody have to?"

"The risks are too high if you don't."

"What are the risks?"

"That you'll end up alone. No one will love you."

"But love has nothing to do with it!"

"Sure it does," she countered. "Jeez, Nick. Why is everything so black and white with you? No matter how bad things are, there's always something that isn't bad. It's a balance, an alternation, a rhythm or dance—good and bad, body and mind, male and female."

"Powerful sex and sexy power?"

"Exactly." She heard no sarcasm in his question. "It's what you learn in yoga. The important thing is the breath. You inspire and you expire. You take air in, and you let air out."

"I hate yoga."

"I know you do," she said, "but you could use it. You don't breathe enough, I can tell. You're tight. You hold the air in."

"I breathe okay," he said, privately admitting that she might have a point. He didn't want to take in the awe that enveloped him in LA like a sulfurous smog. He didn't want to be a happy person on a happy planet. It meant yielding to a millennial present of supernatural significance. The "moment" loomed in its midst like a god demanding sacrifice, at whose feet he was supposed to lay the incense and myrrh.

But he couldn't say why this stubborn urge for resistance had to tighten him up as much as it did. The more he tried to say why, in fact, the tighter he felt, the more tenuous he felt his grasp on any good reasons for resistance. He seemed to be demanding of himself, with a pressure not unlike what one would expect from a different sort of god, an angry god of the wilderness or the desert, that he sink ever further into unhappiness.

He wondered if Carson could feel this conflict in him. She sat by his side with the puzzled expression of those angels Botticelli painted at the feet of the Sistine Madonna, waiting for him to come out of his private torment. Only he couldn't tell just which god she served: the one who offered relief or the one who punished resistance. Perhaps it didn't matter. Perhaps they were the same god, demanding the same sacrifice. Carson would then be sitting on *his* unhappiness without admitting it, wanting from him not universal love but the denial she knew as the only workable strategy for coping with its utter privation.

He recalled her, in the spinning studio, riding her stationary bike with the others. The image warranted more sympathy than he gave it. Even at his most critical, Nick could see that the cyclers, in their imaginary mountains, were trapped in a vicious circle, bearing down on what they rode away from: transactional LA, where well-being came as the reward for making sure one's assets were in shape. This explained the haggard, hunted, look he'd caught in their ecstatic faces. It also explained why acknowledging his own reflection in that look didn't make it any easier for him to yield, to sympathize. On the contrary, he still preferred, stubbornly, to resist.

ᚷ

Not that he knew where this left him, except alone on his hillside, stuck inside himself, feeling his aversions slowly get the better of him. In this state he found it hard to take pleasure even in pastimes he'd once considered immune, like going for walks in the winding streets of his neighborhood, which couldn't be more glorious, especially on the ridge high above Lou's house, where the view invited Olympian comparisons. He used to do that a lot. He'd always been a walker, ever since he was a kid and he accompanied his mother on long peregrinations she did simply for their own sake sometimes, digging in at the fast clip of a woman on the run. He remembered trailing after her, struggling to keep up, homing in on her slight figure as it darted through crowds on Fifth Avenue or Broadway. He wished she would slow down but rarely said so. He had a good idea by then what she was running from.

Walking had ever since been Nick's best antidote to depression. It calmed him to have his thoughts synchronize with his wavering gait. They took on momentum that way, they became physical, and so he could exorcise the specters. It worked in New York and Paris, where the method had first been perfected. It worked less well in LA, although he had plenty of places he liked to go: beaches, Griffith Park, Silver Lake with its gorgeous reservoir. But even before his current doldrums had set in, he'd noticed a tapering off. He'd been in LA long enough to understand that no one was really supposed to walk there. It was embarrassing when you did. Like taking the bus or sitting on a park bench, it hinted at poverty, at second-class status. Eventually Nick tired of this stupid self-consciousness and gave in to privatizing demands as everyone pretty much had to in the end. And now, he feared, even the preference for something else was gone. He thought it was Kierkegaard who said to beware of the man who had lost his desire to walk.

Circumstances, however, wouldn't let him stay in his aversive state for long. Creditors had begun calling at all hours of the day and even night, leaving messages on his voicemail that threatened reprisals if he didn't start paying down his debts. He also had to deal with the new renters, the free-spirited wife and her even more odious husband Bob. They'd both started appearing without notice in his yard, ogling the roses and the view that would soon belong to them. Their intrusions so annoyed Nick that he had to flee the apartment altogether. Mostly he passed the time in cafés, where he drank too much coffee and read books on literary theory, thinking to practice the lingo if by chance he did hear of an interview at the MLA.

6

He wanted very much to see Bojena as the time approached for him to move. One day he left a message on her cell phone, something he'd never done for fear of it coming back to the husband, and begged her to meet with him. A week before he had to clear out of the apartment, she agreed to dinner at an Italian restaurant in Brentwood.

He showed up a few minutes early, sitting at the table she'd reserved on a candlelit back patio and ordering a Bandol wine he knew she would like. The four or five tables surrounding him were still empty, and he felt a little ridiculous enclosed all by himself in brick walls, under a small patch of sky. Every now and then the waitress came to refresh the bowl of olives or bring more breadsticks, so he wouldn't feel so alone. It bothered him that Bojena had chosen this spot for its seclusion.

Time stretched. She was often late, and when she did show up she was often breathless from the exertions of arranging her life so it could go on without her for a few hours. He expected that. But it came to be a half hour after the time, then forty-five minutes, and he began to worry. A couple joined him on the patio, which only added to his discomfort. He poured himself a second glass of wine.

Presently the waitress appeared with a message. "A woman called . . .is it Bojena?" She had trouble pronouncing that second palatal consonant. The name was Polish. Her parents came from Silesia.

"That's right," he said, confused. He felt for the phone in the inside pocket of his jacket. He hadn't forgotten to take it with him.

"She said there's been an emergency, something to do with her son, but it's over now and she'll be here as soon as she can."

"I'll wait, then." Bojena must not have been able to talk—probably involved in some lie to explain the night away.

"Would you like an appetizer?"

"No, thanks. The olives are enough."

He felt a prick of shame force on him questions he mostly preferred not to ask. Why had he gotten involved with a married woman in the first place? Why did he love someone who couldn't love him back without conditions and excuses? Why martyr his heart this way, cutting it out in sacrifice on the altar of a nine-year-old son whose needs would, and must, forever subordinate his own?

Most people, he knew, would have said he chose Bojena because he felt unworthy. No other explanation sounded right. It couldn't have been the other way around. The problem couldn't have been a world where love had no worth, especially when it fit into the conventions permitted it, since then it wasn't love anymore, only what Bojena left behind on coming to see him. He did, however, honestly believe this—whatever else might be the case about him. He didn't love Bojena because of an inferiority complex even if he had one. He didn't love her because she was unavailable even if he did set himself up to fail. He loved her despite his flaws and in the situation such diagnoses were all but designed to exclude—despite a world where love had no chance, where, indeed, love was set up to fail, since there it had to be conventional or it was nothing, and being conventional it boiled down to nothing once again. He should just accept this double bind as fact and without further ado. He should stop blaming himself when nothing was what he ended up with, too.

For a moment he could see down the winding path he was on with this sort of caustic reflection, its distant end point in a hard shell-like self-sufficiency that would be his only consolation for the pride on which he insisted. It scared him as much as a world in which love was set up to fail and had the paradoxical effect of driving him still more to Bojena, to the intimacy he thought they shared. It was all he had right then, even if it didn't mean he had anything at all.

Another hour passed. He went through the whole bottle of wine, eating olives and breadsticks. The waitress came back.

"Your friend's called again," she said, sensing the spot it put him in, even indignant on his behalf. "She wants to talk to you herself this time."

Nick followed her through the bustling restaurant to the reception podium, where he took a phone from the host and stood in the small crowd of people gathered around. He felt unsteady from the wine.

"There's been an accident," he heard Bojena say. Her voice, its plain distress, sounded distant in the line. "My son fell and banged his head on a table. I thought at first it was just a bad bruise, but he felt dizzy afterward. I've taken him to the hospital."

"You're not coming then?"

"I'm sorry, Nick."

"I've been waiting for two hours."

"I know."

"Why didn't you tell me the first time?!"

"I thought I could come," she said, her voice shaking.

"And why didn't you call me directly? I'm standing in front of the whole restaurant."

"This is my husband's phone."

It took him a moment to recover from this lacerating piece of information. "If you'd just told me," he said, struggling to keep his composure. "If you'd just put me out of my misery after half an hour, I might have been able to understand."

"I wanted to come."

He made no reply. That probably was the reason she'd drawn it out.

"I had no choice, Nick." She was on the verge of crying now. "My son needs me. Try to understand."

His shame was intense. It came over him in waves, and the waves hit hard against the walls of his many contradictions, flowing back on themselves in turbid crosscurrents of hurt emotion. He closed his eyes, hearing the noise around him drop into a silence broken only by the sound of Bojena's congested sorrow in the phone. The few seconds it lasted seemed an eternity.

"Of course," he forced himself to say. "You're right. It's no big deal. Take care of your son. We'll talk later." He handed the phone back to the host and looked around for the waitress, hoping she had the check ready. He wanted out of there the way a man locked in a cellar wants the light.

X

Afterward he curled up on his sofa with a bottle of scotch. It was unlike him to drink alone. It reminded him of his mother, in the time before his parents' divorce. There were nights when she'd get quietly potted while they sat in front of the television, surrounded by all those jazz records, wondering when, or if, his father would be coming home. His mother had never been very demonstrative. She held things in as a rule. He could only tell she wasn't in her right mind by a swimming in her eyes or a drawl in her voice. But it was enough for him to feel the moorings slip, the world float. When at last he fell asleep on Castellammare, it was in that feeling, on those nights.

He woke up the next morning to the sound of his screen door creaking open. People, it appeared, were standing in his living room. It seemed a dream at first, matter-of-fact and completely fantastic at the same time. But as he sat up in bed, he understood that Bob Kirschner had entered the apartment with his teenage daughter. Nick pulled the covers back, slipped on some clothes, and went out to confront them. Bob, short with a stocky build, a thick neck, and a bald head, was speaking amiably about an alarm system he planned to install for his new office.

"What the fuck are you doing?" Nick cried.

Jarred, Bob's first thought was for his daughter. He laid a hand on her shoulder and led her toward the door. "Go back to the car," he told her softly.

"Both of you go back to the car!"

"Don't talk that way in front of my daughter."

"I'll talk however I want!"

Bob ushered the scandalized girl outside. He then turned back into the room and planted two very solid feet on the floor, facing Nick with arms akimbo.

"I told Lou we were coming," he said.

"Lou didn't tell me—"

"He said we could start moving in—"

"I'm not out! Understand? I'm still here. I sleep here, I eat here, I work here—"

"So what?"

"So what?!" Nick said incredulously. "You're trespassing. You're breaking the law."

"No," Bob said. "I'm right where I'm supposed to be." Nick had a feeling he was about to hear very truthful words—words too direct to be spoken, but everyone knew what they were, how they sounded. "You're the trespasser."

"You want to ask the police if I'm trespassing?"

"You're the one who's out of place." Bob didn't just mean in the apartment, or in Lou's house. He meant in the whole neighborhood.

"You're standing in my living room!"

"This isn't *your* living room," Bob scoffed. "It doesn't belong to you. Nothing here belongs to you."

"This can't be happening."

"You think you have rights?" Bob took a step forward. They were shoulder to shoulder now. His eyes glittered. He might have been the one whose privacy had been violated. "You don't have rights. Lou Perkins has rights, and I told him I'd be showing up here today."

"That's not how this works," Nick said, trying to pull together thoughts that were in complete disarray. "There are rules, due process, the Fourteenth Amendment, or the Fifth Amendment, whatever—*democracy*, for Christ's sake! Ever hear of that?"

Bob snorted. "Listen," he said, in the blunt manner of someone about to set an idiot straight. "I make more money in a week than you do in a year, understand? That's democracy, you smartass sack of shit—"

"Get out!" Nick shouted, shoving the man. "Get out or I'll kick your fucking ass!"

He could be tough enough when he had to be. He was a New Yorker, after all. But Bob didn't back down, shoving him right back. They traded a few jabbing blows and grabbed each other, tottering in furious embrace around the room. This went on until Bob whacked a lamp with his elbow and crashed against an end table. In the process he lost his balance, and Nick, getting an arm firmly around his neck, wrestled him to the floor. Bob had no choice at that point but to relent. Nick bumped the screen door open with his shoulder and dragged him over the threshold into the yard.

Bob scrambled to his feet, and they both stood breathless for a few moments, taking each other's measure. Nick saw fear in the man's eyes. He'd gotten more than he bargained for. It was probably also dawning on him that the authorities would side with Nick if it came to that, whatever state of ill health the "democracy" was in. But the amazing thing was that Bob still believed in his right to be there. He was even defiant about it. Laws existed for the good of people like him, people with money. When they weren't good, they didn't apply. And thinking otherwise was not only wrong or stupid but an offense to virtue, as palpable to him as Nick's anger in front of his daughter.

Bob might have been right: Nick didn't belong on that terraced hillside. Maybe he never had. Or, maybe, the people who lived there had changed as a class. He was beginning to suspect this was the case. They'd turned vicious in the sense of their own exception, and they were willing to assert their privileges without apology and by brute force if need be, like elites in some Third World country. The beauty of that neighborhood was paid for in blood, in the heart. Its beauty was ugly. That's why Nick had stopped taking pleasure in it a long time ago. The only question was why he'd ever thought it had something to offer him in the first place. He'd have to give that some serious consideration.

"I don't want to see you here again," he said hoarsely, as rigid through the spine as a steel beam.

Bob daubed a split lip with the back of his hand. It was bleeding rather profusely. "I'll be saying the same about you in a few days."

"Fuck off." Nick slammed the screen door shut, swung back into the apartment, and headed straight for the pack of cigarettes.

7

He overcame his pride and called his father. Emmanuele, his little girl, answered the phone, and Nick spent a few minutes chatting with her in French about her life in Paris, her friends, her *école maternelle.* It was the longest conversation they'd ever had. He hardly knew her. Julie refused to raise her in LA. Smart woman.

His father took the phone in a good humor for a change, asking where he'd been hiding himself. Nick hadn't been picking up his calls.

"In a hole," he answered cryptically. "A deep, dark hole."

"A rabbit hole," his father said, by way of gloss. "Your mother used to say that, especially when she got stoned. 'I'm going down my rabbit hole.' Then she'd get very quiet and internal. It drove me nuts. The two of you were exasperating that way."

"I'm not doing well," Nick said, ignoring this rare mention of his mother. "Things have fallen apart on me."

"You're feeling sorry for yourself. I can hear it. You speak from down in your throat. Your voice is small and far away. It doesn't carry."

Nick inhaled, steeling himself. "I need a favor."

"You want money."

"It's just a loan."

"Jesus, Nick. The only thing you ever ask me for is money."

"I'll be able to pay you back in a few months–"

"Since you were a kid," he went on. "You never knew how to ask for simple things, the things that don't cost, emotional things. Love, affection."

"Maybe you shouldn't have to ask for those things."

"Nobody's going to love you if you don't," his father declared. "And you're nobody in this rat race, if nobody loves you."

Nick hated these insipid platitudes from his father, delivered like lines in one of his movies. How so shrewd a man could stand to hear himself say them was simply beyond fathoming.

"Why is it people who are good at taking," he said, on a familiar edge now, "think those who aren't suffer from some sort of deficiency?"

"Because takers have things to give, and they learn a lot about people who need. Needy people."

"Oh, Christ!" Nick cried, all restraint vanishing. "Forget I brought it up, okay? You're impossible. Like a man in a fortress. I can't get in."

"And you're a man in a hole. We have things in common."

"I'll find the money somewhere else."

"I don't care about the money."

"Then why make me feel like shit asking for it?"

"Okay," his father said, in a placating voice. "You're right. I'm sorry. I want something from you I can't seem to get."

"What do you want from me?"

The question struck a chord. Nick could feel his father through the phone touching on limits, on uncertainties he wasn't used to dealing with. When it came to honest feeling, he ran for the hills with the best of them. "I don't know. I want you to love me."

"You have enough of that already," Nick said. "Everybody loves you."

"You don't."

"I *wish* I didn't. That's different."

"Things are falling apart on me, too, you know."

Nick recalled Haley's impression of him shuffling like a homeless man down the rue Oberkampf. "Are you taking care of yourself?" he asked more civilly.

"No."

"Why not?"

"What's the use?" his father said. "My mind slips away day by day, and there's nothing I can do about it. I'm a zombie. A dead man walking."

"How about the drug–what's it called?"

"Duodopa."

"Is it working?"

"I don't know. I'm tired a lot. I've developed a tremor in my hand."

Nick hesitated before his next thought, wondering if he should bring it out. "Maybe I'll come to Paris for a while."

"You come to Paris, and I'll go to LA. God, I miss the sunshine."

Nick smiled wanly. "We're living each other's lives."

"But inside out, or upside down." His father confused himself here. "Shit. I don't understand what I'm saying half the time."

"You mean we're failing at each other's lives."

"Something like that." He shifted to an easier topic. "How much do you need?"

"Five thousand. It's just a loan. I'll pay you back, I promise."

"Send Julie your account number, or whatever it is. I'll have her transfer it over."

"Okay."

Nick felt an upwelling of gratitude. For all the pain his father had caused, he'd also counted on him, and in his own way he'd come through. Nick had to admit that.

"Thanks, Dad."

"Consider it a present, from one fuckup to another. And because I love you. Remember that, Nick. You're a hard kid to love, but I love you."

"I'm not a kid anymore."

"You're still a kid," he told him. "And I don't say that just because I'm your father. You're green that way. You've always been green. Have you noticed?"

Nick sensed him picking out a precise shade of his character, something too subtle for words, but also plain as day when you were subtle. The shade was precise enough, anyway, for Nick not to mind the hint of criticism. "I guess so."

"You were always so touchy, so fucking sensitive. You needed more care, more attention, and I didn't give you that, I know. I was too far up the world's ass to try much either. If it's any consolation, everything smells like shit to me now."

"I don't believe that."

"You wouldn't," his father laughed, "you're green! But that's all right. Be glad you are. If nothing else, you'll age well. You won't end up a shambles of a man like me."

Nick wasn't so sure about that. Innocence had a longer way to fall when it did end, and oversensitivity could wear the body down before its time. But he decided not to worry the point and let his father's conciliatory tone hold through the rest of the conversation, welcoming the relief it gave him. That night he slept better than he had in a long while. The next morning he woke up determined to face his life with more ingenuity than he'd been showing of late, or ever.

ꭗ

He put his things in storage and checked into a Santa Monica motel, plotting out his next move. At least he called it that. He still hit walls when he thought of his options. He could go to Paris, but what he would do there—aside from bonding with his father, a prospect he didn't relish despite the rare fellow feeling they'd shared on the phone—was not immediately clear. He could go back to New York, where he'd been happiest; but that time of his life, bound up with school, had also ended unhappily, in those years spent adjunct teaching at different schools, running himself ragged on subways and trains all over the Tri-state area. He thought of finding a place on the east side of LA, Silver Lake or Echo Park, where he'd lived when he first moved there, and where he imagined it would be easier to avoid Hollywood people. But that wasn't true. Hollywood was unavoidable—a fact brought home to him when he learned that Lou hadn't secured the check Don Torrance still owed him before taking off on his international junket. That meant Nick would have to pry it from the studio on his own—probably with the help of a lawyer. Not having the strength for that or much else right then, and with the holiday season upon him, he resolved to wait until after the New Year before making any decisions.

He went one evening to see Carson in a dance performance. The setting was a women's clothing store on Montana Avenue, near enough for him to walk. When he saw the glass storefront and the people standing outside, he had to fight an urge to turn back. He didn't like the scene on Montana Avenue. To be there was to contact a social boundary in Santa Monica that a friend had once explained to him this way: on one side, young single women (like his friend), on the other, the rich men they aspired to attract in the little restaurants and cafés that lined the street between. The real business of Montana Avenue was marriage, she said. And, of course, divorce.

He crossed the street, joining the small crowd as it funneled through the door. The store had closed for the event, and he stood with the others near the cash register. The sun in the windows cast defined orange beams onto the wood floor, where Carson and a partner lay wrapped head to toe in white sheets. They resembled, Nick thought deliberately, caterpillars in their pupae. They kept still, waiting for people to figure out that the show wasn't going to start until they quieted down. As this sank in, Nick noticed a trancelike electronic music rising steadily in volume. The sunbeams shifted across the floor and up onto the wall as the dancers slowly began to free themselves from their sheets. Both wore loose fitting halter dresses, through which their lean, hard bodies could be enticingly glimpsed. The point, however, as Carson had more than once taken pains to emphasize, wasn't to titillate.

For some time past she'd been fascinated with Butoh dance theater. To Nick's untrained eye the style involved doing different things with different parts of the body, all at the same time. The results made him think of a person suffering in slow motion the agony of a paralytic stroke. Carson and her partner, true to form, staggered onto their feet, lurching off to opposite ends of the store, the looks of rigor mortis in their faces accentuated by a chalky makeup. They gravitated toward racks that had been pushed to either side and inserted themselves between the dresses, wrapping a bare thigh around a pleated skirt, nuzzling up against a stand collar, sniffing at silk ruffles.

Nick detected an allegory of femininity. They were dramatizing the difficulties of becoming a self amid social requirements that the clothes symbolized. Their tics, their spasms, and their pallid reanimated stares suggested the process was traumatic. That would be an interesting impression to leave an audience, Nick granted, if it had, indeed, been the point. But he doubted it. Carson merely applied the style, not letting it disturb her belief that the clothes were accidents, adornments she put on or took off, while the true self she so often liked to praise remained timeless and inviolable. Only the style stripped this self down to its zero degree; only the style understood that the roles were essential and the self an accident, brought to an uncertain being in the vexed element of conventional life. And that meant even the style was an accident. No matter how provocative, or to the extent it was provocative, the dance still reflected that conventional life, if not the business transacted on that social boundary of Santa Monica. Who knows, Nick thought, uncharitably perhaps, a kind of titillation may have been the point after all.

He begged off joining Carson and her friends for drinks afterward, fearing such thoughts would find more corroboration than he could bear at the moment. He wandered instead into the dark residential streets toward his motel. It was a warm night. Some important football game was on in all the condos and apartments he passed. Every significant play set the neighborhood cheering. He felt, each time this happened, as if he was inside a vast abstract game, with abstract pleasures. He could hardly keep from believing it. He had to tell himself that it didn't matter if there *was* a game and that it *did* pervade the world. It was still only a projection, or a metaphor, different from what he thought he was experiencing. This difference, in fact, was all he did know with any confidence. It formed the limit of what he couldn't ever see directly or whole, like the "thing itself" for philosophers, never accessible to the mind as such.

Still he went with it, not because those cheers weren't voices in his head but because they might as well be. His skepticism was as crazy as anything else. Like the metaphor of the game, or the provocation of Carson's dance, it, too, was just an accident, one among many options for getting at the world—"all good," as he imagined Carson saying to her friends back at the bar. And this meant that, as equivalent as anything else, his skepticism put him in the world right at the moment he doubted his own judgment. If it was crazy to think of life as a game, that is, life was a game—arbitrary, factitious, felt in the roles people played and the rules they played by. He saw no point in denying this, when all it did was help him to understand how he *was* crazy. It brought out his irrelevance as a thinking person. Perhaps it also gave some small dignity to the desire for a different game, with less abstract pleasures.

Nick heard the phone in his pocket ring as he walked. He assumed it was his father. His usual reluctance to take the call gave way to a sudden rancor. He wanted to place the blame for the performance principle that he saw now was what most bothered him about life in LA squarely on his father's shoulders. In fact he wanted to throw it back at the man with all the vinegar of a spiteful child. He punched the button without even looking at the screen.

"Hello?" a voice barked. It wasn't his father. He could tell by a near deaf perplexity that it belonged, rather, to an old man who'd been leaving messages by mistake for his service provider to come and fix his cable box.

"You've got the wrong number," Nick said.

"What?"

"*You've got the wrong number!*"

"Helen!" the man bellowed into wherever it was he called from. "There's someone on the line."

"No, there's not—"

"The TV won't work," the man informed him. "We just had it installed a week ago."

"I don't know anything about that."

"Will you take the phone, Helen?" he demanded. "I'll be damned if I understand a word he says."

Nick was about to hang up when the man's wife came on the line.

"Hello?" Her voice had an unexpected gentleness to it, melting all at once the hardness in his heart. Indeed, he felt, with an inexorable force, wall after wall inside him begin to fall. She sounded so lost in the abstract game, the abstract pleasures.

"You've got the wrong number," he told her. "You've been calling the wrong number all along. I'm not Comcast."

"You're not?"

"No."

"I don't understand," she said with dismay. "This is the number the service man gave us."

"You must have written it down wrong."

"Henry!" she cried. "This is not Comcast."

"It's time for *Parks and Recreation*!" her husband hollered irrelevantly in the background.

Nick stood on the sidewalk now, so devastated he felt tears press into his eyes. He could only just hear himself say, "What's wrong with the TV?"

"It won't turn on."

"At all?"

"There's a kind of static," she said, "but the stations won't appear. We press the buttons and nothing happens."

He tried to think what he would do in their same strait. "Can you see the back of the set top box?"

"Henry can."

"Have him pull the cables out."

She relayed the instruction.

"Once that's done, tell him to unplug the box and the TV. Let both sit for a minute, then plug everything back in and turn them on again. Numbers should appear on the front of the box when you do that."

He waited tight of breath while the steps were taken. After a while Helen informed him the numbers still hadn't appeared. "It just says HELP on the little screen."

"Is there a reset button anywhere?"

"Henry, he says to look for a reset button." There was a pause. "Is it red?" she asked.

"Probably."

"Yes, it's there."

"Tell him to press it," Nick said. "Do the numbers come on now?"

"It says 638."

"That's a channel."

"Now it says 9:20."

"That's the time. Press the power button on the remote."

When Henry did so, Helen saw the cable box catch the signal. A few seconds later the TV sparked on, to her immense relief. As if on cue, the neighborhood around Nick erupted in whoops and shouts. Someone must have scored a touchdown.

8

After that Nick gave himself over to the dislocation he'd been feeling for a while now anyway. It hardly seemed a choice. His efforts to find a place, love, work, or just a value for his self-awareness had miserably failed. Resistance ran him straight into what he resisted. All he had left was his situation in that abstract game and the sympathy Helen had managed to flush out in him there. He had to wonder about that. It hinted at another approach to life beyond the resignation he feared if he relinquished what hold he did have on some kind of meaning. Maybe he exaggerated that fear in holding on too tightly. Maybe his idea of a meaningful life had hardened, enough for him to forget what deep down he knew he was: not a true self beset by accidents but an accidental self prone to illusions of an essential nature; not Carson, but a critical Carson. If so, the right thing to do would be to let go. All he'd really be losing were his own illusions. Who knows, he might also be gaining a world.

So he let go. He drifted for a while. He passed into something like the millennial present Carson idealized, into a marvelous freedom from thought, judgment, scruple. As he had nothing else to do, this often meant driving around LA with no aims more solid than passing the time until he could go to bed. He made vast loops on the freeways. He drove down one long boulevard after the next. He felt, in the release from purposeful action, the emptiness of an anonymous circulation. It had its appeal. He understood better why some people liked to drive when they were depressed. In abandon to the tedium of so much concentrated efficiency and the steady depletion of resources it involved, they could feel the different abandon of neutralized qualities and homogenized time, exactly as it was mirrored back to them in the aggregated gas stations, car lots, fast food restaurants, and big box retail stores they passed. The experience was intense, even passionate in its way. At least that was the word that came to Nick's mind when, just before Christmas, he pulled up beside a lone woman in an Audi, stopped at the intersection of Beverly and La Cienega, under the looming shadow of the vast Beverly Center mall. She had Whitney Houston's "I Will Always Love You" playing at full blast on her stereo and sang along with big, glistening tears in her eyes, given over to the senseless pain and ecstasy of somebody who was truly at one with the universe. The sight couldn't have provided a better emblem for the limbo in which Nick now found himself.

ϗ

Carson, sensing he needed help, invited him to a party on New Year's Eve. He resolved to go rather than stay in his motel room, but on coming to his car that night he changed his mind. Instead he walked down to the Santa Monica Pier, blending into the crowd that waited for a firework display at midnight. There again he took that odd comfort in anonymity. It struck him this time as an introverted pleasure, and heading down the pier he realized that LA, for all its garrulous social reputation, had this other side to it as well. Shy people could inhabit their fantasies without the burden of having to test them against the world. They could live vicariously through others.

He came to the end of the pier and gazed out over the languid swell of the water at a crescent moon hanging low over the horizon. Several Latino men were fishing while their kids and wives sat on overturned buckets, bored out of their skulls. The scene stood in pointed contrast to the usual Westside affluence. It revealed another city within the city, where people lived as if in another world. Actually, many worlds coexisted in LA, all laminated together and yet strictly segregated, too, in a kind of four-dimensional apartheid. It worked because one axis of that apartheid was in the mind. It allowed people to see only what they wanted to see.

He soon grew bored with the end of the pier and returned the way he'd come. The roller coaster vibrated in the spongy wood planks under his feet. The lights from the looming Ferris wheel stimulated the phosphene of his obsessions.

He must have gotten too wrapped up in himself this way, because he resented more than it warranted the harassment of a teenager he soon encountered. The kid, with spiky purple hair and a skateboard in his hands, loitered with a few friends by a white railing and cast scornful looks at the passersby. On seeing Nick he started repeating the word "pedophile" into an imaginary police radio. Nick tried his best to ignore the provocation, but the crowd prevented him from moving on, and he had no choice except to linger in earshot. It was obvious the kid picked him out because he was alone, and anyone alone was fair game for ridicule.

"Pedophile! Pedophile! KKKRRRRCCH! Code three! Alert! Possible pedophile!"

Forced to halt altogether, Nick lost his temper. He rushed to the kid and pushed him against the rail. "Stop it!" he commanded.

The kid squared up, his eyes lit with a suddenly incandescent rage. Now Nick was the one intruding on his obsessions, and the prerogative didn't run both ways. In a quick, decisive motion he swung his skateboard over his head and hit Nick with it hard across the jaw.

He fell at once to the pier, both hands pressed to his face, and cried out in terrific searing pain. He saw, in the darkness behind his closed eyes, little points of blue light. There really was such a thing as stars.

"I'll kill you! I'll kill you!" he heard the kid scream, as his friends nonetheless wrested the skateboard out of his hands and restrained him. "You ugly cocksucking shitfaced motherfucker!!!"

A circle of scandalized onlookers had formed around them. No one, Nick noticed, offered to help. They didn't want to get involved. They preferred to stand by until the interest wore off and it was time to melt back into the crowd, into their own obsessions. At that moment, curled up on the rough wood planks, Nick hated the whole world. He hated himself in it, too.

⅄

Shortly after the New Year he received an email from the chair of the English department at King's University in Auckland. It informed him that he was under consideration for a job teaching twentieth-century American literature. Nick sat stunned on the bed in his motel room as he read the message, nursing the livid bruise that had blossomed on his cheek. It apologized for waiting so long to let him know and explained that, given New Zealand's distance, it wasn't feasible for a search committee to attend the MLA conference, just then getting underway. If the position still interested him, they'd like to conduct an interview by phone as soon as possible.

Two days later he spoke to five people on a conference call. They asked a series of rehearsed questions about his teaching style and research interests, to which he gave clumsy answers at best. It lasted an hour, and he figured that was the end of it. He wouldn't have hired him. But he must have done something right, because the next morning he awoke to another email offering him the job, starting in February, the beginning of their fall semester, at an annual salary of 70,000 New Zealand dollars, along with a stipend to pay for moving expenses and an employment visa under the university's sponsorship.

Nick passed the rest of that day in a daze. He couldn't believe it. Nothing had ever come to him so out of the blue–nothing good, at any rate. It felt almost like a miracle, like he'd slipped into this wondrous space of exemption from all the laws of man or nature. New Zealand wasn't much more than that to him. He knew hardly a thing about the country. He'd never visited. He'd never been close to anyone from there. He'd never had much occasion to learn about the culture. A film or two, some basic settler-colonial history, a few clichés about face-pulling Maoris and wingless birds were all he had to go by. As far as he could tell New Zealand really might be the end of the earth. It struck just one consonant chord in his heart. The end of the earth was about as far from LA as he wanted to get now.

Down Under

1

Nick drew his inspiration to be a professor from his mother, who disliked pretense and convention as much as he did. For her scripts, canned words, and easy answers were signs in people of an unwillingness to look closely at the social games they were playing. The tacit conformism in this bothered her most of all, especially when it meant overlooking or slighting idiosyncrasies of character and feeling, voice and manner, that she tended to respect in others.

Not that she was much given to calling people out in their social games. She had a marked preference for listening and observing. But people felt judged anyway, as much by what she didn't say as by what she did, with her typical lapidary precision cutting delicately to the bone. Nick grew up puzzled by this, since his mother in many respects seemed the least judgmental person he knew. She was humane, tender-hearted, a partisan if anything for the underdog, the outsider, the weak and the sensitive.

This compassionate side of her character showed around animals. Some of Nick's fondest memories involved how she related to them, with a sixth sense he didn't have himself. He remembered once, when he was seven, growing frustrated in his attempts to get their cat, Bear, a Russian Blue stray they had found in Morningside Park, to stay on his lap. Every time he placed him there, the cat would run off.

"Don't force it," she advised him. "He senses how you're feeling. If you're patient, he'll sense that, too. Wait, catch his eye, flirt."

"But he might never come then!"

"He won't come any other way, kiddo. Cats are proud. They like their liberty. They know their rights."

She sat beside him on their orange suede sofa for a lesson in feline seduction. She began by drumming her fingers on a crossed knee. Soon enough Bear noticed, gingerly making his approach. When he leapt to the sofa he was still wary, with back arched and tail switching, but

Nick saw a new willingness to negotiate in his eyes. His mother petted him in long unhurried strokes until at length he dug an exploratory claw into the fabric of her jeans. At the same time he shot her an inquiring glance, which she studiously avoided. Bear liked that. Her indifference reassured him. He moved onto her lap and set about lending himself flexibly to its folds. Before long he was curled up in a ball with his chin resting on a forelimb, all skittishness gone.

To Nick his mother seemed just as relaxed as the cat in that moment, at home in herself, more at home than he could even then imagine himself feeling. He loved that native or natural quality about her. It showed ease in more tacit dimensions, where people had a gracefulness so different from what appeared on the surface as to hint at double lives. He even caught himself, in his child's mind, thinking of her as a sprite or pixie moonlighting as a person. She looked a little like one: small, slight of build, with fine, delicate features, fair skin that freckled in the sun, and light gray eyes—a dead ringer for the actress Mia Farrow.

With people, however, his mother's ease often vanished, or suffered in a strange quarantine. She could seem diffident, even cold. The contrast was too stark to go unnoticed, at least to Nick, and she explained it as best she could in terms of a self-consciousness she had trouble overcoming. Here books came to the rescue. Reading for her was a way to contact complexity in the world, to give it the resonance it hardly ever had between people. She still focused on what happened between people, but as a critic more than an artist. The mind was the tangible thing for her. Ideas helped to guide her intuitions out from the thickets of assumption and prejudice, to situate her feelings in larger realities of social emulation, inequity, and exploitation. Nick never saw her happier than when she was doing this kind of work, and even if it didn't exactly help to reduce that contrast, putting her still more at odds with people, the books she had around when he was a kid were signs of possibilities that otherwise seemed shut down in her. They lived in his memory almost as much as she did now. When he wanted to conjure her vanished presence, her lost familiarity, they often provided the associations he needed with their colors, their musty paperback smells, their titles: *Presentation of Self in Everyday Life*, *One-Dimensional Man*, *Soul on Ice*.

ӽ

Around Evan she had no way of claiming her own nature with much authority, as he knew very well how to turn the tables on her. In the many arguments Nick witnessed or overheard in his childhood—often splitting on their different temperaments—his father considered her the one who needed to be in control. She confused shyness with aversion, respect with the denial of appetites he believed from their force in him must belong to everybody. She fought back, but whatever challenge she presented to his father's assertiveness became all the easier to dismiss as he grew more prominent a public figure, more admired for his appetites. Indeed his success, along with his infidelities and the divorce, so undermined a basic pride that she never quite escaped his view of her as too inhibited for her own good.

That view had its share of truth, as Nick better understood when she took him to stay with her parents on a farm in Nebraska. They were odd, slow people who lived a lot in their own minds. His grandmother was a kindly old woman who baked pies and collected Oriental figurines made of porcelain and jade. His grandfather, a hardworking farmer, rarely offered signs of warmth or interest. He would listen in conversation with the ruminative look of a man who had a difficult time believing you were there, and he took in what you said the way a black hole takes in light. In the months after their arrival, when his mother did little more than brood over old choices and mistakes, Nick could see her sinking into the loneliness of her former life, wrestling with limits and loyalties she'd never entirely outgrown. She'd worked out all the problems with that life, and she feared it, but with a keen sadness for her parents' otherworldliness. It struck her as an injustice she didn't want to ignore or forget. A part of her therefore always stayed back with them, feeling any escape, even her own, as a kind of injustice, even though it also set her against herself.

His father may have been right in one respect: his mother needed something like his amour propre for the permission to be a worldlier person, to imagine her independence of spirit in less sacrificial terms. Nick needed it from her, too. He wasn't happy on that farm, lacking her same conflicted allegiances and missing the only home he knew in New York. He had no talent for country life. He hated the school he went to, made no friends, and dealt with his loneliness by burying himself in books, preferring Notre Dame with Quasimodo or Elsinore Castle with Hamlet to cornfields, barnyards, and hay sheds. There was a clear strategy in this refusal to adapt. He was asking her, in so many words, not to give up on the person he knew best, the one who'd long before left Nebraska—even if it was with Evan.

She got the message in the end, coming out of her doldrums and facing up to the challenges of her new life as a single mother. She enrolled at a nearby teacher's college, completed an accelerated credential program, and found a job in a private grade school in Hoboken. When Nick was thirteen they moved back to the east coast, taking up residence in a rented house just blocks from the Hudson River, near the Stevens Institute of Technology. From the other side of the campus they could see the Manhattan skyline, and the PATH train to the city was a ten-minute walk.

Nick saw his mother's mood improve over the next several years, especially when she started taking classes at the CUNY Graduate Center. That, more than anything, helped to put Evan and the divorce behind her. She had projects to work on that interested her more than her own pain. She met like-minded friends and started dating. Best of all, she discovered in herself an acuity of mind stronger than any reticence could disavow. When, in Nick's junior year of high school, she was accepted into the Graduate Center's PhD program in philosophy, everything fell into place. She had a path to her own nature, one that also offered her sense of justice a value and a place: she would become a professor.

But, then, disaster struck. His mother returned one day from a visit to a hematologist with the news that she had lymphocytic leukemia. Forced to postpone her first year of school, she underwent high-dose chemotherapy. The effects were stark. She lost all her hair, shrank to skeletal thinness, struggled all the time with anemia and nausea, and lived in fear of simple infections. The pain was so harsh it broke her will. When, a year later, she learned the chemotherapy hadn't worked, she refused to go to the next step, brain and spinal radiation, no matter how much Nick begged her. Had she known in the first place what it would be like, she told him, she wouldn't have agreed to any treatment at all.

Her bitterness about the suffering she'd been through, about its useless and degrading sacrifices, and at such a turning point in her life, would stay forever branded on Nick's memory. It revealed in her a loneliness far deeper and more thwarted than he'd ever thought possible in anyone. It hurt beyond saying to know she'd never come out of it or come to terms with it either. Her death was all the more devastating because it left nothing resolved and nothing forgiven.

He felt, afterward, obscurely charged with the task of righting this wrong, of living for his mother, or in her memory. He began his first year at Brown a few months later, with all the supports knocked out from under him, and threw himself into the community he found there with an orphan's abandon. His closest friends all took the same literature classes, particularly those taught by a young French professor, Pierre-Yves Ozouf, who'd been instrumental in continuing a tradition on campus of interest in literary theory. Once a student of Jacques Derrida, Ozouf, as everyone affectionately called him, introduced Nick to a European intellectual culture that gave a densely woven texture to his grief. He caught early on its elegiac tone, its sense of history as a tear in the fabric of being, and its feeling for a language haunted by signs, doubles, spirits, specters, and other figural phantasmata. He soon became adept at this semiotic style of thought, shouldering the burdens of that history as if they belonged to him the way they did to his teachers, to the books they had him read. The experience was transformative, mind-altering, even if, in his zeal, he sometimes raced ahead of himself, losing the sound of his own voice in the echo chambers of philosophical allusion.

This abstraction bothered him when he saw it reflected in the social scene to which he belonged. It wasn't pretentious, at least not obviously so, committed to the egalitarian values of the sixties—the French sixties above all—but people in it could still be too exclusive, too ready to make others feel they weren't interesting or smart enough to take part. Nick feared in playing along that he was leaving his mother behind, betraying her outsider allegiances, her loner's self-consciousness. He stayed true to both, or so he thought, by insisting on them in discussions and arguments with a fervor his friends didn't always understand, since, of course, he never brought his mother into it. Still, he tried to raise the political stakes of their deconstructive passions in a manner he knew she'd appreciate, telling himself he wanted them to think twice about their own privilege. He wanted that second thought to be a characteristic of privilege itself.

But he soon came to suspect that his reasons were not as principled as he believed, bound up rather with an image of his mother as an outsider that was more and more his own invention. That's how he knew he was forgetting her, and not by becoming a French snob but, on the contrary, by fighting with his friends for her slowly calcifying image in his mind. He glimpsed a still more painful stage of mourning in the likelihood that he would one day have to break that image apart. He would have to exclude his mother from his circle, leave her unactualized example behind, and for her sake no less than his, for the sake of a link in him back to a shared style and principle that would still be his own. The balancing act that followed from this double requirement led to strange ambivalences, exhausting in their own right.

Fortunately, he found support in his teachers, for whom literary research, the literary sensibility itself, turned out not to be just about initiation or the comforts of insider knowledge. Ozouf, who'd become in the meantime a mentor for Nick, gave him the shorthand he would always remember for that sensibility. Nick had met him in his office one day to discuss Stendhal's book *On Love*, and with too much bluster he criticized what he took to be archness in the writer's account of the different stages through which love passed. He thought it distanced the reader and, in another indirect defense of his mother, accused Stendhal of elitism. It was the winter of his sophomore year, snow swirled outside the professor's window on Waterman Street, and they spoke over a banging radiator in the corner.

"Stendhal comes across as an expert on sex," Nick said. "He uses irony to claim an authority he can't possibly have for what are just disconnected impressions, anecdotes."

"Do you think he expects you to take him seriously?"

"Well, yes. He's not just satirizing the sort of thinking that puts everything in developmental terms. He means it when he says there are seven stages of love, and in the seventh stage the lover's mind vacillates between three ideas."

"In Chapter 9, he worries he might be 'only expressing a sigh' when he thought he was 'stating a truth.'"

"He's still trying to 'state a truth,'" said Nick.

Ozouf fixed him in his steely gaze, wondering now about Nick's deeper need to quarrel with the writer. "I see a stable notion of irony in your mind," he said then. "That's good. You're using it correctly. It implies a constant perspective and an intended meaning. You understand it or you don't. But there are other kinds of irony that work against this inherent hierarchy, too. They're *un*stable, and in these cases there's no perspective not folded back into the ironic effect. Nobody exactly understands them. Nobody's exactly in control of the meaning."

"Not even the writer? Not even Stendhal?"

"Maybe that instability is the truth he's serious about."

Not for the first time around Ozouf, Nick felt a small cognitive push. "The truth that there is no 'truth'," he echoed.

"Or no master."

Nick would always remember this exchange as helping him to unsettle that outsider image of his mother, its authority in his mind. And yet it did so in a curious fashion, by recalling her sensitivity not only to intimidation and power but also, more subtly, to how easily one turned against that sensitivity, denied it, hurt it, in oneself no less than others, and from a need for mastery. Here, his mother helped him to understand Ozouf. For all that Nick's private fidelity to her might have held him back in his new world—for all that everything in it could only ever come for him "after his mother died"—she didn't just stand in the way either. She wasn't just a part of the past. She belonged to the future, to what he still had to learn there.

This more living memory of his mother remained, in any case, even as he did leave her behind, acquiring a sophistication beyond anything she'd known. It also helped to shape the projects that would eventually define him as a scholar in his own right. A focus on modernism as a graduate student became original research when it settled into questions of marginality and borders, edges of various kinds. His dissertation took its title, *Unrecorded Looks*, from a phrase in Djuna Barnes's *Nightwood*, and drew together readings of relatively minor figures from the period—Miguel de Unamuno, Robert Walser, Jean Rhys, H.D., Mina Loy, and the painter-writer Leonora Carrington, who'd once been married to Max Ernst. His feeling for the material, and for close textured analysis, impressed his teachers, including Ozouf, who would be his principal advisor at NYU. His encouragement carried Nick through not only the PhD but also the work that turned the dissertation into a book, which he published, sadly, just as academia was abandoning him. He dedicated it to his mother.

2

He arrived in Auckland after the long flight from LA to find a text message informing him that the colleague who had offered to meet him at the airport would be unable to make it. He took a taxi to the address of the hotel where the department chair had arranged for him to stay, not far from the campus. The city had a haphazard layout, lots of angled and crisscrossing streets, and it disoriented not only Nick but the taxi driver, a Syrian man, who, at one point, had him looking up routes on a map as he drove. The humor in this was not lost on either of them.

After checking into the hotel, a terraced row house with wrought-iron balconies and a pitched roof, he set out to find the English department. It had rained the night before, and the air was humid. He soon found himself sweating through his shirt. February was, of course, summer in New Zealand.

King's University sat atop a ridge overlooking the city toward the harbor. It sported a mixture of modern glass-and-steel buildings and faux medieval halls clad in limestone, with crenellated parapets. At the center of a broad well-manicured qaudrangle bisected by walkways was a campanile in the Gothic style.

The English department was quartered in a brick building with an arcade of cusped arches in front. It faced a green with tall misshapen trees and a pond, where Nick saw black swans for the first time in his life. The man who should have been at the airport, Alan Thill, met him by the entrance, an unassuming priory door under the arcade. He was about Nick's same age, with thinning red hair, a ruddy complexion, and a noticeably small mouth that gave him, unfairly Nick presumed, a petulant air.

Straight off the man took him to a campus cafe called Rick's Place, assuming he needed a refresher before he went on a tour of the department. Alan was a senior lecturer in American literature and spoke with an American accent.

"I'm a Kiwi, though," he said. "Through and through. Born right here in Auckland. I got my PhD at Rutgers."

"And the accent?"

"My mother's Canadian. You have one, too, huh?"

"I guess, yeah. I grew up in New York."

"I can tell," Alan said. "It's faint, but you drop your *r*'s. 'Bought' is 'baught.' 'All' is 'awl.'"

He glanced at his watch, Nick thought nervously.

"You're busy?"

"No, no. It's just habit. This place can get pretty hectic. I guess you'll find out about that."

"I'm still a bit hazy on how it all works," Nick said, hoping to find out more. While in LA, communicating by email with the chair, he had a difficult time deciphering the information he received about his duties. He understood, roughly, that he'd be teaching, that first semester, a large introductory lecture course on "Literary Los Angeles," the syllabus for which he'd had to assemble in a hurry as soon as he accepted the job.

The remark caused Alan some embarrassment. "Yeah, the old Oxbridge model," he said, rolling his eyes as though it were a mythical beast with two backs. "It takes getting used to."

"I'm a quick study," Nick said.

Alan, intent it was clear on not answering his question, shifted his gaze to various posters for the movie *Casablanca* on the walls. "Is it true your father's Evan Moran?"

"Yes." Nick hated this question, even when he heard it on the other side of the world.

"I see the resemblance."

Nick forced a smile. They looked nothing alike, except in their gray eyes.

"I haven't seen him in anything for a while," Alan said.

"He's retired now."

With that irrelevant fact established, his new colleague fell silent. His curiosity left Nick wondering if his father had something to do with him getting the job—a suspicion with which he was all too familiar. Evan Moran was always preceding him.

During the lull an older woman in a dress suit, double-breasted with two parallel rows of gold buttons, appeared at the table. She had a long, angular face from which she stretched her hair back in a bun and sported horn-rimmed glasses that came straight out of the 1950s.

"You must be Nick," she said. "I'm Bernadette Green."

He stood up. "Glad to finally meet you." She was the department chair.

"You must be exhausted after that flight."

"I'm wired, to be honest. I could run a marathon!"

"It might feel like you have after we've finished with you," she warned. "Helman Hall is a bit of a warren."

"We refer to the department by the building it's in," Alan explained.

"We've occupied the same space for fifty years," Bernadette told him. "And I've been here for forty of them." A hint of the deadpan in her voice had Nick cracking a smile. "I began as an undergraduate, just as Alan did. He won our highest prize, the Medal, in his last year."

Alan didn't much appreciate the boast. "One big happy family!" he quipped, suggesting that it might not have been happy at all.

Nick followed them back to Helman Hall, which was indeed a warren of narrow corridors lined with office doors, all closed at the moment. They took him into a corner office as big and cozy as a living room, with wall-to-wall books and a fireplace. There, he met the Head of School, another older woman, with a slight frame and a tremor in her hand as Nick shook it.

"I'm Bernadette," she said.

"You, too?"

"Bernadette Potter."

"There's three Bernadettes in the department," the other Bernadette told him. "You'll have to learn to tell us apart."

"Welcome aboard!" said Bernadette Potter.

"Glad to be here," said Nick.

The will to banter dropped. After an uncomfortable silence, Bernadette Green announced that they had "business to attend to." She said this in just too curt a manner, and it took Nick a moment to realize that she was asking him to leave. He duly withdrew again, glimpsing through the door a pained exchange of glances between the two women as he waited for Alan to follow. He took that to mean informality didn't come easily to either of them.

Alan introduced him to a man in charge of technical support and a woman who managed finances. Each time Nick had the impression they were hiding in their offices. Alan, sensing an explanation was necessary, said, "People are afraid to show themselves. When the semester starts, the hallways become dangerous places."

"Dangerous?"

"Busy, I mean. You have to stop and say hello so often it can feel like you'll never get out. Sometimes it takes half an hour just to reach the mail room. That's why I'm going to show you a back door before we're through."

"It's always good to have one of those," Nick said, wondering why people would be afraid of the hallways when the semester hadn't started yet. Just habit, he supposed.

Alan showed him his office, a plain square room that looked through a leaded pane window on an Illawarra flame tree, ablaze with crimson flowers, and an adjacent parking lot. The technical support man, who had preceded them there, crouched under the desk connecting a computer to its hard drive. There followed his lengthy explanation of programs Nick would be using and the setting up of passwords, which Alan skipped. He returned later to take Nick through that back door to the Human Resources department, where Nick was given various forms to sign and told what his take-home pay would be.

Alan left him where they'd first met, under the arcade, and Nick went back through the apparently deserted building to his office. He sat in the chair, fending off a sudden heaviness of sleep. At that moment he felt the novelty of the situation really sink in. Academia hadn't abandoned him after all. It had opened a door and given him this space right here, about as remote from his former life as he could possibly imagine.

He still had difficulty believing in his good fortune. It would mean a lot of adjustment, and not only because he was in a foreign country. He'd lost the familiarity he used to have with schools. He hadn't stood in front of students in the longest time. In fact, he'd never had much experience of that sort except as an adjunct teaching sketchy composition courses to kids in community colleges. Mostly himself a student, he'd spent his time emulating intellectuals who considered themselves not so much teachers as presenters of their research. People like Ozouf resisted their roles, or their functions, on the assumption that true thinking was resistant like this by definition. It began by testing limits, by jumping out of its skin. Nick would have to adjust on this front as much as any other. He'd have to learn to take himself seriously in all sorts of ways.

Evening had begun to fall by then, and Nick, in his distraction, had neglected to turn on the light. That might have made the knock he presently heard on his door, which he'd left open, even softer. He turned to see a small bespectacled man in a white shirt and suspenders, clutching to his breast a wooden clipboard. Nick, startled, wondered how long he'd been there.

"Sorry to disturb," the man said. "My name's Tom Hatch. My office is just down the hall."

"Nick Moran." He started out of his chair.

"Don't get up!" Tom urged, with a hand raised in warning.

Nick eased back down again.

"This won't take long," he said, speaking to Nick's mind the way a crab walks, backward as well as forward. "I'm in the middle of putting together a course, to be offered next year—that is to say, not this year, but a year from now. It's on the intersection of medicine and literature, and it's designed for doctors, for adults, who might be curious about the subject. It's to be offered online, as part of a community outreach program the department is trying to implement. The idea is there would be different units, reflecting different points of view, different strengths on offer here at King's."

The man waited for some indication from Nick that he was following his drift. "I don't understand," he said at last.

"Well, if you wanted to create one of these units, or even more than one, something to do with doctors in American literature—"

"Uh-huh."

"Just a syllabus, and a few lectures, notes to lectures really, that we could post on the web page."

"So the idea is I would teach that part of the course?"

"You would be responsible, during the unit, or units, for online feedback, yes."

"I see."

"You'd get the hours, of course."

"The hours?"

"They haven't explained hours to you?"

"No."

"Ah!" said Tom. "Then this is perhaps premature. I'm sure someone will straighten that out for you soon."

He clearly didn't want to be that someone. All at once he was eager to leave.

"Think about it," Tom said, backing into the hall. "Doctors and literature, that intersection. William Carlos Williams. Robin Cook."

"Walker Percy."

"Yes," smiled Tom, waving his clipboard goodbye. "Lots of possibilities!"

"I'm sure there are."

He was gone—like a shadow melting into deeper shadows.

ϰ

Nick hadn't asked enough questions about the job beforehand. In his surprise at the opportunity presenting itself as it had, so unexpectedly and at such a time of crisis, he said yes without thinking too much ahead. Even later, when he did have questions and sensed the department chair wasn't all that forthcoming, he allowed her answers to be vague, assuming the work would resemble what he'd known in America, or in France. He had an idea what the British "Oxbridge" meant, too, and shifted his expectations accordingly. But that turned out to be just as misleading. From what he could tell the aim was to blend different systems, taking from each its special power to rationalize the instruction process. Hence, Nick didn't teach his own courses. The department calculated his workload with a formula of hours spent in the classroom and numbers of words graded, or, as New Zealanders put it, "marked." And he had to "get" his hours by guest lecturing and by serving as a teaching assistant in other people's courses, none of which belonged to them either, since their title, like his, was "coordinator," a job confined to managing class lists, arranging rooms and times, hustling lecturers and tutors (in the hallways), and answering email correspondence. Nick understood just what that would entail when he found out the enrollment for "Literary Los Angeles" had topped five hundred students.

He felt overwhelmed at first, not least because he had to find a place to live at the same time as he figured out just what his duties were. Auckland was expensive, somewhere between LA and New York expensive. He spent his weekends looking at high-priced hovels with no light and rooms so hemmed in they felt like closets. To his chagrin he found he'd have to live more or less as he did when he was a graduate student, even though he was working with steady pay for really the first time in his life.

Of his new colleagues, only two, Alba Lynch and Jane Thorne, rail-thin lesbians from Australia who dressed in eccentric vintage clothes and wore bulbous rings of semiprecious stones on most all their fingers, seemed like people with whom he might be friends. As expats themselves, they were more willing to speak about the dysfunction of the department without the usual evasiveness. They also took the time to orient him in the city, showing him around some of the suburbs they thought he might like. This did cheer him. Auckland sprawled not unlike LA; it was clear he'd sooner or later have to buy a car, and frankly he couldn't afford one on his salary. But there were some walkable neighborhoods with character and on bus lines accessible to the university. One, situated by the harbor to the east of the city's downtown, fell off from a ridge line into a maze of intimate streets toward the water. It had a compression of design that reminded him of Cézanne landscapes, an effect derived in part from a number of retaining walls and sea walls that shaped the space out of the hillside.

The one-bedroom apartment he found there was more than he could afford, especially on top of the debt that still followed him from LA, but he went ahead with it anyway. While the building was unremarkable, a hulking concrete structure of vaguely Brutalist design, his apartment looked out over a park to a small cove, had a wood floor instead of the usual Berber carpet, and included a balcony. From its railing he could see one of those sea walls stretch toward a marina.

After signing the lease, however, Nick received his first paycheck with $200 less than he'd been told to expect. When he went to Human Resources and spoke with the director, Sarah Hayes, another formal woman in a dress suit, he found out her staff had neglected to tell him of the deduction for a superannuation scheme.

"Is there another way for me to lower my tax rate?" he asked.

She pursed her lips. "Let's see. Are you married?"

"No."

"Do you have children?"

"No."

"Do you own a house?"

"No."

"I'm afraid not then," she crisply concluded. "There's only one possible bracket for you."

He thought he heard sarcasm in this last remark. She had more brackets to choose from anyway. He knew by the wedding ring on her finger. She was likely a mother, too. They were close in age. He decided not to respond in kind.

"The problem is I've made financial commitments on the basis of what you told me."

"I assure you it was an honest mistake."

"But it puts me in a bind," he said. "I've already signed a lease."

"I'm sorry. There's nothing I can do."

ϗ

He couldn't bring himself to ask people he barely knew if they would be willing to lecture on topics and books he'd chosen for "Literary Los Angeles." It was humiliating even to think of rushing around Helman Hall like Tom Hatch, desperate to fill out his syllabus and grateful when anyone said yes. He decided, therefore, to approach the job in the way he knew: by writing and delivering his own lectures.

"You can't do that," Alan told him on the day he learned of the plan, sitting in Nick's office.

"Why not?"

"Well," he said, in search of a reason, "it's too much work."

"How so? It's the same whether I lecture in my class or yours, right? I'd say it's better, because I can link my lectures together, develop themes, build a structure, tell a story. That would save time."

"We're supposed to collaborate," Alan said.

"We're not collaborating!"

"Sure we are."

"How?! We don't co-teach courses. We don't help one another devise syllabi. We don't attend one another's lectures—do we?"

"No."

"But we'll teach the sections."

"The tutorials," corrected Alan.

"Okay, whatever. We'll teach without hearing the lectures."

"It gives the students more diverse points of view that way," Alan argued. "A course gets boring if it's just one person monopolizing the conversation. Remember William Blake's dictum: beware of 'single vision!'"

Nick, baffled by this reference to one of the more antinomian poets who had ever lived, could only state the obvious: "This is factory production, Alan. An assembly line. I put a door on a hinge, you stick an axle in a hub, and no one makes a car."

"Or everyone makes a car."

"You're still a cog in a wheel."

"Don't you think that's more democratic?"

"Democratic?!"

"Yes. Everybody equal. Everybody contributing."

All Nick managed to say, in place of the disdain he was suddenly beginning to feel for his new colleague, was, "I suppose that's one way of looking at it."

Alba and Jane laughed out loud when Nick told them about this conversation over breakfast the next morning, at a restaurant in his neighborhood.

"What Alan means is you can't do your own lectures because it's against the rules," said Jane, the more voluble of the two. "Conformity is the only principle he understands. I doubt he's ever broken a rule in his life."

"Except one," Alba reminded her.

Some five years before, a graduate student had accused Alan of sexual misconduct. The higher-ups in the department—the two Bernadettes—made the extraordinary decision to bury the scandal, since Alan was their favorite, groomed for a position of power once they retired. The offended student was summarily run out of the department, and they secured Alan's position with a promotion to senior lecturer—at Jane's expense, it turned out, as she still hadn't risen to that eminence after two decades of service. Insult was added to injury when they put Alan in charge of Jane's classes, in effect demoting her to his tutor. She'd heard more than enough of his blather about collaboration and democracy over the years.

"I'll put it this way," she said. "Alan has never broken the rule that matters."

"What rule is that?" asked Nick.

"The one that tells him what's good for Alan Thill," she said, biting into a piece of toast, with egg on it.

"Teach your class the way you want, Nick," said Alba then. "You have them in a bind, because guest lecturing isn't actually a rule. It's a custom. And they can't tell you not to do it without revealing why they don't want you to."

"Why don't they want me to?"

"They don't want you to feel good about yourself," Jane declared. "If you feel good about yourself, they feel the HMS Helman is sinking."

"That doesn't make sense," said Nick.

"It has to be work."

"It can't be fun work?"

"No," said Jane. "Work has to be hard. It has to hurt. The spirit has to be broken. That's how they know who you are."

"Anyone with personality is a threat," said Alba, who was less voluble than her partner, Nick observed, but hit closer to the mark when she did offer an opinion.

3

He went ahead with his plan of delivering all the lectures for "Literary Los Angeles." No one said a word, but it caused consternation in the background. He heard a rumor that the two Bernadettes were thinking of making "collaboration" mandatory, even though, as Alba had said, it would show their true agenda in a brighter light.

Nick had fun with his course. His lectures were personal, sometimes even impassioned, he thought. They had the virtue of catharsis going for them if nothing else. He could work out past frustrations by running them through the filters of Nathanel West, Raymond Chandler, and Joan Didion. The students seemed to appreciate his approach, although he couldn't be sure. They were an unresponsive bunch, accustomed to condescension and impersonal authority. They practiced, with all dominated people he supposed, the art of concealment: they suggested everything and revealed nothing. This art carried over into the tutorials as well, which did resemble American sections whatever Alan might say, with thirty or more students in each. Nick had a hard time breaking down their defenses or persuading them to give more of themselves than was minimally required. He often had the feeling they were conserving their energy, laying low inside themselves.

One of his duties was to serve as a supervisor in an Honours Program, which did approximate the Oxbridge experience of one-on-one relationships between teachers and students. As undergraduates in New Zealand went to school for three years, only those admitted to this program earned the right to a fourth year of seminars, each led mercifully by one person. In the spring Nick would have the chance to teach one of these seminars, on any subject he wanted—a privilege Alba told him not to expect on a regular basis, as they were much coveted by the faculty. In addition, Nick had to supervise one student through to completion of a thesis project. This relationship should be more "personal," the Honours coordinator, John Lurie, told him.

Nick liked this man. He had the same cautious demeanor as so many others, choosing his words with care, but he seemed willing to acknowledge, at least indirectly, the administrative mania gripping the department as a problem. He was devoted to the Honours Program and wanted to preserve its special character. This apparently extended to fighting, when need arose, with Brahmins in the school, who had different ideas about its integrity and purpose. Nick could see the effort took a lot out of him. John was a private, gracious person, slender of build and even a little frail. He was not by nature combative.

In an email Nick suggested to the student assigned to him, Molly Banville, that they meet off campus, intent on breaking through that wary reserve he fully expected to find in her. Sure enough, the young woman he encountered at a busy sidewalk café looked very determined not to be intimidated. She had long hair with a light copper sheen, pale skin, gray eyes, and a quizzical smile that hinted at a sense of humor. Dressed in jeans and a T-shirt, with a small round tattoo of a rose on her neck, she seemed assured yet unpretentious in her neglect of social convention. He liked her at once. But she wasn't giving any ground. Between them lay ramparts and fortifications.

She wanted to do her thesis on Henry James, a choice Nick heartily endorsed.

"What made you decide on him?" he asked her.

"I guess it was reading *Turn of the Screw*," she replied. "That book impressed me a lot."

"What impressed you about it?"

She reflected for a moment. "The way James draws out the children's 'sexual secret,'" she decided. "The uncertainty of that was perfect to me."

"Especially in relation to the crazy consciousness of the governess."

"Why do you say 'crazy'?"

"Not crazy," he said, sensing she knew the book better than he did. It had been years since he'd read it or even thought of it in a serious way. "You're right. That's not the best word."

"I think the ghosts are real."

"They're real and they point to a reality that's hard to fit into ordinary life," he said on a second try. "The governess's world is so true yet so wrong that her perceptions can only be both true and wrong."

Molly found this paradoxical observation more palatable. "I like how James does that. He catches you up in the world."

"He plunges you in."

"Yeah."

"We're at sea in James," Nick said. "Or 'in the blue,' another phrase he liked a lot."

She told him about a philosophy course she'd taken on pragmatism, and how much she admired William James particularly for his fulsome reviling of discipline and systems.

Nick suggested she work on both brothers. "That would be a good way to get at the true and wrong world the governess lives in."

"Have you read 'The Jolly Corner'?" she asked, referring to one of Henry James's late short stories. It, too, featured a ghost.

"No."

"Oh man, you have to!"

"Why?"

"It's even better than *Turn of the Screw*," she said with growing confidence. "James is almost completely opaque there. He won't let you tell the difference between what's real and what's imagined."

"Lend it to me," he urged her. "We can talk about it the next time we meet."

"Okay." She looked harder at him, sifting the warmer tones in his voice for objectionable irony but also pleasantly surprised. He caught a glimmer of light through the walls.

"What is it with you New Zealanders and America?" he ventured to ask. "All I do around here is tell people about the place I've just left."

"We feel pretty stuck with you," she told him. "You're in our heads. We watch your TV, read your books, think your thoughts. It's like static."

"Why not stop watching the TV, reading the books, and thinking the thoughts?"

"It's not that simple." She sought a reason for why it wasn't, without much success Nick inferred from the strain in her eyes. "I guess we wouldn't know what to replace it with."

"Why not your own culture?"

She didn't think much of this option, at least not coming from him. It suggested that he hadn't taken into account just how imposing his own culture could be. America, with its outsized power and influence, was more than one nation among others in this world. Nick knew that. But he could see it now with a new clarity in her eyes.

"What I like about pragmatism," he said then, "was that it did sort of remove the static from people's heads. It cleared a space where they could look around, acquire a sense of who they were, and stop imitating others. It gave them permission to be themselves."

"Isn't that a problem, too, though?" she said in a challenging tone. "Isn't America always going its own way, doing its own thing, trampling over everybody's rights as if its rights were the only ones that mattered?"

"That permission has its dark side," he agreed. "It breeds a bad exceptionalism—"

"For an 'indispensable nation.'"

"Right." The way that wasn't a question impressed him. She'd evidently given American psychology some thought, more perhaps than he had, being too much inside it to get much perspective. And she was right about pragmatism: its stress on practice over theory, means over ends, and truth as a matter of consensus building did lend itself to arbitrary self-assertion and chauvinism. Nick had never been much drawn to the philosophy for this reason.

"I hate that exceptionalism, too, believe me," he assured her. "But still, the permission seems important to give yourself. Don't you think?"

She impressed him again by paraphrasing the philosopher Charles Sanders Peirce: "'There's only one place from which you set out, and that's the place you find yourself in at the time you do set out.'"

"Excellent! You should use that for your thesis."

"It could be an epigraph," she said, excited now, and grateful, too, for the note of encouragement he'd struck with just the right touch. The tension between them cleared out of the air.

She retrieved a pack of cigarettes from the bag she kept on the table between them, holding it up. "You smoke?"

"I thought you'd never ask."

He took one and lit it. They sat for a moment in wondering silence. Neither of them had expected the meeting to go quite this well.

"Is it true your father's a movie star?"

"Yes," he sighed. "Evan Moran."

"Huh." She saw how much he disliked the question. "Never heard of him."

He brightened. "You don't know how happy that makes me."

☓

Nick sat amazed through his first faculty meeting. The central topic was whether or not to change the penalty policy for late essays, which was general over the whole department. He could hardly believe he heard right: either they should keep the current rule of three points per two tardy days or change it to two points per one tardy day. Justifications were offered on both sides, surmises made on the appropriate weight of punishment and the corresponding gain, or loss, in morale they might expect. Nick had never seen so much hair-splitting. Everyone knew it was excessive, too, even those who took a turn holding the floor.

This irritated him at first, but as the meeting progressed he began to detect an element of extortion in the proceedings. People had to play along if they wanted something more from the department. Jane, for instance, put her word in because she was going up yet again for promotion to senior lecturer, which would mean, among other advantages, a sharp increase in pay.

When everyone had exhausted their arguments, Alan, tapped to chair the meeting for that day, turned to Nick and said, "Any thoughts on the matter?"

The question caught him off guard. In a moment all nicety flew out the window. "Let's see," he said. "We're arguing here about a difference of one point every two days—"

"One point in the first two days," said Alan. "Two points in the second two days. The gap widens progressively over time."

"I think we should keep it three points per every second day," Nick said.

"Why?" asked Bernadette Green.

"I don't think students should be penalized more than they already are."

"Statistics suggest there would be less tardy essays with two points each day," Alan put in.

"Why not just leave it up to the individual teacher?"

"Oh no," said Bernadette firmly. "That would be much too confusing."

"The students would figure out who's lax and who isn't," observed Jane, with a sheepish lift of the brow.

"I suppose that's true," he said, relapsing into silence.

He hadn't given this sort of technical detail much thought before, never having been in a position to help run a department. He tended to come down on the side of flexibility, but then he did see there had to be some structure, and it was a good idea to be clear about it, too. That's why he found Helman Hall so mystifying. In it, everything remained murky despite all the clarity, because the one thing that made no sense was the structure, which rose into the clouds on a bottomless foundation. It seemed all he could see was its stratified middle. And what he heard for the most part were the rationalizations of his colleagues, which left him still more mystified. They professed care for students, but they built up baffles and screens with an equal intensity, cutting off possibilities of contact. They dedicated themselves to their vocation, but they ran it through procedures and protocols that left them little more than technicians going through the motions, if not specters behind closed doors. Nick frankly couldn't see himself working in so equivocal a fashion for long without it getting to him.

He relied on Molly to tell him what the place felt like from the other side. She was all outrage, it turned out, at being the recipient of that care, that dedication. Her years at King's University had passed in sullen despair at the transparent fraud of it. She felt helpless in the absence of an outside, of an exit to something else and better, more challenging, more engaged. The English department, shockingly, made no demands on its students beyond a certain number of courses to be completed for the degree. They could take whatever they wanted, and the choices offered them had grown more and more bizarre over time. "Literary Los Angeles" was only a case in point.

It hadn't always been like this. The department used to require the most stultifying coverage of the canon, boring its students to tears and, finally, out the door. Faced with decreasing enrollments and hostile pressures from an administration that thought running the university like a business was a fine idea, the Brahmins embraced Alan's democratic casuistry and turned the students into consumers of their occasional lecturers' fetishes and hobbyhorses.

"It's a beat down," Molly said, succinctly summing up the situation one day over a bowl of phô at a Vietnamese restaurant on Auckland's festive Ponsonby Road. "That's the reason no one responds in class. If you're conscious, if you're sensitive, you've been beat down so long you just go numb. You learn early on to hold back, to pull your head in."

"Pull your head in?"

"You know, like a turtle."

"Oh."

"It's a phrase," she said. "'Pull your head in,' close ranks, don't stand out—don't be a tall poppy. If you are, someone with a sword or a scythe will come through the field to slice your head off."

"Who will?"

"The bogeyman. The Grim Reaper. I don't know. Rupert Murdoch, maybe?"

With this new information it seemed Nick had come upon a missing piece of the puzzle that New Zealand was to him. "Things are pretty sewn up in this country, huh?"

"It's that way in every country, isn't it?" she said, chary all of a sudden. "America's the most sewn up place of all, it seems to me. We just follow your lead."

"I guess," he said dubiously.

"Come on!" she protested. "I detect a little nationalism there. You're secretly a patriot, I can tell."

"Am I? I'd never thought of myself that way before." He sipped his phô, savoring, with the lemongrass and ginger, Molly's growing willingness to talk back, to shed her fear. "I don't much understand your poppies and turtles, I'll say that. The idea, where I come from, is always to stand out, to be the center of attention. If you don't, you get left behind. You feel like a loser."

"'Loser,'" she said disdainfully. "I hate that word."

"Yeah, I know what you mean. People use it in a pretty zero-sum way these days."

"It implies a forced choice I'd rather not make at all, thank you very much."

"Me neither."

"It's not a choice anyway," she added, deadpan. "Winner or loser, in the end everybody's just a wanker."

4

Around the middle of the semester Nick attended a reading on campus by an Irish novelist, who had come for an arts festival in Auckland. On entering the conference hall he waved at Molly, seated some distance away with her friends in the Honours Program. Their interest in this exchange pleased her, he could tell. Apparently other supervisors weren't as attentive or giving with their time as he was.

Afterward, several of his colleagues invited the writer to a nearby pub called the Pig & Whistle. When Molly heard, she took the liberty of asking if students could tag along. Alan had organized the event, and he was eager to ingratiate himself with the writer and control the experience others had with him, so Nick asked if it would be all right. A shadow had fallen between him and Alan as it became clear what Nick thought of his influence in the department. He'd taken sides with Alba and Jane. They formed a faction against Alan and those gathered around him, most of whom were at this reading. But Alan agreed to let the students come, and they all set off.

Nick had to get used to pub culture. He lacked the stamina for drinking that was an indispensable part of it. Molly teased him for being a lightweight, but he preferred to call it common sense, not much adhered to by much of anybody as the night wore on. Still, he liked the conviviality well enough, even if one had to rely on more and more alcohol to keep the inhibitions loose.

The interior of the Pig & Whistle was warm, musty, and intimate, with wood-paneled walls decorated with tacky antique paintings. The only light came from electric sconces and cathode-ray TVs hung from the ceilings.

The group settled around two tables pushed together, the Irish novelist and professors on one side, students on the other. Nick, though, not interested in fawning over the writer or watching Alan do so, sat across from Molly, sipping his Tooheys New and chatting with her friends over pitchers of beer. He saw a more gregarious side of her come out in their company. It combined nicely with the keen intelligence he was coming to admire in her. She liked probing the unexamined backgrounds of social life and caught the subtle signs of vanity or slight in people with a quick wit. It made her attractive at that table. One young man in particular seemed anxious to hold her attention. Brian was his name—husky with tousled hair and a gruff boyish charm. Nick felt just the faintest twinge of jealousy.

The students had all gone the previous evening to another event of the arts festival, a downtown book party for an anthology of short stories by young New Zealand writers.

"It was a bit of a bore," Molly told him, "everyone pretending to be gritty. But at least the food was free."

Brian mentioned his having a story in the book. Molly, with an arch look, promptly changed the subject. "I had another visit from my Peeping Tom."

"Your what?!" cried Nick.

"This guy who sneaks into the bush by my window. Every so often I catch him spying on me through cracks in the blinds. As soon as I do, he bolts off."

"That's awful!"

"No kidding."

"Have you contacted the police?"

She nodded. "They can't do anything about it, though, unless I call right away, and the guy's crafty. He knows not to stay too long."

Silence settled around the table. No one had a ready response to so unusual a problem. Presently Molly asked Nick, "Why do you think a guy would do something like that?"

"I haven't the faintest idea."

"It's so pathetic you can't even feel sorry for him."

"No."

Another lull in the conversation made Molly wish she hadn't brought the subject up. In a second abrupt shift she asked Nick if he wanted to play a game of pool. There was a table in the next room.

"I don't know," he said with some reluctance. "I haven't played in a while." He'd only played a few times in his life was more like it.

"That's all right," she said. "It's just for fun."

"Don't believe her!" Brian warned. "Molly's a pool shark. She pretends to be a novice, and then she kicks your ass."

"I kicked *your* ass anyway."

"She likes beating guys," Brian said. "It gives her a thrill."

"It does not," she retorted, changing her mind a second later. "Okay, maybe it does. But only when the guy comes off as too confident, when he thinks, because I'm a girl, that I can't be as good as he is." She turned to Nick. "What do you say?"

"Maybe later," he said. "After I've had another one of these." He lifted his glass of beer and tipped it toward her.

He asked the other students about their thesis projects, and they spoke for a while about that. Molly commented on how competitive the Honours Program was. She thought it sowed too much mistrust between students.

"I still don't know what most of you are working on," she said. "We act like someone's going to steal our ideas if we so much as whisper them."

"What are you competing for?" asked Nick.

"We're ranked at the end of the year," Brian told him. "They post the results in the department hallway afterward."

"Everybody sees exactly where they stand with everybody else," said Molly.

"No wonder there's mistrust," Nick said.

"They don't do it that way in America?"

"They wouldn't announce the results like that. They'd be considered private. There might be a ranking, but you'd only know who comes out on top."

"You're ranked from the day you start school here," Molly said. "You're always aware of it."

"I see. That explains a lot." Nick meant a lot of what he had to deal with in the department.

"I think the system works pretty well," Brian said. "It keeps us motivated. We try harder."

"I don't!" Molly cried. "I freeze the minute I have to prove myself."

"It doesn't always seem the best way to learn," Nick ventured to say. "Not in an English class anyway. There you have to free associate, think aloud, follow a hunch even if it turns out to be wrong."

"You have to let yourself go," Molly said.

"I don't know," Brian said skeptically. "You get lazy if you let yourself go. You lose your edge, your incentive."

"Not so," she countered. "You start thinking in a different way, that's all."

"A more critical way," Nick put in.

"You start seeing what's really going on," she said. "And you can't see that if you're always trying to outdo the other guy."

"Why can't you?" asked Brian.

"Because what's really going on is that competition, that struggle for power, for status. For some reason we're not honest about that. We pretend it isn't happening, or we assume it's natural when it's not at all. Competition is *un*natural."

Nick admired this observation very much. He'd also finished his beer, and it went to his head enough for him to forget himself a moment. He reached across the table and kissed her on the cheek.

"Bravo!" he cried.

The evening wore on in this same congenial spirit, and Nick let himself drink more than he probably should to keep it alive, in proper pub fashion. He even started to sympathize with some of his colleagues, like Alan, who would've grown up as aware as Molly and her friends of rank, as caught in the need for discipline and system. That was the real pathology in Helman Hall. Nick hadn't much experience with it, except in aversion, and where he came from aversion seemed to be the standard attitude—inherited, no doubt, from William James and that pragmatist tradition. It occurred to him, though, that this might not be so true anymore. Hierarchy was making a comeback everywhere. That had been one of the lessons he'd learned from people like Don Torrance and Bob Kirschner.

He ended up later telling Molly about that stretch of his life in LA. It felt good. He hadn't unburdened himself with anyone in a long time. Molly was also fresh and eager to listen without judgment. She didn't blink even when he related some of the more embarrassing experiences he'd had at the end. She knew just how "in the blue" a person could be.

After a couple of hours, however, Nick decided it was time for him to go home, even though the night had only just started for students and professors alike. Before he left Molly insisted on that game of pool. He followed her to the room with a table. She inserted quarters in the coin slide to release the balls and arranged them in a triangle on the red baize surface.

"I'm no good," he warned her.

"Who cares? I told you it's just for fun. No one has to compete here."

"I thought you liked to humiliate your male opponents?"

"Only the ones with outsized egos." She handed him a pool cue. "You break. That's one thing I'm lousy at."

He bent over, aimed, and split the rack. A solid dropped into a corner pocket. He circled around to find the best angle for his next shot, which went badly awry.

As Molly chalked her cue and studied the table, he noticed Alan approach from the other side of the room. His demeanor was grave to the point of displeasure. "Can I see you a minute, Nick?"

Molly was too intent on her shot to notice the interruption.

Alan drew him aside and said directly: "There's a perception among the Honours students that you're too close with Molly."

"Too close?"

"They're talking about it among themselves."

Nick laughed. "Don't worry. We're just having fun."

"I know."

"Isn't everybody?"

"Pubs aren't the easygoing places they appear," Alan blandly informed him.

"What are they then?"

An answer to that would require more explanation than there was time for. "I'm just saying perception matters," Alan said. "You're still a professor, and she's your student."

"But nothing's going on!"

"That's not the point, Nick. The students still talk. You need to be more careful."

Nick didn't see why student talk should be given so much credence, but he'd also caught the monitory note in Alan's voice. He was serious. "Okay. I'll be more careful."

He returned to the game. Molly had been on a tear. There were far fewer balls on the table. But as she lined up her next shot, Brian and another of the younger lecturers, the third of the Bernadettes, last name Lund, came over, took cues from the wall rack and suggested, or announced, a game of doubles. Before Molly could protest, Nick said, "Good idea! Brian can team up with Molly, and I'll play with Bernadette."

Shocked by this abrupt sanction of the change, Molly could only stand helplessly by and watch while the table was taken over for a new game.

ϡ

She sat crying on the sidewalk afterward. They'd left together, and Nick saw no reason not to tell her what had happened. When she broke down, they stopped right where they were on a night-filled city street, deserted except for an occasional man walking a little furtively in or out of an unmarked door a short distance away.

What rankled her wasn't just the characterization of their behavior as improper but the fact that it wasn't all that surprising. "Every time a good thing happens to me," she fumed, "someone comes along and shits on it. Every time. It's been this way my whole life."

"I'm sorry to hear that."

"It's what this country does. It shits on you. It makes everything ugly."

"It can sure seem like it."

"What were we doing?!"

"Nothing."

"We were just playing a game of pool!"

"It must have been the kiss," he surmised. "I wasn't thinking about how that looked."

"Why should you have to?! It was perfectly natural. I was glad you did it."

"I guess it offended some of your friends."

"Who?"

"I don't know. Alan just said there was 'talk.'"

"It could have been Brian," she reflected. "He asked me out at the beginning of the year, and I rejected him. This might be about getting back at me."

They paused as one of those men, rattled by the two of them sitting on the sidewalk, hurried past and went through the door.

"He's jealous, too," she said. "They all are. They wish they had someone more like you as a supervisor."

"I see." That altered the picture somewhat. It hadn't occurred to him that the effect of the department's equivocal "care" on its students might be quite so emotionally fraught. "I guess I need to be more aware of that."

Molly scarcely heard him. Her thoughts had turned to other facets of the incident. "This is the first time I've ever connected with a professor," she said. "The first time I've ever felt less than a speck, a fly on the wall in that horrible department, you know? But as soon as that happens, this happens, and I have to feel like I've done something wrong."

"You haven't done anything wrong."

"But I feel I have. I feel dirty."

"Don't."

"It's too late!" she cried. "Now I'll have to worry about what people are thinking. I'll have to watch myself. I'll never be able to rest easy in Helman Hall again."

He saw the truth in that, for him as well. "The poison's been administered, hasn't it?"

"You have to feel ashamed even when you're not. You always have to feel ashamed." After a beat she added, significantly, "I won't even be able to feel at ease around you."

Still another man came out of the door and took off into the night.

"Who *are* these men?" Nick complained.

Molly, focusing, slowly hit on the answer. "Fucking hell!" she exclaimed with a snort.

"What?"

She hiked a thumb. "You know what that is?"

He turned back around.

"A brothel, that's what."

"Really?"

"A fucking brothel."

They took a moment to scent the acrid irony this coincidence brought to the situation.

"It's a sick world," Molly observed.

"Yes, it is." He put an arm around her, hoping, with a desire not at all characteristic for him, to keep her from that world a while longer. "I want you to feel at ease around me, okay?" he said. "Maybe we'll have to watch ourselves around other people. I'm not going into a pub with students again, that's for sure. But I see no reason why we can't continue on as we have been, getting to know each other, talking about your project, reading books together."

She wiped her cheeks with a sleeve. "Thanks, Nick."

He heard an off note in his own words. It hinted at more, maybe, than he wanted it to. "Let's face it," he said. "We probably have been too. . .free with each other. I suppose we do like each other in that way."

A sort of wild appeal in her look told Nick it was even truer than he thought.

"I don't see anything wrong with that," he said. "I mean, as a fantasy, of course."

"Of course," she archly concurred.

"Not to be acted on."

"No, never."

They smiled at the inklings this little charade let hang in the air between them.

"I'd even argue it's what should happen between teachers and students," he said, moving ever so slightly onto a more neutral pedagogical ground. "The presence of desire is what makes learning possible. It makes what we learn what we also do."

He saw Molly appreciate how this last sentence folded thought back on action, content back on form, in true pragmatist fashion what's more. It caught them up in the world again—the sick world, but still the only one they had.

"Do you like me?" she gently inquired.

He hesitated long enough to see her face fall. He resolved to be honest. "I don't let myself think about it. I'm trying to be a good teacher, to play that role the best I can. It hasn't been easy. I've been out of practice for a long time. And I don't much like the part either. I hear it falsifying my tone even now. I speak half as an adult would to a child, which really is not how I feel about you at all. So, yes," he said, with more emphasis, "I like you, Molly. I think you're hot."

"Yeah?" she said brightly.

"What time is it?" he asked out of the blue.

She took her cell phone from her bag. "Twelve thirty."

"The next day," he said cryptically.

"So?"

"Guess what that means?"

"What?"

"It's my birthday."

"It is?"

"Why would I lie about a thing like that?"

"How old are you?"

"Why would I admit it at a time like this?" he mused aloud. Then: "I'm forty."

The number towered in her imagination. "Jesus!" she said. "That's old."

"Tell me about it."

They sat in silence, letting the significance of this new data point sink in. Nick allowed himself a regret that her desire for him was shifting into the more transient light of a schoolgirl crush. But she surprised him by saying, "What are we going to do now?"

"About what?"

"About the fact that we like each other."

He weighed his response just longer than it needed. "Pretty much what we've been doing, I'd say. You have a thesis to write. I see it's important you give it your full attention. It's better not to complicate that more than it already is."

"Yeah," she drawled. "You're right."

With this decision made, they'd come to the end of a line.

"Where do you live?" Nick asked.

"Not far."

He stood and offered her a hand. "Let's get out of here," he said. "Someone from Helman Hall might see us loitering in front of a brothel."

5

The next day, a Saturday mercifully, Nick awoke with a lot to think about. Turning forty had snuck up on him, and now that the time had come he wondered if its suggestion of a change, a watershed really, hadn't been in the back of his mind for a while now, making that brittleness of spirit he felt in LA—and still felt in Auckland when it came down to it—less about a sick world than about growing up, or growing older. Recent experience had put him more firmly in the habit of seeking the causes of his frustrations outside himself, in social orders and circumstances that blocked what he considered the legitimate ends of a self-determined life. Now, though, he might need to be looking for those causes a little closer to home: in a garden-variety fear of death or time closing down around him, narrowing options and the room to maneuver. Freedom was not, after all, the same as mere absence of limitation. Maybe he had to stop holding back in the belief that anything was possible.

He saw no reason, however, to concede too quickly this picture of himself as someone driven by a desire to cheat time, to avoid the pain of being one thing, defined and categorized. That struck him as an injustice. He knew time passed whether he deceived himself about it or not. He knew time was the desire for immunity from time, a destiny met in avoidance, like Oedipus leaving Corinth. If he felt subject to external forces beyond his control, it wasn't because he resisted being one thing but because the one thing required of him that he live without this awareness, without the finitude it opened up in the strange truth of error and errancy—even over a table in a pub or on a sidewalk by a brothel. To shift the blame from this requirement to himself as some sort of Peter Pan unwilling to see his own shadow got the problem exactly backward. It implied turning away from time. It implied reducing life simply to what one does, or what is done without question, to going along in a sheer impersonal necessity. He wasn't running from anything except this escape *into* fate, and what responsible person wouldn't try for that?

Still, parsing all this didn't prevent him from feeling sad that day, wistful at the passing away of youth. It unsettled him to think that he was too old for a girl like Molly, or that rules stood between him and another person, setting limits on what they might do with each other that were not up to them. He had to represent an institution now, whether he liked it or not. He'd have to let that function confine him to the one thing a teacher was, to its piece in the puzzle of social *in*finitude. It saddened him that this would have to mean relating to time in bad faith, in the fear of death that produced a phantom youth for middle-aged men. He didn't feel ready for that kind of compromise.

His father would laugh out loud to hear about these rules he had to take so seriously. Evan Moran had never stopped living—until recently at least—with the sense that anything was possible and there were no checks on his impulses, unless you included laws against statutory rape, and Nick felt pretty sure even these hadn't been all that much on his father's mind when he was living high and fast. His sexual freedom had long been a source of confusion for Nick. He often felt like the older man to his father's perpetual adolescent. There'd never been any difference in the field of possible partners available to either of them—Julie, for instance, was only a year older than him. That was the main reason Nick resisted seeing himself in that pejorative image of Peter Pan. He knew, better than most, that a phantom youth could take a variety of forms.

Nick's loneliness that day put him in a mood to talk with his father. At least he could hear the derision when he told him about pub and brothel. He sat on his balcony when he knew it would be morning in Paris, the time his father normally wanted company, and gave him a call. Sunlight spangled the water and a flock of small colorful parrots, called lorikeets, swarmed in a nearby jacaranda tree, squawking loudly. His father, however, was in a fluster. He'd lost his keys.

"I know I put them on the mantelpiece," he grumbled. "I remember leaving them there yesterday."

Nick heard him banging things around.

"They'll turn up," he said.

"I can't find anything around here, goddamn it! I swear there's a genie in the place, moving things around, switching them up on me."

"Stop and wait awhile," Nick advised. "They'll appear when you're not looking for them."

"I suspect my neighbor, François whatever the fuck his name is. Ever since the guy found out who I am, he takes any chance he gets to corner me in a conversation. He keeps his door open on the landing and comes out as soon as he hears me there. I go on the balcony and there he is on his, asking me if I know Roman Polanski. I feel him watching me through the walls."

"He's not watching you through the walls, Dad."

"I even think he comes in here when I'm gone—"

"Dad."

"What?! All he has to do is climb onto my balcony. There's no lock on the doors."

"Come on!"

"I'm telling you, Nick, he's obsessed with me, obsessed, like any fan. He wants to break through the walls, into the privacy he thinks he has as much a right to as you do. He sits next door in his lonely fucking life wondering how he can get inside mine. He's already inside my head."

"Where's Julie?"

"At work. And Emmanuele's on a playdate. I can't stand it when they're gone. That's why I need the keys, so I can get the fuck out of here."

Nick was annoyed now. No matter what the Parkinson's might have to do with it, one more time he had to listen to his father in that absolute self-obsession as it came down on him like a cage. It made no difference, finally, if he was its prisoner, alone with himself and his imaginary wardens. Nick still felt like shit to be around him.

"I'm not doing well," his father muttered, manically opening and closing drawers. "I don't know who I am anymore. There's no one there. All I know is that one day I'll be this pathetic old man who can't even wipe his own ass."

"Calm down—"

"I won't stand for that," he said. "I'll kill myself first. I swear to God, Nick, I'll kill myself. I think about it everyday. I've even been looking up how to do it. I'll buy a helium bag. A fucking helium bag. Just to have it around. Just the thought I could do it, easily, painlessly, keeps me going. Sometimes it's all that keeps me going."

"That's not true." Nick could see how it might be, though. His father's problem was not dying so much as his inability to die. Evan Moran was endlessly dying.

"Don't tell me what's true, you smug prick."

"I was thinking of Julie," he said, through the jar this sudden contempt gave him. "Your daughter. They need you. They want you around."

"I don't know my daughter. She's a little French girl, and I'm a guy from Nebraska who has no idea what's on the other side of a potato field. You want the truth, Nick? The bottom line? *La pura neta*? That's what I've always been: a dirt farmer who pulled the wool over everybody's eyes. The only thing I really had to learn about this world was how easy that could be. People want to be fooled."

He found the keys. He'd dropped them on the shag rug by a nightstand in his bedroom.

"Thank God!" he gasped.

Nick told him to go and have a pastis at the hookah bar near his house. The mood to talk had left him again. He didn't even feel like reminding his father that it was his birthday.

6

At the end of the semester Nick learned of another nuance in the system at Helman Hall. He found in his mailroom box a stack of papers from a course on medieval British poetry that he'd had nothing whatever to do with. As he hadn't yet filled out his complement of words marked, the powers that be, watching the numbers for him, filled it out on their own. He would have to read papers on *Beowulf*. When he asked Bernadette Green about the rationale behind this policy, she said a professional should be able to evaluate whatever was put before him. If anything, his evaluation would be all the more objective because he lacked familiarity with the material. She seemed really to believe this.

He therefore spent the break between semesters in this professional capacity, while also processing marks for "Literary Los Angeles." His other task, and chief pleasure, was preparing his seminar in the Honours Program. He approached it with his own research in mind, as far as he understood what that might be. He had some preliminary ideas. Its focus would be on "the passions," and it would begin with a slow reading—stretched over a whole month—of Proust's *Swann's Way*, interspersed with corollary texts that formed for the novel an echo chamber of allusion, through time and across cultures. The rest of the semester would be devoted to two further novels, Thomas Mann's *Death in Venice* and Djuna Barnes's *Nightwood*. Their common concerns with idealization, sexual jealousy, and eternal recurrence, amor fati, gave to the syllabus the quality of a musical composition in Nick's mind, with themes and harmonic structures he was carefully building up.

The more he worked on it, the more confident he grew that he had the nucleus of a book on his hands, and more than enough desire to write it. The only question was whether King's University would let him. In addition to the seminar, he'd also be teaching nine tutorials in three different courses, not having rustled up any guest lectures on his own. He didn't imagine that kind of workload would leave much time for research.

x

The break was occasion for still more loneliness. He hadn't met many people outside work—certainly no eligible woman who might take his mind off students with crushes on him. He assumed that would eventually change, although he couldn't be quite sure. Auckland was far from a warm place, as taciturn as its people despite the affable reputation they claimed for themselves. Feeling a little desperate, he went against his aversion to online dating and filled out a profile. He sat on his bed one night uploading his information—single, never married, five feet eleven, slender of build but not athletic, with dark hair thinning at the part. In the personal statement he characterized himself as acerbic and critical by nature but not, he hoped, to a fault. He sought a woman of any temperament who had an "inquiring mind" and a "love of conversation." "I'm not interested in games," he wrote, "only in a willingness to engage, question assumptions, and experiment at the limits of convention." That last phrase gave him pause, but he decided its ambiguity might be worth including. He couldn't bring himself to specify the sexual features he preferred in a woman, but the fact that physical attraction would have to be there made him feel a bit of a hypocrite for not spelling his criteria out.

No one responded except teenagers from Nigeria and Russia or Chinese women who "make good wife" and "know how cook well." From adult New Zealanders of similar age and background he received a deafening silence. He found in their profiles a uniform rhetoric of positive thinking, a desire for life lived to its fullest, and at the same time a need for security and trust. In the fields where they indicated their preferences, he saw a pronounced distaste for acerbic and critical men. They were considered negative, emotionally shut down, and a waste of time.

Just before giving up altogether, though, he had one of the stranger encounters of his life. One evening a woman with the name Cytherea sent him a message that said, *I'm not interested in games either*. It included a headshot of a brunette looking back over her shoulder with limpid brown eyes and a puckered smile. He answered, and she sent him back a link to a website, where he saw more photographs of a frankly sexual nature, along with poems by Rilke and quotations from Carl Jung. They traded messages, tested waters, flirted. She was direct to the point of insult, doubting if he was interested in "experiments at the limits of convention" and alleging a prudishness that would in all likelihood bore her. He wondered if she wasn't playing another game but nonetheless went along. *I'm open-minded*, he wrote. *Let's meet*. She put him off, however, with vague aspersions cast on his manhood, which had him defending himself in a manner she clearly enjoyed. Over the next several nights they went back and forth. She varied the pattern by sending him ethereal songs by Sinead O'Connor that filled Nick's bedroom with her unique sensibility. It was odd, she was odd, but he found it all intriguing enough.

It sent him one night, after a flurry of posts, back to the dating site, where he went again through the seemingly endless lists of women seeking men, to see if there weren't others he might find intriguing, too. But in the process he saw a message pop up on his screen—from Cytherea, sent through the site. She was furious. *What are you doing!? No cherry-picking!!!* That came as a shock. It seemed as if she were right there in the room with him. He tapped in, *How did you know what I was doing?* She answered, *It has to be me and no one else, or you can go fuck yourself!!!* He replied, *Maybe I am fucking myself. Who are you?* She didn't answer for two days. He tried in further texts to reassure her of his intentions, apologizing although he couldn't say for what, even promising fidelity from then on. He didn't peruse the lists again for fear of her finding out.

She did finally answer, and they resumed their exchange, to the verge of exasperation for Nick, who went on proposing they meet in the flesh. She still resisted, needing more time, she said, to be "sure" about him. He went along for a few more nights, after which he told her the ritual was starting to irritate him. At that point she sent him a link to another website she'd made, this one, formatted like the last, with a new set of photographs, poems, and quotes, profiling a Russian spy clad in a white fur hat and coat. Then she wanted to chat using a program he didn't have on his computer. He had to download it while she derided his digital ineptitude, equating it with sexual timidity and threatening to terminate their relationship on the spot if he didn't hurry up. When at last the program was installed, they started dialoguing in real time. There followed an attempt to have the written equivalent of sex. It turned into a hunt for the Russian spy, which led him to corners of the website where she took the fur coat off.

This appeared to be Cytherea's preferred mode of sexual relation, as the next night she revealed yet another website devoted to a cosmopolitan socialite in lingerie. That was the last straw. It was one thing to be a prude, another to be shamed into collaborating in the fantasy life of a complete stranger who might be off her rocker. He issued an ultimatum: they must meet or call it off.

She reluctantly agreed to lunch at a dim sum restaurant in Auckland's Chinatown, hinting at inevitable anticlimax. This turned out to be an understatement, as he met there a mousy tax attorney named Doris who attributed her obsessions to overwork and insomnia, looking nothing like her photographs and lacking any trace of queenly pride. It was heartbreaking. She seemed totally split off in her virtual self, or selves, with almost no ability for immediate human contact.

Not that sympathy changed Nick's mind about her. He couldn't wait to get out of that restaurant, to flee the glimpse she afforded into the secret life of a "professional" like the one he imagined King's University saw in him. For this reason among others, all he could think about as they miserably swallowed their steamed dumplings and buns was Molly, living and breathing Molly in her ratty jeans and T-shirt, denied him as absolutely as Doris was not Cytherea. It was a sick world all right.

ϗ

Nick welcomed the new semester rather more eagerly after that lamentable episode, hoping the Honours seminar would lift his spirits. When, on the first day, he sat with the students around an oval table in a bright, pleasant room looking out toward Auckland Harbour, good fortune did seem to fill the air.

He started with a lecture on a short text from Plato's *Symposium*, part of a speech given by the priestess Diotima to a young Socrates, which Nick thought would nicely encapsulate a central paradox of the course. This paradox turned on a metaphysical definition of "beauty" as something outside the world in which it nonetheless appeared. Timeless and immune to change or death, "subsisting of itself and by itself in an eternal oneness," as Diotima had it, this "beauty" remained a quality of definite and material things. Yet such beautiful things, Nick told them, paid a heavy price: they suggested a transcendence they were only ever able to represent. They failed to match up, or "coincide," with themselves, being only what they were not.

"When we give to people this same discrepant unity," he said, "we use a particular figure: we say of them that they are 'beloved.' This figure is paradoxical, too, being simultaneously an object of beauty and beauty's substitute, the present symbol of its absent spiritual character. Two consequences follow: we love those whom we consider 'beloved' because of their perfection or purity, but we resent them because they're neither perfect nor pure. They remind us of what they fail to be. To put this a different way, with Marcel Proust, 'what attracts us in another is always something else.'"

The students took this in at a sort of startled attention. They weren't sure just what he was driving at, or if they liked how it sounded, but they seemed willing to suspend judgment for the time being. He could feel Molly, in any event, firmly on his side from her place across the table.

He turned next to an essay he had them read over the break, Heidegger's "The Thing." He hoped it would give more epistemological depth to that figure of the beloved. He asked the students to imagine it together with the essay's distinction between, on the one hand, an object logically determined in space and time, and, on the other, what in that object cannot be so determined, cannot be put into perspective by consciousness. "The beloved is for the lover this absence of perspective," he said, "this disorientation of the rational mind that Heidegger considered ethical in the relation to a nonobjective 'thing.' Love, that is, never exactly leads to a reassuring sense that we understand the other's or even our own feelings." He cited Djuna Barnes: "'The more we learn of a person, the less we know.'"

He threw a lot at them in this associative manner on that first day, as much to set the scene as to arouse feelings that would emerge as motifs of the course. He wanted that ethical disorientation to be at stake in how they understood what they were reading and also the place where they read, with its manifest hostility to being seen, to being held to any critical account. That was the whole point of teaching, as far as Nick had ever understood it. No matter what the topic, even love, it should reveal what was happening in the moment. The point for teachers like Pierre-Yves Ozouf was always to bring out the tacit patterns and connections on which people relied to be or act in the world. Interpretation, like any serious art, was, in a nice phrase Nick picked up from the philosopher Charles Taylor, "an exploration of order through personal resonance." It was a genuine pleasure for Nick to practice it this way for once. It gave him the sense of vocation he'd always wanted.

Afterward he went against his resolve not to socialize with students and joined them for coffee on facing sofas at Rick's Place. He sat away from Molly, next to a girl he hadn't met before, Eunice Notley, who had a shock of wiry red hair and skin so white she might have been albinic. She wore a miniskirt and fishnet tights, along with a pair of brightly colored cowboy boots. On one hand she wore a suede glove with the Brown University seal—a demi-sun under argent clouds over a red cross—stitched into it. Nick recognized the symbol right away.

"You must have gotten that in Providence," he said.

She nodded. "My boyfriend and I visited last summer."

"Did you like it?"

"Yeah," she said. "It seemed a fun place to study."

"Maybe you should apply, once you've finished your degree."

"My boyfriend's a postgrad here."

"Well, you can go."

She took that seriously for a moment, shifting in the sofa. He sensed her connecting the topics raised in class to her own experience, just as he hoped she would. At length she asked, "What did you mean when you said we don't know another person, even when we do?"

"Especially when we do. What we think we know isn't the same as the thing we think we know."

"That's circular!"

"It is," he conceded. "It's a way of stripping gears. I like to hurt the mind a little."

"I think love's simpler than that," she declared. "No one can tell me I don't know what I know, or like what I like."

"I wouldn't presume," he assured her. "I just think it's interesting to inquire into assumptions we make about others. Literature unsettles our beliefs. Maybe that's all it does."

He could tell from the frown on her face that he wasn't persuading her. Literature might qualify as a "passion" in her mind, but it wasn't the "ethical disorientation" he had alleged. As an idea or an attitude that was too "confronting," a word Nick noticed New Zealanders often used to signal a social discomfort they tended to avoid. He didn't much respect this habit in them, truth be told.

"Take what happened to me and Molly a few weeks ago," he said, pushing out impulsively into uncharted waters. "You heard about that I suppose?"

"Yes."

"People formed an idea about the two of us based on what they saw, yet what they saw didn't match the idea they'd formed."

"I would say they saw what they saw."

"But their perceptions were colored by suppositions, and those suppositions affected their judgment."

"They weren't 'suppositions,'" she said with a flash of annoyance. "They saw something that shouldn't have been happening."

"But nothing was happening!"

"It looked that way."

"That's why looks can be deceiving."

Nick could say the same about Eunice Notley by this point. He now regretted starting the conversation.

"You don't think there's anything wrong with student-teacher relationships, do you?" she asked him then.

"I didn't say that! I agree it would be wrong for Molly and me to be romantically involved." He wondered, though, riled now, pushed to a wall, whether he really did believe it. "But that aside, I don't see why in principle it would be anybody's business what we did together, if it was consensual."

"I see."

"You think that's wrong?"

"It sounds like moral relativism to me."

"What's relative here," he shot back with more vehemence than he should, "is your interest in the private lives of other people."

Startled to the point of offense by this show of temper, she turned to chat with Brian, who sat on her other, and, for Nick, now grotesquely overexposed flank. Their sparring match was over.

ϰ

He wouldn't make the same mistake again. Whenever he felt lulled into addressing students as adults, answering the invitation to candor they themselves offered, he had to remember that it wasn't sincere. They didn't want what they appeared to want: the respect that comes with tearing down the barriers of formality. Instead of unstudied moments, improvised exchanges, and the care that followed from breaking rules, or at least acknowledging them for the guidelines they ought to be, they preferred an illusion of freedom, of nonconformity, as plausible as Eunice Notley's fishnet tights.

This forced him and Molly to be still more discreet about their friendship, which had thankfully continued to grow. He needed it, to be honest. He had no one else in New Zealand he could talk to as he could to her. She didn't share her peers'—or, for that matter, his peers'—tacit deference to authority, and she had a desire to break through those illusions of freedom. That primed her for a way of thinking and acting that rested on the always shaky ground of experience. That's where she instinctively wanted to be, however precarious it might feel. And she was courageous enough to stay there without needing any other support than what she herself could provide.

In his role as supervisor he assembled a number of secondary texts for her to work with on her thesis project. They read Henry and William James as well as Peirce, weaving concepts and metaphors from a variety of sources into the affection that had grown up between them. This affection once again had no need for rules. It set its own limits and obligations. Both of them were part of the world they thought about, not its detached observers; and if just this constituted the impropriety of their relationship in the eyes of other students, they at least found the reasons, the permission, for it in the material itself. Existence followed upon action, as the pragmatists had it. Action didn't conform to some objective order or truth. Nick had no trouble seeing in this precept a "moral relativism" he could stand behind.

As Molly professed a broader interest in the American culture that grew from the pragmatist way of thinking, they started exploring its different corners—things like 1940s romantic comedies and Beat poetry. One evening Nick went to her apartment to watch *No Direction Home*, the Martin Scorsese documentary on Bob Dylan. It happened to afford an excellent social history of the Greenwich Village music scene in the early sixties.

Nick was surprised to find that Molly had only one room, and only one place to sit and watch the television: her queen-size bed. They had to lie together more intimately than propriety allowed, elbows grazing and thoughts wandering to those limits and obligations. Molly enjoyed his embarrassment a lot the way a teacher would. She was testing him. To be part of the world was also to be thrown, or "plunged" into it, as he had said. But if nothing there could be "put into perspective by consciousness," she all but told him, that ethical disorientation also couldn't be tamed or sanitized. The stakes had to be high if Nick wasn't just talking out of his ass.

He took the point. They even laughed about it, and the documentary they went on to watch became still more compelling because of the camaraderie it made possible. He loved seeing the New York of the postwar era through her eyes—the restless crowds on black and white streets, Cafe Wha?, The Bitter End, the original Cedar Tavern dotted with abstract expressionists, jazz musicians, and poets. It evoked a time when candor and improvisation mattered, and the rules were made to be broken.

This pleasure, however, was interrupted when Molly, returning from the bathroom, let forth an ear piercing "Fuck!" and pointed behind him to the window. "My Peeping Tom!"

Nick twisted around in time to glimpse someone through the jalousie blinds crashing back into the bushes. He reacted alertly, darting out the door and taking off after whoever it was—a young man with a backpack. Nick chased him down the residential street where Molly lived to a small park with acacia trees. At its far end he came upon a wall made of rough-hewn stone over which his quarry had scrambled. Nick jammed his foot into a crevice and lifted himself up. On the other side he saw an empty street slanting along a hill and lined with Edwardian terrace houses, each slightly higher than the last. No Peeping Tom.

Back at her apartment the two of them sat on the bed and puzzled over the guy's motives. They seemed compulsive yet also premeditated. He'd clearly devoted time and strategy to what he was doing. Nick had the impression he'd even planned out his escape route beforehand. He must have cased the apartment. . .and cased Molly, too. In all likelihood he'd been following her around the neighborhood to get a sense of her habits. Nick decided not to mention this unsettling possibility.

"It makes me so mad," she was saying. "How could anyone want to be intimate without getting to know me first, without even wanting to know me?"

Nick thought again of Cytherea, that other fantasist. Life really must feel too risky, the self too fragile, for such people. Experience could only be split off in private obsessions. Perhaps this wasn't so hard to understand in a compartmentalized world. Perhaps Cytherea and the Peeping Tom were just exaggerated versions of everyone who had no choice but to live in one. Nick didn't want to consider just what that might mean for him and Molly, if true.

"Once he saw me in the shower," she told him. "There's a small screened window in there, high up, too. He had to drag a cinder block from a neighbor's yard to stand on. When I reached to the sill for shampoo, I saw these two big spider eyes staring back at me."

She shuddered in the memory.

"At least he's harmless," Nick said, hoping to set her easy. "I could tell from what I did see of him—probably another college student."

"He's not harmless!" she countered. "Shit, Nick, he affects everything I do. I'm always thinking I might be watched, which means I act as if I am watched even when I'm not. He gets in my head that way. He robs me of my solitude."

That wasn't so hard for Nick to understand either. As he'd had occasion to say before, the world was always trespassing. "Maybe you'll have to find a new place to live."

"Great!" she cracked. "Fucking great. I have to change my whole life because some dickhead has a hang-up. It's not fair."

"No."

On the television a young Bob Dylan was throwing cue cards to the ground and singing "Subterranean Homesick Blues" to the camera. Allen Ginsberg lurked in the background. Neither Nick nor Molly much felt like watching them anymore. Their antics seemed a bit juvenile now. She saw him think it might be time to go home.

"I don't want to be alone," she said, letting the hope in her words hang between them in its faintest of overtones. If he wasn't mistaken, she was asking him to stay the night.

He looked around the room, cluttered with books and clothes. It felt still smaller because she'd covered the walls in the graffiti of her wilder imaginings—words, song lyrics, drawings.

"There's no place for me to sleep here, Molly."

An underhanded smile played into her face. "We could share my bed," she said, with a pat on the mattress. "I've had lots of friends sleep over."

"I bet you've never had your professors sleep over."

"The guy might come back," she pleaded. "He might be out there right now, waiting for you to leave."

"You're seducing me."

"No, I'm not," she said, with a gleam in her eyes that suggested otherwise.

He left the bed and went to lean against a desk, considering his options. They weren't as clear-cut as he'd thought a moment before. "Okay," he said finally, grabbing a chair and pushing it into the adjacent kitchen. He started kicking dropped clothes out of the way. "I'm going to sleep on this floor, and you're going to sleep on that bed—"

"You don't have to."

"No, no," he insisted. "I don't want you to be alone either. We're going to stay in our separate zones and think of what the two Bernadettes would do if they found out—which is wheel out the guillotine and cut off my head. How does that sound?"

"What? Cutting off your head?"

"No." He rolled his eyes. "You're a smart-ass, aren't you?"

"Sometimes."

He held out a hand. "Give me a pillow."

7

The semester wore on without further criticism of their relationship, and Nick let himself hope the problem would soon be forgotten. He taught his seminar with more caution than he liked, and he never went again to Rick's Place afterward, even though the students had made it a ritual. They'd warmed to what they were learning, and also to his comparative approach—all, that is, except Eunice Notley, who had the habit of mocking every writer he assigned, from Ovid to Roland Barthes. In her view they made things more complicated than they needed to be. She liked to kick Zeno's stone by turning the discussions to trivialities like the tattoo she got on her ass while on vacation in Thailand. For a sexual moralist of her caliber, she certainly had no problem sticking her bum in other people's faces. She lost all credibility when Nick found out from Molly that she'd hooked up with her current boyfriend, the postgrad, while he served as her tutor in a course Alan had taught on postmodernism.

Molly showed an interest in going to graduate school in the United States, and Nick thought of NYU as a good choice. After one seminar he met her in his office, and together they did some research online, sending information and application forms from his computer to the printer in the mailroom. He'd closed the door in the meantime. But when he opened it again, and the two of them stepped into the hallway to retrieve their printed documents, Alba and Jane happened to walk by. It was late, night had fallen, and Nick feared the way it looked. Professors were expected to keep their doors open when a student was in the room.

He had nothing to worry about, however. Jane was in tears.

"What's the matter?" he asked.

"They denied her application for senior lecturer," said Alba. "Again!"

"I thought for sure I had it," Jane said. "They made me jump through so many damn hoops I thought even they couldn't say no. I feel like a circus animal."

"I'm so sorry," Nick said, shuddering to think what the Helman Hall ringmasters would be like when they had you—or him—in their clutches. "Listen, I'm about finished here. I've been helping Molly with applications for grad school. You want to meet at the Pig & Whistle?"

"We were planning a bitch session somewhere," said Alba.

"I can be there in half an hour."

"Okay," Jane said gratefully.

They left on a collegial note. Nick headed with Molly for the mailroom.

"That was close!" he said in a low voice.

ᛯ

He found the two women in a corner of the pub with a pitcher of beer, intent on drowning their sorrows. He hadn't seen them much lately, either in the department or in his neighborhood, and not only because they were all so busy. It had stopped being much fun for Nick to spend time with them. Now that he'd been at King's University awhile, he mentally divided his colleagues into two camps. The rationalizers, with Alan as their captain, believed bureaucratic intrusion into every crevice of university life marked an advance over previous orders. The accommodators, like Alba and Jane, had resigned themselves to the new status quo. They could tell the hawk of democracy from the handsaw of corporate managerialism, but they were helpless to do anything about it. They therefore drifted inward, taking their solitary comfort in complaint, losing themselves in idle gossip as a substitute for open confrontation.

Around them Nick felt he had little choice but to drift inward, too, and less because they did than because it had its appeal, its draw in the heart. But he didn't want to be an accommodator anymore than a rationalizer, even if the other choice, open confrontation, would be the quickest way to cut his own throat.

Jane was asking why she didn't just quit when he sat down. "That's what they want me to do. They're daring me to do it."

"You're not going to do it," said Alba.

"They're seeing how much humiliation I can take before I crack."

"Just remember what kind of people they are. It has nothing to do with you. It has everything to do with the torture chamber in their minds."

"But I'm the one being tortured!"

"Why is that torture chamber in their minds?" Nick asked.

"When women like Bernadette Green and Bernadette Potter first started teaching at King's," Alba explained, "the department was dominated by misogynist old men who ran the place like a colony."

"They humiliated anyone under their sway."

"With dangled promotions," Alba said, "and heavy workloads that left no time for research."

"Worse things than that," said Jane darkly.

"So these women pass on to others what happened to them," Nick said, trying to understand. "The frustration. The sense of injury. The resentment. In a cycle. A cycle of bad conscience."

"'The instinct for freedom forcibly made latent,'" said Alba, citing what Nietzsche had to say about it, "'pushed back and repressed, incarcerated, and finally able to vent itself only on itself.'"

"The academic is a slave," declared Jane.

Nick took this in with a jolt of recognition. It was, sad to say, no idle claim. "At least we're different, though, right?" he asked hopefully. "We jump out of the cycle? We see it for what it is?"

Both women dropped their eyes. They wondered if he was right. He wondered himself.

"Pain has a way of leaving nothing else around it," said Alba solemnly.

"No place to jump to," put in Jane. "And no one who jumps."

Nick tilted his chair back. It was a reflex motion. He sought in recoil to escape the vision that these two women had of the world they all shared. He could say he didn't much feel like a slave sitting there. But then again, maybe he just hadn't felt enough pain.

X

On his way to a bus stop afterward, Nick let this last thought close around him, meld with the warm New Zealand night and the scents and sounds that were still so exotic to him. He wondered what it would be like to live there for a long time. He'd never faced this possibility—at bottom he was just passing through, on the way to somewhere else even though he couldn't say with any confidence exactly where. But he might be kidding himself. He might *have* to stay there. He might have to suffer that incarceration of instinct, that inward turn of pride to self-loathing the job would force on him, in the long run at any rate.

He imagined how the change would play out: years of resistance resolving slowly into the acquiescence he saw in all his colleagues without exception, blunting whatever sense he had of himself as his own person. He was in fact already acquiescing, already compromising. One sign of this was the "good" teacher he tried to be with Molly, the right thing he did by her and for the professional identity his job held out for him even knowing how hollow it was. That pulled him up short on the sidewalk. He wouldn't say the right thing to do was necessarily a compromise—there were many ways to approach being an ethical person. But he wondered how hollow that identity had to get before *it* undercut any good reason to do the right thing. And when it did, was it ethical anymore not to sleep with his student? Or was resistance as ridiculous as sleeping with his student was wrong, and never more so than when he knew his student wanted to sleep with him?

Or when she lived a few blocks away, for that matter. This broke the deadlock, and he continued on, but not to his bus stop. He wanted Molly's company now with an emotion akin to longing. A voice in his head said turn back, avoid temptation, think what you're doing, get a hold of the reasons why sacrifice matters at this stage of your life. But he couldn't do it. He heard nothing to respect in that voice, in its punitive tone. It sounded like the rational mind telling him the difference between desire and lust. Who, though, could believe that desire lay back at his bus stop and not forward in Molly's apartment? The way back meant the heart's stupid compartmentalizing. It meant fantasies of the kind Cytherea indulged on the internet or experiences unassuming doors on deserted night streets offered to the men who passed through them. It had nothing to do with the desire that sought contact and took risks, that thrilled to the intuitive touch. Only Molly offered him that right now.

He paused on the street outside her apartment, looking through the bushes at the light in her window. He heard the faint sounds of her television. That his compunction only made him more like the Peeping Tom the longer he stood there precipitated him to the door. He knocked and called out her name. Moments later he was in her studio, catching a heavy odor of marijuana.

"I'm high," she said.

"I can smell."

She went to lie on the bed, grabbing a remote control to mute the television, on which Nick noted some kind of reality TV show about teenage girls. His attention made her sheepish, and she turned it off.

"I'm interrupting," he said, sitting on the chair she kept by the desk, next to a computer.

"No, you're not. But I don't know if I should offer you some pot—unless it's part of the research. Eh, Professor Moran?"

"I wonder if you need my help with that part of the research."

"Of course I do. It requires the professor get high, too."

She lifted herself up to load a bong. "Come on," she urged while picking out a bud from a plastic baggy. "There's nothing wrong with this stuff, believe me. Pot is very kind. The kindness of pot knows no bounds."

She lit the bong for him while he took a drag. "I don't know what I'm doing," he said as she swayed too near for him to ignore her hip curving out from her small waist. It came as a revelation to learn from the quiver of her breasts that there was nothing between her and her shirt.

"I think you know what you're doing all right."

She set the bong on the desk behind him and fell lightly onto his lap, letting her coppery red hair graze his cheek. He had no choice but to raise an arm and drop it around her shoulders—not in the avuncular way he'd done it the first time on that night-filled street.

"You're nervous," she observed.

"I'm an idiot," he corrected. "I should be home in bed, working on spreadsheets and thinking up ways to protect the innocence of children."

"I'm not a child."

"So I gather."

"I'm twenty-two."

"So much?"

"I think deep down you're shy."

He smiled. "Now you know my secret. I don't ask for things."

"You make the girl do all the work?"

"Something like that."

She looked at him with quizzing eyes. It disconcerted him. They suggested more sexual experience than he had, for all the difference in their ages.

"You know what your problem is?" she then playfully inquired.

"What?"

"You're a 'good' person."

"Am I?"

"I hate 'good' people."

"You do?"

"They're so boring."

"I imagine that's true."

"What you need is to work on being less of a 'good' person."

"That's a tall order."

"I'm serious."

"I know you are," he said. "Should I start now?"

"I don't see why not."

He still wavered.

"You don't want to," she said in a disappointed voice.

"It's not that."

"What then?"

"My head's full of what other people think I should do."

"Fuckers."

"Part of me thinks they're right."

"What does the rest of you say?"

"The rest of me?"

"The rest of you," she said, digging into his ribs.

He reflected. "I guess it doesn't understand how simple pleasures come to be so hard. It wishes for simple pleasures."

She put a hand on his cheek and drew her lips to his. "Shit," he said in a sudden breaching of inner dams, kissing back, kissing harder.

He took her in his arms and led her onto the bed with a heedlessness the more exciting to him because it thrilled her, too. All at once they were in a world of their own, free from prying eyes, moralizing hypocrites, and Nietzschean resentment. Nothing mattered now but improvisation and candor. Among the many things he intended to do, with his whole being if he could swing it, was to nestle into the crook of her neck and find that rose tattoo.

8

Two days later Nick received a call from Bernadette Potter, asking him to drop by her office before his seminar. On arriving at the appointed time he met her with Bernadette Green and that officious director of Human Resources, Sarah Hayes, all three in conservative dress suits. Sarah had a clipboard on her smooth polyester lap.

He sat down.

"This is an informal meeting," began Bernadette Potter with a hare-eyed look. "But I've asked Sarah to be here anyway, as a matter has come up that falls under her jurisdiction."

"Is something wrong?"

"There's been an allegation made about your relationship with Molly Banville."

He felt strangely supported in his plastered smile.

"A student contacted a member of staff," Bernadette Green informed him, "who then related to me what had been said."

"What had been said?"

Sarah was taking notes.

"We can't go into the specific nature of the allegation," Bernadette Green replied, "except that it concerns your adherence to the university code of conduct."

"Who made the allegation?"

"I'm afraid we can't divulge that information."

"Who was the member of staff?"

"That's not important now."

"This is still preliminary," put in Bernadette Potter.

He pointed at Sarah Hayes. "Then why is she writing down what I say?"

"It's routine in cases like this," Bernadette Green assured him.

Struggling through the shock of the moment, he asked what they were able to tell him about the allegation.

Bernadette Green pushed an opened pamphlet across the table. "Have you read the university code of conduct?"

"I didn't know there was one."

The three women watched him peruse the pamphlet. "The pertinent clause falls in subsection C.7," Bernadette Green added helpfully.

Nick read a sentence about the impropriety of "personal, sexual, or family relations" with a student.

"Would you characterize your relationship with Molly as improper in any of these senses?" asked Bernadette Green.

"We're friends," he said. "I'm her supervisor. I interpreted my responsibility in that role to include liking her, yes."

The two Bernadettes shot each other somber looks. He saw very distinctly that the truth bothered them as much as the lie.

"John Lurie told me the relationship between an Honours supervisor and his student should be more personal," he said. "Is that not true?"

"It's professional," said Bernadette Green brusquely. "You're expected to maintain the dignity of your position at the same time that you establish a rapport with the student."

"So I'm accused of having an improper 'personal,' but not 'sexual,' relationship with Molly?"

"I'm afraid we can't divulge that information," said Bernadette Green.

He felt his temper rise. He didn't have to be a saint here for her evasiveness to be infuriating. In a tight voice he asked, "What do you want from me?"

"Your side of the story."

"There *is* no story."

His firmness unnerved the old women. Like everyone else in that place, they had no stomach for confrontation.

"Please," Bernadette Potter urged, as leporine as ever. She was the kindlier of the two. "There's no reason at this stage to get upset."

"I'm not upset," he said more calmly. "I just don't understand what's happening. If you like, I'll admit to a 'personal' relationship with Molly. No one told me how you define 'personal,' and I notice the language of subsection C.7 is broad and open to interpretation. All I did was go ahead and define it for myself—to include friendship."

Bernadette Green eyed him suspiciously—feminine intuition, he supposed, tripping one alarm after another. "Well," she said with a sharp intake of breath, "I think it safe to say, at the very least, that there's been a breach of your objectivity, and until this issue is resolved, it's better that you stop being Molly's supervisor."

Sarah leaned over to whisper in the chair's ear.

"In fact," the old woman continued, "it's better you not mark any work by an Honours student until we can sort all this out."

That told him an Honours student had made the allegation.

"Have you talked to Molly about this?" he asked.

"Not yet."

"What happens if she denies any wrongdoing?"

"We'll take in all information and assess the validity of the charge," said Bernadette Green.

"Even if we both deny it?"

No one offered a response to this. It was evidently enough that something might have happened for them to act as if it had. Indeed, since they couldn't possibly know what had happened, everything now would be happening the same way even if it hadn't. The right thing to do would have been just as wrong.

"I can't believe this," he murmured.

"You haven't been officially charged," Bernadette Potter reminded him.

"It's informal," said Bernadette Green.

"And preliminary," said Bernadette Potter a second time.

"Did you get that?" Nick asked Sarah, the lesser of the three Fates but the one he imagined cutting the threads of destiny, with a sarcasm he couldn't bring himself to hide.

⅄

His seminar fell directly afterward. He entered the room with the feeling of shock still strong in him. He glanced at Molly as he sat down, purposefully enough to alert her to a problem. He started in on a wavering introduction of the book he'd asked them to read for that day, Stendhal's *On Love*, sketching out the life of the author and the circumstances of the book's writing. Then he drew the students' attention to a chapter entitled "Concerning Intimacy." He proceeded too precipitately to avoid the impression that he was rattled.

"Stendhal makes a distinction in this chapter between nature and habit," he said. "To act naturally implies spontaneity, an absence of forethought or calculation. To act habitually, on the other hand, implies pattern, routine, a familiar environment. Imagine yourself getting up in the middle of the night for a drink of water and passing through the house without turning the lights on, because you know where everything is. Habit is canny this way. By contrast, the natural act takes place in unfamiliar environments, where we're not at home, where we're strangers. Stendhal draws here the counterintuitive conclusion that the natural act, and the spontaneous person—the lover, in other words, the person aroused by passion—is by definition self-conscious. Stendhal thus assigns to the lover the attribute of reticence or scruple. Do you follow?"

His eyes roamed around the room. The students sat stonily listening, as they mostly did. He thought he saw smirks on Eunice and Brian's faces, but he couldn't be sure. Nick settled his gaze on Molly and waited for her to nod.

"It's counterintuitive," he said, "because we're used to confusing nature with habit, and more significantly passion with comfort, ecstasy with confidence. Stendhal pries these states apart for us, associating love with a particular kind of awareness rather than, say, an animal impulse. That's why, when his friend Salviati gives his arm to his girlfriend Léonore in the chapter, he feels he is about to fall and has to 'think how to walk.'"

A stir in the room told him someone had entered while he was speaking. He turned and saw Tom Hatch, with his idiotic suspenders, standing as vaporously as ever just inside the door.

"Can I help you?"

Tom tipped his head and looked through the top of his bifocal glasses at the class. "Is Molly Banville here?"

She raised a tentative hand. The son of a bitch didn't even know who she was.

“We need you a moment, Molly.”

Everyone sat scandalized as she rose to her feet, circled around the table, and followed Tom out the door. By the time she left, for Bernadette Potter’s corner office no doubt, Nick had forgotten what he was trying to say about Stendhal.

ᚸ

That evening he met Molly at a café well away from campus. She told him she had categorically denied any wrongdoing to the three women. She had praised him as a supervisor and challenged the idea that they had her best interests at heart, as they all took pains to emphasize. Molly’s biggest worry was the catastrophe this turn of events had made of her Honours year.

“Who’s going to mark my thesis now?” she cried. “Someone who doesn’t know me? Someone who doesn’t give a shit?”

“I’ll talk to John Lurie. He can make sure a sympathetic reader is chosen.”

“I’m fucked!” she said bitterly. “This is all about fucking me.”

Nick tried not to dwell on the several ways this remark might be taken. He kept to the main issue. “Whoever made the complaint must think I give you too much of an advantage,” he surmised. “There’s no other explanation, unless the answer is simple spite.”

“So I have to suffer because other people are jealous I have a supportive supervisor? Why is that fair?”

“It’s not fair.”

“How am I even going to write now?” she said. “Under these conditions?! How am I supposed to concentrate? Who am I supposed to write for?”

“None of this means I can’t keep helping you. I’ll read, I’ll edit, I’ll give you deadlines if that’s what you need.”

“I’m fucked.”

“I wish you’d stop saying that!”

In the pause that followed this remonstrance they sipped their skim flat whites and tried to settle down. The cafe where they sat, on a commercial street visible through a glass wall, was bustling. People, when not waiting to order at a counter, spoke at tables like theirs over the hiss of baristas steaming milk behind an espresso machine. The world went on its usual course, as indifferent as ever to the human comedy.

"This can't go any further," Nick decided. "All that's happened is a third party has complained about our relationship, and we've both denied it. That should be the end of it—unless they had some sort of evidence or eyewitness. Have you told anybody about the other night?"

"No, Nick. I swear. Nobody knows a thing."

"Then there can't be anything to the charge," he said. "All they can do is reprimand me for what I've already admitted—a 'personal' relationship with a student."

He frowned. The word was deceptive. It carried a sexual connotation whatever it was supposed to mean. If it went into his record this way, with his confession, he'd be as good as guilty of harassment. For the first time he began to understand just what kind of power flowed in the background of Helman Hall.

Neither he nor Molly heard a word from anybody of authority for the next two weeks. The whole affair dropped from sight. Nick went about his business, presiding over tutorials and marking essays. Everyone in the department acted as if nothing was going on, even though they all had to know. The pressure of so much pretense was unbearable. One day he let it get the better of him when Bernadette Lund turned into a ridiculously long corridor about five steps ahead of him, pretending he wasn't there. He followed her for a good twenty feet, closing the gap between them. Unable to help himself he burst out, "Are you never going to admit I'm here?"

She paused and looked back, the color rising in her cheeks. She was a small woman of around thirty-five, insecure in her junior status on the faculty and easily rattled. "I don't have time to talk," she stammered.

"A simple hello would do." He didn't give a damn about civility with these people. Most of the time he didn't want anything to do with them either. If he persisted now, it was only because he didn't know which was the faster way to become like them: pretend they were ghosts, or pretend he was. "Just a smile and a nod. Even English professors manage that around here."

"I have a lot to do."

"Just a smile and a nod," he said. "Then you can go back to rolling your rock up the fucking hill."

"You're making me uncomfortable."

Fear shot up through his outrage. He'd gone too far. He was always, it seemed, going too far. "Fine," he said, stalking off. "Have a nice day."

Once at his office he closed the door, opened the window, and sat on the sill smoking a cigarette, forbidden in Helman Hall. He was too beside himself to wait until he could get out of the building.

⅄

He finally received a message from Sarah Hayes informing him that he had a meeting with a dean named George Prashad the next day. He'd never heard of the man. Sarah said nothing about what they might discuss, but of course it would have to be the allegation. She did say, ominously, that he had a right to bring a witness.

He asked the Honours coordinator, John Lurie. He could think of no one as trustworthy, although he, like everyone else, had avoided any mention of the scandal. Nick couldn't tell if he even knew, or if he did, what conclusions he'd come to in private.

He told John his version of what happened. "I'd like you to know," he finished, hoping the lie wouldn't show, "that none of it is true. I've just tried to be as supportive a supervisor as I can."

John looked at him in astonishment. "That's strange."

"Why?"

"When I talked to Bernadette Green, I came away with the distinct impression that you had admitted to a sexual relationship with Molly Banville."

"She *said* that?!"

John ran back over the exchange in his mind. "In so many words," he said. "The implication was clear anyway. She certainly had no doubts."

"Both Molly and I have denied the allegation."

"I see."

"How can they *do* that?!" Nick demanded hotly. "How can they just decide I'm guilty without either charge or evidence?!"

"I'm afraid I couldn't say," that very civil professor replied, suggesting, however, that he wasn't entirely surprised by it.

The two men went to the dean's office together. Nick was prepared to concede he'd made a mistake, albeit a reasonable one based on his coming from a different country, where his ideas about personal relationships might not have been quite so out of line. He'd agree to modify his behavior in the future, knowing now what the standards were at King's University.

They sat down in George Prashad's office, which had a splendor fit for a CEO. The ceiling was twenty feet high, and a rank of lancet windows looked out over a quadrangle of closely mown bluegrass. Nick noticed books by Michel Foucault on the shelves. George Prashad was a sociologist as well as a dean. When Nick, in an effort to be informal, asked about them, he found out the man was a specialist on conflicts between modern and traditional cultures in the global south. He'd used Foucault's work as a theoretical rubric for an influential study of matrimonial customs and honor killing in India. Nick took this as a good sign.

But all hope evaporated when the dean began to speak about his case. "I'm afraid I have bad news, Dr. Moran. Multiple allegations of sexual harassment have been lodged against you."

The dean awaited a response. Nick was scarcely able to register what he was hearing. "I don't understand," he stammered. "Two weeks ago there was only one allegation, and it wasn't sexual harassment. The problem, at worst, was me having a consensual 'personal' relationship with my student."

"The records indicate multiple charges."

"And they've come up since I last spoke with Bernadette Green?"

"I'm not sure when they first surfaced."

"Just what are they?"

"I couldn't say."

"Do they all allege my sexual harassment of Molly Banville, or am I sexually harassing other people?"

"Again I couldn't say."

"Who made them?"

"I can't reveal that information."

"Were they other Honours students?"

"I don't know."

"What *do* you know?!" Nick snapped, unable to hold himself back.

The lapse brought out a frosty side in the dean. Nick had to remember that anger never worked with these people. Their right to indirection was absolute and nonnegotiable.

"I have to say this is a surprise to me," put in John, hoping to lower the temperature. "No Honours student came to me about it, and that would be a logical first step in situations like this."

"They must have gone directly to Bernadette Green," said Nick.

"It may not only be students," the dean offered.

"Not only students?!"

Nick's mind shot straight to Bernadette Lund. That had been a stupid mistake.

"Human Resources is now exploring whether or not the allegations have merit," the dean continued, turning a page from the documents before him. "It's not yet a formal inquiry."

"What is it then?"

"If they decide the allegations have merit, an inquiry will follow, with possibility of censure."

"They being Sarah Hayes?"

"And her staff."

"How long will this inquiry on whether to have an inquiry take?"

"I can't commit to any time frame," the dean said. "I would hope it happens as quickly as possible."

Nick needed a pause to arrange his thoughts. "Let me get this straight," he said slowly. "You're telling me that I have to wait an unspecified length of time to see if unspecified allegations made by and to unspecified people are going to be investigated or not?"

"I'm afraid so."

"And that seems reasonable to you?"

"It's how it is anyway."

"What am I supposed to do in the meantime? Am I expected to go on teaching as though nothing's changed?"

The dean gave no answer to this. He hadn't finished with his disclosures. "You should know," he said with the somber demeanor of someone about to administer a coup de grâce, "that we may be dealing in this case with human rights violations, actionable by the Anti-Discrimination Board of New Zealand or the Human Rights Commission of the British Commonwealth."

Nick stared aghast. These were words in a nightmare. They sank right into the brain stem.

"It very well might not come to that," the dean hastened to add. "But it's my responsibility to inform you it could."

"This can't be happening," Nick mumbled. He licked his lips and swallowed, trying to get rid of a parched dryness in his mouth. His whole body felt numb. "None of it has any basis in fact. It's all rumor and innuendo."

That prompted another thought in the dean's mind. "Under no circumstances should you take steps to find out the identity of those making the allegations," he said firmly. "That would make it much worse for you."

"It gets worse?"

The dean eased up, growing less formal. "I realize this must be difficult. Believe me, I understand completely. We have a duty of care for everyone involved. If you like, I can offer the services of a counselor to help you cope with the situation."

"Would the counselor come from Human Resources, too?"

"No."

"Would the counselor's notes be part of the inquiry into whether there is going to be an inquiry?"

"Of course not."

"I don't need a counselor," Nick said, rising to his feet. Fear, if nothing else, had gotten the better of incredulity. "What I need, obviously, is a lawyer."

He went in a state of fugue for the door, forcing a bewildered John Lurie to follow. At the last second Nick turned on his heel and pointed to the books by Foucault in the shelves.

"You should look again at *Discipline and Punish*," he said to the dean. "Especially the part about human rights being little more than the rights of some to decide on the rights of others."

He didn't know if Foucault even said that. In fact, he had a vague suspicion he was thinking of someone else—if he wasn't mistaken, Foucault had become an advocate for human rights late in his career. But the dean only stared at him, suggesting he might be as out of his depth as Nick here. With this odd acknowledgement of a collapsing common ground, he left the office.

☧

He had a tutorial right after, but there was no question, in his state, of teaching. John offered to take care of it for him, and Nick headed straight off campus. He walked erratically for a long while through the busy Auckland streets, animated only by a sense of clear and present danger in the terrace houses, the pubs, the convenience stores, the traffic on the wrong side. He tried to make sense of what had just happened, but the amazing thing was that nothing had just happened. There were no charges, no accusers, no inquiry. All he could do was feel the shadowy quality of events diffused everywhere he turned, in everything and everyone he saw. He felt like a prisoner, released from his cell, who knew at the same time that it was only a dream and he hadn't escaped anything. The whole world was his prison.

He jumped on a bus that took him to the harbour at Mission Bay, from which he could walk home along a promenade in view of Rangitoto Island, its volcanic cone limned by a clear blue sky.

As he went his thoughts began to focus. Just what was happening? He saw two possibilities. Either the department didn't want him there or it was breaking him down, letting him know what kind of person he had to be if he expected to fit in. He couldn't tell if this discipline was deliberate or merely an accident. George Prashad may well not have known anything about the allegations relayed to him. That was John's opinion. No one directly communicated with anyone else. People mined their particular seam of duty without asking after the big picture, the structure, cause and effect. If you did ask, wires were tripped, passages sealed off, the mine itself locked down.

But all of this he soon realized was beside the point. That discipline wormed its way into his heart regardless. He could feel it already inciting a harsh analysis of impulses and desires, words and deeds, that drew him closer and closer to the stigmatized person. His accusers plainly counted on this conscientiousness. They hoped he would do the punishing for them. And he might, if he wasn't careful. Even his best reasons for what he did with Molly now felt suspect to him. It made little difference, whatever line he'd crossed, that no one had been coerced and everything was consensual—unless you believed Molly's consent impossible because he was her teacher, and he had no problem rejecting that as paternalism once she did. Still it felt like he was making excuses, like he was asserting a right to ignore the rules, to hide in the law—much as the university was doing with him. Even his belief that the only moral lines crossed were those protecting people's right to work out for themselves what it means to be human with one another, on a case-by-case basis, had become, in the shadow of "human rights" violations, strangely the property of his superiors. They had, by this deft maneuver, taken from him any ground apart from their exercise of arbitrary power. All he could do was feel the presumption of innocence (at least until proven guilty) and the right to privacy become rationalizations even in his own mind.

It didn't help that they aimed so cannily at his sense of himself as a man. He reflected glumly on a sad fact about his sexual identity. Fraught by relations with women who wouldn't or couldn't love him back, it had long rested on a simple premise: he was not supposed to love. If he did, it was always in some sense an infraction, a trespass. As ridiculous as this feeling might have been, he knew it pointed to ambivalent investments he'd never quite managed to unravel. It suggested a static emotional structure that was always generating the same scenarios of eroticized defiance, disappointment, and shame. He suspected this at least partly explained why he'd been attracted to academia in the first place. The constraints under which a teacher had to work were versions of older inhibitions in his character, courted for the pretexts they gave him, the way an actor might play a role.

He did, however, recognize this emotional structure in himself. And because he did, he wanted to believe now that it didn't entirely define him. He wasn't *just* an actor. It could be that he wasn't enough of one for his superiors' taste. They pushed him into that inner theater as much as he brought it with him, and not only because it was what they understood as teachers themselves; they were betting that, there, he would see himself as they did and so do the punishing for them. The real question was, would he oblige? Or would he respect his self-awareness enough to hold fast in the other person it made him, the person who was neither innocent nor guilty of what they alleged?

That he couldn't say sent him reeling back into his own psychic history, where that emotional structure had its deeper foundations. Haley sprang to mind, and the intricacy she in particular had given it. He needed to talk to her right away. He found a bench that overlooked an inlet of spangled water, rimmed by a long curving sea wall, and called. It was morning in Paris.

"*Allô?*" he heard.

"Haley."

"Nick! What a coincidence. I was just thinking of you."

"Me, too."

She caught the distress in his voice. "What's wrong?"

He gave her the shortest brief he could. When he finished there was silence on the line.

"I don't get it," she said at last.

"Me neither."

"What did you do to set them off like that?"

"Nothing," he said. "Just be myself. That's the way it feels anyway. It's illegal to be me in New Zealand."

"You must have done something. Did you sleep with your student?"

His hesitation was answer enough. "Nick," she said.

"It was consensual, Haley. She's not the one making the accusation. She denied it, too. From what I can tell, third parties are characterizing my relationship with her as sexual harassment. And they're inventing stories about further relationships, either with them or others."

"Is there evidence?"

"No."

"Are you sure?"

"I'm positive."

His sharp tone rattled her. It also brought the gravity of his situation into clearer focus.

"I'm just trying to figure out what's going on," she assured him.

"I know. I'm sorry."

"I don't care what you've done with your student. I don't think it's anybody's business if you did sleep together. It's completely ludicrous."

"I'm sensitive to the assumption I've done something wrong."

"Do you feel like you've done something wrong?"

"I fear it doesn't matter what I feel. The aim is to define the truth for other people—to establish what's real without my having any say in it."

"That sounds irrational."

"I know."

"You care too much what other people think," she said. "You give them that power over you."

"That doesn't make the power less real."

"True." She pondered this new dimension he gave to the problem. "You have to fight it in yourself, but you can't let people define you either. It won't be easy, especially for you."

"Why me?"

"Because you don't believe there is a self not defined by others," she said. "It's socially constructed. 'Relational.'"

"Is that wrong?"

"It's conceptual anyway. And it's dangerous, when you're a moralist at heart."

"I thought I was a sexual harasser!"

"No," she said with a laugh. "That's the funny part. You're not the type to go around taking advantage of your students. If anything, you're a bit of a Puritan."

"Oh come on!"

"It's true," she insisted. "You have a fixed sense of right and wrong. It's not relative. You don't think people should be free to work their private feelings out for themselves—especially sexual feelings."

She was touching on past experiences now, on one above all, which Nick still couldn't easily talk about with her.

"For instance," she went on, "I've been seeing this Tunisian man lately, and I haven't wanted to tell you about it."

"Why not?!"

"I imagine you making all kinds of judgments. He's younger than me, poor, uneducated. We don't have a lot in common, it's just about sex, I'm an orientalizing westerner, et cetera."

"That's ridiculous, Haley."

"Maybe so. But still, that moral training in you makes me hesitate. I'm not sure I can trust you."

"You sound like the one who's worried, not me."

He heard another person in the background speaking French. She dropped the phone and answered in kind.

"You're not alone?" he asked.

"That's my housemate."

"Your housemate?"

"I've moved out of the apartment," she told him. "I live with friends near the Gare du Nord now. They're part of that atelier I told you about—actors, writers, set designers. I'm very involved with them."

"Huh."

"I've quit my job, too," she said. "I couldn't bring myself to translate another software manual. It was literally making me sick. I'm writing that screenplay about the American woman in Paris."

"I see."

"I'm excited about it, Nick, like I haven't been about anything in years. And I'm determined. I won't stop until it's finished. Jean-Claude thinks he'd like to direct it. The idea is it would be a French-American co-production. That way we could look for money both here and in the States."

Nick was at a loss for words. Her enthusiasm all but stymied him. Feeling suddenly drained, he cast a weary eye over the scene before him. A heavyset man jogged past on the promenade, lost to the music in his earbuds. Out on the inlet beyond a fast-moving motorboat, packed with revelers all in red life vests, was busy churning the water. Everything had a hard-edged radiance to it.

"He told me he'd like to meet you," Haley added.

"Jean-Claude?"

"Yes." Nick sensed her tactfully shifting ground. "He also said he'd like to meet your father. He was interested to find out he lived in Paris. I said I'd ask you about it."

She knew this would bother him. His whole life people had been interested in meeting Evan Moran. His whole life he'd had to wonder if it was a reason for them getting to know him. The children of famous people had the worst of two worlds: they shared next to nothing of the celebrity they lived with, but they worried, as celebrities do, if others just wanted something from them. It hurt whenever the question came up, but it especially hurt when it was a close friend who asked—Haley, above all.

"I don't know if it's a good idea."

"I told Jean-Claude he was sick," she half-agreed.

"That's not it." Nick refrained from saying more. He saw no way his feelings could come across as anything but petty. "You don't need my permission. I'm not my father's keeper. You know him, too."

"Are you sure?"

"I'll email you his number when we're through."

"Thanks, Nick. It means a lot to me."

He wanted off the phone now, fearing his vexed emotions might overflow in misdirected anger. When he hung up and resumed his walk around that seawall, his thoughts swirled like clouds in a storm cell, mixing his present calamity up with the past, in particular with the time he first met Haley and that one experience he couldn't remember without pain.

9

Whatever moralism Nick harbored about sex had a lot to do with his father, who had the libidinal constitution of a satyr. Evan thought of sex all the time by his own admission, and because he was attractive and powerful it came to him so easily he lost any inhibitions he might have had, especially after he moved to LA. There it became the dominant mode of his relationship to people. He didn't look at a woman so much as size her up. To be a man around him was immediately to feel ranked and judged by the intensity of one's urges. He claimed to understand what others wanted more than they did, or more than they were prepared to admit, and the proof was always the mere fact of knowing him. If people registered in his awareness it was because they wanted him, or wanted something from him, some version of his sexual freedom most of all. His credo, as he had put it many times, was that nothing in life should ever be repressed.

Behind this confidence Nick could see that farm kid from Nebraska, terrified of death and loneliness. For him, sex was a compulsion. He went from one woman to another, seeking a strangely impersonal transcendence that reduced every feeling, every sensation, to its exhausted state. Satiation was his father's Achilles' heel. It revealed the very death and loneliness he tried to cheat. With age this contradiction had become a torment. It trapped him in a boredom all the harder to take because it was so much a result of what he wanted, of what everybody wanted. To his credit, he showed no interest in whitewashing this endgame. He even embraced it. He became supremely bored, looking on the world with a jaundiced eye, given over to the pursuit of more and more empty pleasures until limits were reached that even he couldn't withstand. At that point he had to change course or die.

Nick, growing up without the benefit of hindsight, suffered his father's example as a wound that never quite healed. Around him, or even simply with the idea of him in mind, Nick couldn't experience his own desire except as a deficit, and he couldn't meet his father's standard any more than he could altogether reject it—he was still a man, after all. This double bind became in itself a source of anxiety, aggravating the split he naturally enough had to live with as a child of divorce. If he felt inadequate in LA, he also felt guilty in Hoboken, where his erotic life seemed, however irrationally, like a betrayal of his mother. His first sexual experiences, with indifferent girls he met through his father, were secrets he couldn't divulge at home, where he tended to sublimate his desire for others in romantic fantasies gleaned from books, which stopped well short of consummation.

In college he grew out of this double bind, meeting men who were unlike his father, neither oversexed nor sexually ashamed because of it, and women who defined themselves in explicit opposition to his father's chauvinism. They helped Nick to be himself and still imagine a shared love. He met Haley during his sophomore year, in his first tentative apprehension of this state. One night he'd gone to the basement of his old residence hall to use a pay phone. He found her there before him, in tears, seated on the floor gripping the receiver with both hands, telling her father how bewildered she felt—only a few weeks into her first term—and how much she missed home. She was tall, slender, with that gangly beauty of a fashion model, but it went easily missed in her heedless manner and casual style—she wore that first night, Nick still remembered, a ripped T-shirt with a solarized image of Chrissie Hynde on it. They suggested that other things interested her more than caring about her looks or other people's opinions. Right away Nick thought he detected a loneliness they had in common. He thought they missed the same tenderness, the same trust, in the games people played, the pretenses they required, the conditions they made. The sudden love that befell him didn't so much take the form of a crystallizing fantasy, one that had nothing to do with her, that failed to see her as a separate person; it was more because of her separateness, or her introspectiveness, that Nick loved her. The image in his mind, borrowed from the poet Rilke, was of an ageless couple, neither old nor young, moving serenely in orbit around the same sun, apart and together, each "guarding the solitude of the other." This image, in any case, was central to the way he did idealize her.

He introduced himself when she hung up the phone, assuring her Brown was a less forbidding place than it seemed, and promising to introduce her to his friends the first chance he got. A few nights later he invited her to see the movie *Hiroshima, Mon Amour*, screened in a dining hall by one of the many film societies that existed then on campus. They sat side by side on metal folding chairs as the sixteen-millimeter print rattled through the projector at the back of the room, letting the cool, intelligent film collapse the boundaries between them as it did between its two protagonists, the French actress and the Japanese architect, their illicit passions caught in dissolves of bedroom and street, private and public grief, trust and betrayal. They were the exact type of Nick's idealized lovers: inward, engaged, self-assured. If for him life imitated art, he'd often said that at least the art looked like an Alain Resnais film.

The first tear in the fabric of his illusions came afterward, when he discovered that Haley hadn't been as seduced by the film as he had.

"I thought it a bit mannered," she told him, "juxtaposing a one-night stand with nuclear holocaust. The one just trivialized the other."

"How can you say that?!" he said. "Love happens in the world, in the moment of its impossibility. Its evanescence is not an escape, or a fantasy, but a breach, a violation. It hurts to love."

She glanced sideways at him, suppressing a smile. "You're pretty sure of yourself there, Professor Moran."

With a shrug he conceded his didactic tone. He had, in fact, been paraphrasing an essay he wrote for a French cinema class, of which he'd been especially proud. The professor, a celebrated French film critic, had given it an enthusiastic *A*.

"I liked the ambivalence the film sustained anyway," he said. "It didn't defuse the tension in sentiment."

"It wasn't sentimental," she agreed. "It held off from that."

"You're not either, I can tell."

"Yeah," she drawled, tactfully shifting ground the same way she would all those years later when Nick sat talking to her on the bench by Auckland Harbor. "That's what my boyfriend says, too."

The news hit hard. The boyfriend was a statuesque six-foot-seven captain of the rowing team at Harvard. He and Haley had gone to the same high school in Atlanta. Nick rallied at once, though. He could tell, or he wanted to believe, that the relationship wasn't going to last. The boyfriend belonged to the past, and Nick had every advantage being a part of her new life at Brown. He just had to make her see that image he had of them both as companionable lovers. He felt sure, if she did, that she'd want it, too.

He may have been right, only her version of that image had another man in it. She liked him, yes, very much, but not with a burning erotic attraction. When he persisted in trying to win her over, she had to tell him bluntly: the chemistry between them was all in his head.

Her rejection sent him into a tailspin that combined disastrously with the sadness he'd pent up with his mother's illness and death. He stopped concentrating on his studies, neglected his appearance, and lost all appetite, starving himself sometimes for days at a stretch. At night he walked the Providence streets alone, stupidly crying his eyes out. And he had no one to confide his feelings to, no one to talk him out of his belief that Haley was the only woman for him. He knew then that his mother really was gone, and that her absence isolated him in his life more completely than he thought he could bear. It seemed he'd fallen into a solipsism that overpowered every effort at resistance, like someone caught in a riptide starting to sink, to take in water.

He went on for the rest of that year in this drowning state. He threw up his best fronts for Haley but failed miserably, putting her through emotional scenes that included tears, pleas, and sullen silences, which she sat through not always patiently, but she sat through. It grew even worse for Nick when she split up with the boyfriend, raising his hopes for a time, only to get together, shortly afterward, with a thirty-five-year-old Russian graduate student in the Slavic department. Then Nick had jealousy to deal with as well. He had to contend with a desire in Haley that shot past him to men uniquely qualified to hurt his pride—strong, decisive men, father figures. That's what Haley, in her own insecurities, seemed to need. She lacked confidence as a student at Brown, where so many of her peers knew what they wanted and also what to expect from the world. She was open-ended, vague about the future, a little spacey even—"touched," as the Irish say.

The best way to end his lovesickness turned out to be going abroad to study. He spent his junior year in Paris without seeing her. During that time he threw himself into the French literature courses he took at the University of Paris. In particular he liked the symbolists Joris-Karl Huysmans and Remy de Goncourt. The first time he read Proust was a revelation; it felt like he was seeing, in Swann's relation to Odette or Marcel's to Albertine, the phosphene of his own heart. These writers helped him to sublimate his feelings for Haley, to inflect his romanticism in the literary history he was starting to care about as much as he cared about anything, even her.

On returning to Brown for his senior year he felt more polished, less of an adolescent. She noticed the change in him, and he sensed her responding on deeper levels of affection and need. Strong, decisive men were a problem for her. Their support came at a price: increasingly, she had to fight her way out of their confining demands. And Nick had begun to learn how to talk about this sort of romantic complication, how to get a more articulate grasp of one's drives, one's motives, running them through filters as old as Provençal poetry or as recent as Lacanian psychoanalysis. She followed his lead here, pursuing the same understanding in her studies. It became the basis for an intimacy between them that bore, indeed, some resemblance to that image of two solitary lovers in his mind. And as much as it still depended for her on friendship without love or sex, Nick let himself hope they might go together at some future point. But he never spoke of this, and never made a move either, having learned in the meantime how to bluff.

He lost all hope, however, when his father came for a visit during his final semester. It caused a stir on campus when the news got around. Evan Moran was at the pinnacle of his career in Hollywood, working all the time, landing solid roles in big-ticket movies, making money hand over fist. He was at his most insufferable, too, but no one would have thought it looking at him. He could be perfectly charming, the life of the party, having long since mastered the art of being what others wanted him to be. It left Nick thinking of the emperor's new clothes, but he'd given up trying to convince people of the naked man.

His father hung around with Nick for a week, acting with a faintly insulting presumption as if they were brothers. He ate in his college dining hall, held forth with his friends, and fraternized with the black food service workers—once playing craps with the head cook and dishwasher in the kitchen. He took Nick to see *King Lear* at the Providence Performing Arts Center, and afterward they hung out backstage with the cast. The two of them attended an Ellsworth Kelly exhibition at RISD and a regatta on the Seekonk River. His father even sat in on a class or two.

One morning he met Nick on the Main Green and started an impromptu soccer match. Before long there was a crowd gathered to watch him play. Haley stopped by, too, basking in his glow along with everyone else. Later she and several of their friends took him out for lunch. Nick, with a seminar to attend as well as a paper to finish, forgot about them through the rest of that day. Only in the evening did he wonder where his father had gotten to and think to go looking for him at his hotel in downtown Providence.

When he slipped in the key card he'd been given and opened the door, he had the shock of his life. On the king-size bed he saw his father and Haley, both naked, their backs turned to him, pressed side by side in a double *S* shape. His father had his penis thrust inside her, with one toned shoulder arched up and a hand firmly gripping her undulant hip. She had her face twisted back toward him, her eyes closed on a pleasure Nick had never seen in her before, while his father kissed her neck. Nick startled them out of this pose, but he didn't want to hear what they had to say or what he might say if it came to that. Instead, he jumped back into the hallway and ran to the elevator, banging on the buttons until he couldn't wait and took the stairs. When he reached the street, he sprinted several blocks to the Providence River, crossed to the east side, and didn't let up on the riverwalk until he reached Memorial Park. There he sat on a bench by the bronze statue of a kneeling soldier, too exhausted by then to hate or cry. He did, though, feel sick to his stomach—enough to vomit into a nearby trashcan.

10

Back in Auckland Nick stopped going to work altogether. He couldn't keep up any pretense of normalcy while the inquiry about whether to have an inquiry settled into its attrition phase. He talked to a lawyer retained by the teachers' union, who advised him to see a doctor for medical notes, excusing him on account of stress and ensuring that he continued to get paid. He faxed them to Bernadette Potter's secretary.

No one in the department contacted him except John Lurie, who cared enough to ask how he was doing from time to time. Alba and Jane left him alone. He tried to explain his side of the story to them in an email. Alba sent back a curt reply, letting him know she'd come to conclusions in line with the general perception the scandal was designed to ratify. The quickest way to convince otherwise reasonable women to suspend their judgment, he supposed, was to tar a man with the feathers of sexual impropriety.

Days and then weeks passed in this isolated state. He had no choice but to stay, to dwell, with the knowledge that his life, in a real sense, wasn't his own, that it had its locus in a situation he didn't control. At some level he knew this was always the case. As Haley had said of him, he thought of the self as socially constructed; it depended on conditions of shared practice, language, law, institutions, and systems. That had been the main theme of his education from his first year at Brown. There the target of criticism had been the liberal individual with its abstract autonomy, its rational self-mastery, not to mention its tacit male privilege. Even when intentions and choices could be imputed to this individual, they implied no true self behind them. "Identity," "will," "reflection," and even "consciousness" were categories of a suspect metaphysical wholeness.

But King's University understood better than he did what a world without individuals looked like. It caught him in the paradox of claiming an autonomy he couldn't credit, when the other choice was to feel the will broken down, humiliated, if not vaporized in a technocratic transparency. He wondered if that was why Dean Prashad had Foucault's books on his shelves: because the critical style they modeled, with its lack of realism where hard power was concerned, and its leveling of the substantial subject into surface "effects of discourse," lent itself to a complacency about civil rights, due process, privacy, the very idea that people could have or lead their own lives. At least Nick saw no other way than in the light of a dubious antihumanism to explain the moral high ground the university had taken, quarantining him in a *hetero*nomy he could credit. It left him not a little confused about his own commitment to basic democratic principles. Had he gotten himself into this mess by failing to take responsibility for himself as a liberal individual? Or was it the other way around: Did he believe in that autonomy, with something of that moral fixity Haley had attributed to him, and so affirm the right of people to work out for themselves what it means to be human, on a case-by-case basis?

Whatever answers he might find to these questions, he ended where he started, with a feeling of exclusion. He knew, too, that the feeling had still more complicated harmonics than he was hearing on conceptual registers. Its keynote lay, finally, in the memory of his dead mother. Mourning her peculiar loneliness had always been for him a stake in teaching, writing, and also loving. He felt it with Molly in that private space they made with each other, where teaching, writing, and loving were happening in the right spirit as far as he was concerned. True, sleeping with a student didn't exactly fit his own picture of proper conduct. Haley was right there, too. Had the university offered conditions for the professional he aspired to be—not a dispassionate expert, but still aware of authority, ethical about it—he may have acted otherwise. But the absence of such conditions, either at King's or ever in his life, he nonetheless considered a good reason for treating Molly as he would anyone met in the world, as an equal. He'd even say it was why he hadn't taken his authority over her all that seriously. Why should he? It had no legitimacy, no right to his respect. All it amounted to was a marginal benefit of his own exploitation. They both knew it, too. They'd bonded over it.

There was, to be sure, a less wholesome aspect to that feeling he took from his mother—or, rather, from the idealized image he had of her as an outsider. Under its sway he fell too easily into a mood of familiar fatalism. And though he didn't always care to admit it, he knew this tendency as much as anything explained why he found himself so often detained on fitful edges, adrift like a man in limbo, dislocated from any purpose or fixed identity—not because the world deprived him of purpose or fixed identity but because he held back in any life that failed to meet some impossible standard of fidelity to her, condemning himself to equivocation in the face of inevitable compromise. He'd never considered himself all that averse to compromise; it seemed he'd been doing a lot of it in his time. But it was clear enough by now that he lacked a talent for it. He missed opportunities not just to get what he wanted from the roles he had to play but to be more fully himself in them. He could hear his father judging him here—not for sleeping with Molly, but for getting caught.

In any event, Nick ended up back in old habits on those days with nothing to do but brood over these nuances of his disastrous situation. He took to wandering through Auckland streets without a destination, anonymous, there and not there, observing the come and go of daily life like the ghost he'd been so afraid of becoming *in* those roles. He was a foreigner to boot, without the right of citizenship or simple belonging, which intensified that tonality of exclusion to an almost excruciating pitch. He'd left LA all right, that other limbo, those aimless drives on freeways and commercial strips, that pier in Santa Monica, pressed against the rough wood planks and horribly revealed to scandalized eyes. Now, it seemed, he truly had slipped through a crack in the world.

ᚷ

A month, then two months, passed without a word from anyone at school. Nick gathered information through Molly, most of it heaping outrage on top of outrage. The department, in its zeal to restore its compromised reputation for "objectivity," had assigned Alan Thill, the known sex harasser, as the principal marker of Molly's thesis. John Lurie objected, even strenuously, to no avail. Fortunately, in what was the standard procedure there would also be two others—Alba Lynch for one—forming a small committee, with the marks to be averaged. Then he heard that Jane, of all people, had told the Honours student she supervised that Nick reminded her of a "sexual predator" in some well-known television series, a comment that circulated in a network of gossip rendered still more dense and ramified in the background by the aid of social media. That hurt like a dagger thrust. Nick had been ready to stand with those two women on the political battlegrounds of the department, probably undermining whatever power base he had when he first arrived. Now he imagined the different factions, the Bernadettes, the Alans, the Albas and Janes, whoever else there might be, hating and fearing each other with a sullen passion for years, come together at last in their common hatred of him. The point of a scapegoat, after all, was to reunite a straying community. Maybe they all met for a pint at the Pig & Whistle.

His other concern was that they'd find out about him and Molly sleeping together. That hadn't stopped in the meantime, neither much feeling like other people's opinions should have any sway with them now that they had no official relation. Of course, this didn't mean other people stopped making what they did together their business. Nick feared private investigators aiming cameras at his balcony or hackers breaking into his computer. Molly discouraged such paranoid fears, and he resisted them as best he could. But he thought it entirely plausible that King's University would stoop so low.

Molly spent most nights at his apartment, as the Peeping Tom also hadn't gone away, making periodic appearances at her windows. Usually she came in the evening and worked late on her thesis. Nick watched it develop into a textured examination of Henry James that teased from the stylistic features of his prose—unclear pronoun antecedents or double negatives in the passive voice—a sensibility for the deeper ideological pressures of social life. She argued for an essential awkwardness in the way James wrote, finding it in registrations of a sexually exploitive status quo that might be sustained in many moral guises, not least concern for the innocence of young women. She also made allusions to their current situation, nesting them in citations from pragmatists on the importance of the knower implying herself in what she knows. Her thesis had a swing to it, a bravura, which suggested to Nick unquestionable talent as a writer. He encouraged her to keep working on her application to NYU.

She had the idea of getting him away from his apartment with a trip out of Auckland. Her mother owned a small cottage not far from the Whakarewarewa Rainforest that she used for occasional retreats. He'd never been outside the city before, and the car ride up onto the volcanic plateau of North Island gave him his first inkling of the wider countryside with its splintered peaks, rust-red craters, and shooting geysers. The town where they stayed had a counter-cultural feel, reminding him of rural places in central California, like Ohai. It went a long way toward blunting the sharp edge of prejudice he'd formed toward the New Zealand he knew at King's University. Molly had to remind him not to equate the two.

"It's my country," she told him. "You can't hate it. Only I can hate it."

"As long as you hate it enough for the two of us."

"I could say the same about you and your country."

"Fair enough," he said. "Every society is hateful in its own way."

The house faced into the bush, where flashes of light and color denoted parrots and rosellas. Other birds, called tuis, made a maniacal racket all through the evening. The sound stirred Molly to nostalgia, and she regaled him with stories of vacations that she'd spent there as a kid. She grew up in Auckland's inner suburbs, comfortably from what Nick could tell. Both her parents were professionals. They had, however, divorced when Molly was ten. The good times near the Whakarewarewa Rainforest mostly preceded the jolt that gave her. It was something else they had in common.

Nick hadn't experienced much sentiment of this sort in New Zealanders he knew. He wondered if it was kept from him on purpose. He only experienced it now because all the rules had been broken.

This widening of his sympathies, however, contracted once again when the phone rang around nine thirty that night. He saw Molly's face fall on answering. She waved him to a second line in another room.

"How did you get this number?" he heard as he picked up.

"Your mother gave it to me," said Sarah Hayes.

"You talked to my mother?!"

Sarah hesitated. "Yes. I thought it was all right after she called Dr. Green to ask about the investigation."

"And you think it's all right to call me on a Saturday night?"

Sarah ignored the implications of this risible fact. "We're trying to wrap things up here," she said, "and I wanted to talk to you one more time about your relationship with Dr. Moran."

"I've already told you what happened."

"I want to make sure you feel completely free to confide in me, without any worry there might be to. . .well, protect Dr. Moran."

"I've told you he did nothing wrong."

"We have your best interests at heart, Miss Banville. I want you to know that. We have a duty of care—"

"No, you don't," she bravely returned. "You don't care about me. If you did, you'd understand how this makes *me* feel."

"If you like, I can arrange for the services of a counselor."

"I don't need a counselor."

"Did Dr. Moran ever say anything that made you at all uncomfortable?"

"No."

"Did he ever suggest that you change your story with me or anyone at the university?"

"No!"

"Did he ever touch you—"

"No!" cried Molly. "Jesus. The only time I've felt molested is now. *You're* molesting me."

Nick must have made some slight noise in the receiver at this point, because Sarah asked, "Is somebody listening?"

Molly panicked. "No," she said, slamming the phone into its cradle.

Nick was alone with Sarah on the line. He heard the faint sound of her breath, the rise and fall of it, as she quietly assessed the significance of Molly's abrupt departure. Then, as she hung up the phone, Nick heard her tell someone else, "I think the guy's up there with her now. . ."

He was so livid at that moment he could have killed. He could have extinguished the life he felt in that woman's voice with his bare hands. Nothing was more hateful to him than the prurience it revealed.

ꭗ

Sarah Hayes didn't end her "investigation" after that phone call, and two months stretched into three without a single new development. Apparently the aim was to keep him on an edge until the strain tore him apart or he lashed out. It almost worked. He carried anger around with him in a way he never had before, afraid he might erupt at a chance encounter with a colleague or even just annoying strangers met on the street. It scared him enough to wonder if he should even leave his apartment, or rather it would if he weren't still more scared of giving in to phobic tendencies. The last thing he needed right then was to be alone with that strain. His sanity could well be at stake.

Anger, however, concentrates the mind. Nick began to write, not anything coherent enough to form an essay, or essays—certainly not that book on love, as dead as his seminar—but more rants on the topics that preoccupied him: human rights, liberal individuals, the blurred boundaries of public and private life, women who treated him as they did in the conviction that his feelings were not just irrelevant but inherently wrong. This, indeed, galled him most of all: preemptive response made moral sense to them because he could only be guilty in their eyes. He remembered Alba and Jane telling him about old men who ran Helman Hall like a boy's club. He imagined Bernadette Green and Bernadette Potter, frightened young lecturers in a nightmare of male chauvinism, forced to endure who knew what indignity to keep going. The lack of power would have been horrible, and a desire for justice strong even decades later. He understood that. But why they would go so far as to confuse those old men's abuses with anything he had done—whatever authority he might have mishandled or narcissism he might have betrayed—just boggled his mind. What possible interest could be served by so clouding the idea of subordination that it became, in effect, useless for understanding how and where subordination actually happened?

An answer came into focus for him with the simple trick of replacing those old men in their minds with his father. Then, he couldn't but think, the real violence popped right out of its patriarchal frame. Power was sexy. Law and transgression were linked, even inseparably so, the one called forth by the other or sustained in eroticized fantasies of the other. Sarah Hayes might define her duty as policing power or standing in for it; she might hate it or have it. But either way she wanted to fuck it. That was why she, why all of them, could only see violence between him and Molly. It was also why Evan Moran stood, or reclined as he once did with Haley in that Providence hotel, one more time between him and what he loved.

ϰ

This made Molly all the more remarkable a person in Nick's life. By virtue of their common predicament and just plain character on her part, she saw through the fake concern for her, and she didn't see his father—the pervert Oedipus—in him. He wondered if that wasn't the even more fundamental offense here, and the source of the hostility directed at Molly by Sarah Hayes no less than by her peers in the Honours program, who'd gone to that "member of staff"—he suspected Tom Hatch now—and started the gears of scandal turning. No one was supposed to escape that economy of transgressive law, with its libidinal exchange rate converting all moral concern into the coin of fantasy, traded as gossip by anonymous Janes. If Molly and he did manage to escape it, they would have to pay a price.

Not that their solidarity kept Nick from bouts of panic. Maybe especially when they were intimate, when they were learning how to please and excite each other in spite of the pressures they were under, he had to fight to remember why it wasn't a moral problem for them to be together. His anger helped and hindered at the same time. With it he resisted the image others had of him as, in short, a sexist man, but it also brought his paranoia to such a boil that he could hardly keep from turning against everyone, against Molly even, against the friendship she offered, and, what came to the same thing, against his own capacities for trust and sympathy. Resistance thus merged with a resentment that only drew him closer to that image of the sexist man. In this manner, he suspected, chauvinists truly were made, not born.

He received aid from unexpected quarters. The world could be merciful, too. On a day Molly had come over and noticed the lorikeets in the jacaranda tree—an unusual event it turned out as they were rare in New Zealand, not being native and often targeted as pests—she suggested he lure them to the balcony with green apples. She said they liked eating them enough sometimes to overcome their shyness around people. And, indeed, after just a few days' effort, a bird lit on the rail and let him ease a slice under its beak. It dug the flesh out from the skin and chewed it into pulp, looking him guardedly in the eye. Then a second, its mate Nick presumed, appeared as well. The rest of the flock soon followed.

Feeding them became a companionable ritual made possible, ironically, by his free time. To his surprise they lost their fear of him almost completely, and before long he had them standing on his arms and shoulders like Burt Lancaster with his pigeons in *The Birdman of Alcatraz*. He'd never experienced anything like that before. Nick was a city person with a city person's mistrust of nature, so it came as a shock to find nature so capable of trusting him. His mother would have been proud.

He'd also begun to meet people in his neighborhood, where he spent the days in nearby cafés reading or trying to write. In particular he befriended a Somalian émigré named Ahmad, who also seemed to have nothing else to do. He came around the cafés with his dog, a brown merle Australian shepherd, and they took walks in the park that stretched around the marina. Ahmad was an unemployed medical technician who'd left his country as a political refugee fifteen years before. When he wanted to describe the violence there—involving sectarian ethnic groups, warlords, and corrupt elites, stretched over decades of military and economic meddling by foreign powers, notably the United States—he pointed back over gently swaying sailboats at their neighborhood, where Nick could see his apartment building, and asked him to imagine it destroyed by missiles or car bombs in great plumes of fire and smoke. "That's what it's like in my country," he said. "Civil society is a war zone."

The man had a gentle disposition. He was almost wholly without aggression, or at least on the other side of experiences that had drained it out of him. Nothing in the human capacity for cruelty surprised Ahmad. He took it all in with a fatalism that left him unruffled, if also disappointed and hurt. That the cruelty still did get to him, Nick could tell from a glassy expression in his eyes, which indicated that he was drunk, or perhaps stoned, even in the morning.

He needed that help to keep his equanimity. But still, Nick sensed in him a different way of dealing with adversity: not deceived, but not mean either; wounded, but not resentful.

Ahmad learned of Nick's situation without batting an eye. He had a vision of New Zealand and its people that was finally as critical as he was gentle. "It's a sad place," he told him. "There's too much that can't be talked about. Things go unaccounted for, they go missing, and people grow used to that. They even miss themselves. It's easier to coast, to drift inside the rules, which do the work of drawing people together more than people. This makes for strange loyalties. People complain—they 'whinge,' a proper New Zealand expression—all the time, but it never really means anything, and never releases them from their inertia, because they don't know what to do without it. They think they need it to get along. Everyone's nice, polite, on the outside, but inside no one much likes one another, or likes themselves for that matter."

Nick tried to imagine himself living in so dispirited a fashion. "How do you stand it?" he asked.

"Oh," Ahmad smiled, "I coast, I drift. I vanish into the woodwork. I try not to bother anybody. It's easy enough to do, even for a black man, if you stick pretty close to suburbs like this one."

Molly had said disparaging things about New Zealand, too. He'd also seen her hide in the midst of unaccountable power. She continued on in her Honours courses, as she had to, but she also hung around the other students without the affair ever coming up between them. They could go to a pub together, drink beer, play pool, and not once allude to what some of them were doing, and all of them were wondering about, in the background. Nick couldn't conceive how such dissembling was possible. It upset Molly when he declared as much one night at his apartment.

"What good would it do for me to confront Eunice Notley?" she said. "She's a bully, she thinks she's right, and the whole school is on her side."

"So you pull your head in."

"I have to!"

"I wouldn't," he averred. "I'd be in everybody's face, and I wouldn't stop until I knew exactly where they stood. I'd have it all out."

"Why don't you, then? Why don't you stand with a picket sign in the department hallways and insist they end this witch hunt?"

He had no answer to that. They, or the school, did have him cowed. He acted as if he had something to defend, a job, a reputation, even though it was clear now that neither would survive the outcome, whatever it might be. Molly saw this thought take shape behind his eyes.

"I have to go on living here," she reminded him. "I have to keep going or I won't even finish my degree. Then where will I be?"

"In a tough spot," he acknowledged. "You're right."

X

He had more to defend than his position at the university. The scandal also threatened any chance of him getting another job, since the aspersions cast on his character would follow him, if not as rumor then in the embarrassment he'd feel whenever he had to explain why he left his position so soon upon getting it. He had to consider what sort of outcome he'd need to minimize this risk. He might fight back, as Molly had said, in the spirit of a worker on strike. But just what principle would he be standing up for that could survive a public opinion skewed by charges of sexual harassment? He could sue the university for slander, but when he raised this possibility with the union lawyer, she told him the chances of success were slim and the satisfaction, if he won, symbolic, as courts didn't tend to award exorbitant damages. Defamation of character, she told him, was a rich man's sport in New Zealand. If he went that route, moreover, he'd have to sever any connection with Molly, since the merest hint of a relationship, no matter what kind, would be enough to dissuade a jury of his innocence. Once again, the disciplinary ends of the university would be served.

His other option was to quit outright, although that, too, would play wonderfully into their hands. It would look like an admission of guilt. They could feel their power to disgrace ratified and return to their holes with their virtue intact, ready like eels to strike again at the next "personality" that came around. The only gain would be a quicker end to his current ordeal—not insignificant, as he discovered when John Lurie, his only supporter, invited him to lunch at a restaurant overlooking Auckland Harbour and confided to him the story of another professor in the distant past of the English department. He also stood accused of shadowy sexual crimes, passing a full year in virtual lockdown before the whole affair was quietly dropped and he returned to his job—this time, of course, as a ghost, speaking to no one, catching no one's eye.

"I'll go mad well before then," Nick said as they sat on a veranda looking out through sunshot gardens to the sparkly harbour waters. In the distance a massive supertanker, loaded down with containers, slid slowly out to sea.

"He had a wife and family as well," John added.

"And he was innocent, I take it?"

John shrugged. "Whatever that means. No one accused him directly anyway. When it concerns matters of the heart, I don't consider it my place to judge."

"You'd be in a minority at King's, I suspect."

"You might be surprised," John said. "No one much wants a genuine reckoning. There are skeletons in the closets of Helman Hall."

He shifted in his chair, violating, Nick could tell, his own judgment with what he brought out next. "Bernadette Potter, for instance. She met her husband when she was his undergraduate in the department, over forty years ago now."

"And let me guess," Nick said. "She's about twenty years younger than he is."

"Was, I'm afraid. The man passed away a month ago. I suspect that may have something to do with the unconscionable delay in your inquiry. Bernadette hasn't been the same since."

Nick asked if John would mind excusing him so he could go outside for a cigarette. He needed its brief high to help absorb this proof of the burden it appeared he really did share with all scapegoats: the sins of others. With the prosecco the two of them had been liberally drinking, he hoped it would be enough.

11

It turned out he wouldn't have to wait like his predecessor in limbo for as long as a year. As the semester drew to a close, and Molly submitted her Honours thesis, word came through the union lawyer of a request from someone with the apt job title of Human Resources relationship manager in the vice-chancellor's office. The university wanted him to name a price for quietly disappearing from view. He asked the union lawyer how someone who'd disappeared as completely as he had could disappear still more, but then said the first thing that popped into his head: two years' pay with moving expenses. The union lawyer doubted they would part with that kind of money, but she went ahead and relayed the demand. About a week later, to her surprise, the Human Resources relationship manager came back with an offer of one year's pay. No charges would be filed and Nick's employment contract would be terminated without explanation.

His disbelief on hearing this was anticlimactic. It drained the whole affair of any substance. All along he may have been dealing not with malicious intent but simple stupidity—incompetent officials going by the book in a risk-averse institution that was only concerned with covering its own ass. In this light all his obsessive worry about motives, actions, and rights had been a waste of time, a futile bid to generate on his own the recourse or closure he wasn't going to get from the world.

Molly came over the same day he found out, flush with excitement because her marks had been posted and she did much better than she'd expected, placing second in the overall ranking. Alan Thill had given her thesis the mark it deserved. Alba had given her the lowest score of all, dragging the average down. Had her mark been as high as the other two, Molly would have won the Medal. She was still pleased with the result.

"Finally, some justice!" Nick cried with enough effusiveness to arouse suspicion.

"What's wrong?"

"Nothing. I have news, too, though."

He told her about the offer.

"And you're going to take it?"

"I have no choice."

Her face fell. "That means you'll be leaving."

He nodded. "I don't know where I'm going to go. Or what I'm going to do."

"What about me?" she asked in bewilderment. "Where am I going to go? What am I going to do?"

"What do you want to do?"

"I don't know," she said. "Shit. I was so happy, and now I'm so sad."

"You could go to NYU."

"They have to accept me first!"

"You have a good shot now, right? With your second-place finish?"

"Are you going to New York?"

"It's as good a place as any."

"I could join you there next year," she reflected.

"You could." He felt an upsurge of tenderness for her sticking by him through all these paralyzed months. It hadn't been easy on her either. She'd been under tremendous strain, too, more maybe than he was able to appreciate in his distraction. For this among other reasons, he didn't see why she should have to go on there without him. "You could even come earlier, wait to see what happens with your application. I could show you around New York."

"I do have a friend there: Sean."

"Then you have two reasons to go. Think of it as a vacation."

"Are you sure? You really want me to come?"

"Yes, Molly," he said, drawing her close. "I want you to come."

ⵅ

He remained in Auckland another few weeks, awaiting the transfer of the year's pay into his bank account and wrapping up his affairs. It rained a lot in that time. Eerie thunderstorms passed over the city, throwing up bolts of lightning that were fearsome to behold. In between the skies would clear, or striking formations of wind-sheared clouds would tower into the atmosphere, scattering an opalescent sunlight over his neighborhood. Those storms were unlike anything Nick had ever seen: capricious, moody, tropical. He felt how alien it must have been for the first settlers from Britain, deposited there as if at the end of the earth. And he wondered what it must have been for the original settlers, the Maoris, crossing the Pacific in their catamarans: the "land of the long white cloud" they called it. Paradise, he supposed, though it didn't seem that way to him. Of course, the truth was he had no real feeling for the place at all. He was more a stranger in it than he ever was, and far from presuming that told him anything about the legacies of belonging there.

He felt bad cutting off the ritual with the lorikeets, which he'd miss about as much as he wouldn't most everything else in that country. It had been a pleasure feeding them green apples, and they'd come to rely on it, he suspected, as much as he did, even neglecting other sources of sustenance. Molly had said that was a drawback of befriending them as he did. They grew tame.

But as it happened he didn't have to cut them off. A few days before his departure, a couple of black-and-white magpies swooped onto the balcony, frightening the lorikeets away in the hope of horning in on the feast. Nick pelted them with ornamental stones he took from his building's front garden, but they started reappearing whenever the lorikeets did, claiming the balcony as their territory, until the lorikeets stopped coming altogether. He hated those magpies for that, even though he had to say they did provide a fitting end to his disastrous stay down under.

A Perfect Trap

1

New York had always been two cities for Nick: one, marvelously frenetic, that swept him up in its obsessions, and another, still and silent, seen over the Hudson River from the cliffs at Stevens Tech or the Hoboken waterfront, stretching from the George Washington Bridge to Battery Park. The first he grew up in until his parents' divorce, and there he felt, not exactly an outsider, but on terrain his father controlled, inhabiting it with a princely ease. The feeling might have been exaggerated, bound up with inhibitions, private grievances, and even an ambivalent pride Nick took in his father's accomplishments. Nonetheless, it weighed in Nick's heart right up to the present. New York, psychosexually speaking, belonged to the Broadway actor Evan Moran; Nick was a bit of an interloper, feeling, with his mother, neglected and left behind.

The silent New York did belong to him, though, or to him and his mother both. The perspective it offered helped them to find a way into it that broke the old painful isolation. When Nick lived as a graduate student in the East Village—in a studio apartment he was lucky to get on the corner of Twelfth Street and Avenue A—this perspective, this silence, carried over in the work that filled his days with reading, courses, lectures, and writing. It formed the basis of an identity that allowed him to leave the world, or to absorb himself in other worlds, without feeling disqualified for it. He could strike the right balance between the insider and the outsider, the participant and the observer. It made him unafraid to be thoughtful, skeptical, self-aware. Reticence was a quality he didn't mind owning, as long as it still recommended him to others. In those days, that seemed a fair bet.

Of course, success depended on the support school gave him, and without that his confidence began to fray. His last years in New York, after he finished his PhD, were shadowed by the discovery that he'd been laboring under an illusion, riding too high, and the world wouldn't let him remain in his state of intellectual grace for long. The city had changed, too, become more expensive, conservative, unequal, and frankly authoritarian. What he mistook as a horizon was, in fact, the walls of an artificially maintained enclave; Manhattan, meanwhile, had filled with a newly assertive breed of Wall Street brokers, pharmaceutical marketers, and IT specialists who were his same age, went to the same schools, and frequented the same restaurants and bars, but with whom he otherwise had little in common. For a long time he ignored them, or held them in polite disdain, but the minute he had to make money to live, he understood that the city belonged to them, that it required their attitudes and their ambitions just to keep up a minimal middle-class existence. He'd been pushed out of New York when he moved to LA as much as anything else. And he could only wonder, coming back all these years later, if the place wouldn't be as challenging for him now as it had been then.

⅄

He stayed his first weeks back in the apartment of a friend who'd left town for the Christmas holidays. It was located in Inwood, a neighborhood on the far northern tip of Manhattan. From one fourth-floor window he could see the Harlem River bending toward the Hudson under the parkway bridge. From another he could just glimpse the Romanesque bell tower of the Cloisters. Across the open fields of Inwood Hill Park stood a steep wooded ridge that reminded him of wilderness.

He welcomed the sequestered feeling it gave him up there, especially when a nor'easter hit the city, dumping two feet of snow. Everything stopped. People stayed home from work, school was canceled, kids spent the days sledding in the park, and everyone grew uncharacteristically civil with one another. It reminded Nick of similar snow days in his childhood. He hoped the pause it afforded him would aid in the recovery of strength he needed now, faced once more with an uncertain future.

As the days passed, however, he began to suspect he was mistaken. He took walks along the river or up to the wooded ridge, hoping for a simple pleasure that didn't come. He patronized a wine bar down the street, reading in an easy chair while the snow gusted against the windowpanes, but his book didn't open itself up to him. He wrote on his laptop, adding to those fragmentary rants in Auckland, but he couldn't give any satisfactory form to his experience. By the time Christmas rolled around and he spent the day miserably by himself, he saw he'd miscalculated. Introspection wasn't working. The shock, brought back with him from New Zealand, ran more insidiously into his "reticent" character than he knew how to address on his own.

At that point he got out of Inwood, taking the long ride downtown on the A train to visit old friends. They were people he hadn't lost touch with, thanks to the internet, but he didn't really know them anymore. Most were married and raising children, on the far side of careers Nick had never started, looking to settle down even more, eyeing rustic houses in the Hudson River Valley and gearing up for a final retreat from their younger selves. This made it difficult to find much in common beyond a nostalgia that discomfited Nick as much as the stresses of family life he ended up hearing about. Predictably he felt a stranger in their midst, interrupted in awkward conversation by needy children, judging as false the sentimentality that entering into domestic arrangements seemed to require, and resenting the odd condescension directed at the "bachelor," a word that made him wince when a friend's precocious eight-year-old daughter used it on him one day in the playground at Bleecker and Hudson.

He did better with friends who were still single, although the commonality with them seemed to be confusion at the dead ends they'd reached. One friend, Dylan Porter, an intense sharp-tongued man who grew up in the West Bronx, shared Nick's general experience with academia. He had a PhD in film studies from Columbia, and he'd published a book on Werner Herzog, yet all it had gotten him was adjunct teaching at New York City Technical College, where he'd been toiling away for the past ten years. Just recently, tired of living poor in New York, he'd decided to take a one-year visiting position at a university in Pusan, South Korea, with a vague understanding from his employers that the contract might be extended.

This proved fortunate for Nick, who offered to sublet Dylan's apartment in Hell's Kitchen while he was gone. They met one evening to sort out the details, heading for two stools in a bar on Eighth

Avenue afterward. There, talk over drinks turned to the reasons why they'd had such trouble establishing themselves. Neither could help finding them in the ways New York had changed since they were kids. Dylan, it turned out, had well-formed opinions on the subject.

"I hate that every bar has flat-screen TVs," he declared, feasting his eyes on the six such screens that faced them from every wall. They disclosed a football game in triplicate, a tennis match, an NY1 newscaster relating the story of an elderly woman hit by a car near Prospect Park, and a plate of pasta prepared by some expert chef. "It didn't used to be true. Bars used to be places people talked. Now we watch things. Even when we try not to, we have to compete with images, we have to resist the temptation to stare." He stared at the plate of pasta. "Look at that. Just like a porn film. It's shot exactly the way sex is shot, in tight close ups."

"The same people are probably making both," Nick said.

"It's no accident either. The aim is to make distraction permanent, to hold our attention at every point by covering every possible surface with media. We're cave painters."

"Cave painters?!"

"I'm thinking of this Herzog documentary," Dylan said. "*Cave of Forgotten Dreams.* It's about the urge to imprint and represent—also to animate. That's why Cro-Magnon man painted in caves: the rock's contours, along with the light from their torches, simulated motion. Movies were there from the beginning, in other words. They're a later phase of the same desire to make the world a cave—to fill it all up with signs."

Nick thought of Times Square, one long crosstown block away. It did resemble a huge, lit up cave when you stood in it, or even when you looked on from a distance, down the canyon-like avenues that intersected there.

"Don't get me wrong," Dylan was quick to add. "No one likes images more than me. But they're easier than words and concepts. They don't require articulation. They don't have to be argued out. We absorb them without contradiction."

"They're safer, too," Nick observed, "like a cleaned-up Times Square. They imply a public culture that carries no risk."

"Why should it?!" Dylan cried. "Why should we have to take a position in respect of anyone or anything for that matter? Why should we have to work out what we think, test our beliefs, or confront our fears and prejudices? It doesn't make sense. Virtual reality makes sense! Dreaming our lives away makes sense! The point is to be positive, pretend to be tolerant, pretend to transgress—like a Republican dressed up as a hippie."

Nick burst out laughing.

"It's not funny." Dylan's clipped tone conveyed just how seriously he took this new variation on his theme of living in Plato's cave. "New York is full of multicultural libertarians who get their values from Ayn Rand. That is what you discover when you *do* talk to people."

He mentioned a black lesbian he'd met in a bar a while back. She taught PE at a charter school and thought big government was evil, CEO's were geniuses on the cutting edge of human evolution, and inheritance taxes were discriminatory. "We ended up in a no-holds-barred fight," he said, "and a young hip bartender joined in, too, taking her side, of course. They both thought their only responsibility was to themselves, to trust in themselves. All they needed was the freedom to manage their aspirational projects without the meddling of bureaucrats and pessimists. No one owed them a thing, and if they failed it was because they were lazy. They accepted handouts and lost contact with the 'discipline of the market,' which gave them energy and built character. Really, that's what they said. *The discipline of the market!* Can you believe it? Who talks like that?!"

"People who should know better?"

Dylan settled his gaze on the glass of beer before him, shaking his head in fresh bewilderment. "It's not unusual either," he went on. "I hear the same things from people all the time. And no one backs down. If you suggest that the market doesn't work for them, or work at all, they reproach you for being negative. If you call them on their narcissism, suddenly they feel threatened. Their confidence is challenged, and it feels like abuse, like a violation. You, of course, as the violator are just one among the class of social undesirables that needs to be purged from their comfort zones, sacrificed to their fantasies. That's why New York feels so unreal, so sanitized. No matter how gritty or granular things still appear, the fact is the grit has been removed. The grain is gone."

"Sounds like you need a break, Dylan."

"It's driving me crazy," he admitted. "Nothing makes sense anymore. Discourse isn't working. Distinctions don't matter. If you want them to matter it's because you're stupid or bitter, it's because you romanticize the past, it's because you're a socialist or a nationalist or a racist or a sexist—believe me, I've heard *all* these strategies for stopping thought before. And they disarm me every time, because I haven't got a leg to stand on. I'm a loser in people's eyes—hell, in my own eyes. How can I deny it? I spent ten years writing the book on Herzog, and all I was doing the whole time was writing my way into irrelevance. Even those who care about Herzog don't care about somebody else's interpretation of Herzog. The only person I know who read the book through was the copy editor at Routledge. No one gives a shit about reading, you know?"

"I know," Nick said, with a trace of impatience Dylan caught.

"Sorry." He made an effort to check the prodigious flow of his thoughts. "I get carried away. Before I know it, I'm ranting."

"No need to apologize," he assured him. "I understand the impulse perfectly."

"It's hard to resist when nothing you say matters."

"Yes."

"The less relevant what you say becomes, the harder you try to make what you say relevant again."

"Only you can't do it."

"You strip out. You start spinning wheels."

"Like everyone else."

"Exactly!" said Dylan. "It's not a choice. There's no resistance in an electronically mediated society. We float in huge word clouds."

They sat in silence for a moment, wrestling with the implication that no more of a difference existed between irrelevance and relevance than between anything else. The world was ranting, and the ranter was only a creature of the world.

"I can't stand it sometimes," Dylan said. "I feel this pressure, you know, only it's not just coming from the sides." He patted his ears with the palms of his hands. "It's coming from above and below, and all at once. It won't let the head squeeze up or out."

"You feel trapped."

"Like there's no escape."

"And the compression's killing you."

"Just killing me."

"What happens when you can't take it anymore?"

Dylan reflected. "There's the option of collapsing into a black hole, right?" he said, deadpan. "I think you disappear that way. Or do you explode first, like a supernova?"

"Or a raisin in the sun?"

"Ha! Tell that to the black lesbian, man! Langston Hughes must be turning over in his grave."

They both laughed this time. "You haven't lost your sense of humor anyway," Nick said, although he wasn't sure about that, despite the new levity in his friend's voice. He also wasn't sure how much help conversations like this one were going to be for him. As good as it felt to share his frustrations with someone, he could see it provided no relief and no direction for the future either. On some level he was glad Dylan was also leaving.

He couldn't escape the fact that, if he were to resume living in New York, it would have to be by starting over, from scratch almost. He'd have to make new friends and new associations—hardly a straightforward wager when the culture had indeed become so incoherent, so alien, and he had to fight with the past, too, with old hopes and fears busy knitting themselves together on city blocks, in subway stations or parks, in sudden vistas or smells or even simple qualities of air and light. This haunted feeling made it difficult to imagine beginning much of anything new.

He also had to find a job. The money from King's University, or what was left of it after he'd paid down as much of his credit card debt as he could, wouldn't last long in New York. Dylan thought he could get him adjunct work teaching freshman composition at City Tech, and Haley had contacts in software companies, where he'd probably be writing manuals in some midtown skyscraper. Neither prospect did much to brighten his mood.

2

He moved in to Hell's Kitchen just after the New Year. It was a neighborhood he remembered from childhood as a place to avoid, but its fortunes had improved with the Times Square renovation. Ninth Avenue was a hub for an eclectic mix of aspiring actors and dancers, working people both old and young, white and ethnic—also, notably, straight and gay. He liked it better than he thought he would.

He picked Molly up at JFK a few days later, happy to see her come through the door from customs, looking excited if worse for wear after the long flight. He'd been missing her more than he cared to admit. He worried about the burden this might put on her. They hadn't worked out just what kind of relationship they were going to have, everything being so open-ended, but nothing suggested they wouldn't go on as they had before or even grow more serious if she did get into NYU. For the sake of this possibility he suspected it would be better to keep the hope, or the need he had for her, in check. He didn't want to overwhelm her in circumstances that would likely be overwhelming anyway.

Not that it would bother him if she did raise his spirits, and, indeed, he felt a salutary boost in this department straight off. Everything was new to Molly. Her first views of Manhattan in the cab from the airport were awe-inspiring. She didn't mind navigating the dirty slush and hectic passersby on Ninth Avenue. She looked past the flies that hovered in the vestibule of the dilapidated building where she'd be living for the next few months. The third-floor apartment wasn't too cramped, dark, or dingy. The kitchenette was all she needed to keep herself fed and moving. Even the lonely old man they could see watching TV in his window across the courtyard formed part of a drama in her mind.

At first she wanted to make the usual tourist stops, and Nick enjoyed showing her around even when it meant he had to go to the top of the Empire State building, hire a horse-drawn carriage in Central Park, or ride the Staten Island Ferry. He gradually refined the agenda to include things he liked more: dining at little restaurants he remembered from the past, visits to the Vermeers at the Met and the Frick or the Henry Moore sculpture in the reflecting pool at Lincoln Center, with its hint of gravity-defying warp in the surface of the water. On her suggestion he also showed her different places where he'd grown up, like the brownstone apartment in Morningside Heights. She was particularly curious about a nearby grammar school he attended, with its paved playground enclosed in a tall chain-link fence and divided by a white painted line that, in his day at least, separated the boys from the girls during recess. She said it helped her to fill out his past this way. He became less of a professor, more of a person.

One place she didn't want to see was NYU. She resisted him showing her around the campus, for fear of unduly raising her hopes . . .or jinxing her chances. She wasn't used to good things happening for her, and her customary way of dealing with the anxiety was to suppress the possibility that they might happen. That made it difficult to spend time in Greenwich Village. When they did, Nick walked her past the university buildings without mention, even though both knew what they were. He hit on the idea of taking her to the various landmarks of postwar culture they'd seen in that Scorsese documentary. He noticed, however, a drop in her enthusiasm here. He might have been overplaying the interest for these things, or falling too much back into that professor role. It struck an off note now, in this different situation, where they had to figure out how to be close to each other outside an institutional setting. While they spoke for the most part around this new fact, Molly gave clear enough signals that she didn't enjoy feeling like a student around him anymore.

He caught some of these signals the night they went to see *Hedda Gabler* on Forty-Second Street. It was a wretched production, with some mediocre television actress playing the lead. Molly had an allergic reaction not only to the usual Broadway ceremony but to the play itself, which she considered boring and dated. During the intermission, Nick spoke about the play's significance in a nineteenth-century preoccupied with neurasthenia and the "Woman

Question," but Molly's cool demeanor made him hear his own didactic tone. He suggested they ditch the rest of the show and have dinner, "anywhere you like." He hoped her choice would be nearer to Ninth Avenue, but it turned out to be B.B. Kings right next door to the theater, a gaudy house of ribs lit in bright neon and packed, for the most part, with middle-class people from the outer boroughs, enjoying a night on the town.

They sat down to obscenely sized meals—roasted half chickens with steak, shrimp, and fries. Molly loved it. "This is *so* decadent," she said over the thumping music. Leaning forward to sip a raspberry martini, she glanced surreptitiously at several black girls as they hobbled past on high heels, their curvy bodies squeezed into tight dresses.

"They said the same thing about Ibsen's play when it first came out," Nick remarked.

"Yeah, but that's not *our* decadence," she said. "It belongs to another time, right? For us it's more of a fantasy. It diverts attention from what's going on now, in the present."

"Just next door."

"Yeah." She pointed over his shoulder. "The play's happening on the other side of that wall, isn't it?"

"Strange, huh?"

"Bizarre."

"I wonder, though, which is more of a fantasy." He fought past misgiving here. "I mean, this restaurant's a fantasy, too, right? People come to distract themselves from the prosaic things they do most of the time, to feel those things are worth the chance for distraction. But it doesn't offer any reflection on whether they're worth it."

"You think that's what people are doing in the theater?"

"Maybe not. It doesn't mean there's no difference between art and distraction."

"But they can be the same thing."

"Sure," he said, his assent a little grudging. "I suppose I've tended to care more about the difference."

"Is it always clear?"

"We're certainly capable of being fooled," was his only reply.

He felt, in exchanges like this, the emphasis shift subtly to how he might be fooling himself. There would be no more uncritical admiration from Molly for his understanding or experience. It was also clear that she had to draw this line, for the sake not only of being her own person in New York but so that they could be together on a more equal footing. Nick saw the challenge for him right away. It meant he'd have to let her resistance be a provocation to that younger "reticent" self, formed in school but nowhere much at home. They were going to succeed as a couple, that is, only with a change in his whole relationship to the world that wouldn't be easy for him to make. He hoped he had it in him.

3

There were practical difficulties with living together in Dylan's apartment. It had a bedroom that allowed for some privacy, but it was hardly bigger than the futon Dylan kept in there. The living room, moreover, was crammed with a couch, a TV, a coffee table, and a desk, along with a voluminous DVD collection stored in shelves. It felt like the cockpit of an airplane.

The arrangement might have worked had they the same habits. Molly, however, had trouble falling asleep, so much so that she often spent the whole night awake. She watched TV to alleviate the boredom, and Nick, an early riser, often found her passed out on the couch with the TV still on. It turned out she'd been this way a long time. Nick hadn't noticed before. She did often enough stay up all night in Auckland, too, but he'd presumed it was because of her thesis project. He saw now that it wasn't an anomaly. Insomnia was a chronic problem for her, and watching TV to cope with it formed a central part of her life.

She also didn't think it was such a big deal. She even liked staying awake through the night. On her account only conventional people woke up in the morning; especially when they didn't have to, it savored of a dull conformism. When Nick said he didn't see how watching so much TV constituted rebellion against the status quo, Molly turned the tables on him. She claimed it was better than sitting around with nothing to do but stare at the walls. That stung, since he had a hard time occupying himself with much else right then, and she knew it. His only option was to back off, not wanting his paralysis to become yet another problem between them.

It meant, in practice, that Molly's habits began to predominate. He stayed up late and watched a lot of TV. It was hard for him. He hated what he saw, or, more specifically, what Molly liked: reality shows devoted to housewives, aspiring models, teens rowdy or pregnant, girls out to marry a millionaire or find a "sugar daddy," food, home improvement, cops, and criminals. The worst of these shows for Nick involved ritual scenes of judgment that were always plugging the virtues of a competitive individualism. They reminded him of LA—particularly when one contestant on a cooking show turned out to be Big John, the Jamaican man whose party he had fled more than a year before. One night seated side by side on the couch, they saw him on the screen making étouffée under a deadline, his long dreadlocks flying around his stately head.

"I can't believe you know Big John!" Molly cried.

"I could say the same about you."

"He's very popular," she told him. "He's always voted the one viewers most want to win. People think of him as the wise man on the show. He never talks shit about the others."

"Viewers vote?"

"They do these polls."

Nick imagined the pleasure producers like Don Torrance took inventing that sort of gimmick, turning their contempt for people into cheap product and quick profit—not least by cutting out writers like Nick altogether. It baffled him how Molly could have such a high tolerance for the results, watching one show after the other with an avidity that seemed more like ensorcellment than interest.

She bristled at this patronizing characterization. The shows didn't control her mind or condition her feelings, she averred. She didn't "identify" with the people on them; she engaged with the world they revealed—curious, amazed, even shocked, but never taken in or fooled. "When I watch them, I also 'frame' them," she said. "I observe people in their traps. That's how I keep them at a distance."

"But there's no distance! You watch them all the time!"

"Not *all* the time."

"A lot of the time, anyway." He disliked the corner she put him in. Normally he wouldn't care if she watched TV. He'd be happy to keep his opinions to himself, provided he didn't have to watch, too. Now, though, with no other place to go and no outlet of his own, he felt compelled to bring them out.

"What is it we're doing here, after all?" he pressed. "I mean really doing? We sit and stare for hours on end—come on, not unlike two people cast in a spell! Things happen to us, or for us. We don't process and synthesize what we see."

"I do."

"It's not like reading a book."

"Why not?"

"It gives us nothing to read, Molly! Just crude formulas and banal emotions! There's no depth to any of it."

"Why isn't that worth 'reading'?" she asked curtly.

"What?"

"The lack of depth."

A bell rang on the cooking show, forcing their attention back to the screen. Big John stopped. He looked exhausted, like he'd just run a race. In a subsequent interview he mused on his own performance. He thought he'd done pretty well. There were one or two things he would have done differently, but he was confident he'd survive the round in good shape. He followed this assertion with the same welcoming smile he'd given Nick by that makeshift bar in his Playa Del Rey yard.

"Okay," he conceded, back in his frame of mind at the time. "The show captures something true about the world we live in. It dramatizes people struggling to achieve their goals, closing the gaps between what they have and what they want, or think they deserve. I'm *one* of those people, so I get it. But the show is no less manipulative for that. And it doesn't illuminate what's frustrating people either. It twists our dreams and hopes into metaphors of complicity."

"I guess that doesn't bother me so much. I don't take it so personally."

"But it *is* personal," he insisted. "The show works on our sense of ourselves. It catches us up in this nasty evaluative gaze. It turns us into the kind of people it assumes we are: passive, inert, in need of discipline."

"Don't we need discipline?"

That threw him coming from her. "Sure," he said. "We have to take control of our lives. We have to become our own masters. But the show isn't about that. The aim isn't freedom or self-determination or even success. That's all a sham. It diverts attention from the real aim, which is to…govern how we govern ourselves."

The cooking show had moved to an assessment stage. A plump girl with a nose ring and spiky orange hair awaited the feedback of the judges, who were busy pursing lips, grimacing, and widening their eyes in response to the various sensations they had tasting her moussaka. The verdict wasn't good. A man with a craggy face found too much salt in the béchamel sauce. A woman who looked like an aging fashion model thought the eggplant too chewy. The girl fought back tears. She hadn't been doing well and now risked elimination. The man with a craggy face questioned her commitment to being a first-rate chef. A hint of defensiveness in her response had him reproaching her for "whining," which everyone else experienced as akin to a bad smell. Nick couldn't imagine the scene proving his point about discipline any better.

"It's so obvious," he said sadly. "That's the worst part. Nothing is hidden or even pretended. Democracy is technocracy, or plutocracy. Experts and millionaires tell us what kind of people to be if we want to be like them, or at least to serve them in the right way. They tell us what to do, how to do it, how to feel when we do it. We're not supposed to trust ourselves at all."

"That seems more honest to me."

"Why?! Because the agenda's explicit?"

"Because it's dishonest to offer an alternative where there is none," she countered. "That's why I don't like watching dramas. They're so earnest. All they do is confirm us in our self-importance. At least reality TV admits the catharsis is fake."

"Does it follow we just give in to the cynicism?"

"That's not what I'm doing!" she shot back. "Shit, Nick. You're so quick to judge. I can still be critical—maybe more critical than you are when you don't watch TV. It doesn't make me a zombie."

"I didn't say you were a zombie."

"I have to feel a part of something," she said, in a plaintive tone now. Deeper anxieties were surfacing. "If the only world out there is ugly, vile, and stupid, it doesn't mean I can just tune it out. I have to find my way in it somehow."

"What would happen if you did tune it out?"

"Nothing. That's the point. Nothing would happen, and nothing would change. It would go on just as it did before. And I'd still have to find my way in it. That's what you don't understand: the distance I have is *no* distance. We start from where we're at, right?" She pointed to the TV. "Well, that's where I'm at. It's where you're at, too, only you don't want to say so."

To Nick this sounded like an excuse, since she wasn't finding her way in the world so much as withdrawing from it, fearing it. But he doubted himself now. The impulse he had to take her outside, to show her the world—equally in the spirit of that pragmatist philosophy she was recalling he would've thought—had been checked one too many times in his life. He couldn't be sure if he had more to offer Molly than his own fear of finding his way in an electronically mediated society. She knew it, too. She saw his wavering faith as a refutation of his disdain for TV and yet another reason for pessimism.

4

Late one morning Nick went to meet his former professor Pierre-Yves Ozouf for lunch at the restaurant in Bryant Park, adjacent to the Public Library where he was spending the day on a research project. Nick hadn't seen Ozouf in years, and he was a little nervous, never having quite lost his awe of him. A self-assured Parisian of Tunisian descent, with a straight, classic nose and a slight flare of the nostril suggesting fierceness of spirit, he could be an intimidating interlocutor. For all his sophistication, though, Ozouf had been both open and generous with Nick. He was a genuinely curious person, dedicated to the practice of thinking wherever it might lead and without conditions or agendas either. For him, intelligence had an absolute quality. When you encountered it, or when it happened, you felt the arbitrary nature of social differences and rules. They might still exist, and Ozouf might even be invested in them, caught up the same as everyone else in status games. But the mind for him was fundamentally an egalitarian organ.

Nick found him seated in the restaurant by tall windows that looked out on a promenade, wearing a fitted black blazer and a blue necktie. It disconcerted Nick to see how much he'd aged. His youthful looks had faded, his refined features were lost in a new fleshiness, and his hair had turned a shocking white. Worse for Nick, his expression lacked some of its old candor. It was more guarded than it used to be.

He learned why over lunch. Ozouf was no longer on the faculty at NYU. He worked at John Jay College, a strange choice for someone of his reputation. He taught seminars in critical legal theory, which made sense, but also introductory survey courses in the humanities for largely unmotivated students, which didn't make sense at all.

"It was the only way for me to stay in New York," he said. "My wife has her work"—Carolyn Ozouf was a research psychiatrist at the Columbia University medical school—"and my children are settled here as well. I might consider a position in Paris, but so far there haven't been any offers."

"What happened?"

With a mischievous lift of the brow Ozouf said, "Thereby hangs a tale." A waitress brought their wine, relieving him of having to elaborate straight off. They waited while the bottle was uncorked and poured. Ozouf proposed a toast to their reunion. They drank, and he set his glass down, pausing still another moment longer.

"I don't quite know where to start," he said apologetically. "There are two versions. In one, I'm a stupid man who gets what he deserves. In the other, I'm a target of character assassination. In one, I'm punished as a teacher for abusing his authority. In the other, I'm abused as a public intellectual for speaking his mind. Both have their grains of truth, I'm afraid. I alternate rather painfully between them."

"I know the feeling."

"Do you?" Ozouf seemed to doubt it. Nick chose not to say more, urging him to continue. But he felt a strange anticipation stealing over him.

"The first version began with a visit by two police detectives," Ozouf told him, "who said they'd come upon evidence of an affair I'd had with a graduate student some years back. The affair had been entirely consensual, and it ended with no one the wiser. Apparently, another graduate student, whom I barely know, overheard me mention the relationship to a close friend at a party, and she recorded her impressions of that conversation in a diary. That, too, was years ago. Time passed, and this person I barely know found herself embroiled in a lawsuit which had nothing to do with me or the university. Her diary was entered as evidence in a trial. A lawyer noticed, I'm told perfectly by chance, the entry recording the overheard conversation. He took the extraordinary step of informing the police about it."

"Why?!"

"That's what I asked the two detectives," Ozouf said. "I was shocked, as you might imagine. But they gave me no satisfactory answer, announcing only that they intended to present their evidence to the university authorities. To head things off, I told Harvey Brand, the chair at the time, who had no interest in this becoming a public matter. I was more or less well liked in the department. I thought it would end there, but the news came to the attention of a dean, who was so outraged, and so emboldened by the evidence in her possession—a rare event, it turns out, in cases of sexual impropriety—that she insisted, not on inquiry or censure, but outright dismissal. I was fired, Nick, and not before my wife found out about the affair, seriously damaging my marriage. That's the first version."

"There's another reason you were targeted," Nick inferred.

"I believe so." Ozouf fretted over how best to frame the second version. He decided to be direct: "I've antagonized powerful people over things I've said on the subject of Israel's occupation of Palestine—in writing, in the classroom, and, more recently, in fact more stridently, in public speeches."

"Powerful people?"

"It sounds preposterous, I know. Even paranoid. That's what people whisper behind my back, if they don't proclaim it to my face. They tell me I've succumbed to conspiracy theories, to imagining secret Jewish plots. And I have no credible answer, because, of course, I have no evidence. This is what I do know: an undergraduate student, enrolled two years before in my literary theory course, turned out to be in the employ of a right-wing media group—not Jewish, but Zionist in its sympathies and, I suspect, funding—dedicated to smearing the reputations of people it disliked. This student filmed some of my lectures. These were then deceptively edited and released on the internet, suggesting far more extremism in my views than anyone could reasonably assign to them. This sparked a controversy, until it was discovered—by the happy coincidence of another student's having recorded the same lectures—just how much my views had been distorted."

"I didn't hear about that."

"It caused quite a stir at the time," Ozouf said. "It also made me still more outspoken than I was before. I gave interviews to reporters, and I participated in a moderated discussion on France 24, where I was very pointed in my analysis. I stopped caring if people thought me irrational. And now I really don't care. The only plausible explanation for the appearance of those detectives in my office is that someone of authority put them up to it. I was neutralized, 'taken out' as you Americans say, and the only reason I see—the only reason

I could possibly be a threat to anyone–is that I publicly criticize the state of Israel."

Nick had no idea what to say. All he could come up with was, "I've never thought of you as a political man, Pierre-Yves. Not in the activist sense, I mean."

Ozouf laughed. "You're right. I've always been more receptive on the register of scruple, or qualm. But there are times when the misrepresentation of facts and history becomes so outrageous, the censorship so gross, the consensus so hypocritical, that one has to speak out."

After the waitress came and took their order, Nick related, as simply as he could, what had happened to him in Auckland.

Ozouf listened with sympathy but not surprise. "I don't put anything past the academic institution anymore," he said. "Since the idea has taken hold that it should model itself on the corporation, it's adopted the pathologies of the corporation, too."

"Its bad conscience."

"Which engages people at basic levels of belief, desire, and fear. Either they see themselves as managers, since that is the road to prestige, or they feel isolated and irrelevant, prone to nurse their narcissistic wounds and finally to lash out."

"In such a personal way, too."

"They make you feel their own compromises. I daresay that's the true aim of ad hominem attack. Inflict your narcissistic wounds on others. Make them as bitter and resentful as you are."

Nick shook his head in raw and painful recollection. After a pause he said, in subdued tones, "I don't understand how anyone could do that."

"No?" Ozouf doubted him here, too. "I've seen it often enough, I'm afraid. People spend so long in social hierarchies they know nothing else. They become attached to the roles that simultaneously underdescribe them. At once unique and generic, they start to live for the semblance of their own nonequivalence, insisting on it with others, defending it from others."

Nick recalled Jane declaring over breakfast that the academic was a slave, and Alba quoting Nietzsche on the instinct for freedom forced down and turned upon the self. The thing was it didn't matter what the two women understood when they said these things; they were still slaves, still determined by that repressed instinct. Awareness made no difference. It changed exactly nothing. That had been Nietzsche's point, Nick supposed. Consciousness was a prison house. It suggested, among other things, that the problem ran deeper than he even realized—right into the belief that he, or anyone, could think himself out of it. Feeling uncomfortably close in spirit to Nietzsche's Last Man, he asked, "Is there no choice then? Is bad conscience in social hierarchies all we have?"

"I'd ask, rather, if there are social hierarchies, or arrangements, that allow for something else," Ozouf said. "And the answer nowadays seems to be no. Not under that corporatizing influence, felt through the whole fabric of society as the effect of a radicalized capitalist project. Both of us probably need to situate our experiences more consciously in this context."

"How would you do that?"

Ozouf took a moment to compose his thoughts. They were, as usual, multidimensional. "The first thing to say," he began, "is that the power behind that project cannot be declared. It's founded on a prohibition, and by this I mean not simply that it's censored or ruled out of official discourse. It defines itself negatively, in the prohibition, over and against any positive form of power."

"As an *anti*power."

"Yes." Ozouf liked this word. It fit nicely into his account. "One hears this 'antipower' in the rhetoric of Wall Street bankers, for instance, when they claim the complexity of financial markets as something no one could possibly comprehend, or see whole, from a God's eye view. That's why, they allege, there can never be effective regulation—indeed, there shouldn't be. Regulation involves an illegitimate power, an absolute power, associated with the very idea of a state that would ground economics in the laws and rights of a people. To their way of thinking, the power of the market isn't power at all. It's the freedom that resists power."

"So laws and rights are violated with impunity."

"Or reduced to tactics used for profit and not for defending people from the profit seekers."

"And another such tactic would be ad hominem attack?"

"I'd call it rather exemplary in this regard."

"Right."

"But it might not be quite apt to speak here of tactics," Ozouf said, pursuing still more refinement in his thoughts. "The modern constitutional state has always been an instrument of private interests, after all. And it has always concealed this fact in a language of self-limitation and disengagement. State power, then, is already an 'antipower.' It not only guarantees a free market but models itself on it. That's how, for Adam Smith, let's say, the state governs the uncoordinated actions of individuals and also their subjectivity, their inner motives and drives."

"By leaving them alone."

"Not only that."

Ozouf took a sip of his wine, needing the pause it gave him. His eyes were tense with the effort of compression he was now making.

"In one sense those motives and drives *are* determined," he said, "since they're not simply off-limits to regulation, and we're not simply free to supply them with what content we will. They're also opaque. We can't know *why* we want what we want. All we can know is *what* we want, the objects of desire. Introspection is a 'painful probe,' Bentham said, a useless form of metaphysical speculation. For his sort of liberalism, the deeper ideal of the citizen has always been the consumer, defined by his needs, guided by a pleasure principle, and subject to a psychologized behaviorism. This bias feels persuasive, of course, because the axioms of political freedom have proven so malleable."

"What axioms?"

"That autonomy is self-ownership. That it entails a property in the person, something to be bought and sold, exchanged, alienated, also managed and monitored. These are the terms on which the consumer aligns his interests with those who prey upon his needs, converting them to the debts and data that are the predators' assets. In today's economic theology, all capital is 'human capital.'"

"That's why its register is sexual."

"It's 'sex itself,' in Foucault's estimable phrase!" cried Ozouf, pleased by the turn back to the starting point of their conversation. "Whatever one thinks of sleeping with one's students—and I don't defend it, even if I do think it's nobody's business what consenting people do together in private—the most important rule will always be the one that shelters an autonomous sexual reason, since that is 'antipower' on the most intimate levels of one's being."

"Even for those who accuse you of exploiting someone sexually?"

"To a man with a hammer, everything looks like a nail."

"To a woman with a hammer, in my case!"

The hint of bitterness in this remark was too strong. Nick feared it revealed his own narcissistic wounds, brought with him from New Zealand if not from still further back in his life as a man. But he also couldn't bring himself to renounce it. "Anti-power" had a feminine quality. He needed to say that now, even at the risk of prejudice.

"One of the more irritating motifs I see in public discourse these days," Ozouf remarked, trying to address this need in Nick without the same acrid tone, "is the concern in Western democracies for women's sexual freedom. In France, laws are passed forbidding Muslim girls from wearing the hijab in school, on the grounds that covering their bodies in public violates their right to self-expression. I'm not against this right, but I do reject what its defenders mean when they invoke it: the idea that people are nothing but human capital—'entrepreneurs of themselves,' as Foucault put it, though it might be better to speak now of 'investors in themselves'—charged to bolster the credit-worthiness of what they *are* as well as have to offer. Sexual freedom then becomes a stalking horse for everything from economic austerity to zenophobic immigration laws to military intervention. I don't know how many times I'd heard it said that the US occupation of Afghanistan enabled more little girls going to school."

"I guess it works because it's easy to support little girls going to school," Nick said pensively. The moral of Ozouf's digression had not been lost on him. "They become flashpoints for our own innocence."

"They help us to sustain a neoliberal political and economic project as natural, right, even good—with the corresponding decay in discourse that brings. Everything then becomes perfectly circular: democracy is antidemocratic, inequality is the same for all, social security is totalitarian, elites are anti-elitist, and those who deplore the prerogatives of rich people are discriminating against them."

Nick fell silent, again at a loss for words. Ozouf was giving him a lot to ponder. He was, in fact, giving him a framework for his whole life. "People really do think in that circular fashion," he ventured presently. "I've been noticing it for a long time. But it's like a vortex when I do. It sucks me in. It swallows me up. The circles become vicious. I can't find the same. . .remove you have."

"It's not easy."

"The consensus runs, I fear, deeper than we even know."

"In the body and the soul," Ozouf agreed. "In schemes of perception, cognition, and feeling, where structures and systems are lived out—which is to say, in the world itself. That's what we're talking about, Nick. Contemporary institutions—political, economic, social, and cultural, above all in America but at almost every point in the global system it tries to control—are manifestly vacuous. 'Antipower' is like anti-matter in this regard. It volatilizes what it touches."

"That makes it hard to take a stand."

"You have to anyway," said Ozouf. "You have to speak out."

"But how do you know what to say when the terms have been so confused?"

"And your words have lost their value."

"You've been 'taken out' of the game."

Ozouf entered into this new dimension Nick gave the problem. "You've learned the lessons of your teachers well," he said. "We need foundational concepts—law, right, property, contract, testament, the state, not to mention reason and truth itself—even as they betray us to contradictions we can't readily resolve. We have to assert or criticize them depending on the context—even assert and criticize them at the same time."

"How is that possible?"

"Maybe it's not. Derrida liked to say it was *im*possible. That didn't mean an experience wasn't implied."

Nick could only wonder what such an experience might be—his, he supposed, but that didn't clarify much. Ozouf caught some of this vexation in his eyes. More delicately he said, "Maybe it's true the sort of pragmatics, or polysemy, Derrida had in mind is no longer sufficient for the contexts we face."

"It becomes equivocal."

Ozouf nodded. "I'm reminded of Wittgenstein's drawing of a duck, the one that also looks like a rabbit. Do you know it?"

"Sure."

"Stanley Cavell uses it to criticize Derrida's deconstructive aporias in one of his books. He argues that it's all very well, or 'charming,' I think is his word, to say it's both a duck and a rabbit, or even sometimes a duck and sometimes a rabbit. But if the aim is to decide, to make a decision, he wonders just what is to be gained by maintaining the ambiguity."

"I take his point."

"Of course, the wager is that social contexts are ambiguous in just this fashion, and they require careful deliberation—"

"Scruple and qualm."

"Yes." Ozouf smiled. "That isn't to say decision is impossible, but it does imply that every decision is wrong, even violent. One is forced into the element of a difficult freedom, and claiming that freedom can only ever be—"

"Wrong or violent?"

"Or paranoid, let's say."

"So you speak anyway, even if that means you speak as an anti-Semite or a sexual predator?"

"Sometimes that turns out to be the only way to speak," Ozouf said. "I confess the experience gives a new twist to the wager—one I had never quite considered in the same light before."

The waitress came with their food. As she laid it on the table and poured them more wine, Ozouf looked suddenly tired. That new twist pained him more than he let on. It saddened Nick to see his mentor, his model really for the kind of man he'd long wanted to be, affected by the same demoralizing forces that had plowed him under and churned him up. It frightened Nick, too, the glimpse Ozouf afforded of their magnitude. It seemed the very coherence of the thinking person was at risk now, and right across the world, too. Nick wondered if a time was coming when that person would have no place left to stand, no ground for the perspective he sought. What would remain then? Circles, he glumly concluded. Vicious circles. . .

5

Nick returned home to a cascade of messages and missed calls from Haley on his cell phone, which he'd neglected to bring with him.

"Finally!" she gasped when he called her back. "Where have you been?!"

"I was having lunch with Ozouf."

"Are you free now?"

"Sure."

"Can we Skype?"

"I don't know," he said, fearing it might wake Molly up. She was asleep in the bedroom.

"I have to see you."

"Why?"

"Please," she urged. "It's important."

"Okay. Hang on a minute."

He went to close the bedroom door and open his laptop on the coffee table by the sofa. She looked upset when he got her onscreen—more than upset. Her eyes were glazed and cheeks bloated as if she had the flu. That telltale vein down the middle of her forehead suggested considerable strain.

"What's wrong?"

"I've had a terrible day." The sound of people talking in the background startled her. She waited to make sure no one could hear. "Your father," she said, in a lowered voice. "Jesus, Nick. It was awful."

"My father?"

"I took Jean-Claude to see him."

"Oh."

"You were right. It was a mistake. I shouldn't have done it. I thought so myself. I'd even been putting it off, hoping Jean-Claude would forget, but he kept insisting. He wanted to meet him. So I called."

"It didn't go well."

"No." She took a moment to order the details of what had happened in her head. "He seemed okay at first. He said he was glad to hear from me, and that it would be all right if I came over. I told him I'd be bringing Jean-Claude, but I guess he didn't remember that afterward. When we showed up he was surprised to see me with this strange man. We sat uncomfortably in the living room and talked. Jean-Claude told him how much he admired him. He mentioned some movies of his. But everything he said only seemed to wind Evan up more. When Jean-Claude let it drop that he was a director, your father lost his temper altogether and turned into this angry, bitter man. I've never seen that in him before, Nick. He said terrible things about French people. He called Jean-Claude a 'fucking opportunist' and a 'bloodsucker.' We were practically chased out the door."

"I see."

"He hated Jean-Claude. Just hated him."

"I don't think it had anything to do with Jean-Claude."

"But it was *so* personal," she said. "It really shook Jean-Claude up. The more he thought about it afterward, the more insulted he felt."

That irked Nick. He wasn't sure he liked Jean-Claude either. He probably *was* an opportunist.

"I think he's mad at me now," she said. "Or at all Americans."

"Is that why you're speaking in a whisper?"

"No. He's not here." She started rolling a cigarette. That was a new habit. She'd always smoked the red Gauloises. "My housemates are protective of him. It makes me nervous talking about it. I'm not sure what they'll think or tell him."

"It's not your fault my father's an asshole."

"I know." She hesitated, her thoughts moving back into the past. "He's not the man he used to be."

"No," Nick objected with sudden asperity. "He's *always* been an asshole, Haley. Celebrity makes you an asshole. No one should ever forget that—especially if they want something from a celebrity."

"Jean-Claude didn't want anything from your dad."

"Maybe not," he said, hearing his own mixed motives here. "It's hard for me to be objective about that."

"And he certainly didn't deserve what he got."

"No."

She let up, in no mood herself to quarrel. "I wish I'd never brought it up."

"He isn't the man he used to be. You're right."

"It's complicated things."

"How?"

Rather than answer, she licked the edge of the rolling paper and slid it between her fingers. Then she said, "I don't need the aggravation now."

"You're not comfortable in your apartment," he surmised.

"I'm not used to living with other people." She lit the finished cigarette. "There's not enough privacy."

"How's your screenplay going?"

She groaned. "It's not. I can't concentrate at all. There's too much distraction."

"Maybe you should go to a library. Beaubourg, or the BnF."

She shook her head. "I can't work in public."

"Why not?"

"What I'm doing is too intimate," she said. "When I'm writing it feels like someone's watching me, or tapping in to my thoughts."

"Tapping in?"

"No," she said, dissatisfied with her own phrase. She sought a better one. "It's more that I feel exposed. I'm too close to the story—it exposes me to the world, and that's exactly what I'm trying to capture, too. The protagonist is exposed in this same way."

"Makes sense," he said, unsure, though, if it really did.

"Yeah?" She brightened. He saw the worry about his father ebb in her eyes. "I can't tell sometimes. It gets so complex. There are too many details, and they keep spreading out, unraveling. They form patterns I can't reconstruct or put on the page. It's like trying to grab water."

"Maybe you should write it as a novel."

"Why do you say that?" she asked suspiciously.

"No reason. It seems to need a personal touch, that's all. The screenplay's so diagrammatic."

"But that's what I like about it," she said. "It's a map—a celestial map. I've been working with that metaphor. Listen." She reached out of the frame to retrieve a notebook. "I found this quote by Giordano Bruno."

Just then Molly emerged from the bedroom, dressed in one of Nick's sweaters. Her hair was bedraggled, her eyes bleary.

"'Let us remove from the heaven of our mind the bear of roughness,' he says, 'the arrow of envy, the foal of levity, the dog of evil calumny, the bitch of flattery; let us ban the Hercules of violence, the lyre of conspiracy, the Cepheus of hardheartedness.'" She broke off. "You get the idea: man-as-microcosm, intellectual heavens, the mind containing the world. I love the nonobjective connections that implies."

"More than Giordano Bruno it seems," Nick said, aware of Molly circling around the cramped room and keeping out of Haley's view. "He's criticizing superstition, right?"

"He's clearing the way for infinite space, or geometric space. That's what I want to criticize."

"Sounds like your dissertation." As he recalled, her focus in graduate school had been on seventeenth-century French neoclassicism. She was working on some similar problem in writers like Racine and Pascal when she quit.

"The one I'm *not* writing," she assured him. "I was thinking of making that quote an epigraph, though. Is someone there?"

"Yes." He beckoned to Molly, who silently protested.

"Molly Banville," he said, urging her over.

"The student from New Zealand."

"That's right."

Molly eased onto the sofa beside him.

"This is Haley, an old friend of mine."

"Hi."

Haley leaned back in her chair. "*Very* old," she said, with an expression Nick thought just too bemused for comfort.

"Okay," said Molly, sensing the same thing.

"You've moved to New York?"

"I'm visiting."

"She might," said Nick. "She's applied to the English department at NYU."

"I'm waiting to hear."

"Haley was there the same time I was."

"Oh."

No one spoke. They all felt embarrassed for some reason. Haley drew tensely on her cigarette. She leaned forward and said, "Do you think I should include the quote as an epigraph?"

"You don't usually see that sort of thing in a script," Nick said.

"Mine's not the usual script."

"Go ahead, then, if it helps you to understand the story."

"I think David Lynch approaches his films in the same way," she said. "Not in terms of plot or even character, but of constellations. He's always putting things in scenes that either come back later or appear where they can't logically be. Like the blue box in *Mulholland Drive*. Or the vacuum cleaner."

"Those always seemed like non sequiturs to me."

"No," said Haley firmly. "They're part of the design. They distort the diegetic space in this very precise way, mixing up time and place. They demand a different kind of interpretation."

Molly moved off the sofa and headed for the kitchenette to make herself a cup of tea. "Try for that then," Nick said. "As long as you're working with a director who understands what you're doing, it's fine."

"Jean-Claude likes the idea. He's waiting for a draft—at least I hope he is, after what happened."

"Don't worry about it. Tell him my father's sick and it's hard on him."

"He's not happy in Paris, is he?"

"No."

"Maybe he should move back to LA."

"I don't think his wife would go for that."

"Even if it was better for his health?"

"I'm not sure that's the case. He was out of control in LA. It made sense to get him away from temptation."

Haley's thoughts drifted one more time back over the day's events. But she was feeling easier about them, too. "Thanks, Nick. I needed to talk things through."

"Don't let it bother you," he said. "Go work on your screenplay."

"No, not tonight. My head's pounding."

"In the morning then."

"I'll try."

He wanted out of the conversation now. He had the feeling Molly was unhappy with the encounter.

"When are you coming for a visit?" Haley asked.

"A visit?" He glanced at Molly, who stood by the stove waiting for water to boil in the kettle. The question plainly irritated her.

"It'd be nice to see you."

"I'm still trying to find my bearings here," he said noncommittally. At the same time he heard an urgent note in Haley's voice. It sounded as if she really did need his company. Once more it struck him how unwell she looked on that screen. She seemed overwhelmed, scared even, like a figure trapped in strange depths. For a moment he felt in her the same loneliness that had inspired such anguished yet illusory love in him so many years before.

"Think about it, okay?" she asked.

"I will."

"Take care."

"You, too."

Skype cut out. He shut the laptop and walked to the kitchenette. Molly avoided his gaze. She dropped a tea bag in a cup and opened the refrigerator for milk. The water approached boiling. The refrigerator door slammed shut again.

"You're mad," he said.

She shrugged.

"You didn't like Haley."

"Not really."

"Why not?"

"She ignored me, Nick."

"What do you mean?"

"She acted like I wasn't there. She drew a nice private perimeter around the two of you and made it crystal clear where I stood: outside."

With some caution he said, "I'm not sure it was that deliberate."

"Oh yeah?" She turned to face him. There was an angry gleam in her eyes. "I spent twelve years in an all-girls' Catholic school, Nick.

She'd fit perfectly there. I know her exact type: superior, competitive, and pretentious. 'The diegetic space is distorted,'" she mocked, exaggerating Haley's American accent. "'Time and place are all mixed up.' Fucking hell."

"You're being a little harsh."

"Do you know how many times she called here?" she demanded. "Your phone has been ringing off the hook all day."

"I know."

"Girls like that think the world revolves around them. When they want you, you're supposed to jump—you're supposed to drop everything and go to Paris."

Nick saw her regret this remark, or what it revealed: jealousy behind the anger, something like her own pretensions behind the jealousy, the risk of wanting a life she didn't have and might not be able to get.

More gently he said, "I think you've got her wrong."

"I don't."

The kettle whistled. She stared at it. They both wondered how long she was going to let it go on. Haley aroused ambivalence, too. Desire vied with aversion, like winners with losers, in Molly's heart, tightening a knot she couldn't easily undo. "Oh bugger!" she said, opening the valve on the spout. The kettle went silent again.

x

Molly did have that friend in New York. Sean Tiernan, a fellow New Zealander, went to the same all-girls' school and fit the type Molly saw in Haley much more completely, it seemed to Nick. Tall and blonde, with an attractive oval face, powdery skin, and pearl-gray eyes, Sean wore elaborate makeup and tight revealing dresses with an almost haughty self-assurance. For the past year, since her arrival in New York, she'd been working as a salesperson at Bloomingdale's, hoping one day to become a buyer. Meanwhile she'd been living fast in the East Village, not far from Nick's old apartment in fact. As he learned the first time they met, Sean combined sexual liberation with traditional values. She was a strong woman who spoke her mind and liked cooking her man a proper meal. A favorite pastime, one she was quite good at apparently, was pole dancing at parties.

She didn't stand out all that much in the East Village, Nick noticed. Her self-styled "power" feminism seemed all the rage and sharply at odds with what he knew when he was that age. Then, the squaring of gender circles seemed a lot more political. The ethos was just as performative, and just as feminist, but it challenged heterosexual norms and mocked the banalities of consumer society. It looked back to David Bowie and Cindy Sherman, not forward to Lady Gaga.

Now, as far as Nick could tell, the point was to be or have what you wanted, to emulation without the derisive energies in parody or even any critical edge at all. At least Sean didn't seem to reach much further, and even Molly admitted to an absence of negativity that made her friend's confident persona just too literal and self-contained, like a piece of cork bobbing on the sea, forever resilient in adversity. Molly was too shrewd a judge of character to miss the pretense in that.

Still, the two of them got on well, and not only because they'd grown up together. They liked similar things—*Sex in the City* bus tours, obsessive texting, Instagram, and most of all reality TV, especially the shows about bickering housewives. Molly started going over to Sean's apartment to watch them, a change Nick welcomed for the relief it gave him, although in the quiet of her absence he did also find himself better appreciating what she was coping with in a mediatized market culture. It was the same thing he was coping with finally: an "economic theology" (in Ozouf's resonant phrase) that pressured every bid for a viable social identity. He learned just how true this was, at least for young women in New York, when Molly told him Sean moonlighted as an escort for Wall Street bankers, who took her out for expensive dinners, plied her with drugs, and fucked her in fancy hotel suites. For her services she received astronomical sums of money—so much, in fact, that she'd begun to wonder if she needed her day job at Bloomingdale's.

Molly was right: they were in something together, and if it hardly afforded a world in which a viable social identity made much social sense to Nick, it didn't mean another world offered itself. Nor did it mean he offered a better way to handle the world they had. His way, in fact, only seemed to end in no identity whatever, if not in any identity whatever—in that nonequivalent semblance Ozouf had discerned in the corporate personality. Bad conscience, in other words, seemed all but inescapable now, met as much coming as going, as much in confrontation as in recoil. He had no idea what it would take to break free from that. Worse, he wondered if he should even try. Maybe there was no such thing as a good conscience.

In the meantime he tried to be less critical around Molly, or at least critical in a fashion that acknowledged the shared challenge of living in a mediatized market culture. He watched TV, keeping in mind that any account of it he might give would be false as long as he himself lacked credible alternatives. Again, it was hard. When, in an episode they were watching of *America's Next Top Model*, the contestants had to sell a soft drink while skating on the Venice Beach boardwalk, tested in their ability to be at ease and natural for the camera, he couldn't help launching into a tirade about human capital and entrepreneurial selves. Molly rolled her eyes, not because she disagreed but because it was obvious. Too obvious to mention, like air or gravity. In her view he had to accept the general condition the show implied and stop using his mind to secure a bogus immunity. He had to see himself in those aspiring models even when they shared the attitudes of their more successful judges, craving recognition and confidence. And frankly he didn't know how to do that. It scared him. He might feel for those young women in their traps of sexual reason, but he couldn't ignore a panicky fear of the desire to be trapped dragging him under. Sympathy was a deluge. He wasn't cork-like enough to know for sure if he'd be able to rise to the top again. Molly felt this in him, too, and didn't much respect it he could tell. She sensed the deficiency was one of courage.

6

The trouble between them came to a head the night of a Tribeca party to which Sean had invited them. They found it in a cast-iron industrial building near the West Side Highway. A doorman checked off their names on a list, and they passed up five flights of stairs to a top floor warehouse with T-beams spaced at regular intervals, a few old sofas along the walls, and a bar crowded with backlit bottles of gin and vodka. The place throbbed with electronic beats and colored lights flashed in moody darkness. On one wall the movie *Tron* unfolded its weird blue-toned geometric landscapes.

Only a few people were dancing as yet. Most had gathered on the roof to talk and look over the Hudson River toward the Jersey City skyline. Nick and Molly followed suit, mounting a flight of stairs at the back and trailing through the crowd in search of Sean, the only other person there they knew. Not finding her, they huddled together by a hooped wooden water tower, holding drinks and smoking cigarettes while their bare fingers burned in the cold air. At one point, seeing Molly shiver, he put his arm around her shoulders. He felt her, pressed against him, more willing than she'd lately been to yield or trust. It came home to him how new everything must be for her, enough to explain all nervous resistance. The worry about their differences momentarily faded, and an older camaraderie returned.

She pointed her cigarette at the dark mass of a nearby skyscraper. "That's the new World Trade Center, huh?"

"Yeah."

The specter of 9/11 loomed, with the building, in her mind. "Can you imagine being here on that day, watching the towers blow up?"

He remained silent.

"You don't like talking about that, do you?"

"I don't like the way it's made into this existential event, no. Maybe I'd think otherwise if I had been here, watching them blow up."

"Where were you?"

"In Paris."

"I was at home," she said. "The TV show I was watching cut out and I saw the first plane plow into the building. I'll never forget that. I knew nothing would ever be the same again. It felt like some kind of innocence was lost."

"You were just a kid!"

"I was old enough," she tersely replied.

He regretted his remark. "I didn't mean to sound dismissive," he said. "You're right. It was difficult for everyone."

He tried to sort out his own feelings about 9/11. He'd lived through its disastrous aftermath aghast at the reactionary patriotism, the shameless warmongering, and the breakdown of democratic common sense, hoping the fever would at last abate. He remembered when it sunk in for him that it wasn't going to abate, that the nervous change in people was far more durable. Walking along a street in LA some years back, he'd come upon a teacher guiding her young charges in pairs down the sidewalk. She was singing "When Johnny Comes Marching Home," the song heard on the soundtrack to the movie *Dr. Strangelove* as the rogue B-52 flies over Siberian wastes. "There was no irony in it," he said, on relating the anecdote to Molly. "That was the weird part. The cognitive dissonance the movie satirized had become normal to the woman. She was innocent of the Strangelovian way it sounded."

"Maybe she just hadn't seen the movie."

"I'm not sure that matters."

Molly nodded, letting the point sink in: that the world was innocent of the Strangelovian way *it* sounded. "9/11 exposed the insanity of American power, it's true," she said. "The innocence I lost was about that, in case you were wondering. I saw how much of a bully you are."

"Me?!"

"Well, your country. But you are American, Nick. You need to take responsibility for that."

"You don't think I do?"

"Sometimes it seems like you want to defend the culture," she said. "You believe America hasn't always been an insane power. You think there's this other, better country that used to be there or became something else."

"It did seem different when I was a kid."

"More innocent?"

"No," he said, smiling. "Just alert to sentimentalized violence. No one back then, for instance, saw the Twin Towers as symbols of something important or essential about themselves. Just the opposite. They resented them. They were considered an abstraction forced on the city. My mother once compared them to a huge bar graph, and I've thought of them that way ever since. She said they ruined the downtown. They *did* ruin the downtown."

Molly listened with bent head. "That's as much as I've ever heard you say about your mother," she remarked.

"Yeah?"

"Why is that?"

"I don't know." Suddenly he felt on the defensive. "I guess she's part of a painful past."

"You weren't happy as a kid?"

"Not really."

"Maybe you should talk about that more."

"I don't *avoid* it. It hasn't come up, that's all."

They saw Sean in the crowd, her face pillowed in the white fur collar of her coat, approaching with some friends. "Give it time," he advised, "and you'll probably hear more than you want. Or maybe one day you'll meet my father, and you'll understand better."

Sean pounced as he spoke, drawing Molly into an ostentatious hug and hearty introductions. Nick lingered with the discomfort it caused him to think of Molly meeting his father. He wondered how true it was that she'd understand better. Practically no one in his life had.

Sean kicked the party into higher gear by giving them each an Ecstasy pill, which they both swallowed, Nick with some trepidation. It had been a while since he'd indulged in that sort of thing.

The roof was pronounced too cold, and everyone moved back inside. They deposited their coats on a bed in a side room and had more drinks. Soon the warm fellow feeling of the drug stole over Nick and Molly both. They let their guards down, smiling at each other, catching each other's eye in sly complicity as everyone else became interesting, too. Nick ended up talking over the pounding music to a Russian man, formerly a physicist at Harvard but now working as a financial analyst at Goldman Sachs—located, it turned out, only a few blocks away. The thought that he might've been one of Sean's clients didn't bother Nick as much as it otherwise might have.

Not long after he saw Molly on the floor, crowded now, dancing with Sean and her friends. She'd fully accepted the invitation to abandon. He wondered if he should join her. Before he could decide, though, Molly and Sean pulled him off toward a bathroom, where they locked themselves in and proceeded to do lines of cocaine off the closed toilet lid, with a rolled up fifty-dollar New Zealand bill.

Nick followed them onto the floor this time, that heedless feeling stronger than ever. They all spun off on their own. Sinewy and loose, Nick moved effortlessly through the space, in and out of the other bodies and the steel piers standing like sentinels in their midst. Awareness became for him a fabric that stretched and curved in very physical fashion. It all but eliminated the sense of separation having a body gave him. He spent a long time marveling at this effect, coming out of it only when he started missing those sly looks of complicity from Molly. In the effort to resolve the mass of people around him into individuals, he spotted her dancing with another man around her same age. The pang this produced was unexpectedly sharp. He tried to reason the feeling away, without success.

It was clear that Molly thought nothing of their flirtation, even if the other man had his own ideas. Nick watched him insinuate his body ever closer to hers, close enough for gyrating hips to brush and bump. At one point he stopped dancing altogether. Both of them stood stock still on the floor as she listened to him speak into her ear, his hand resting on her shoulder. When she understood what he meant—plainly some sort of proposition—she did look over at Nick, and with a smile flooding him with affection, she spoke back and pointed. Nick pretended not to notice, but he could feel the man's eyes on him.

The event was jarring nonetheless, so he withdrew for the bar, pretending he wanted another drink and not the time to settle confounded feelings. He sat on a sofa for what must have been too long, because Molly came up a while later and said, "Jeez, Nick, I couldn't find you!"

"I've been right here."

"I thought you'd left!"

"I felt dizzy, that's all."

"You okay?"

"Couldn't be better."

She grabbed the drink from his hand and took a sip. Just as she was about to squeeze in next to him, however, Sean appeared, pulling her away one more time to that bathroom.

By then Nick felt he'd calmed down enough for trust to get the upper hand. He danced again, resolved to give Molly as much latitude as she wanted. But as he watched her grow more and more abandoned, his insecurity only increased. She seemed to be moving off into a realm forbidden to him, as light and easy as he was weighed down by this heavy burden of consciousness. He thought of what she'd remarked on earlier: that he didn't speak much about his past. He wasn't a nostalgic person. Not for the first time it occurred to him that many things he loved did give themselves over to remembrance and longing. It had always seemed like he knew how that felt. But a principal ingredient of any feeling for the past was letting go, yielding to memory, or rather to the immemorial, to a kind of forgetfulness that was more connected to memory than it might seem, and here Molly was right: it wasn't part of his makeup. He admired the past from a critical distance. He read it in its alienated reflection, like, he feared, a fetishist with little talent for what he loved. It worried him that this was also the opinion slowly forming in Molly's mind.

Meanwhile, he saw that she'd befriended a light-skinned black girl and her white boyfriend. They appeared more straightlaced than he would've thought Molly liked, even high: people who worked through the week in office buildings she wouldn't be caught dead in. Still they formed a small privileged circle on the dance floor, and Nick couldn't help noticing the sly looks of complicity they shared between them. His mind went on all sorts of tangents then, like those long glowing lines in *Tron*. He excused his reaction as concern for Molly: he wanted to make sure she was all right and nothing got out of hand. But as the fact of her intimacy with the two strangers grew ever larger in his mind, this effort at self-control resolved into what really preoccupied him: his total absence now from Molly's thoughts.

A while later they broke away. He watched them enter the side room where the coats were kept and reemerge dressed for the cold. He guessed they were headed upstairs for cigarettes.

He went to a corner and slumped onto the floor, fighting an urge to go up there, too. "It's none of your business," he told himself. "She's her own person. You're in your own world." But no persuasion worked. Against his better judgment he retrieved his coat and went upstairs.

The roof was less crowded than before, but still it took a while to locate Molly by a fire that burned in a charcoal grill. She sat in a low-slung chair opposite the black girl and the boyfriend, perched beside her on an armrest. They were engaged in an animated discussion. Molly had a wild expression in her eyes that Nick had never seen before. She seemed older, more self-possessed, and more alluring, too.

He stayed off to the side, smoking a cigarette and pretending not to care. He forced his attention out over the river to a tugboat pulling after it a long slender barge. It cut the water like a knife.

"Got a light?" he heard. Sean had quietly come up beside him, holding her own cigarette.

"Sure."

"Quite a party, eh?"

"Yes." His arm pressed into her quilted coat as he lit the cigarette for her. The contact was distinctly arousing. Despite his distraction, it made him want to press more.

She took a drag and exhaled, swiping at the smoke with a gloved hand. Then she shifted her gaze straight at Molly. It was too deliberate to ignore.

"You know what you should do?" she said.

"Do?"

"Come on. Don't play dumb."

He turned toward Molly, sensing depth in Sean for the first time. "Okay. What should I do?"

"Find the best looking girl on this roof and talk to her. Don't stop until Molly notices. Make her feel what you're feeling."

"I think I am talking to the best looking girl here," he said, noticing a breeze stir the haze of her fur collar.

"I don't count."

"Are my feelings so obvious?"

Sean smiled. "I'd say Molly's the one being obvious now."

After a moment's reflection he said, "I can't do it."

"Why not?"

"It's too tactical."

"You're a gentleman!"

"No," he said, under the impression that she didn't much like gentlemen. "But I'm not very tactical."

"Well, you better do something," she said. "Go over there and get between them. Make it clear you're here."

He could tell he wouldn't be able to do that either.

"Sometimes a man's gotta step up to the plate," she said.

As if to confirm the wisdom of this homely advice, Molly lifted herself off her chair and slid onto the lap of the black girl, planting a firm kiss on her lips. It went on and on. Her passion proved infectious for the boyfriend, who at length wedged himself in beside them, laying his head on the chair back so that he could observe them both from up close. At the same time his hand slid surreptitiously to Molly's ass, and the touch prompted a shift of her attention. They started kissing.

Nick glanced sideways at Sean, at her steady witness, and felt indignant, humiliated, and insulted all at once. Flicking his cigarette to the ground, he swung off without a word and marched straight down the stairs toward the exit. Pride, he told himself, demanded he not stay another instant. In the middle of the building, though, he faltered. It looked worse than it was. She had no idea what she was doing. He shouldn't overreact. When he reached the foyer with the doorman still checking people in, he turned around and went back up.

The stairs leading to the roof ran along the back wall, and at their foot a kind of platform had been built where a newel post should be. From a short distance he saw Molly standing over it, flanked by the black girl and her boyfriend. They were doing more lines of coke while people filed by on the stairs. The party had gotten to that stage of oblivion. Nick took a few tentative steps nearer, wondering how to get her attention, finally calling out her name. Her new friends were the ones who heard, though, and gazing at him over her hunched back, they appeared to know exactly who, or what, he was in that situation. He read the antic gleam in their eyes as frank derision.

When Molly straightened he called to her again, waving her over. Without any awareness of his state, she came to greet him.

"Nick!"

"I want to go," he said coldly.

"What?"

"Now."

She looked back, feeling the night wasn't over. This prompted him to start for the exit once more, forcing her to follow.

They descended to the entrance without a word. Nick darted through the crowd gathered there, thinking he might find a cab on Greenwich Street. As they went darkness and silence closed around them. The block was otherwise deserted.

"What's wrong?" she called after him. "Hey, slow down."

"I was on the roof, Molly."

"So?"

Too rashly he swung around and grabbed her wrist.

"Ow!" she cried.

"I saw you kiss those two people."

"That hurts, Nick."

He released her.

"What are you talking about?" she said. "What people?"

"The black girl and her boyfriend."

Pieces of the puzzle fell together in her mind.

"Lisa," she murmured.

"You meant it, too."

"I didn't *mean* anything," Molly said. "We're on Ecstasy, for fuck's sake! It's all a blur. I don't remember kissing anybody. . .exactly."

"Oh Jesus," he said, darting off again.

"Are you just going to leave me here?"

He heard the fear mingled with anger in her voice and halted. "No."

"I hate that!" she cried. "I hate the way men cut out the second they don't know how to handle something."

"I wasn't going anywhere."

"No, you just wanted to remind me I'm here at your discretion."

"Not true."

"You have no right to be upset."

"I think I have every right."

"I'm high off my tits, Nick!"

"So what?"

"I thought things were looser than that."

"Looser?!"

"You're the one saying how temporary things are," she said, determined now to bring her own complaints to the fore. "How we have to wait and see about school, how everything's up in the air. I thought that's what you wanted."

"It doesn't mean we're just two people keeping our options open."

"I don't know what kind of relationship this is," she went on. "Nothing's clear between us. I don't know what you want from me."

"I would've thought that was easy to figure out."

"You haven't said anything—"

"For starters, I want you to want me."

"All you do say, or hint, is that I'm too dependent. You're always going on about your 'space,' your time to yourself. You make me feel I'm in the way."

"You're missing the point, Molly."

"But what happens when I'm more *in*dependent? You shoot me down. You shit on what I do."

"And your way of telling me this is to flirt with other people?"

"No," she said. "I wasn't thinking of you at all."

"Right."

"I mean I wasn't thinking of anything. Shit, Nick. We can't *always* be thinking."

"That's not the point either."

He could see where this was going: the insensitivity on his side, the problem his temperament, not her actions. His feelings could only be illegitimate, not feelings at all but disguised abstractions. He'd heard this before. It worked because it matched so well the private judgments he made of himself. He lifted his gaze to the wall of cast-iron facades sheering off down the block.

"What am I supposed to do?" he said then. "Pretend it doesn't hurt my feelings to see you kiss other people? Not have any hurt feelings? Would that suit you better? Would that make me a more sympathetic man?"

"You're a 'sympathetic man,'" she cracked.

"Fuck you!"

"Fuck you, too."

"What other way is there for me to tell you I *do* care than that it bothers me to see you making out with someone else?!"

"We weren't making out."

"The three of you were practically having sex!"

"No."

"No?"

"It's not like that."

"Why?!"

"You can't have sex on Ecstasy," she told him. "It's erotic and sensual, but you can't cum. It's about fantasy. It draws fantasies out. It makes them real."

"But not really?"

"That's right."

"What if our roles were reversed, and I wasn't really kissing somebody else?"

That gave her pause.

"It would end the relationship right there," he said. "You wouldn't take it. No self-respecting person would."

"I wasn't thinking," she said, not in a spirit of concession.

"No."

"I was only trying to have fun."

"Just because games are erotic," he said, too sententiously even for his taste, "doesn't mean eroticism is a game."

7

Nick wasn't so wounded, or so narcissistic, as to miss in that night further signs of Molly's discontent. That eroticism was more than a game didn't mean he had a feeling for what else it might be. She wanted from him an intimacy beyond the caricatures that formed under the pressure of inner correction in his personality, especially now, and arousing jealousy may have been the only way she knew to get this across. To be sure, that seemed disingenuous to him. She didn't want his anger or his possessiveness. From what he could tell she wanted feelings without risk, and that meant games played without consequence, genuine intimacy. But it didn't follow, just because he might have a point, that she was wrong to miss genuine intimacy from him, even if she didn't know what it was any more than he did.

Be this as it may, the Tribeca party put him on alert. It let him know Molly had a life of her own, feelings of her own, and they very well might not include him. This set off a speculative panic in his heart. He needed assurances no one could give, and if he knew that, if he knew security beyond any doubt was never possible where another person's feelings were concerned, he nonetheless couldn't stop obsessing about them. He'd never felt this way before—at least not with the same intensity. He had never considered himself the jealous type. He might blame Molly's provocation for the change, of course, but he knew that wasn't the reason. The truth was the successive shocks of his life were catching up with him. They'd disturbed a deeper sense of self. He was shakier than he'd maybe ever been.

He wondered if he should take a high road, concede their incompatibility and resign himself to the transience of the relationship. She deserved the chance to discover who she was on her own. He needed to step back and get some perspective; only then would he be able even to imagine committing to another person. It also wouldn't be fair to involve Molly in those shocks more than she already was. A young woman at the beginning of her life had enough to worry about.

She caught the false note in these thoughts when he later brought them out, in the cleared air that confrontation brings. "You're pushing me away," she told him. "You don't think you are. You think it's the other way around, but it's not."

"I don't want to push you away."

"Then relax!" she cried. "Stop trying to control things all the time. That's the real problem, Nick. You end up isolating yourself too much."

He couldn't relax. The more he tried, the less of a grip he had on his newly volatile emotions. But the more in their grip he was, the stronger became the need for control that set him apart from Molly, or from the man she wanted him to be, which only further compounded his insecurities. It seemed a true double bind. A perfect trap.

X

One path to the intimacy Molly missed involved the sharing of fantasies. She'd done this with other boyfriends and thought it might help them out of their impasse now if they tried it. Lying beside him in bed one night, she asked for an example.

He drew a blank. "I guess I don't have worked out scenarios in my mind."

"What do you have?"

"I don't know," he said, searching within himself for how fantasy *did* work for him. "Particular situations, I suppose. I meet someone, or I see someone, and it gives me a feeling I might conjure up later, recalling little details of her person or manner. But I guess it doesn't last much beyond the initial experience. It fades without new experience."

This answer disappointed her. It indicated the problem all over again. She tried to help with a fantasy of her own. It put her with two men in a limousine.

"Who are the men?"

"No one," she said. "Just generic men."

"Not someone you may have seen or met?"

"Well, sometimes, but often not: they're faceless, too. They show up, and they melt away again."

Nick made the mistake of trying to enter into this scenario with her, as one of those men. The sex didn't work. He ended up eroticizing the experience of her pleasure with others and from that same critical distance he felt at the Tribeca party. If he could do that well enough, imagining spontaneous threesomes in limousines or coatrooms from some neutral God's eye view, it didn't fit her fantasy at all. In fact, as a fantasy he might have had, it seemed no more shareable by her than vice versa.

Something else about Molly became clear at this time, and it made Nick's feelings still more untamable. Those men came suddenly on the scene, and their motives were far from benign. They hinted at an overpowering that Molly finally admitted drew her better than anything into an erotic mood. She kept such hints strictly separate from actual violence, she told him. They were nothing *but* fantasy. Their inconsequence meant that difference. It even formed a barrier against actual violence. As she put it, "If I want to be raped, I can't be raped."

This had Nick scratching his head. Even if he saw, in the fantasy she was driving at, a strategy for containing or managing fear, he couldn't see the difference between actual violence and that aggression which drew out the freer, more unfathomable submission she wanted to feel with him. At least he couldn't easily separate the two. He found it hard to be the dominant man even in fantasy. It went against a conditioning that ran far back in his life. If rough sex he could do on occasion, when the signs were right and it lacked premeditation, he couldn't keep it up for long without triggering bad associations—mostly involving his father.

It proved too much on the one occasion they did venture in this direction a few nights later. Nick felt so clumsy and conscious of Molly's unresponsive body beneath him that he stopped in the middle of sex. He leapt off the bed and retreated into the bathroom. A minute later he came back to find her fuming.

"You cut out again," she said.

"I'm sorry."

"It's such a petulant thing to do."

"I know."

"What's wrong now?!"

"I'm not getting what you want," he said. "I have to be a brute, but not really. I have to be a harmless nice guy, but not really. I feel like I'm walking on a tightrope."

"I guess I don't know what I want." Her rather too civil tone suggested disdain for his obtuseness. She didn't see why anyone should have to "know" what they wanted.

"All this is supposed to be natural," he went on, "but it's not. It's performance, theater. I'm supposed to play a role."

He thought of another man playing that role for her, making love to her with just the sort of command she wanted. This image, bright and hard as a shard of glass in his mind, cut him to the quick.

"Maybe I'm not the one for you, Molly."

"Don't say that!" she cried. "It makes me feel I can't trust you. I'm mixed up, okay? I don't understand why I'm like this. But I need it to be all right that I am. I don't need to feel guilty about it."

"I don't want you to feel guilty."

"Yes, you do. You have some idea of natural sex in your mind, I can tell. At heart it's healthy, lyrical, human, and sweet."

This litany of traits plainly nauseated her. And she might have been right. When it came down to it, Nick was a fairly conventional romantic about sex. He hadn't had a lot of experience with women who wanted much else either. On the contrary, they tended to mistrust precisely the sort of fantasy Molly was fishing for in him. *It* betrayed a need for control.

"What would arouse you?" he asked then.

"That's a dumb question."

"What would you do on your own, to get that feeling?"

He caught her short with this. "You mean, if I were doing it myself?"

"Yeah."

"You wouldn't like it if I told you."

"Tell me."

A crafty smile played into her face. "I'd go online."

"The internet?"

"Yeah."

"Porn, you mean."

"Sometimes. Or there's this interactive program. . ."

With a sinking feeling he asked, "What program?"

"I can't describe it."

"Show it to me."

She tried to picture this. "No," she said with an uneasy laugh. "You'd hate it."

"You don't know that. Come on. Show me."

"Are you sure?"

"Yes," he lied.

She reluctantly rose from the bed and put on a shirt, moving into the other room to set up her computer on the desk. He followed after her.

"Do you want to be involved?" she asked.

"Involved?"

"Do you want to be onscreen?"

"No. I'll just watch."

He sat naked on the floor by the desk while she retrieved a beer from the refrigerator.

"You're going to think it's creepy," she warned.

"No, I won't."

"You've never looked at porn before?"

"I haven't sought it out anyway."

"I can't believe that."

"Why?"

"Everybody looks at porn. It's so common. I've been living with it since I was twelve."

"Maybe that's the difference," he said. "It wasn't much around when I was a kid."

She went to the website and clicked a link. The two hands of an animated clock spun at the center of the screen. Then a live video image appeared of a man's erect cock. She clicked again: this time they saw a fat man with a full beard and no clothes seated before a desk in what appeared to be a warehouse office.

"Can they see you?" he whispered.

Her answer was to make a smaller image of her in the room appear onscreen.

"Do you talk to each other?"

"You can if you want," she said. "I'm just going to text."

She clicked through a half dozen or so candidates before coming to someone who interested her: a naked young man reclining in bed, seen straight on. He was lean of build, with a crew cut, a full-sleeve tattoo, and a very large penis. He might have been in the military. The words *hello who r u?* appeared in a chat box. She tapped in: *im carla who r u?*

He answered on a keyboard by his side.

—chas

He started touching himself. She sipped her beer.

—ur sexy

—u 2

—where u from?

—nyc u?

—charlotte

—what u doing?

—nothing bored

—me 2

—what do u like?

—i like to watch guys cum

—gotta show me somethin first

Molly stood, hesitating one more time. "Are you sure you won't hate me?"

"I won't hate you."

She pushed the chair away and pulled off her shirt. She turned half around so the man could see the curve of her ass. His penis was now fully erect. Nick looked on aghast, his heart heavy. All he could think was that he'd been wrong the whole time, in every respect. Eroticism was a game. And his place in the game was—had always been—this sideline, this margin, where the preference for something else contracted into a dumb spectatorship. He read on the screen:

—u got a nice body

Molly reached forward to key in her response. Nick watched her breasts loom into the smaller image, her body receding past her ribcage to her flat stomach and cunt.

—so do u

—sure like to fuck u

—u would?

The man was finding his stroke now. He *was* fucking her. The fantasy of sex was sex itself. Nick could only marvel at the cunning of it. She reached down with her hand and touched her clit.

He added: *fuck u hard*

With one finger she keyed in: *how hard?*

—jackhammer hard

—its big enuf

—u like?

—yes

—bet ud like 2 suckt

Molly's only reply was to take a swig of the beer and begin swiveling her hips in slow-motion imitation of a stripper—always with her eyes glued to the screen. Nick saw grow in them that same wild expression she had just before she kissed Lisa at the party.

The boy wrote, *say ud like 2 suckt*

She laughed through the bottle in her mouth.

—say it or i wont cum

She wagged her head no.

—i swear i wont cum

They continued on in this same bantering fashion. Molly danced and the man watched. He stroked his dick with an intermittent vigor, bringing himself to the edge of climax, pausing, squeezing hard until the pleasure subsided, then working himself up again. He had apparently convinced himself she was sucking him off when at one point he tapped in, *i luv it when u go deep*. The idea proved enough of a catalyst to push him over the edge. He lost all restraint, his exertions intensifying into frenzy. He threw back his shoulders, thrust up his pelvis with its chiseled *V* lines, and came with what, on the grainy surface of the screen, looked like an animal cry, spurting semen all over his torso. The tension drained from his face as he sank into post-coital bliss. Molly looked on, her smile by contrast sly like a fox. She typed *thanx* and annihilated his image.

Nick, however, was still aroused. In a state half way between desire and detachment—like someone cast in a spell—he bent Molly over the back of the sofa and took her forcefully from behind. He felt no unresponsive frustration from her this time. In fact, her submission was freer and more unfathomable than he'd ever felt it before.

Ϫ

Such experiments may have drawn them closer, but not in a way Nick found reassuring. The more he tried to meet Molly on her terms, the more exacting the cost to what he could only call his pride. Debasement seemed a requirement of attraction. The proof came from many quarters. He found it, for instance, in the world Sean shared with them: the bars and parties they went to with more frequency now. If Nick's jealousy spiked in the general promiscuity he found in them, the expectation wasn't so much that he shake the habit of realism, its sensitivity to provocation in lines blurred or crossed, as that he let the "real" fantasies excite him. His problem was only the wrong kind of jealousy, which both women made clear enough felt like a dishonest bid for sympathy, if not, worse still, resentment of their sexual freedom.

In any event, Nick had a hard time obliging with the right kind of jealousy. Its orgiastic allusion, however arousing—he was only human—struck too personal a chord. The feedback, the static of strange masochism, invariably conjured the New York that had always pushed him to the margins of a conscious exclusion, the New York that had always been, for him, his father's territory. He knew he was there now by how many of the men who ended up circling around Molly and Sean on any given night at those bars and parties resembled his father in their looks and their swagger.

He'd been putting off a talk with his father, who was also desperate to reach him to judge by the many messages he'd lately been leaving on his voice mail. Nick rarely felt like answering, but his current state of mind also begged for some kind of reckoning. It wouldn't be easy. He had next to no idea how to broach longstanding grievances without anger whipsawing back at him. His father could be formidable in his vision of the world, all the more so given his worldly success. And it didn't help that Nick had always more or less felt his place in that vision was emasculated and pathetic. At least the way to something else had always led for his father in the same direction: toward a projective male identity. Anything less fixed

Nick all over again in the condescension it seemed he'd been living with his whole life.

He'd still not settled on an approach when he did call. But it turned out not to matter. His father was in no mood for a father-and-son talk.

"Where the fuck are you?" were his first words.

That demanded a literal response. "I'm in New York, Dad."

"What are you doing there?"

"I live there now, remember?"

"No, I don't," his father groaned. "I don't remember anything. How can I? I'm beset. I'm besieged."

"What do you mean?"

"François."

"François?"

"The guy who lives next door."

"He's bothering you?"

"I told you he sneaks in to the apartment."

"Dad."

"He moves things around."

"*Dad.*"

"I'm serious, goddammit! Don't you dare try and tell me I'm imagining it. Fuck you, if you think I'm imagining it. He does it just to mess with my head."

"How do you know?"

"I know!" he snapped, and, then, to the neighbor, he all but screamed: "Get out! Get out of my head, you weaselly-assed French motherfucker!!!"

"Calm down," Nick said, concerned now. "It's all right. The man is not in your head."

"I'm telling you he's obsessed with me."

"Is Julie there?"

"She took Emmanuele to see her mother. He knows that, too. He knows when they're gone. He knows how hard it is for me to be alone. And every time I go out, he comes in. I know he does. He leaves things just slightly out of place, just slightly changed."

Hoping a different topic would settle his father down, Nick said, "I take it you saw Haley."

"With her French pimp, yeah."

"He was a friend, dad."

"He knocked her up anyway."

"What?"

"They're all pimps," his father sneered. "This country's one big fucking whorehouse. They gender everything. Haven't you ever wondered about that? About why they do it?"

"Dad," he said, wanting him to focus now. "Haley's pregnant?"

"Yes."

"How do you know?"

"It was obvious," he said. "She'd gained weight, her tits were huge, she looked like she'd just vomited. I think she *did* vomit in my toilet."

That would explain her pallid face on Skype. She hadn't been herself at all. "What was the guy like?"

"Like every Frenchman," his father said. "He wanted to get inside my head. I wouldn't let him, though. No fucking way. I wouldn't give the sonofabitch that satisfaction."

"Are you taking your drugs?"

"François changes the pills on me! He mixes them up so I don't know which is which. I'm always taking the wrong ones at the wrong times, and they don't work anymore. I just get worse. I can't believe this," he muttered to himself. "A fucking French mailman is persecuting me."

Nick presumed that was what his neighbor did for a living.

"He's like a mole."

"You–"

"I don't want to be what you want me to be anymore!" he railed at François or the universe.

"Talk to me, dad."

"That's what he wants. He wants what I am to him. He wants inside my head the way I'm inside his. That's why he sneaks in here. He pretends to be me. He puts on my shoes. He shaves with my razor. He eats my bread at my fucking dinner table. He imagines fucking my wife."

"Dad."

"I try to keep him out. I change the locks on the doors. I put locks on the windows. Even the balcony has a lock on it now."

"Then he couldn't possibly get in—"

"Yes, he can."

"How?"

"He comes through the walls."

Nick's heart stopped. His father meant that in a way he'd never heard from him, or anyone, before.

"Where's Julie?" he asked, shaken.

"In the south somewhere."

"When's she coming back?"

"Wednesday."

Three days away.

"Does she have a cell phone?"

"It's not working," his father told him. "She's in a remote place. Ardennes or Ardèche. Her mother's on a project."

Her mother, Nick recalled, was an archeologist.

"Do you have a phone number for her?"

"It's in my address book, which I can't fucking find!"

"What's her mom's name again?"

"Jeanne."

"Breillat?"

Julie's name.

"No. She married somebody else. Bernard something or other."

"I want you to look for that address book, Dad."

"It's not here. François took it. I'm sure he uses it for the names, so he can drop them in the mail room."

"Will you try for me?"

"I've *been* trying."

"Is there a friend you can call?"

"No one wants to see me like this. I don't want anybody to see me. I don't have friends anyway—not here. Who's friends with anybody here? There's no one home in these people. They have no fucking idea what friendship means. They're talking heads."

"I know you have friends."

"My life is Julie and Emmanuele. That's it. *C'est tout.* They're the only ones I'm close to—the only ones who calm me down. Without them, I'm lost."

Sadly, this sounded more lucid. "Why didn't you go with them?"

"Julie didn't want me there."

Nick could see why. He could also see the time was approaching when his father couldn't be left alone like this. He'd need live-in care. Dementia may not be far off.

His father seemed to guess this last thought in him when he ended the pause that followed with, "Sometimes I just want to fucking explode."

8

Not long after Molly received word that she'd been accepted into the graduate program at NYU. The offer included a full scholarship plus living expenses for the six years they estimated it would take to complete the PhD. It came as a shock and challenged her pessimism on a lot of levels. Good fortune didn't just happen to other people. The world wasn't so parsimonious as to deny her chances for accomplishment and recognition, not to mention the means to support herself. As difficult as it might be for her, from then on she'd have to permit herself the luxury of thinking life could be had on favorable terms.

The news left Nick a little downcast. As happy as he was for her, as hopeful, too, that the challenge might extend to other things (but on that he was silent), he foresaw himself cutting an incongruous figure in her new life, as someone older who'd been through it all before and also failed at it before. It might even be that his sense of injury, together with his lack of prospects now, would hold her back. This brought him sharply up before the task of figuring out what to do with his own life—a task becoming more imperative by the day. The money from King's University was running out. He had to find a job.

He came across a possible lead through an acquaintance he'd made at a café on Ninth Avenue—an older Puerto Rican man named Gelacio. Nick had noticed him one day reading *The New York Review of Books*, and they'd struck up a conversation. Gelacio worked as a sales representative for an academic publisher. Nick remembered seeing people like him haunt the faculty hallways in his student days, approaching standoffish professors in their offices, hoping to interest them in textbooks for their classes. Gelacio warned him it was dismal work. The only good thing he could say about it was that he got to keep his own hours.

Nick saw that the job weighed on Gelacio because he admired the professors whose good graces he needed to court and who were often rude to him. He had little formal education, having grown up above his father's pawnshop just down the street—in the old Hell's Kitchen, as he put it—without any encouragement or support. He figured early on that, if learning how to read books as a professional was impossible, at least he could be around people who read books, so after high school he started working at bookstores, graduating over time from salesman to buyer. From there he progressed naturally enough to the publishing business. None of this meant he didn't read or, Nick quickly came to appreciate, understand what he read. But he was modest to a fault, considering himself an amateur who dabbled, an autodidact—"kind of a spick Jude the Obscure," he said laughingly. Nick heard, in the tenor of this remark, a notable absence of the self-pity that was all he could muster at the thought of filling Gelacio's shoes. It shamed him enough to wonder if he might, at some future point, find the moral backbone to face the downclassing that was the main fact of his life now.

With this question in mind he called Haley, intent on asking her about technical writing. It also gave him an excuse to find out in more detail what was going on with her. At first she insisted everything was fine, but after some probing she admitted that she was pregnant. The father wasn't Jean-Claude but the Tunisian boyfriend she'd mentioned before.

"What are you going to do?" he asked.

"Keep it. Raise it myself."

"Without the father?"

"I haven't told him."

"Won't he find out?"

"We don't see each other anymore," she said. "I broke it off."

"You're going to hide it from him?"

"Yes." Her laconic tone warned Nick not even to hint at the man having rights in the matter.

"How will you live?"

"I'll go back to technical writing if I have to," she said. "But first I want to finish the screenplay. Maybe I'll sell it for a million dollars and solve all my problems."

Here, too, Nick had to watch his words.

"You're taking a big step, Haley."

"Don't sound so bloody discouraging!"

His silence was enough for her to hear her own touchiness.

"I'm sorry," she said. "I'm not myself."

"How do you feel?"

"Awful. The nausea is constant, and I have the worst cramps. I've never experienced pain like this."

"Do you see a doctor? Do you have what you need?"

"Yes."

"Are your housemates supportive?"

She groaned. "I haven't told them about it. We don't really get along."

"Why not?"

"Everybody's so serious. Motherhood doesn't fit the *esprit de corps*."

"Maybe you should move."

"I can't. I have no money."

"Go home then. Rely on your parents for a while."

"No," she said emphatically. "I haven't told them yet either. My dad would kill me."

Nick knew vaguely of her father that he was a conservative man, a Republican and also a fervent Christian, given to harsh judgments that often had Haley tied in knots.

"I want the kid to be born in France anyway," she said. "I want it to have French citizenship."

"At least ask them for help."

"No."

"But—"

"Drop it, Nick. There's nothing to worry about. I'm good where I'm at."

It sounded like she was trying to convince herself of this, but he decided, nonetheless, to drop it. He asked instead about those contacts in software companies.

ϗ

He and Molly spent an afternoon in Greenwich Village. This time they visited the various buildings that comprised the NYU campus, her earlier reluctance gone. The sun was shining as it hadn't in weeks. Washington Square Park buzzed with activity. There was a noisy demonstration against the Israeli occupation of Palestine taking place under the Arch. Two different jazz trios performed on the walkways. Students read on benches beside prim old ladies in babushkas or homeless men clutching their meager possessions. Molly took it all in with a new relish, wanting to draw the day out as long as it would go.

That evening they met Sean at a wine bar off Second Avenue. The cozy interior was wood paneled with rough-hewn beams overhead. A gas fire burned in a stone hearth near the table where Sean sat flipping through an issue of *Vogue*. She could have been in the magazine the way she looked: her shoulders bare in a silk-embroidered basque, her blonde hair braided into an intricate coif, and an immaculate makeup that drew out her sculpted features to advantage. A scent of perfume filled the air as they sat down.

"I've taken the liberty of ordering the wine," she told them, filling their glasses. "I just quit my job, so I'm celebrating."

"Is that why the new hairdo?" asked Molly.

"And the earrings." She turned her head to show them off: two oval sapphires dangling from silver chains. "You like?"

"Very classy."

"I've been coveting them at Bloomingdale's for months. I thought them a fitting way to end my tenure there."

"What do you think?" Molly asked Nick.

"They match your eyes."

This was too flatly conveyed for Sean's taste. She worried the edge of her mouth with her tongue in the pause that followed. . . reading his thoughts, Nick presumed. They had in fact drifted to what she was going to do without a job.

"Yeah," she drawled. "And all I gotta do to pay for them is fuck a few extra bankers this month!"

"Easy!" Nick couldn't help blurting out.

Molly glared at him.

"Nick doesn't approve of my career choice," Sean coolly observed.

"I didn't say that."

"He thinks I should keep folding clothes for twelve dollars an hour."

"No, I don't."

"To him I'm a working girl, his girl Friday, Rosie the Riveter—"

"Come on," he protested. It's not true. I think you should be designing clothes, or modeling them, that's all. You're a talented person. You should be aiming high."

She relented in the suspicion that her sarcasm revealed more than she wanted it to. Nick saw the career choice wasn't as easy for her as she pretended. For a second she let mixed feelings show through the usual bluff confidence.

"I don't disapprove," he said. "I don't understand choosing to be an escort, I'll say that."

"What's so hard to understand?! The part about three-thousand-dollar weekends or the part about eight hundred dollars for forty hours of wage slavery?"

"I don't understand how you combine being a social subject and a sexual object like that."

"I don't 'combine' anything," she scoffed. "It was done for me a long time ago. I just work with what's there."

"Why not work against it?"

"For twelve dollars an hour?!"

"That's not what I mean."

"Besides, I don't see much difference," she said. "At Bloomingdale's I wear the same clothes, I put on the same makeup, I wax the same skin, and I exert the same feminine charm. The only difference is I don't fuck anybody. Plus, it's no fun."

"Fucking bankers is fun?"

"For money, yeah."

The ambiguity in that hung in the air for all of them. Sean decided she didn't mind keeping it that way. She waited to see how Nick was going to avoid admitting he had a problem with both connotations. To tell the truth, he did feel a little checked.

"Nick's a purist," Molly interposed. "He doesn't accept the world as it is."

"Do you?!"

"I accept that I'm in it."

He felt a wrench of anger. Why should he accept that he was "in" the world, he wanted to rail at her, when the world had so completely locked him out—so completely it threatened a basic dignity, a basic feeling of his own existence? How dare she expect him to absorb this threat of ghostliness without complaint, without a fight! He thought she'd understood, having gone through so much with him, just how deep the alienation ran. It hurt to feel she wasn't—perhaps she'd never been—quite as much of an ally as he'd thought.

They hadn't really known each other in Auckland. That much was clear by now. He could only wonder what was going through his mind when he put so much at risk with her. The idea of them both as up against that horrible school must have been just another fantasy. Perhaps it even involved that transgressive law he'd glimpsed in Sarah Hayes, the Human Resources director. Had Molly seen (or fucked) his father in him after all? he wondered. Worse, had he invited her to it? Had he counted on a glamor like his father's when he crossed the line with her—and not to take his pleasure, or liberty, which his father would at least have approved, but to bring his own stupid masochism covertly into the picture? Was this a reason for him to have refrained, played by the rules, held on in the job even if it offered only another kind of masochism? Or had he missed what else the job offered simply because masochism was all he could see?

Bewildered by these inklings of a deeper error into which he'd fallen, he also saw no way to frame a response that wouldn't sound petulant. "I'm not judging anybody, okay?" he said. "I just don't see why the alternative has to be so stark. Either prostitution is wonderful or I'm a prude. Something has to be wrong with that."

"I didn't say you were a prude," said Molly.

"A purist is next door to a puritan. You both think I'm sexually repressed or, worse, trying to repress you. I limit your freedom when it bothers me to hear you want the same thing bankers want."

"That's not what bothers you," said Sean.

"No?"

"I don't feel like a victim, and you don't understand that because you don't know how to see me any other way."

"I'm saying don't let others treat you as a sexual object!"

"Women are victims in your mind," she continued, not hearing this at all. "It bothers you that I resist fear."

"In the boardroom at least," Nick cracked.

"I bet in the bedroom, too."

"I'm sure you're a real superhero there."

"If it feels good," she declared, "my motto is, 'fuck it.'"

⅄

They moved on to more neutral topics, going through the bottle of wine and a few appetizers. Later they headed for a cellar bar where Sean knew they would be able to play pool. On arriving, both women worked into the mix of people at the table, located near the door. By the time Nick had come back with the first round of beers, they'd made fast friends of total strangers.

Sean played the first game and won in short order. After that they teamed up, making it their goal to hold the table against all comers. They managed to do it—both of them were pretty good. As the night progressed, and the beer flowed, they grew more and more animated, laughing, high-fiving, yelling at errant balls, cheering at a well-executed shot. Nick could see they were looking for the camaraderie of a pub. They wanted to feel at home.

He fought with the suspicion that their pleasure came at his expense. It seemed as though they were punishing him for his earlier peevishness. He might have been wrong, but then it didn't much matter. Even right, he betrayed a childish need for their attention that could only keep him quiet. He took it that this was what the world meant by him accepting his own ghostliness with a better grace.

He stood off to the side, trying to stay bemused but gradually losing the battle with discomfort and distance. It grew still harder when Molly and Sean lost to two men, both the type Nick had such trouble separating from his father: rakish, cocksure, good at innuendo. Their victory prompted vigorous calls from Molly and Sean for a rematch; but as the two men were better at pool, they decided to split the teams instead. From then on Nick had to notice all the blurred or crossed lines. He watched Molly reconnoiter with her partner, drawing close, tipping her head to hear, letting her hair graze his cheek. An impressive shot on her part had them clasped in a tight embrace. The man lingered in it longer than he should. . .or a boyfriend should let him. Nick's exasperation became acute in a break between games, when he found himself observing the backs of both men obscure the two women against an opposite wall. All he could see of them were their gesticulating hands.

He went outside to cool his head with a cigarette. He stood on the sidewalk beside other refugees from the bar, mentally rehearsing the different things he might say to Molly the next time she managed to remember he was there. He hadn't gotten too far in this pointless exercise, however, when a fight broke out between the two men standing next to him. Nick had to shy away to keep from getting hit. It startled him because they had seemed to be friends. They'd come from the bar together. But a quarrel had quickly escalated; as far as Nick could tell it concerned a woman over whom both felt a proprietary right.

He joined with a couple of passersby to break them up. In the process a thrown elbow landed at his mouth, giving him a fat lip. He wanted to slug someone then, too, and the scene might have turned into a melee if the bar's floor manager, a large black man unused to taking shit, hadn't shown up and stood everybody down with a menacing glare. He shunted the instigators off in opposite directions, both continuing to hurl invective at each other as they melted into the night. The manager ordered everyone else to disperse.

Only Nick stayed behind. He turned toward the stairs and glanced through a basement window at the two men still pinning Molly and Sean to that wall. Nothing changed there. He decided it would be a bad idea for him to go back down. With his own feeling of proprietary right strangely inflamed, he might not be able to avoid making a scene himself. Thinking to take a short walk to settle his nerves, he crossed the street and went up the block. But as he advanced it became clear he wasn't going back. Everything about the bar repulsed him. The only thing he wanted was escape and the night.

He headed west on Fourteenth Street, crossing Union Square to thread the long diagonal of Broadway. In the distance Times Square resembled a huge cave filled with hectic light. It was the most direct route back to Hell's Kitchen, but as he drew closer the thought of waiting for Molly to come home, or not to come home, held no appeal. At Herald Square he saw the little blue sign for a PATH train station. On a sudden impulse he descended the stairs, bought a ticket, and boarded a waiting car. The aim seemed to be a visit to the neighborhood in Hoboken where he'd lived as a teenager, although why he couldn't say. Misgiving grew in him with each stop. By the time he reached the ferry terminal on the other side of the river, he resolved to go back. But as the wait for a returning train stretched, he changed his mind yet again. He exited to the waterfront and followed the river north, just as he used to do.

He had no interest in seeing the house he shared with his mother, located beyond a soccer field and an adjacent park. Instead he mounted a hill to the Stevens Tech campus and found a bench where he used to sit now and then, on a bluff overlooking the river.

From there he could see the Manhattan skyline, alluding from across the dark expanse of water to the salutary perspective it had once afforded him. With its help he tried to untangle knotted feelings. He was angry at Molly, that was clear, hurt by what seemed her callous neglect, and jealous of those other men, not to mention of Sean's influence on her. He was, moreover, in the midst of a disastrous collapse in his sexual confidence. It made him so tentative. He second-guessed everything. Did he have a right to be angry or was he overreacting? Had Molly hurt his feelings or was he blaming her for a pain he'd brought on himself? Was it honor or vanity that had been offended in the bar? Unable to decide either way, he reproached both his desire to be part of Molly's life and this sacrificial retreat from it. Yet if both were unacceptable, he reflected, what else could he do? If he stayed without desire, would he not leave without self-pity? That seemed to be more or less what she wanted: a man who stayed with no other motive than the one for leaving.

He might have called such a creature mythical, and her desire for one perverse, if it wasn't in fact easy to explain. Such creatures existed everywhere. They were known, otherwise, as young men. Molly wanted to be with people her own age. Nothing could be more natural, he reminded himself. The one standing in the way here was him. He should step aside, and he should do it gracefully, like the mature person he was in the situation, blaming no one.

He could see that would be difficult. Molly herself would resist it. Even if she wanted out of the relationship, the hint of still more sacrifice on his part would suggest less wisdom or bigness than, again, simple cowardice. He'd be running from the challenge of a desire that was only ever risky, dangerous even. He should welcome this challenge, he heard her say, not insist on some impossible harmony for love to work. He thought he had. He thought they shared a feeling for the right way to live with uncertainty, against the grain of formulas and conventions. Wasn't that what had drawn them together in the first place? Or was it, too, another fantasy, another error into which he'd fallen?

A terrible verdict formed in his mind then: he'd stopped living with any sort of passion. Maybe he'd never started living with it. Indeed, the reproach of pleasure denied seemed all he'd ever known—spoken, naturally, in his father's voice. He'd worked out good reasons for why he shouldn't listen to that voice: pleasure demanded was little more than pleasure made into the hard, cold, positive thing of circulation and exchange, and accepting it really meant adjusting to a world without pleasure. He'd always thought refusing to adjust this way still put him somewhere on the side of passion.

Now, though, he wasn't sure. What he considered refusal might have been too stark, too black-and-white a position for him, or anyone, to take in this day and age. It presumed, as Molly had intimated, a point outside the commodified world that no one could really occupy except at the price of self-deception. There was only the commodified world, and as he'd seen too many times to need reminding, its formulas and conventions were not negotiable. They had to be taken up, played with, mocked or satirized in the performative style Sean had learned along with her sexual politics. He hadn't much evidence of the difference that style made even before performance started looking like a fun way to fuck bankers, but he agreed that something like its dissident right of self-fashioning fit the times better than his refusal, or his *pudeur*. It had going for it a playfulness, a theatricality, that he lacked, and maybe lacked by temperament. Sean and Molly were right to sense the limitation in this—especially now, he thought with a sharp pang of regret on that bench, wrapped tight in his coat against the cold. It brought him up before a painful fact. However deep the break with passion might or might not be in him, he wasn't handling his life well at all. Too much adversity in the commodified world was hardening his heart; too much frustration with its formulas and conventions was making him bitter.

He went on to ask himself if he blamed women generally for this change, or revelation, of his character. He did sometimes think of them as victims, with his mother's unhappy life a distant point of reference. At bottom women were tragic figures to him. The autonomy they wanted just never seemed in reach. He supposed Sean was right to mistrust this presumption in him, too. She hadn't been the first. Some had suspected even the sympathy it implied of a backhanded disdain. And those who didn't, those who trusted that sympathy, could still wonder at the underlying tone he took from his mother. Either they judged it in the same manner his father did, as inhibition and fear, or they suspected Nick had so distorted in appropriating it that even his mother wouldn't recognize the man who based so much of himself on fidelity to her.

This sent him rummaging through the past, not so much for reminders of the bond he had with her—its sinew of fierce and abiding love that nothing would ever be able to cut—as for the moments of tension in which that tonal distortion might have its source. They hadn't always gotten along in the house set back there in the darkness behind him. Even when they did, he'd had her solitary nature to deal with. He lived ambivalently enough on its edges, attuning his loneliness to hers but also frustrated by what he could scarcely admit was more diffidence than he needed. She could go on for too long engrossed in a book or in her own thoughts, and while it was never mean, it could be too inward and aloof. She knew it, but in a fashion mostly despairing of any change that suited him. She could only give so much and still remain herself. But while he accepted that, it didn't feel like she gave enough, and to his unmet needs he responded, for the most part, with shame.

A memory from even further back in time came to him. About seven years old, he sat on that orange suede sofa in the Morningside

Heights apartment. Wrapped in a pink mohair blanket that felt scratchy to the touch, he couldn't concentrate on the TV in front of him because he knew his mother was distraught. It was late and his father hadn't come home, maybe one of the first times he didn't. The implications were too overwhelming for her even to pretend to hide her feelings, and as he watched her move restlessly around the apartment, something of her pain passed to him. Tears sprang into his eyes, despite his best efforts to suppress them. This confused her. It made a claim on her attention she hadn't the wherewithal to meet. It called for candor more than comfort. When she addressed him it was with a tone that, though it just missed being cold, lacked any trace of condescension. It suggested an equality in suffering that was what he would always remember about it. She said, "Nick, promise me you will never do this to another person."

Her words felt as present to him now as they ever did. They seemed to address him through all the intervening years, through the changes that buried not only her but that whole countercultural era of the '70s he associated with her, and which that equality in suffering anchored in his heart. Now, though, he detected another note in them: a suspicion that his need of her would only feed into inevitable betrayal. She spoke not just as a mother but as a woman. He wasn't just a son but a man in the making. This difference, or this schism, became part of the pain she communicated to him. It placed him on the other side of trust; it linked him to the specter of heartless self-assertion that had appeared in the apartment with his father's absence. Love was caught impossibly in a transitive relation between allegiance and defection. It still was for Nick. He'd been confusing one with the other ever since. In fact he'd done it again tonight, leaving Molly at the bar for this place of detached reflection and with a feeling he'd omitted from the memory until that very moment: reproach of his mother for making him promise.

⚔

He returned to the apartment around three a.m., hoping to find Molly there. As he guessed, no one was home. She'd probably decided to stay the night at Sean's. The possibility that the relationship was already over threw him into a tailspin. He thought to head back to the East Village, but fear of what he might find, or how Molly might feel about him checking up on her, dissuaded him. Instead, he broke open a bottle of scotch that Dylan had left behind in a cupboard.

He waited stupidly for the phone to ring or the bolt in the door to catch, growing more and more flustered. He kept imagining Molly with one (or both) of those men, giving in to a desire he couldn't share or meet, acting out her "real" fantasies—anything was possible. He tried to dismiss such lurid fears, but his heart thumped very distinctly against his chest, ache sweated out in him, and despondence swayed the will. Nothing seemed more real. The pure form of human fallibility was flesh dissolving in prismatic obsession, the body caught in the act of its own falling.

He soon became aware that he wasn't alone in the apartment: through the window and across the courtyard he could see the old man who sat most nights watching TV in his living room. Nick had noticed him from time to time at the café on Ninth Avenue. A tall, slender retiree of some kind, he would sit by himself on a stool at a counter that faced the street, huddled in a worn coat and cupping his coffee with both hands. The stoic look in his eyes, combined with a fastidious manner, suggested a sensitivity that hadn't made life easy for him at all.

In the torpor to which Nick had by then reduced himself with the scotch, he could hardly avoid taking the old man as a warning for his own future. He had only to extrapolate from the present to see how the change was going to play out. One by one the lights would turn off in his life. Old consolations would cease to work. Writing and even reading would lose any connection to the world. The effort of meeting other people's conditions and standards would become all but impossible to bear. He already didn't know how much more failure he could take before he concluded that no one related to anybody. The only recourse from the loneliness that followed would be the cold comforts offered by TV and internet, which would slowly pass into the body no less than the mind, petrifying social and sexual impulses, if not, finally, simple sensations. From then on he'd have to live the way he imagined most people did in this world: neutralized of spirit, unable to be or do anything completely, like a man in a cage designed so that he could neither sit nor stand up. He remembered hearing somewhere that that was a technique used in torture.

He kept telling himself these thoughts had no actual traction. They were a delirium talking, and they'd pass away in time, yield to a sober view of things that, whatever it afforded, wouldn't be what he assumed it was now. But he also had to fight with their deadly plausibility in his mind. He had to argue with a sharp, berating voice that insisted every exit was closed, every bid for hope or care a lie folding him back into the same resignation, the same sad opacity of a private life centered on nothing but itself.

He finally drifted off as the first light of day welled blue on the windowsill, but even in sleep he found no relief. He dreamed he went looking for Molly at a party in a maze-like warehouse. In each room he met people from different phases of his life: New York, Providence, Paris, LA. He asked Carson, of all people, if she'd seen her, and with a broad smile that could have meant anything at all, she pointed to a red sofa below a yellow neon sign that said in blinking letters "The Last Man." There he found Molly seated on the lap of a rakish boy. He had his arms all the way up her shirt, yellow like the sign, and he was very pleasurably fondling her breasts. Both paused on seeing him; they gazed back with a curious gleam in their eyes, wondering if they should stop. But they decided nothing so insignificant as his feelings should keep them from gratifying their own and went on with what they were doing, fully aware of the pain it caused him. They even took satisfaction in it.

Nick bolted awake from this scene of gratuitous cruelty some hours later, feeling his cell phone vibrate in his pocket. He wriggled off the sofa and fished it out, thinking it might be Molly. It wasn't.

"Hello."

"Hi Nick."

He didn't recognize the voice: a woman, with an accent. His head throbbed.

"It's Julie."

He rubbed his face, trying to bring himself back to the present. He winced on touching the sore lip.

"Yes, of course," he said. "Julie. How are you?"

He heard crying through the line.

"Not good."

"Is something wrong?"

"Evan's dead, Nick."

All vagaries of thought, pain, and dream went rushing out of his head.

"He killed himself," she said. "Or it was an accident. I don't know. He left no note."

He sat slowly down again.

"He went over the balcony and fell to the sidewalk."

His eyes snapped shut. In the phosphene he saw his father in strobe-like flashes crash brutally against the pavement.

"He took Emmanuele to school this morning. He seemed fine. I had no reason to think anything was wrong."

"He threatened that before."

"I know. I never took it seriously."

"Me neither."

Julie's grief overcame her. "I'm sorry. It's too much. I can't talk anymore."

"Of course."

"I wanted you to hear it from me first."

"Yes," he said. "Thanks, Julie."

9

He remained where he was on that sofa for he didn't know how long, too stunned to think or feel, his heart squeezed tight like a fist. The apartment was silent except for the compressor humming in the refrigerator and a faint sound of someone practicing scales on a violin higher up in one of the adjacent buildings. A gray afternoon light filled the courtyard. The air in the room had a pressure that suggested rain. It seemed the very atoms might break like storm clouds. That he would be able to feel. In the very fabric of time and space was conflagration.

He reached for a cigarette and saw that he was out. He'd been smoking one after the other all night. He rose and went to the door, descending automatically down the stairs to the bodega on the corner, returning with a new pack and a cup of coffee. Again he sat on the sofa, acknowledging now, as one reason for his state of mind, a fear so intense it froze everything else out, or up. He wondered how long it would last, or if he knew anyone who might be able to help him melt the ice. The thought that it might never melt only added to his fear.

He remembered that Dylan owned one of his father's movies, not Nick's favorite but much acclaimed by critics. In it, his father played an inmate in a prison for the criminally insane, and he gave to the role a menace impressive enough to warrant his only Oscar nomination. Nick retrieved it from the shelves and put it in the DVD player. The story concerned a rebellion his father had fomented against an authoritarian warden. As the violence escalated on both sides, the plot became convoluted and surreal. Slowly the audience learns that much of the action takes place in his father's head and that he'd once been a warden confronting a similar rebellion, with means so brutal he ends up crossing a line into mass murder. The other warden turns out to be a psychiatrist who, like Dr. Caligari, is trying to make him understand what had really happened.

The movie came out a few years after his parents' divorce, and Nick watched it with an eye to the man his father was then. It gave him little to go on. His father wore a vicious scar down the side of his face and was lit to look like a maniac in nearly every shot. It might as well have been a stranger on the screen, and that, Nick supposed, was the evidence he sought of the man he'd been: immersed in his roles, way out in a life that included his son only incidentally. Evan came through for him rather in the stylized morality tale, which set up mirror relations between law and crime that delivered, with a small dose of profundity, exactly the image of power that powerful people had. It made no difference that, as a study in self-deception, it asked of us that we reflect upon radical evil. All Nick saw confirmed in the supercharged naturalism were beliefs and rationalizations his father had peddled to him his whole life. The more he watched, the cooler he became. The experiment in resensitization wasn't working. About midway through the movie, he turned it off.

The apartment proved too confining then, and he went into the light rain that had begun to fall, fighting the crowds up Eighth Avenue to Columbus Circle. On the way he fancied he could see his own reflection in the faces of the people he passed, everyone resolved in themselves and going nowhere fast. He saw nothing at all, of course, only his own disconnection, but it amounted to the same thing. He was still becoming a citizen of the world.

He entered the park and headed north, taking random turns in the networks of forking paths, under rachitic trees, in the livid grisaille of a winter dusk. He exited near the Met and walked downtown again on Fifth Avenue. Near Rockefeller Center he came upon a clothing store with a large reverse projection screen on the wall. It livestreamed blue undulating waters off Santa Monica Beach, or so a placard said. He halted amid the crowd on the broad sidewalk and stood gazing upon it. It reminded him of old frescoes. People used to call them the souls of the churches they decorated, and this, too, he decided, was a soul, or the closest thing to a soul that one was liable to find these days—a corporate soul, glassy, tranquil, blatant, vacuous.

In this reverie he heard two bleating tones from the phone in his coat pocket. He took it out and found a message from Molly: *come to seans – please.* He guessed she preferred not to call because of last night's vanishing act. That would have to be talked out in person. Perhaps she also had confessions to make. But against the pull of these thoughts he also felt a terseness in her words hint at a different problem. He texted back saying he'd be right there and hailed a cab for his old corner of Twelfth and A.

ϗ

When he knocked on Sean's door, he heard Molly apprehensively inquire, "Who is it?"

"Nick."

Three bolts turned and the door opened a crack. Through it he saw her retreat. He stepped into a square studio, large by East Village standards. Against the wall opposite stood a queen-size bed with the covers in disarray. To the side, a sofa and a faded leather recliner were constellated around a sheepskin rug. A flat-screen television took up one corner, tuned to another reality TV show. Clothes had been dropped here and there on the floor. Someone in the bathroom was taking a shower. Sean, he presumed.

Molly flitted with a quick birdlike motion onto the sofa, flexing her knees and hugging her legs. She avoided his look. He could see she'd been crying.

Sensing the delicacy of the moment, he eased himself into the recliner before gently asking, "What's the matter?"

She struggled to get her words out. Her thoughts were scattered. "I woke up an hour ago. I didn't have any clothes on. Neither did Sean."

"Uh-huh."

"We don't know how we got that way," she said. "Neither of us remembers falling asleep."

He made the best of this he could. "When did you get home?"

"I'm not sure. Late. We brought these guys." She looked at him for the first time, to see if he knew what guys she meant. He gave no sign, but his already heavy heart sank. "We were drunk, and we'd done coke, so they offered to walk us home. On the way they talked about more drinks. We stopped at a store, and they bought some beer."

She waited for a reaction. He could tell she feared it might be angry, even violent. Not knowing what to say, he wedged his hands between his thighs and stared at the television.

"I didn't want them to come," she said. "I told Sean I didn't think it was a good idea. But she said not to worry. She knew how to handle them."

"What were they imagining would happen?"

"She told them we had boyfriends, and they said that was okay. They promised it would just be drinks."

"Was it?"

"We sat right here talking, and everything seemed normal."

Her lip curled and her jaw started sliding back and forth. Tears pressed into her eyes. "But I don't remember what happened next. I don't remember passing out. I don't remember when they left. Everything's a blank until I woke up next to Sean."

"They drugged you?"

"They could've put something in our beers."

Why they would have done that came into sudden devastating relief. "They sexually assaulted you?"

She broke down altogether. "I can't tell. I feel sore down there. I have a bruise on my neck. It might be a hickey."

He sprang to his feet, in a panic himself now. "You have to see a doctor," he said, mentally rehearsing the steps that would have to be taken for that to happen. "Get your shoes on. You'll need a coat. It's raining."

"We have to wait for Sean."

At that point she emerged from the bathroom, wrapped in a towel. She looked at them through a pair of thick-lensed glasses, dramatically changed from her glamorous self. In a cold fury she announced, "I'm bleeding."

⅄

Nick took them to the NYU medical center on First Avenue. They had trouble with the receptionist in the urgent care ward. Because neither had insurance she wouldn't let them see a doctor unless they paid a whopping $4,000 for two rape kits. Nick handed her a credit card—both women having been relieved of their wallets as well.

They were quickly ushered in for tests and consultations. Nick waited in the lobby. Before long two police officers showed up and went inside, he guessed to make some kind of report.

Molly came out first a while later. Without a word she sat in the chair next to him.

"Well?"

"I was raped," she said flatly. "They left no incriminating traces. They might have used condoms. The doctor gave me a morning-after pill, just in case."

They sat in silence, feeling the space between them drop into a gulf of awful mistrust. Neither had any idea how to close or cross it, Nick most of all. Molly slowly began to sense as much. He could see her mistaking his exhaustion for coldness, his bewilderment for judgment.

"Are you mad?"

He shook his head. "I'm sorry I left the bar, that's all. Very, very sorry."

She took that in for a beat before saying, "I wasn't ever going to speak to you again."

"I wouldn't blame you."

"Why did you go?!"

"I was feeling left out. It's an old feeling. I tried to run from it, but I just ran into it. Pain makes me self-centered."

"At least you could have let me know," she said. "That would have made a difference."

His eyes snapped shut, just as they had earlier in the day on the phone with Julie. He drew a hand to his face. Molly mistook this gesture, too. She turned to him, not understanding why he was the one in need of comfort. Moments later she turned back again. The tension went out of her body. The space between them reasserted itself. But as she directed her gaze away, events shifted into a more definite pattern in her mind.

"I knew how you were feeling," she admitted. "I knew the effect it had on you, me playing pool with those guys. I did it anyway. I didn't want to be responsible for your pain."

"You're not."

"I wasn't going to let you ruin the chance for pleasure, just because you can't feel it."

His thoughts went to the many reasons why that chance might have no chance in this world, or why the feeling for it might die in a person.

"I was mad," she went on. "I've always been mad. I see that now. I'm mad at the whole stupid obscene male world. All it makes me want to do is sit alone in a dark room and watch TV. Why should I care? I'm nothing in it. Nothing at all. Just a hole for you to fuck."

She shot him a glance, worried how that might land. He remained with his face covered, his eyes closed.

"I'm sorry," she said. "I didn't mean that. I know you're not like the others. I take things out on you because you're the one who's there. I suppose that's not fair."

He slumped further in his chair.

"You ask something of me I'm not sure I can give."

He saw two distinct choices for what she thought he might be asking of her, and he couldn't tell if even she knew which it was. But her next words threw the emphasis more decidedly on one side.

"It's new for me," she said, "not to fantasize about the hateful other."

This acknowledgement fairly blazed into the darkness of Nick's mind. In its bright light he saw his life like a kaleidoscope make one fateful turn, its parts dividing, sliding, and overlapping much as he did for Molly with the hateful other, confusing figure and ground, attraction and repulsion, friend and foe. It also brought into view his hateful other. As he put himself in Molly's place, sympathy shifting with more turns of the kaleidoscope, he once again saw his father fall from the balcony. He saw the mass of his body crushed on the pavement. He saw it receive in return for its vitality a brute force that broke his whole frame, emptying the space in his blue eyes—Nick's eyes, the one clear trait they shared.

All at once he felt his situation horribly crumble. The grief that had proven so inaccessible to him all day now broke through, building in a crescendo that soon became more than he could bear. It erupted in a weird strangled cry, more noise than pitch, and fragmented into an uncontrollable sobbing. Unstrung, ashamed, utterly bereft, he threw himself on an astonished Molly, burying that cry with his face in her shoulder and clinging to her with all his strength.

10

Molly stayed with Sean over the next few days. Test results showed no evidence of drugs typically used to assist in sexual assault, but that wasn't surprising: they were designed to leave the system quickly. There were no signs of AIDS or other STDs. Both of them could rest easy about that. A deeper sense of violation, of course, would prove just as much a disease, one no treatment would be able to cure. It didn't help that the authorities were unable to ascertain who the two men might be. They had a single clue to go on: at least one had been in the military. But after many hours' perusal of photographs taken from government databases, it became apparent that the field of suspects was impossibly large. Efforts would continue to be made, but no one thought the chances good. Time would close up on the event and leave no trace beyond the shock of a gross injustice.

Molly's mother arranged a flight home as soon as she learned of what happened. Molly, in her current state, wasn't sure if she wanted to start school in the fall. New York had become a hostile place to her. Nick hoped her feelings would change, but he could offer no reasons why they should. The city felt hostile to him, too. It bore little relation to the place he'd always called home, the place he loved for its exciting and sociable character. Life wasn't happening on the streets anymore; it was up above, in the lofts and penthouses of the very rich, hidden from view. There really was something obscene about New York now.

He found a kind of proof for this in that café on Ninth Avenue. It was closing its doors in a week's time, driven out of business by high rent. Soon it would be a bar like so many others in Hell's Kitchen, called Dillinger's. The clientele would be the bond traders on Sixth Avenue, with their imitators.

Gelacio told him the news. Nick ran into him there one morning. To his surprise, the man had both hands in casts laid on the table in front of him, drinking his coffee through a straw. A few days before he'd taken part in a political action connected with a boycott of Chase Manhattan Bank. When he tried, along with a few dozen others, to close out his checking account at a midtown branch, the police arrested everyone in sight. While he did nothing to resist, having been specially trained for the occasion to go limp when accosted, officers nevertheless wrestled him to the ground and broke both his wrists in the process of handcuffing him. He now faced a felony count of "obstructing public space in front of a bank."

"The thing is they wouldn't let us in," Gelacio told him, "and they wouldn't let us stay outside either. We didn't have the right *not* to be customers. One way or the other, we were going to have to deal with JPMorgan Chase. I still haven't closed out my account."

"That's just outrageous."

Gelacio couldn't get over the broader significance of the event. "There's no public space anymore," he lamented. "Hell, there's no public anymore! The banks make sure of that—in more ways than one." He mentioned a book he'd been reading on the subject. Its thesis was that finance, a highly concentrated industry of computerized high-frequency trading, ran more or less on its own. It constructed a "shadow" economy that destroyed jobs and assets, reducing everyone to structurally dependent paupers or serfs—"dead souls." "And the state's in on it," Gelacio said. "That's the worst part. Politicians and CEOs have the same dream: to govern without people."

"I fear people have the same dream, too." Nick was thinking of those two men and their necrophiliac desire for sex with unconscious girls. It made an awful sense finally. They were picking up on, even channeling, that general hostility to the human. They were taking the cues of a power as omnipresent as it was negative—an *anti*power, volatilizing the whole of society as it trapped everyone in the speculative schemes of their plutocratic superiors. "It gets in our heads anyway."

Gelacio glumly concurred. "I guess it has to be faced. This country's had one idea its whole history, from the beginning: the free market. It's an obsession. Nothing else matters, and all things have to fit back into it, from health care to social security to war to work—"

"To love?"

"Yes, even to love. The market absorbs everything it touches, and it tries to touch everything it can. It eliminates any margin, any remainder, and any chance at something else, too."

"I wish I could accuse you of pessimism."

Gelacio laughed. "Oh, well, what is it they say? Pessimism of the intellect, optimism of the will? I'll settle for that. At least I know where I stand."

Nick wondered. At least he had no more of an idea where he stood than he ever did. Erosion in the ground, illusions of the will—he had a hard time picturing alternatives to either. But Gelacio was right in one respect, in the same respect Ozouf was right: you had to take a stand, from wherever you happened to find yourself and regardless of misgiving. Things couldn't go on in this spectralizing fashion. If his own sojourns in limbo weren't proof enough of that, he only had to look at Gelacio's broken wrists to remind him.

ϗ

Evan's death meant Nick would have to go to Paris for the funeral. He booked a flight that departed on the same day and from the same terminal as Molly. They met at Sean's place that afternoon and together took a taxi to JFK. All their former frustrations with each other had fallen away; in some respects they were closer than ever. But they had to contend with a new formality between them. That gulf of strange mistrust remained without either much wanting it to be there. Their lives were going in opposite directions now, their choices no longer exactly weighed in consideration of the other. He planned on staying in Paris for a couple of weeks, but he hadn't ruled out extending his visit, depending on what he found there. Molly very much wanted to go home. Both spoke around the possibility that this might be the last time they saw each other.

They went together through security—that ritual threshold of controlled intimacy—and Nick stayed with her at her gate until the time came to board. Neither spoke much, but building in the silences was a tenderness that had been there all along, in the background. It left them wondering how they'd let themselves forget it as much as they had. When her announcement came, they stood and held each other, across that gulf but with more fellow feeling than ever. As they drew apart again, Molly met his eyes.

"I might return in the fall, you know," she said. "I haven't decided yet."

"You should. It's too good a deal to pass up."

She nodded, hoisting her bag on her shoulder. Then she said, "It's been a disaster, hasn't it? A mind fuck on top of a mind fuck."

"Yes."

"I'm surprised one of us hasn't blown a gasket."

"I suspect we're both made of sterner stuff."

"Yeah." She wondered if he was right but saw no point in arguing. With a shrug she said, "Guess I'll be seeing you."

"We'll keep in touch."

With a nod she made off toward the gate. After a few steps she thought of something else and swung around. "You know, back in Auckland, there was a lot of pressure on me to turn on you. I never told you how much. Not just from the school, but from friends, family. I almost did. It seemed easier to see myself the way they saw me, as a victim."

He sensed more than one reason why she wanted him to hear this now. He tried his best to weigh his response in their light. "I'm glad you didn't," he said. "I don't think you were a victim."

"No. It's what other people thought. I got pretty confused about the difference, though."

"Other people are also in our heads."

"Aye."

A silence fell between them. She hesitated still. There was more to say, but words failed her. Abashed, she said what she could: "I love you, Nick."

He heard in that a tone different from what it might have been before, but genuine still. It had the color of the unsayable to it.

"I love you too, Molly."

She smiled. "Good."

With a quick wave she broke away for the podium and the agent taking tickets. He stood watching her disappear into the jet bridge . . .and, it may be, into someone he just used to know.

His flight didn't leave for another few hours, so he went to a bar and had a drink on its patio, open to the concourse. From there he could observe people as they streamed past in the usual frictionless way. The two most obvious fixed elements in view were advertisements. One, on a digital screen, said "CHASE What Matters." It showed a child running after a balloon on a green hillside. He wagered Gelacio would have a lot to say about that. The other was a poster put out by the Office of Homeland Security. Over the earnest face of an Asian woman holding a cell phone to her ear it read: "On the front lines/Stay alert and stay alive/Notice something odd or out of place?/Call or text against terror." Hating everything this vile quatrain implied about people in society—informers in a police state was more like it—and feeling more than ever both odd and out of place, he had to fight an urge to march over there and rip it down.

In Limbo

1

Haley had promised to meet him at the Charles de Gaulle airport the next morning, but on emerging from customs he didn't find her in the terminal, and there was no answer on her phone. He waited until it was clear she wouldn't be coming and headed for the RER station, from which he took a train to the Gare du Nord, near where she now lived.

At a loss for what to do, he stopped at a café in the lobby of the station. He watched people come on and off the platforms that stretched out from under the immense glass shed, fearing something was amiss. He knew Haley could be unreliable, but she was typically quicker with her excuses. He'd also sensed, when he spoke to her from New York, that she wanted very much to see him. The arrangement seemed firm in her mind. They'd planned on having lunch at a North African restaurant.

He had to meet Julie in her apartment at two. That gave him four hours to kill, and in a state of complete exhaustion. He decided to head for the restaurant, letting Haley know he'd be there when she woke up or freed herself from whatever entanglements were keeping her away.

He took the metro two stops to the Jacques Bonsergent station. Rolling his suitcase behind him, he crossed the placid green waters of the Canal Saint-Martin and walked south to a side street off the avenue Parmentier. He found the restaurant under an arcade. It faced a small plaza crowded with vegetable stalls and sandwich stands. While seated at a sidewalk table he ate couscous *méchoui*, staying awake with Turkish coffee and the diverting street life. Still no Haley.

Later he set out on foot for Julie's apartment. On the way he came upon the odd sight of a dozen or so burned scooters on the center strip of the boulevard de Belleville. It looked as though they'd been doused in gasoline and set alight. He wondered if it were vandalism or some sort of art project. The scooters had a certain stark beauty, and people passed them by without apparent concern. This brought a smile to his face. For the first time he felt really back in Paris.

He passed through a neighborhood of modern apartment complexes to the rue Julien Lacroix. Still early, he ascended the steep covered stairs in the Parc de Belleville to a platform at the top, which offered a view of the city. It was one of the more unusual parks Nick had ever come across: shaped like a crescent on the flank of a rising hill, it crammed gardens, playgrounds, tennis courts, fountains, and even a small vineyard into terraces so compressed you might not have known they were there.

He stood by a railing and looked through haze at the lone skyscraper on Montparnasse and the Eiffel Tower to the west. He had to fend off young African men who thought he might be interested in the drugs they were selling. They wouldn't take no for an answer. Something about a weary American with a suitcase made them think he could be brought around.

At two he came into the rue des Couronnes, a curving narrow street with the secluded feel of some Ménilmontant neighborhoods. The building where his father had lived for six years stood next to a corner brasserie. The brick on its exposed side was covered with graffiti as high as one could reach standing on the brasserie's tiled roof. Over its front entrance an octopus, with tiny humans, a man and a woman, caught in its tentacles, had been expressively drawn in the black-and-white tones of a nineteenth-century lithograph.

He waited for Julie to buzz him in, ignoring the spot where his father's death must have taken place, and hurried up the stairwell to the fifth floor. He hadn't thought ahead to the difficulty of staying there and contending with this macabre fact. Julie wasn't going to do it a day longer than she had to: she planned on leaving with Emmanuele to her mother's house in Tours right after the funeral. She told Nick he could have the place for as long as he wanted through the summer. Right then, though, he wondered how long that would be.

She let him into the apartment, a bright space that had been expanded to include the attic floor above. The living room and open American-style kitchen had one arched ceiling and faced the balcony with its wrought-iron rail and a view over rooftops to the park.

The wall to the adjacent bedroom had been replaced with folding French doors, so it could expand the living room when need be. A spiral staircase with mahogany treads led up to other bedrooms.

Julie had lived in the apartment for years before she met Evan. She wasn't sure what she would do with it now. "Sell it, I suppose," she said when asked. "Start over somewhere else."

As they sat on opposite sofas, she pulled up her feet and crossed her legs at the ankles, arching her back. An athletic, muscular woman, she could make her body do things Nick had never seen in anyone else. As a kid she'd trained to be a gymnast, aspiring for a spot on the French Olympic team. But she lacked suppleness despite her impressive flexibility. Tension tended to show. She drew in her breath and tried for a relaxation he could tell she needed.

"How are you holding up?" he asked.

"As well as can be expected. There's been so much to arrange I haven't had time to think of anything else. Death is a lot of work—especially when it's Evan who dies."

This hinted at older and deeper difficulties that she left for him to imagine. As long as they'd known each other there was a tacit understanding between them about his father's character. In the beginning Nick would try, in so many words, to warn her about his unreliability, his violent swings of mood, his willingness to lie. No matter how clear about these vices she might have been, nothing could prepare her for their full-spectrum dominance in daily life. She knew how to defend herself, how also to insist on her vision of right and wrong through the distortions to which Evan would invariably submit it. But intimacy with him could only be a struggle, and a lonely one at that, if you didn't have some corroboration from others who'd wagered as much emotionally as you did in it. That's what she ended up finding with Nick. They were like veterans of a foreign war. Their intimacy consisted in the looks, starts, and nods of a secret recognition.

"How's Emmanuele?"

"Fine. She bounces back. Of course, I'm not always sure what's going on underneath. She's good at hiding her feelings. She wants to be an actress."

They laughed at the drop in enthusiasm both felt at this prospect.

"I'm not too worried," she said. "She's a smart kid."

They sat in silence for a moment. Nick's thoughts stayed with Emmanuele. He'd really be meeting her for the first time. It struck him as an injustice that he hadn't taken more of an interest in her. She was his sister, after all. His habits as an only child had prevented him from thinking of her that way. He made a mental promise to change this in the future.

Julie, meanwhile, grew solemn, reflecting on the various practicalities with which she had to contend. One, in particular, involved topics she knew would be indelicate to broach.

"Evan left a will," she said. "I suppose you were wondering about that. It includes a trust fund set up in Emmanuele's name."

"Of course."

"And it stipulates dividing his remaining assets between the two of us."

"Okay."

"I'm afraid there isn't a lot there to divide. You know how Evan was with money." She braced herself for the next disclosure. "All told, and after expenses for the funeral and some miscellaneous debts, it comes to about eighty thousand euros."

"That's fine," Nick said with a fixed smile. He'd run through the money from King's University now and hoped it would be more. "You should subtract the five thousand he gave me last year from my half. It was only a loan."

"That won't be necessary—"

He insisted. "You should have it all, Julie, after what you've been through."

She tried to meet his suddenly evasive eyes. Both knew he meant more than just the tribulations of the last week. And behind his acknowledgement of her pain lay the whole landscape of his pain, of a life spent feeling the brunt of his father's love.

"It seems like—I don't know the word in English—*un prix de rachat, n'est-ce pas?*"

"Blood money."

"Yes."

She hovered on the edge of disclosures she wanted to make, uncertain, though, if the time was right to speak ill of the dead. Instead she glanced at a clock on the wall and said, "I should fetch Emmanuele. She's at school. Would you like to come?"

"Sure."

"You can stay and settle in, if you prefer—"

"No," he said, not wanting to be alone there right away, even though he could have fallen asleep on his feet by then. "I'd love to go."

They descended to the street and found Julie's red Citroën. She drove down the hill to the third arrondissement and parked by a school located through a porte cochère at the back of a cobblestone courtyard. Parents stood waiting for their kids to emerge from a tall double door in what turned into a charming ritual. The teachers released them two at a time, and the kids thrilled to the moment when they first saw their parents or heard their names called out. Adrenalin ran so high they couldn't keep from chasing one another around the courtyard. The parents didn't seem to mind. It afforded them time to talk among themselves.

Nick caught Emmanuele's attention right away. She took an immediate liking to him and in no time lost all shyness around him. He had more trouble, not having had much experience with children. But she disarmed him, too: she had her father's and Nick's eyes, and also Nick's straight dark hair, which fell in a long braid down her back. The family resemblance was striking.

At the car she held out against her mother's protests and maneuvered herself into the front seat with him. As they made off, she set her hands on the dashboard and perched on his lap with a weight that soon had his leg shaking. For a while they both pretended it wasn't happening, but it became too much for her to ignore. She twisted around and said, "Why do you tremble?"

Pourquoi tu trembles?

The question, or the fact of it, embarrassed him for some reason. He grew aware of Julie listening in while she drove. "I don't know," he replied. "You've gotten to be such a big girl."

She doubted this explanation but went with it, telling him about the relative heights of other students in her class. She was taller than most of the boys her age. It wasn't the only sign of her precociousness.

ᚷ

The funeral took place in the Belleville Cemetery. A leaden sky threatened rain, but it was warm out and easy to stand through the service, which was mercifully brief, if a little rote and impersonal. The grave would be covered by a stone slab with Evan's name, dates, and also profession inscribed in it—not a vault or pillar of the sort that ranged around them. Nick considered it an improbable spot for a farm boy from Nebraska, or even an actor from LA, to end up. Had his father been there next to him, he would have agreed.

Dozens of people attended, friends of Julie's but also others Evan had known in the film business. Among them Nick recognized Lou Perkins. He stood at the back by himself, looking particularly shaken. Lou had admired his father with an intensity that bordered on infatuation; less handsome, less dashing, and less talented, he came across sometimes as Evan's biggest fan. That had bothered Nick in the past, but now he found it touching. It suggested genuine emotion, or the closest thing to it that a Hollywood agent could muster. Lou seemed more given over to abandon than anyone else in the crowd, like a bereft lover.

Nick couldn't say exactly what he was feeling—numb pain, an exhausted grief that called for more than he could reach or show. He'd felt embarrassed turning down an invitation to offer a eulogy, but he didn't have it in him even to tug at the knot of his relation to his father in any public fashion. The tears, when they came, fell a little cold down his cheeks. If anything they had the memory of his mother as their source. In particular he recalled, with a wincing pain, the last time he saw her cancer-ravaged face as she lay on her deathbed in a Newark hospital. The thought that he was losing her one more time brought home to him just how much of an orphan he was now.

With that he did feel the bond connecting him to his father, through all the difficulties, across all the distance. He belonged as much as his mother to that countercultural time from which Nick had taken his tenderer emotional as well as ethical bearings. His father's values might have been different, more hedonist, less political, and they would mesh all too easily with the meaner individualism of the eighties and nineties–his heyday in Hollywood. But they made for a dissident streak that Nick had respected well enough. The only authority his father really cared about was his own, a dubious distinction for an overbearing man, to be sure, but it was all Nick often had to rely on. He'd miss its hint of iconoclasm.

He refused Julie's offer of a ride to the apartment afterward, guessing she needed time to change and pack for her trip. He also didn't mind walking back on his own. They said goodbye at the cemetery gate. Julie raised the possibility of him coming to Tours for a visit before he returned to New York. He had no definite plans, so he didn't see why not.

Lou approached as they parted. Up close he looked even worse for wear: his clothes crumpled, his hair unkempt, his face unshaven. He'd gained weight, too.

"Hello, Nick," he said, extending his hand. "How are you?"

"I'm okay, Lou."

"Do you have a smoke?"

Nick pulled two out of his pack, and they both lit up.

"I can't tell you how sorry I am," Lou said.

"Me, too."

"It went through me like a knife in the heart when I found out."

"Have you come from LA?"

Lou shook his head. "Bangkok." His eyes darted around the cemetery. He seemed distracted, even shifty. Not at all like the man Nick used to know.

"What are you doing now?" Lou asked.

"Nothing much. Probably head back to Julie's apartment at some point."

"Mind if I tag along?"

"Sure."

"The truth is I have no idea where I am. This city's a maze."

They exited the cemetery toward the rue Ménilmontant, following the long sloping groove it cut down the hillside. As they went, Nick learned that Lou had passed much of the last year and a half in Asia, mostly on islands off the coast of Thailand. Clearly he'd let himself go in that time, slipping into a rich man's limbo. Nick couldn't say it had done him much good. It seemed he'd lost his confidence in himself. He walked in halting fashion, too sensitive to the rights of other pedestrians, before whom he was perpetually giving way. Nick thought their exoticism might have had something to do with that: lots of tall black men in djellabas and Middle Eastern women in hijabs. The neighborhood was diverse in the extreme. But the change in Lou ran deeper. Nick could see him listening to himself as he spoke. His voice rose and fell with the worry that his words didn't fit the meaning he wanted to give them.

As they drew close to the rue des Couronnes, Nick suggested a drink at the nearby hookah bar. Evan would often spend time there on those mornings when Julie and Emmanuele were away. He'd smoke tobacco from the hookahs and strike up casual friendships with the men who shared their mouthpieces with him.

They sat on the front terrace of the bar, next to a small square with a Wallace fountain and in view of a broad stone stairway that led up to the church Notre-Dame-de-la-Croix. Nick persuaded Lou to try a pastis after he said he'd never had one. As they drank, blending the liqueur with the water also provided, conversation turned more animated. Lou spoke about his recent adventures with a candor that soon crossed over into confession. Apparently he'd done terrible things in Thailand, things he couldn't square with his own moral sense of himself, such as it was.

"It makes me wonder if I'm not some kind of monster," he said, "because only a monster could act on the impulses I have. Really, only a monster."

Nick suppressed a laugh. He sounded melodramatic.

"I have a hard time believing you're a monster, Lou."

"I feel like I've woken up inside a dream," he said, "and it seems like the terrible things happening in the dream are real. The dream is that they are a dream."

"I hope you're not going to tell me you've killed somebody," Nick said, still amused. But Lou was completely serious.

"It's as bad as that. Worse, in a way, because it's so mixed up with my nature, with what I've always been. I can admit that. It's not that this monster got a hold of me. I'm not possessed by a demon. It's always been there, growing little by little more assertive. I can't even say how I came to the point when I was monstrous, when I started doing monstrous things. Before I knew it, I was simply doing them."

"What did you do?" Nick was annoyed now. His indirection felt a little manipulative.

"Before I left for Thailand, when I was still in LA, I bought these girls."

"You *bought* girls?!"

"I purchased them, just like slaves. There's no other way to put it. Three of them. I paid a man in North Hollywood thirty thousand dollars for the right to spend a week with each. I'd have them to myself, and I could do with them whatever I liked. I booked rooms in different resorts. These old women dropped them off and picked them up again. In between they lived with me, ate with me, slept with me, and did everything I asked of them."

This couldn't come as altogether a shock to Nick, given what he remembered of Lou's sexual proclivities. But he wasn't sure he wanted his picture of the man confirmed in this blunt a fashion either– certainly not on the heels of what had just happened in New York. Lou was taking more liberties than he even knew.

"The thing is they were twelve years old," he said. "That's all. Kids. Their parents sell them to this prostitution ring so men like me can have their way with them."

"Lou," he remonstrated.

"And I didn't just do it three times. I did it over and over, each time with a different girl, hopping from resort to resort, using the money I made on rent from my house each month. I couldn't stop."

Nick sought refuge from these appalling disclosures in the Neo-Roman facade of the church across the street: the portal, the round tympanum, the rose window, the triangular gable. It didn't offer much relief. Lou sounded strangely Catholic–moral and depraved at the same time, like Saint Paul wanting to do good but continuing to do evil.

He did stop, finally. Something still more terrible happened. "On Ko Samui, back in the resort where it all started, I learned that the first girl I purchased this way had been killed. She was working in a brothel, and a man cut her up with a knife. He left her a bloody lump of flesh in tangled sheets, and then he killed himself. He put a gun into his mouth and fired."

"Jesus, Lou."

"I couldn't keep going after that. It scared the hell out of me. What is it they say? 'There but for the grace of God go I'? Well, that's how I felt. I'd go a step further. I *am* a murderer, Nick, because the girl's fate was sealed the year before, when I paid for the right to take her virginity. That's the appeal for the men who do this. An old Thai masseur explained it to me. The girl's parents indentured her to that brothel because they considered her tarnished goods after I got through with her. I was the reason she was there."

"Why do I need to know this?"

"I felt like I had to tell somebody," he said sheepishly, "and the only person in the world who'd listen or care was Evan. Now, with him gone, I'm alone with it. I guess I'm using you as a proxy."

"A priest, more like it."

He smiled. "Okay, a priest. Except it's not forgiveness I'm after. I don't think that's possible. It's just that I have a hard time seeing how to live with myself right now. I'm kind of groping in the dark. I took a chance you might be able to help me understand."

"What don't you understand?"

"Why I'm like this. Why I do what I do."

"You have no idea?"

"Not deep down, no."

Nick didn't know which was worse: the question or the corner it put him in. He had little desire to help Lou in a backhanded bid for expiation. "I don't believe that," he said anyway. "You're not possessed by a demon. You said so yourself. You know exactly what you're doing. You make choices. You can choose otherwise."

"Do you remember that script you wrote, by the Mexican guy?"

"Cuban."

"Right. You said it was about people caught in a loop, doing the same things over and over. Well, I'm caught in a loop."

This took Nick by surprise. He hadn't expected to have his own words thrown back at him. "Okay," he said, trying to sort himself out now. "But you know you're caught in a loop. There's a difference between the characters and the reader, or the writer. That has to count for something."

"Did Donnie ever pay you the money he owed you?"

"No."

"Sonofabitch!" Lou cried, snapping back again into a tough-minded agent. "I'm going to get that for you, I promise. I'll sue his ass. I'll sue the whole studio. There'll be damages."

Nick heard only the cadences of this. It had struck him with a rather devastating force that he could no longer say the difference he wanted to make between character and reader, or writer, did count for something. He used to find it reasonable enough that a principle of eternal recurrence governed one's life. It meant that nothing ever quite happened without a certain foreknowing, a certain savoir vivre entering into events. One shouldered the weight—the "greatest weight" Nietzsche had called it—of things happening down to their finest details exactly as one expected, hoped, or even remembered they would, in accordance with a will one had only to trust against all remorse, all hankering to do over, or do better. But now life seemed just too galling, the will too much in jeopardy, for him to go on believing the difference at stake in this commitment to the irrational, this amor fati, was more than a conceit or led to more than acquiescence, if not a worse complicity, in a monstrous world. His eyes drifted back to the church façade. Somewhere up on the steeple, below the rather severe astylar cross into which it tapered high above, he wondered if there might not be a gargoyle or two.

2

On his return to the apartment Nick found Haley seated on a step of the front entrance, her knees folded up to her chin and a plastic Monoprix bag beside her, stuffed with clothes. Something was definitely wrong. Her skin was pale, her eyes were bloodshot, and her high cheekbones were too pronounced in her sunken face. In a ragged plaid coat and flat shoes, she looked like a skinny homeless woman loitering there.

"Thank God," she said, springing to her feet. "I thought you'd never come."

"Why didn't you tell me you were here?!"

"I lost my phone."

This didn't explain why she hadn't called. She had a landline, too. But before asking about that, he opened the door and led her up to the apartment. As she trudged in silence on the stairs behind him, he guessed at one reason for her dishevelment. She was *too* skinny. She was no longer pregnant.

Straight off she took a shower. In the meantime Nick sliced some oranges and tomatoes Julie had left on the kitchen counter, laying them one on top of the other and dressing them with olive oil. When Haley appeared again, she found this with also a pot of tea on the glass table between the two sofas. Evening had set in by then. He turned on the lights, which made the space still more inviting. He was glad Haley had come when she did: it absorbed the first shock of being there alone. With her help he might wrest the apartment from its ghost.

She needed help more than he did, though. As he surmised, a week ago she'd suffered a miscarriage. The nausea and cramps she'd felt all through the pregnancy had combined with a crippling back pain, and spotting turned into heavy bleeding. Tests at a clinic confirmed her worst fears.

"I'm so sorry, Haley."

She made no reply, preoccupied with a rolling paper she had laid flat on the coffee table. He watched as she took a Gauloise cigarette from a pack and pulled it apart.

"What are you doing?"

Without answering, she transferred the loosened tobacco to the paper and produced a small plastic bag with a chunk of hashish in it. She drew it out and cut off resinous fragments with a small pair of scissors.

"The doctors said I could use this for the pain." She carefully added the fragments to the tobacco, placed a roach on one end, and slid the paper into a cylinder. "Actually, that's not true." She tucked one edge in, licked the other, and tightened it. "It works for that, but I've been doing it for a while now. It's a habit I picked up."

"You're an old hand, I see."

A smile creased her lips as she lit the joint and drew on it. She caught his eyes for the first time, blowing vapor out the side of her mouth.

"I'm a mess," she said.

"You're not the only one." Poor, penitent Lou flashed into his mind. "It seems to be going around."

She asked about the funeral and listened distantly to his description. It interested her only as an excuse to avoid explaining herself in more detail. The pressure for this was, however, equally strong. At a lull in the conversation he gently inquired about the clothes.

"They're not mine," she said. "A friend lent them to me."

"Why?"

Her face fell. "I did a stupid thing, Nick. I bounced a rent check. You can't do that here. Even one month's slip is enough to get you evicted. My housemates are livid."

"So you can't go home."

"They won't let me in. Not until I pay what I owe, and then they want me to leave."

"How much is it?"

"Six hundred euros."

He offered to cover it for her. It would have to go on the credit card, along with what he'd paid to the NYU medical center and also his plane ticket.

"I don't know what to do," she confessed. "They have all my stuff: my computer, my clothes, my books, everything."

"Your phone, too?"

She groaned. "I'm such a fuckup."

"When did this happen?"

"A couple of days ago."

"Don't they care that you've been ill?"

"We haven't been on speaking terms for a while now," she said. "I've become something of a pariah. It's my fault. I kind of closed up."

"Where have you been staying?"

"With a friend, Margaux. But I can't for much longer. She lives in a studio. We've been sharing a bed."

"Stay here then."

"I was hoping you'd say that."

"As long as you need to, Haley."

Her relief was palpable. "Thanks." She placed her still-lit joint on the edge of the table and reached for the teapot, pouring herself a cup. "I bet you weren't expecting this."

"No."

"I'm lucky you arrived when you did," she said, adding with another faint smile, "just in the nick of time."

⅄

Soon after she retired to the master bedroom, where she slept all through the rest of that night. When Nick awoke the next morning, he found her smoking quietly on the sofa. It was early still, dim in the apartment, and she hadn't turned on any lights. He could tell she'd been there for a while, listening to the silence and the darkness.

He made coffee and joined her, not forcing the conversation, letting her set the tone. After a while she spoke more about her current predicament, especially in connection with her housemates and that Belleville atelier. The whole experiment had proven a disaster. The people turned out to be devious and self-serving, not at all what they'd seemed when she first met them. The final clue that she'd misread Jean-Claude was a script he gave her to read only two weeks before.

"It was awful," she told him. "A puerile misogynist fantasy. It took me completely by surprise." She thought twice about this. "No, not completely. There were inklings of something wrong before that."

She told him of a party about six months back, thrown in honor of a film producer Jean-Claude had hoped might provide financing for the script. "Everyone went on about it as though it was going to be the most brilliant movie ever made, sure to revolutionize French cinema, to lay bare the French soul. That's what I thought, too. I believed Jean-Claude's opinion of himself: that he was going to be the next Claude Chabrol. I suppose I wanted to believe it more than anything."

Nick refrained from telling her what he thought of the claims people in the film business made for themselves. In LA they extended pretty much to the moon.

"I played along, just like everybody else," she said. "I talked up the promise and talent of our little atelier. But at a certain point I had the feeling from my friends that I was expected to sleep with the producer. That was how committed to Jean-Claude's project I had to be."

"They *said* that?"

"Not in so many words, no. Sandrine, one of my housemates, just said the man liked me and suggested I show an interest in him, despite my horror of the idea. He was the least interesting person there, exactly the type I loathe: a conservative businessman from Neuilly. At the end of the night I politely excused myself and went to my room. But the next day I felt everyone silently reproaching me, as if to let me know I hadn't been enough of a team player. Again, none of this was explicit. I couldn't be sure if I was imagining it or not. In fact I decided I was imagining it. But it put me on my guard."

"Probably a good thing."

She flashed him a doubtful look. "It threw me off anyway. I stopped feeling at home there. I never have. I don't like the neighborhood by the Gare du Nord. It's not a neighborhood at all really. The Gare de l'Est is there, too, along with two big hospitals. Also, there's a lot of sex shops and prostitution. It's close to the rue Saint Denis, or the faubourg it runs down into. It made me extremely sensitive to what was happening around me. It also made reading Jean-Claude's script even more of a blow."

"It isn't brilliant and revolutionary?"

"Oh God!" she groaned. "It's the worst, Nick. Pretentious, soft-core porn. It gets off on what it pretends to expose: cold, impersonal, commercialized sex. I'd be embarrassed to show it to anyone. . .even Evan."

"They asked you to give it to him."

"Not exactly. His reception of Jean-Claude nixed that possibility." She paused, deciding how to bring out her next thought: "He did ask me if I'd give it to you."

"Me?"

"And you'd help with your father."

"Ah."

"I'm sorry, Nick. I know how much that bothers you. I overplayed your importance in their minds. I wanted them to take me seriously. I made out like you were this powerful contact I had in Hollywood."

"Don't apologize," he said. "That's how it's done. You exaggerate everything. You create an impression of your value."

"Now I think it's the only reason they included me."

"I wouldn't be so sure of that. There are many ways to generate 'value.' It sounds to me like Jean-Claude's more likely to get his feature with *your* screenplay, for instance."

That didn't have the reassuring effect he hoped it might. In silence she set to work on rolling another of those joints. When it came time to add the hashish, she held up the plastic bag and eyed its contents. "Damn," she muttered. "I'm almost out."

ϰ

Nick left to buy groceries at a Franprix he'd noticed on the walk with Lou. There, pushing a cart down the aisles and choosing items he thought Haley might like, he reflected on the strange similarity between her story and his father's rant about France being "one big whorehouse." He hadn't then registered the oddity of this coming from his father of all people, but now it puzzled him. It had something of the same paranoid character as Lou's confession—indignant about his own sins, a perception and a projection at once. In the further light of what Haley had told him, it suggested conjunctions of sex and power that drew everything, even Haley's story and even his own now thoroughly mixed-up opinions on the subject, closer to his father believing his neighbor walked through walls or, for that matter, throwing himself off his balcony—if that's what he did.

Once again Nick sensed a lack of separation in that darkness where Lou groped. It hinted at an obscene dimension of everyone's freedom, where people touched so closely on an underlying violence in the world that no divergence, no distance, and no perspective was possible. It couldn't even be named without either rationalizing it or going mad. . .or both.

He came back intent on fixing Haley a hearty breakfast. By the look of her she'd been starving herself for weeks. But she had no appetite for the scrambled eggs and toast he made. All she wanted was coffee, cigarettes, and hashish. Her dwindling supply concerned her so much that she arranged to meet a man for more. Her need for it pointed straightforwardly to the mental state of an addict.

Nick accompanied her the following afternoon to a rendezvous on a small pedestrian street next to, of all places, the police prefecture on the Île de la Cité. From the entrance to the metro station, and a busy flower market there, he watched Haley approach a man standing under a plane tree, by a row of iron bollards. They spoke amiably, their coats flapping in the wind of a blustery spring day. Nick didn't see the transaction when it must have happened, even though he looked for it.

Haley made no mention of the man afterward. They walked over a bridge on the Seine to the Hôtel de Ville, where they could catch the train on which they'd just come, back to Belleville. When they were far enough away, Nick remarked on the irony of the exchange taking place where it did. "Law and transgression stand revealed," he said drily, "in their hidden complicity."

Haley told him the man had some business in the prefecture but conceded he might have chosen the spot for other reasons than simple convenience. "The best place to hide a tree is in a forest," she quipped.

This had Nick thinking back to the events in New York. As they sat in the metro station, he related to her what had happened to Molly and Sean. The story fit seamlessly into her own preoccupations. She connected its hint of an obscene sexual power—or *anti*power—to the men who solicited prostitutes near her apartment, disappearing into doorways and coming out a short while later with stupid smirks on their faces.

"I don't see what the appeal is," she said. "Why would anyone want to have sex with total strangers like that?"

Nick could see the idea pressed on her not simply because she'd witnessed prostitution up close. The novelty was that she should satisfy that abstract desire, meet its need, or present herself as its object to get something she wanted from the world. Prostitution as an underlying logic of all social as well as sexual "exchange" was what mystified her now.

"I don't know," he said with a shrug.

"Do you do it?"

"No."

"Are you ever tempted?"

The question bothered him. It brought to mind Molly's poor opinion of his preference for mutual or "natural" sex. "I won't say I've never felt the urge," he said. "How could I, without sounding like a liar or a prude? I'm not sure what it proves, though. Only that a man is a category shaped by social imperatives, or penetrated by social rules. I will say I don't much like those rules, those imperatives. I resent the category. It feels pretty much as cold and alien to me as the rooms where prostitutes take their clients."

Haley eyed him sideways. "That's a good answer."

"You think so? I'll have to remember it then—for the next time I'm asked."

"I guess it's not a fair question."

He heard the confusion in her voice. The topic, it was clear, had her in knots. "It's fair enough. I'd want to know, too, if I were you."

"Sex doesn't have much to do with people, does it?"

He considered this. In the past he might have argued with her. He might have held out for the possibility of a genuine sexual love, if only in general, only for others luckier or more talented than he was. Now, however, he couldn't say. Genuine sexual love honestly seemed little more than a dream to him at this point.

The train rumbled into the station. The cars were full, and they had to stand pressed against the other riders. Haley tensed up from the proximity. It made her uncomfortable in a manner it wouldn't have before. Nick thought relief would come at Belleville. Unfortunately, everyone flowed out of the train with them, and they had to move in a mass off the platform. The scene turned even more chaotic as people, streaming by in the other direction, made for much jostling through a corridor. Right in front of them a middle-aged woman abruptly started shouting racist epithets at a girl in a hijab who sat on the floor selling roses. She tried to ignore the volley of insults. "*Espèce de salopard! Espèce de con!*" The woman lost all restraint and kicked her. Enraged, the girl sprang to her feet, returning fire in her own language. Seconds later they came to blows. The woman dropped the bag she carried to the ground, spilling tomatoes, carrots, and apples at the feet of passersby. That paralyzed the crowd altogether.

Nick took Haley's arm and pushed through, fighting his way up two flights of stairs. It seemed they'd never get out before they finally did.

"Jesus," he said on reaching the street. "What a madhouse."

"I want to go home," Haley curtly announced. The altercation had shaken her. He could tell by a strange expression in her eyes: crossed or askance, as if she suspected someone was looking at her, or, rather, as if she was trying to see herself from behind, from a blind spot. They'd spoken of stopping somewhere for an *apéro*, but he abandoned the idea at once, quickening his steps with hers back to the rue des Couronnes.

3

In the days that followed it became clear Haley's problems ran deeper than Nick even thought. They preceded the miscarriage and the conflict with her housemates, encompassing her whole relationship to the city where she'd been living for more than ten years. That was the subject of her screenplay about the American woman in Paris, which sat unfinished in the computer on her desk and lost to her with everything else. It was all she cared to talk about. The story proceeded as a series of small coincidences that gradually assumed an overarching significance in her character's mind. They were *too* coincidental, she said. They formed synchronicities that were impossible yet undeniable, irrational yet true. Her character sensed dire events happening behind but also in or, better, *to* surface appearances. And it wasn't just that the world seemed to be something else, something other than what it was. The world was so much what it was not that it disclosed a "pure seeming," by which Nick gathered she meant a lack of foundation in some ultimate reality. The world was "false" in the very physical connotation that word had up to the Renaissance: "false as water," Haley told him, was a locution typical in Shakespeare's time.

Nick found the premise still more intriguing than on the previous occasions he'd heard it. She had hit on an ingenious way of combining one person's private unraveling with a more general epistemological crisis in late modern societies. He saw it also afforded a vehicle for the expression of elliptical personal qualities Haley had long struggled to bring out in her relations to others. As much as she prided herself on a canny knowingness, nothing was really so direct for her as evasion.

They spent hours discussing her project, but while this improved her spirits, it also meshed with phobic tendencies. She was plainly in a state of mental exhaustion. One sign was a hypersensitivity to light, which aggravated the migraines that had been plaguing her for so long. On those days of engaged conversation, the curtains would be drawn and the apartment plunged in gloom.

At the same time Haley insistently brought the topic back to her own situation, closing the distance between her life and her screenplay. She experienced the same improbable coincidences as her character. She might notice a woman on the street carrying a Louis Vuitton handbag and see that handbag all over Paris, in ads on billboards or buses, in a friend's house, at a restaurant, on a TV show. She might find herself thinking of a name—Barbara was her example—and suddenly the name would appear in other things she saw, read, or overheard. These coincidences were so frequent now that she'd been hesitating even to leave her room, for fear they would further multiply and confound her.

"They happen every time I go out now."

"Every time?"

She nodded.

"Did it happen when we went to buy the hashish?"

She sat up in the same spot on the sofa she now usually occupied. "Do you remember the man who was tying together bunches of freesias at the flower shop?"

"Vaguely."

"He had a lazy eye, and afterward I kept seeing people with lazy eyes: two near me on the metro—they might have been twins—then that horrible woman who attacked the girl, and finally a poster on the back side of a newsstand on the boulevard de Belleville, for a movie called *Fragments*. On it, the actor Forrest Whittaker appears in this spiderlike design of a broken window."

"And he has a lazy eye."

"That's right."

Nick wasn't sure what to make of such claims, but having no reason to think Haley was lying or even exaggerating, he gave her sufficient benefit of the doubt to assume there must be some plausible explanation. And in fact one wasn't all that hard to come by. Chance could very well be the measure of determining forces. It could reveal a systematic coordination of belief and behavior at unconscious levels, in a more profound symbolic order of tacit norms and unspoken directives. Ideas, like fantasies and dreams, weren't simply "in" the mind. People didn't simply "have" them, they inhabited them. They acted them out. It made sense, then, that a change in one's perceptions of the world could also be, or at least indicate, a fact about the world itself.

Nick would even say Haley helped him to understand his own experience, and with a poetic clarity he'd never managed to give it on his own. Whenever he'd tried to get a hold of the independent patterns or structures he felt in his life, the words failed him and he fell into ambiguities. Such failures frustrated him not so much because they betrayed some self-deception on his part, which a sober realism should catch and correct. As he'd had many occasions to observe by now, even the value of that realism was in question when basic polarities of inside and outside, individual and society, reality and appearance, stopped doing their work as completely as it seemed they had. Haley resolved this deadlock to which a "false" consciousness had so often reduced him by taking the simple step of declaring the metaphysical breakdown real. As a move, it seemed even inspired.

To better explain herself, she brought up the Roman Polanski movie *Rosemary's Baby*—a current cinematic obsession. "Do you remember the scene when a drugged Mia Farrow wakes up as the devil is raping her?"

"A little." It'd been a long time since Nick saw it. He had to find his way back to the impression it first made on him. That moment, however, was hard to forget—not least because of how much Mia Farrow resembled his mother.

"As she's coming to she says to herself, 'This is no dream. This is really happening!'"

"Right."

"That's how the coincidences are 'real' to me."

"Of course, what's happening is the husband—"

"His name is Guy."

"Okay," he said, smiling. "*Guy* pimps his wife to a coven of witches so he can advance his acting career."

"That's the story, yes."

"But it's absurd, right? You can't believe it." The sober way he saw in her steady gaze that she did believe it disconcerted him for the first time. "Part of its reality is that you can only be crazy to see it."

"Sure."

She gave this concession a firmer emphasis than he would have. "The question is just how that exchange between Guy and the witches is real," he said more carefully.

"Or that scene of sexual violence."

"How it inheres in our lives—"

"Literally," she declared. "It forms the fabric of laws, words, images, rights, bodies, gestures, decisions, contracts."

"I might say figuratively and mean the same thing."

She weighed this for possible equivocation of that sexual violence. He could see it furnished all the moral pressure behind her insistence that the world was revealing something to her. It also suggested a pain she might have been only too content to speak around or deflect in associated forms like *Rosemary's Baby*. But he decided not point this out. It would be more than a little like the pot calling the kettle black.

ϗ

Julie had removed Evan's things from the apartment, thinking their presence might bother Nick. She collected them in a closet next to the WC in the upstairs hallway, and while he wondered about them he nonetheless kept the door firmly shut. He preferred to live with Julie's taste, even though it wasn't his own. She had a New Age bent, decorating the apartment with Buddhist statues and Tibetan wall hangings. It reminded him of Carson and the two women's friendship, unlikely despite their shared commitments to yoga and health food. Julie had a lot more going on than warmed-over Orientalism. Nick could see that in the apartment, too. The books on her shelves revealed a thinking person: not only the Dalai Lama but Saint Augustine and Rousseau; not only *The Power of Now* but *The Phenomenology of Perception* and *Tristes Tropiques*. She also had an impressive collection of art books that drew both his and Haley's special attention.

At the end of a day that had been particularly sultry, prompting them to open the doors to the balcony, Haley took one of those books, on Vermeer, to the sofa and opened it in the glow of a small lamp. The last rays of sunlight glinted through gaps in the curtains, slowly losing their glare and melting into the darkness. Nick came to sit by her side, and together they perused the reproductions of Vermeer's paintings. Haley was most struck by those with figures in rooms reading letters and consulting maps, often near windows that cast a strong diagonal light. She compared the windows to eyes and the rooms to heads or skulls. They suggested to her less interiors than interiority, less private spaces than the inner lives of the people in them, who existed, as she laconically put it, "inside themselves."

Nick admired this interpretation a lot. It helped him to see what was so dynamic in the contemplative stillness of each painting. The figures weren't engaged just with things in the world but with the contents of their own minds; their mental representations, on the other hand, acquired the substantial qualities of the things they were holding or that surrounded them. Haley had a definite feeling for this blending or emulsifying of subject and object, mind and world, that seemed very much to be the point for Vermeer.

She turned a page to the painting entitled *Woman Holding a Balance*. The expression of the figure in the frame, with her covered head slightly canted and her eyes lowered to the scale she held up, was closer to reverie than others they'd seen. The task in which she was so absorbed shifted the focus from representations of the world to abstract concepts like justice and value—those other entities taking up residence in the human mind.

"He's not just after private experience, is he?" Haley observed. "Its public conditions are there, too, in the background. Equality and equivalence. The market. Private property."

"Property in the person," Nick said, recalling his lunch in New York with Ozouf, who'd used that phrase with his customary precision.

Haley nodded. "Vermeer might even have had that idea in mind. It was an artifact of the time, after all."

"Right."

"He's combining inwardness and calculation, conscience and self-interest, value and price. I suppose the one's just an alibi for the other when it comes down to it. That would be a subtext of his perspective, of the care he takes rendering objects in space."

Nick took her point. The impulse behind the painting's design and execution was proto-photographic. It mirrored, in its form, the objectified relations between people that would have been increasingly common in the early modern period. Nonetheless, he found her view a little harsh. "I see an objection, too. The cost of holding the incongruities together is there, in the melancholy tension. The woman also looks trapped in her bourgeois ideology."

"You think so?"

"Bored at least."

"Hmm. Maybe. . ."

Her hesitation brought to Nick's mind the comment his father had once made about him being "green." He wondered if the same might be said of Haley. She was certainly suffering an allergic reaction to economic demands in her personal life. The casual opportunism she felt in her friends had forced underlying sensitivities to the surface. She couldn't pretend it was easy or natural for her to go along without feeling alienated. Nick guessed she also resented the conformity going along required at an instinctive level. It made resistance impossible without also disqualifying her as a person, without making her impossible in all the senses of the word. The price of that objection in Vermeer's painting, if it was there, he conceded, could be high indeed.

"Would you like to sit on the balcony?" she asked.

He wavered. "I'm not sure. I've been afraid to go out." He meant because of his father. "It's been working for me to have the curtains drawn."

"Of course," she said. "I hadn't thought of that."

She shut the book. He could see she wanted the air. The heat in the room was oppressive.

"Let's do it," he said, changing his mind. "It's okay." He stood up. "It'll be cool out now."

He lit a candle and brought it outside to place on a wire mesh side table between two low-slung chairs. They sat under a cobalt-blue sky flecked with the darting swallows that seemed everywhere over Paris at the time.

Both soon settled their attention on the apartment building opposite. Most every window was open. The rich hum and bustle of domestic life filled the space between. They observed people in their warmly lit rooms talking at dinner tables, watching TV, or reading books. Through a gauze curtain one floor down there was a couple making love on a bed. The sight left them both a little embarrassed. Something of the old sexual tension between them came to the surface.

Moments later a door opened on the balcony adjoining theirs and a heavyset man of about fifty appeared. He wore round wire-rim glasses that caught the twilight. With his bald pate it gave him an owlish look.

"*Bonsoir!*" he called out cheerfully. "You must be Nick."

Haley shrank into her chair and turned away, annoyed by the interruption. Nick rose toward the man.

"Yes."

"François Cenac," he said, extending his hand across the rail that separated the balconies. In halting English he added, "Happy to make your acquaintance."

"Same here," said Nick, also in English.

François glanced over Nick's shoulder.

"This is Haley Dunne."

She waved feebly but didn't otherwise engage him. "We've met before," François said, reverting to French. Nick gathered from how he addressed him that she hadn't been all that forthcoming the first time either.

"I'm terribly sorry for your loss," François said. "It was such a shock. I'm not quite recovered myself."

Nick gave a noncommittal nod. He didn't want to discuss his father. The idea that François might also be in mourning struck an odd note.

"Settling in nicely?" François asked.

"Yes, thanks."

"Do you have everything you need?"

"Need?"

"Have you found stores and services, things like that?"

"Oh," said Nick. "Yes, I have."

"Don't hesitate to ask, if you have any questions. I've lived in the neighborhood on and off most of my life."

"Okay."

Silence settled between them. François would've liked to stay and chat, but it being obvious they preferred to be alone, he started to withdraw again. "Let me know if you have any trouble," he said. "I mean with plumbing or wiring, things like that. I'm also an unofficial concierge for the building."

"I will."

"*Bonne soirée!*"

With a slight deferential bow François exited the balcony and shut his door. Nick resumed his seat, feeling sorry for the man. He seemed lonely. Haley wasn't so sympathetic. In a low voice she told him that François had accosted her on the landing a couple of days before, and she hadn't cared for the exchange at all.

"Why not?"

"He wouldn't stop talking," she said with evident disdain. "I had the feeling he was trying to pry secrets out of me."

Nick heard this in fresh bewilderment. For a second he thought she was about to tell him that François wanted to get inside her head.

4

Haley's affairs would eventually have to be straightened out: her housemates confronted, a new place to live arranged, a new job found. It was all too much for her to face. She needed time to gather her strength. That meant she'd need Nick's help in the interim. He decided to put his departure back and stay through the summer if it came to that. The only limit would be Julie's return in early September.

Over the next several weeks they settled nicely into the apartment. It was ideal for two people. Haley slept in the main bedroom, while he took one of the smaller bedrooms upstairs. They assembled for their talks and retreated into privacy as they wished. The only drawback was just how comfortable in their respective holding patterns it left them.

Whatever worries Nick harbored about Haley on this score were tempered by his memory of the person she used to be: self-reliant, levelheaded, and for the most part cheerful in outlook. Her Parisian life had often struck him as charmed. She had a variety of friends, and she pursued her interests with a grace that left him feeling poorer in the contrast. Past visits had been occasions for him to revive his flagging spirits, not the other way around. That had been especially true as his life in LA began to deteriorate.

He found it hard, recalling those times, to keep from blaming the crash in Haley's fortunes on her decision to write that screenplay, to be part of a film business that was toxic wherever it operated. He knew it wasn't as simple as that. A volatile mix of aspirations, inhibitions, and emotional history lay in the background as well. But she had changed significantly from the moment she started talking about Jean-Claude and the atelier. Nick hoped she might change again, with that episode behind her.

Unfortunately, the friend Haley had mentioned to him, Margaux, shook his confidence here. He'd gone one day for cigarettes at a *tabac* on the rue des Pyrenées, buying red Gauloises from a thin old crow of a man who ran the counter with a brisk bonhomie. There was typically a small group of his friends gathered there, and Nick liked to linger and listen in on the repartee. They spoke an idiomatic French that stretched what he knew of the language. On this occasion, standing in the cramped store as usual, he heard his phone ring. It was a woman asking for Haley.

"She's not here," he told her, stepping out to the sidewalk. "I can tell her you called."

"Is this Nick?"

"Yes."

She introduced herself with a long last name that sounded Polish. "I've heard a lot about you," she said.

"Really?" He couldn't say the same for her. She must have been one of Haley's more recent friends. "Some of it good, I hope!"

"Most even," she said, in the same bantering tone. "Perhaps we can meet while you're here."

He started back to the apartment, turning into an alley that cut downhill to the rue des Couronnes. "I'd like that."

"How's Haley?"

"Well enough, under the circumstances."

"I'm worried about her."

"Me too," he said. "But I think she's all right."

The silence on the line went on long enough for him to sense a reservation.

"How much has she told you about what happened?" Margaux asked.

"Everything, as far as I know."

"Did she mention the coincidences?"

"Yes."

"They don't strike you as strange?" She gave this last word its fuller French significance: *singulier*.

"Well, yes," he said, hesitant now. For the first time he heard how Haley's claims might sound to someone else. "I wouldn't make too much of it, though. She's dramatizing her thoughts, her experience. It's a form of self-analysis."

"It's more than that."

He slackened his pace down a flight of stone stairs.

"What do you mean?"

"She's been acting in an erratic manner for some time," Margaux informed him, "even before she started talking about the world conspiring against her. She says one thing and does another. She fails to show up when she promises she will. She borrows money and doesn't pay it back. When confronted, she quarrels. Her friends are angry with her. Frankly, when her housemates kicked her out, I was the only one who was willing to take her in."

He paused in the alley below. "That doesn't sound like Haley," he said, realizing in the same breath that it could, with the right degree of exaggeration.

"I'd say she needs psychiatric help."

He stepped to the stone wall of an adjacent building and sank into a crouch. "What?"

"I think she's in serious trouble."

His first impulse was to disagree, strongly even. Haley wasn't crazy. If anything, Margaux's diagnosis, her idea of health. was crazy. It reflected a toxic consensus Haley was rightly trying to criticize, to see as a problem. He worried, though, that this construction–its inverse relation of terms, held as in a mirror image–was too neat, too formal. He could tell Margaux thought so when he tried roughly to convey his opinion to her. She conceded that some sort of psychoanalysis might be in order but insisted the help would have to be professional. "It might even have to come in an institutional setting."

"You think she should be hospitalized?!"

"She isn't coping well at all right now."

"But there are reasons for that!"

Margaux let another silence on the line emphasize why those same reasons might warrant a more radical explanation.

"Perhaps you should ask Haley about it," she suggested.

"Why? Has she brought it up?"

"She's done research into different places she might go, yes."

That threw him completely into confusion. Still in a crouch, he stared down a shallow gutter that ran through the flagged pavement before him, wondering if he was crazy, too.

ϗ

He kept what Margaux said to himself, assuming Haley would bring her concerns out when she was ready. But if restraint was a well-worn path of respect here, it also hinted at a new complacency on his part. If he didn't want to believe she was crazy or say as much to her, he also couldn't go on forever confirming her wilder intuitions as if they were entirely rational. He might have to challenge her in a fashion that was challenging to his sense of tact. At some point both of them would probably have to acknowledge more mundane sources of their difficulties—choices and mistakes they'd made, dead ends they'd reached, weaknesses they'd hid from themselves. He suspected this was true for Haley in connection not only with the screenplay and the aspirations it signified to her but with the pregnancy, which she conspicuously didn't want to discuss. The wound was too raw and tender.

Still, he started pushing, clumsily, into sensitive emotional territory with her. He asked about the Tunisian boyfriend and what the decision to have the baby by herself had to do with turning forty. He wondered if the difficulty she had writing the screenplay stemmed from anxieties about not having made something of herself, from a reluctance to take the measure of an identity she'd only ever incompletely embraced. He alleged that the coincidences she was seeing in her daily life were also cues for the more dynamic narrative account she needed to give, and with respect not just to writing but simply to being in Paris *tout court*, to taking her life in the directions she had, away from the middle-class person who grew up in Atlanta. Her fear of triviality might only be avoidance of how trivial the world really was.

She agreed enough to admit her shortcomings and also the challenge of honestly accounting for them in her screenplay. But facing a trivial world wasn't the same as accepting it, she insisted, since that only undermined the motives for writing in the first place. Realism was a dead letter when it just persuaded you to be trivial along with everyone else.

"The problem isn't personal," she said one day, inclining forward on the sofa with an air of quiet gravity that impressed him. She had thought her position through and knew how to defend herself. "It isn't about denying something in myself or trying to be something

I'm not. It isn't about anything in my control. It's independent of me altogether."

"Objective."

"A paradigm that's reasonable, without being the result exactly of anyone's conscious choices."

"It can still be reasoned out, though."

"That's what I'm doing!"

"I mean the paradigm is present in our own behavior, in what we do practically with one another."

"Of course," she said. "That's why I'm writing a screenplay. But the behavioral patterns aren't linear or causal. They're abstract, as I've said before, like constellations in a celestial map. They configure feelings and incidents, ideas and acts, names and places, bodies and minds in virtual diagrams that sort of stretch through the order of things. People don't stand over against this order. They identify with it. They meld with it."

"That might be too abstract, Haley."

She felt a turn in his sympathies here. "What's more abstract than this externalized visual world we all have in common?!" she said, bristling. "Maybe it's easy for you, Nick, as a man. But why should I have to see myself the way others see me? Why should I have to be the caricature of a woman that demands, always afraid of dropping masks? I'm so fucking tired of that! I'm tired of pretending I feel beautiful when I have to worry obsessively about flabby triceps."

"That's following a train of thought!"

"The world we have in common is insane. That's my point."

"You don't have to worry about your looks, Haley."

She raised an arm, hooked the sleeve of her blouse on a shoulder, and pinched the flesh above the elbow. The muscle might have lacked in tone, but the chief impression was one of thinness–if anything, too much thinness.

"It's not flabby," he said.

"It didn't used to jiggle."

"That doesn't matter. It's a girl's arm. You look great."

"Thanks," she said. "I feel like shit."

He regretted the comment. It made her case for a male visual abstraction a little too well. "I only meant there isn't just one way of seeing."

"You wouldn't say that if you were a woman," she said. "Femininity is a full-time job, unpaid and without benefits—especially in France. Even committed feminists accept the conventions as natural. '*Chacun sa place!*' is their rallying cry. Men on one side, women on the other. Sexual difference is absolute. Its fixed law anchors the whole symbolic order. Without it every other analytic difference falls apart. You can't think—men can't, anyway."

"That sounds like the true subject of your story."

"No woman thinks," she said, in damascene tones, "unless she thinks this thinking, and from the bottom up."

"Because it structures social and sexual relations."

"It positions people in social and sexual space. It orients them in social and sexual time. That's why it's *real*."

This word indicated, once again, the only questionable element Nick heard in anything she maintained. "I agree that symbolic order is real," he said. "It exerts a real force in our lives. But even by your own reckoning it's not real the way we think it is. Because it operates in the mind, we wrestle with it in ourselves. We engage it by challenging our beliefs and presuppositions. We become *self*-critical."

"I sense a dodge in that."

"Why?"

"It's too psychological, for one thing. What you're telling me is that I have to second-guess myself all the time. I can't ask why things happen to me as they do."

"However they happen, your assurance of their meaning is still in question."

"But *that* they happen isn't," she said. "I can't deny the evidence of my senses. If something appears to me as horrible, it *is* horrible." Her thoughts shifted to another register. "Did I mention I witnessed an accident a while back?"

"No."

"A boy was hit by a car in the nineteenth, and I was standing on the corner when it happened. The driver made the jag from the rue de Meaux to the rue Petit too quickly. As he did, I was looking at one of those blue placards on the side of a building, where someone had blacked out the *e* in *Meaux*."

"So?"

She picked a piece of lint from the arm of the sofa, waiting for him to make the connections. *Maux* was a plural form of *mal*, the word for *bad* or *evil. Petit* could refer to a small boy.

"The street names connote the accident for you?"

"Mm-hmm."

"That's an unusual coincidence," he admitted. "But it could still be just a coincidence, right? You're not saying the person who changed *Meaux* to *maux* knew an accident was going to happen there, or that the corner is especially hazardous for children. Are you?"

"All I know is it happened, and I was there to experience it. At that moment, the signifiers fell into the real."

"It's still not clear the event means what you think it does," he said. "We can't step behind things, or see them in the round that way, as much as we might want to."

"That hardly matters."

"But it has to, Haley."

"Why?"

"Because otherwise it sounds a little crazy."

Her face fell. He noted the vertical vein in her forehead, always there these days, livid to the point of pulsation. She saw that he was taking the side of a toxic consensus. The hush in the room deepened as her eyes went roaming through the surrounding gloom.

"That was too strong," he said.

"You don't understand," she muttered half to herself. "You're just like everybody else."

"I'm trying to understand."

"You think in that symbolic order, with its fixed distinctions."

"Not true," he said. "Believe me, I couldn't be more at odds with it than I am right now."

"I can't trust you." Her eyes locked on his. "I've never been able to really."

"Never?"

"Not when it comes down to it," she said. "You're opaque to me, Nick. I don't know who you are, what you feel, what you stand for. In some respects you seem a conventional man."

"You mean in my attitudes toward women?"

"Among others."

His answer here was prompt: "I don't make any assumptions about people based on what they are, okay? I place no limits on you because of anything you can't control or change. We're not puppets of biology or prejudice. All I will say is, I'm often disappointed in people when they act as if they are puppets."

"That's what I mistrust in you."

"Why?!"

"You're too much of a rationalist," she said. "You believe we should all be masters of our impulses and desires. You don't have a feeling for what it is to be *over*mastered."

Now it was his turn to take offense. She had deliberately struck a tender nerve. "I don't think that's fair," he said on an edge of his own now. "Maybe I am too reticent for my own good, and maybe it does point to a deficient sympathy—"

"That's not what I meant."

"I know," he shot back. "You meant I lack spontaneity or daring as a man. Fine. Maybe that's also true. But I can't help wondering what the standard there is. Where does it come from? It seems pretty conventional, too, if you ask me. I've certainly felt judged by it often enough. It reminds me of this producer in LA once telling me I had 'no heart' because the character in my script wasn't trying to fuck everything that moved. Really, Haley. Maybe you're the one thinking in that symbolic order."

With this expostulation they were on dangerous ground, and neither felt up to the rash words they were likely to say to each other if the conversation turned more heated. Both decided, therefore, that it would be wiser to change the subject.

ᚷ

What Nick really had in mind was the incident at Brown with his father, and afterward he found himself revisiting the pain it caused him, buried in some remote corner of his heart. Haley had explained what happened as a one-night stand that wouldn't be repeated (although he suspected it was, another time, in New York), and he knew enough of his father to believe her when she spoke of his seduction. That was by far the worse betrayal. But while she did feel regret about the whole affair, she resisted the idea that she owed him an apology. However ill-advised and even unkind it had been for her to sleep with his father, he still had no right to influence her sexual choices. She shouldn't have to feel responsible for his infatuation.

That had been the issue in college anyway, and Nick hardly needed convincing. He knew he had no claim on her. They were only friends. Even his father had assumed as much, since Nick had never bothered to confide in him his feelings for her. No one had set out to hurt him. He'd had to accept as his lot an injury largely of his own making, and it seemed to him he'd done so well enough over the years, all things considered.

What bothered him now, or still, was how this injury, this narcissistic wound, fit into the derogatory picture of his intellectualizing character. It wasn't enough for Haley that he dealt with his feelings by trying to understand them; he also had to experience them more passionately, with some more total thrust of the self. And to be fair, he didn't fail in this double imperative because he was insufficiently like his father in her mind. He failed, rather, out of a fear that feelings were overmastering in every sense of the word, just as selfish and cruel as Evan following his creed that nothing should ever be repressed. In her view, paradoxically, this image of his father was his true problem. It became a caricature that kept him from exploring other more expressive ways of handling pain, approaching love, even being a friend. It blocked the possibility of a deeper connection with himself no less than others. For Haley, or so he imagined her saying, not all masters were tyrannical. Some helped to free us from our inhibitions. They instructed us in the art, not just of becoming ourselves, but, more subtly, of establishing how we are to count for others.

But such a distinction, important as it may have been for him to draw, frankly blurred in the light of what happened in college. At least it didn't much help him to understand the attraction for a man like his father. Nor from what he could see did it get Haley out of that insane world she was trying to step behind. And it definitely didn't make her unconventional. If no one failed to condemn coercion when it threatened their autonomy, everyone defended the particular sublimation that made power into a cue for pleasure or happiness. "If I want to be raped, I can't be raped," Molly had said to him back in New York. Okay. Why, though, should he have to consider this less of a formula than his self-consciousness for the fantasy that anchored *one* insane world in everybody's minds? Why, in the scenario of rape Haley had introduced between them, was his sympathy for Rosemary and his hatred of the actor-husband's egoism both suspect? Just what criterion of emotional honesty was really at stake here?

He wanted to bring all this up in the days that followed, but it churned too chaotically inside him to sort criticism from grievance. It was clear as well that Haley didn't need to hear either right then. Her hope of establishing herself in that insane world—while keeping the contact with her own feelings—had taken a serious hit. Pointing this out would only make matters worse. But he did allow himself the thought, petulant though it might be, that one reason not to go crazy was the complicity going crazy implied in a law, symbolic or otherwise, that came down on everyone in the requirement of a stupid ecstasy.

5

A month passed with little change, and Nick grew anxious about Haley's lack of resolve. She dreaded any practical moves, putting them off to a time when the light burned her eyes less and the headaches subsided. These symptoms were serious enough to make deference the best response, but he also saw her counting on this in him. He might have to push her to act anyway, with pain and short of readiness. If he didn't, she might hide in that apartment all summer.

He did at last persuade her to confront her housemates, give them the rent money, and arrange for the removal of her things. He offered to go with her, predicting the exchange, however awkward, would at least be brief. The aim would be to start the process rolling.

But on the appointed day she was loath to leave the apartment. When he insisted, she bristled at the pressure. She trudged beside him up the hill to the rue des Pyrenées, where they could catch a bus to the street where she lived, making sure he felt the barb in her silence.

At the stop she spoke again of turning back. She wondered just what end would be served by a face-to-face meeting.

"It's already been arranged," he said. "Your housemates will be waiting."

"I can send the money."

"What about your clothes? You've been wearing the same things for weeks!"

The bus came into view up the street, squealing to a halt in front of them. The doors swung open, and he waited for her to pass inside. She placed a foot on the first step, aware of the driver, a clearly impatient man, eyeing her sideways from his seat. He must have been running late.

"Go on," Nick urged.

"I don't want to—"

"Haley," he said firmly. "You have to do this."

"I don't *have* to do anything."

"Get on or get off!" the driver barked. "*Nom de Dieu!*"

Nick crowded in behind her, leaving her no choice but to mount the stairs into the bus.

"Don't push me!" she cried.

"I'm not."

"You are, dammit!" She glared so openly at him that he lost his temper.

"I feel pushed into pushing you!" he said, inserting their tickets into the machine. "How's that for a mind fuck?"

Galled by the sudden opprobrium she stalked off to find a seat. He followed after as the bus lurched forward. Seeing her avoid his look, he decided to keep his distance.

He stood by himself, fuming as much as she did. He felt caught in a bind. The help he had no choice but to give was also resented. It confirmed once more her poor opinion of his character. Why would anyone stand to be cornered this way even an instant? he wondered. *He* was the one who should turn around and go home. At least then he'd have his self-respect. Hell, he'd even have her respect. He'd come closer to the kind of man she evidently did prefer. His father wouldn't have been caught dead playing the Good Samaritan like this. He would've understood the insincerity in any attempt to save people from themselves.

These thoughts absorbed him the whole ride down the avenue Simon Bolivar to the Place de Stalingrad and around to the rue La Fayette, where they exited a couple of long stops short of Haley's apartment. She told him she needed time to collect herself. They set out at a slow pace down the broad sidewalk.

Tensions drained away as they went. She knew she'd put him in an untenable position. He knew he'd verged on an aggression she probably should suspect at its older sources. Neither much liked what the situation revealed of them.

"This isn't easy for me either," he said at length, in a cadence of apology.

"I know."

"We can call it off, if you really don't want to do it. We can have lunch at that North African restaurant instead."

"No," she said, more fortified against the inevitable. "Let's get it over with."

They walked on in silence. Nick sensed her slowly sinking into the more troubled depths of her predicament. "I feel so detached," she said presently. "So remote from myself. Like I'm not here."

"You're here," Nick assured her, thinking, though, how a certain spaciness had always been an attribute of hers. It was part of her charm as a person. Noticing it had often stirred in him a protective feeling. She could seem at times just a little too sensitive for this world.

"I'm like a character in a play," she said, "only the play isn't a play at the same time. It's real."

"A real falsity?"

"Yes. And the only way out of that feeling, or the only way to it, is to force it, to push its theatricality through to the end."

"'The play's the thing, wherein I'll catch the conscience of the king?'"

She laughed. "That's right. I'm a female Hamlet. I hate how things 'seem,' yet in my inky cloak I only 'seem' to be anything."

Nick regretted the allusion. If everything she suggested through the detour to Shakespeare was lucid, he preferred to hear it right then in plainer speech. "You mean you're depressed."

"'Everything weary, stale, and flat,'" she went on, citing the play once more. "'All custom of exercise foregone, man just a quintessence of dust.'"

"Haley."

"No?"

"It's not as bad as that," he said. "The mood is exaggerated even in the play, right? That's how I understand the hints of Hamlet faking it."

"You don't think he's mad."

"At least his feelings are hystericized. That's not to belittle the suffering they imply. But part of what makes them real is their banality. He can't take them, or himself, seriously."

"He's drowning in two inches of water."

"That doesn't mean he isn't drowning," Nick said. "The problem is a world in which nothing has any weight or gravity."

"'Its frame a sterile promontory, holding only this foul congregation of vapors.'"

"Those vapors can be words, too, Haley."

"Yes," she said with a sigh. "'Words, words, words.'"

He looked out over the train yards of the Gare de l'Est, which had in the meantime opened up across the rue La Fayette behind a ceramic parapet of trellised beams. He sought there still blunter terms for their situation.

"Things are too abstract," he said then. "Too reified. That's the real problem. Taking care of ourselves demands too much compromise with that. We can't question or even reflect on the reified world without putting ourselves at odds with it. You're not forcing the relevance of *Hamlet*. The irrelevance of *Hamlet* is forced on you."

"I don't want to accept that."

"Me neither! But we still have to take care of ourselves. We can't just give up. We have to find some workable compromise. If we don't, that reified world will come down around us like a cage."

She placed a hand on his arm as he finished, slackening her pace. He noticed again the strange expression in her face of someone trying to see herself from behind, from a blind spot.

"Do you hear that?" she whispered.

"What?"

She pulled him off to the side. Her glance alerted him to two middle-aged men who'd been walking in their rear for a while now. As they ambled past, Nick caught the mingled tones of their conversation. To his astonishment they were talking about *Hamlet*, specifically the traps laid for testimony and speech when Horatio first sees the father's ghost. He even heard one of the men use the phrase "pure seeming"—*la pure apparence.*

☧

Haley was still less ready to confront her housemates after that. They walked past her building and turned a corner, sitting for a cigarette on the curb of a service road that wound down under the Gare du Nord. Nick tried to minimize what happened, speculating that the two men must have overheard them mention *Hamlet* and somehow picked up the thread. But he and Haley hadn't been speaking loudly enough to be heard over the traffic. And even had they been, the conversation between the two men felt very much their own, intimate and involved. It was a bona fide coincidence, and Nick would've left it there had it not been for Haley's claim about its frequency in her life. He had no idea how to fit that within a reasonable tolerance for random chance.

After the cigarette he rose from the curb and urged her to the reckoning with her housemates. They walked back to the building, a typical Second Empire structure faced with gray *pierre de taille* and a bronze mansard roof. It was as functional as the place in which it was situated. As Haley had said, it wasn't much of a neighborhood, just a transit point for people on the way to somewhere else.

Haley entered a code on a keypad by the front entrance and waited to be buzzed in. They walked up to the fourth floor and met, outside the apartment, a woman of about thirty, dressed in sweatpants and a T-shirt. Her eyes smoldered with an indignation dampened only by disappointment at Nick's presence. She'd hoped to find Haley alone. That would have made the tirade she had in store for her easier to unleash.

First she demanded the rent. Nick had given it in cash to Haley before they left, and she handed it over, so cowed she had difficulty introducing him. The woman, Sandrine, cut her off.

"I still shouldn't let you in," she said.

"I'll just be a few minutes."

"That's all you have. I'm about to leave, and no one else is here."

"There's just a few things—"

"I should throw them all out the window," Sandrine said. "You can pick them up off the sidewalk for all I care."

"There's no reason to get upset," Nick broke in. "You have the money. She has a right to be here—"

"No reason?!" She kept her eyes on Haley. "Because of your bounced check we're all getting evicted. Do you understand? Everyone has to leave by the end of the month."

The news didn't catch Haley as short as it should have. She'd known it was a risk. "How can that be?" she stammered.

"Oh come on," Sandrine sneered. "Don't play dumb. You gave the landlord an excuse knowing he wanted one. Everybody told you so, more than once."

"I didn't think it would be that easy."

"You didn't think at all, Haley."

"So much was going on—"

"It always is!" Sandrine cried. "You're in a perpetual state of emergency. It's a perfect excuse."

"Can we try to be civil?" Nick implored.

"No!" she said, addressing him for the first time. "I don't want to be civil. I don't feel civil. She's ruined everything. She's walked all over my rights as if they didn't concern her in the least. I'm so mad I could scream."

"I'm sorry," Haley said miserably.

"I don't care if you're sorry. What good does that do now? I still have to find a new place to live, you stupid bitch."

"This isn't helping anyone," Nick said, cutting to the chase. "Just let us in, and we'll be out again in five minutes."

Sandrine stood aside. He positioned himself so Haley could pass through the open door unmolested.

"I want all your shit out on Friday!" Sandrine shouted after her. "What's left goes on the street."

That gave them three days. It also brought home to Nick his own mistake. Haley was right: it would've been better to send the money by mail and avoid this pointless scene. In all likelihood no one would be there on Friday but a concierge.

He passed through the apartment and found Haley standing in her bedroom. It had wainscoted walls papered in pastel blue, on which could just be seen the faded garlands of brown leaves, and a ceiling medallion over a tacky chandelier. Tall French windows opened onto the rue La Fayette.

"I don't know where to start," she murmured, her presence of mind completely shot.

"Concentrate on what you need."

She went to a packed wardrobe and began transferring clothes into her Monoprix bag. Nick waited by the door, noting familiar signs of her domestic life: an Art Deco lamp standing on an old paint-flaked *guéridon* they'd once found together at the Clignancourt flea market, a framed Gustav Moreau print of a woman with a winged angel standing behind her, a tapestry of Renaissance design tacked to the wall above her bed. They reminded him of happier times on the Canal Saint-Martin.

"Can you open the window?" Haley asked. "It's stuffy in here."

When he complied, noise from the street rushed into the room, collapsing the sense of separation between inside and outside. Through the window he glimpsed a sex shop next to a bistro that curved around a corner. He could see why Haley would feel so exposed to the world living there.

She filled a second bag with clothes and a milk crate with whatever miscellaneous things she had to hand. Then she perused a bookshelf, withdrawing a few volumes she threw into the crate as well. At that she paused, thinking over what she might have forgotten.

"Do you have your phone?" he asked.

She patted her pants pocket. "Yes."

"Do you want anything from your desk?" He pointed to the notebooks and scraps of paper there—elements of her screenplay project, he presumed.

"No. That can wait."

"Let's go, then." He picked up the crate. "This place gives me the creeps."

She couldn't agree more. "I hope I never see it again."

6

They hired movers to deliver her things to Julie's apartment. Nick suggested renting a storage space, but Haley said no. She thought she'd be able through friends to find places for the boxes and furniture that soon dominated the living room. This proved more complicated than she imagined, however. Persuading her friends to help was hard—even at their most sympathetic they didn't much trust her anymore—and, once she had persuaded them, spaces needed to be cleared out, convenient times set up for delivery, and social effort spent making people feel their good will went appreciated.

The experience left Haley still more brittle than before, and her appetite for conversation dropped. More and more she kept to herself even in the apartment, wearing earphones and listening to music, intent on shutting out a growing number of irritants. Among them were sounds that came through the wall from François's apartment. Several times she complained about them. She never crossed a line into his father's paranoia, but the temptation had even her worried about an eroding self-control. Nick tried to console himself with the thought that this concern only proved she wasn't losing her mind, just wrestling at an edge from which her keen intelligence would pull her back in the end. But even if that was true, it didn't mean she'd be able to dig herself out of her hole any time soon.

Nick also found himself alone more. It had him asking if his reliance on her wasn't an excuse for delaying difficult decisions of his own. He sensed a bad faith in this now. He, too, could well compare himself to Hamlet, with his excessive self-probing, his irresolution, his need for solid ground in a world without weight or gravity. This reflective approach to life had seemed honest to him. He tried not to be dogmatic. He tried to challenge his beliefs. He never assumed events or people were the same as his ideas of them, even if he tried to understand them in his own way. Now, though, he wondered just how honest he was. Or, worse, he feared trying for honesty was itself the mistake. It made him too much the rationalist Haley criticized; it had him depending too much on a picture of himself that had become hard, reified. Holding fast to that picture in a world that separated him from his own substance, from what defined him, as completely as this one, he'd forgotten just how unfounded things were, or he was, and so lost the suppleness (not to say playfulness) self-care required if it was to be more than fearful accommodation. That would make his pleas for "workable compromises" hard to take, if not further proof of a reified world.

He saw, too, that his bad faith had a lot to do with that image of his father in his mind, with reactions to its hypermasculine example that had never been all that rational. In fact, now that his father was dead, Nick saw more distinctly than ever just how spectral a figure he'd long been for him, bound up with an absence that was also too present, too large, too much there in its disturbing, vulgar, obtrusive excess. More "satyr" than King Hamlet's "Hyperion," Evan was still a standard for Nick, an ideal point of comparison from which he saw himself as diminished and insufficient, yet to which he was strangely attached, on which he strangely relied for whatever sense of identity he had. The question now was whether he'd ever be able to free himself from this psychic trap. He was, truth be told, tired of it. Its alienated inwardness had left him, in his way, as paralyzed as Haley.

She had a larger-than-life father as well. Nick had never met him, but it was obvious all through the years he'd known her that this successful realtor in Atlanta cast a long shadow over her. They were emotionally close—more so than she was with her mother—yet worlds apart in their beliefs and values. As a politically and sexually conservative man, he posed a formidable barrier to her independence of mind, disapproving of basic choices she had to make in reactions of her own, strong enough to explain their occasional recklessness. Nick suspected she'd gone to school at NYU but also quit and moved to Paris for this reason. The distances, both physical and spiritual, provided a measure of both her need and his reach.

This history complicated her situation still more, since the thought of going home aroused fierce resistance even as she seemed to be narrowing her options to little else. On the one occasion Nick suggested she might have to go home, at least for a while, she shut him down as sharply as she'd done when he had brought the subject up before. She might have shut him out more, too, feeling, if not her father in him, then at least a pressure to be responsible on his terms. Nick considered this a baseless fear, but it did hint for him at another analogy to Hamlet: prone in his Oedipal frustrations to lash out at the women in his life, to blame them for his psychic traps. He supposed this propensity could never be discounted in a man.

ꭓ

Margaux jolted him once more from his complacent mood. He met her, finally, when she came over one night with Haley. Later she called him, hoping to arrange a time to meet alone. The next day they sat down together at a sidewalk café on the boulevard de Belleville, in view of the crowded market that took over the median strip once a week. In a crisp matter-of-fact fashion—he could tell Margaux was that kind of person, practical and efficient, well put together—she sketched out a scenario in which Haley wouldn't dig herself out of her hole before she had to leave Julie's apartment. Without money, a job, a place to live, or the wherewithal to provide these things for herself, she might fall apart completely. "In my opinion this has to be faced," she said.

Nick still resisted. "I don't feel the same urgency. She's perfectly clear-minded in my opinion, however bottled up she is."

"You might feel differently if you'd been around her these last months."

"Maybe." He didn't, however, think much of this claim.

"The worst thing would be that she ends up back with Amir."

"Her boyfriend?"

"He's been pestering me about her for weeks."

"He doesn't know where she is?"

"Nick, she's hiding from him."

"Oh."

"He found out about the pregnancy. He wants to see her."

"So she'll turn to him for help," he inferred.

"And that would be a terrible idea, believe me. They're not good for each other."

"No?"

"All they do together is sit around and smoke hashish," she said. "They're too much alike in that way. They confuse reality with what they imagine."

Nick frowned. He wanted not to believe Margaux knew as much about Haley as she said, but it didn't help that she kept revealing details about her he didn't know.

"It's hard for me," he confessed. "I keep waiting for her to snap back into herself."

"That might not be much of a strategy now."

"What else can I do?"

"Nothing, by yourself." She met his eyes. "We could do something together, though."

"What?"

"An intervention. Have you thought of that?"

"What would it mean exactly?"

Margaux told him of her experience going through one with her brother. Without warning, she and her mother confronted him about his alcoholism. They gave him a plane ticket for a rehab center in Marseilles and said they'd have nothing more to do with him if he didn't go. It would be a complete rupture, and he had to choose right away. The reservation required he leave immediately, without the time even to pack his bags.

Nick, on hearing this, flatly declared that it wasn't a good idea.

"Why not?"

"Where would she go?"

"A clinic."

"What clinic?!"

"We would have to pick one," Margaux admitted.

"She's the only one who could do that."

"Maybe she should go home then."

"She doesn't want to go home."

"What if you spoke to her family about it?"

"No," he said, more emphatically still. "She'd be furious if I went behind her back like that."

Margaux turned to take in the market hubbub across the street. It was apparent now that she didn't have the ally in him she'd hoped.

“Haley’s resourceful,” he told her. “More resourceful than you think. She knows what she has to do. She’s not a child. I’m not prepared to treat her like one, anyway.”

“That’s not what I’m doing!” she cried, taking offense. “I see how much she’s changed, that’s all, how solitary and unreachable she’s become. I don’t think that’s sunk in for you yet, and it needs to, Nick. There’s no use mincing words. Haley has suffered a nervous breakdown.”

“I’m not so sure of that.”

“Nothing else explains why she insists on things that can’t be true! I hate when she does that. Every time I want to force her to stop.” She mimed this desire from where she sat, grabbing the air over the table with both hands as if it were Haley’s coat and sternly addressing her: “‘There are no supernatural powers! You’re not a woman in a horror movie!’”

The suspicion that Margaux wouldn’t appreciate how Haley *was* in a horror movie, and why nothing might be wrong with understanding oneself and the world through such cultural analogies, kept him silent.

“I’m not the only one who thinks steps might have to be taken on her behalf,” Margaux told him then.

“You’ve talked about this with others?”

“We’ve wondered what will happen after you leave, yes.”

His heart seized. That sounded like a threat.

ꭓ

Nick related the substance of this conversation to Haley later that day. He omitted Margaux’s idea of an intervention, but she was still angry. “How ridiculous,” she grumbled. “What a busybody!”

“She’s worried about you.”

“No, she’s not. She’s too self-important for that. She just senses a chance to orchestrate the situation.”

“She likes being in charge?”

“She’s a manager at heart,” Haley said. “That’s what she does for a living. She’s part of a ‘sustainability team’ at Crédit Immobilier.”

“What’s a ‘sustainability team’?”

“Something to do with human resources. She runs ‘sensitivity training’ seminars.”

"Oh."

"Really, Nick. Trust me. Don't listen to a word she says. She's mixed up. She sees no difference between personal life and the crap she peddles at work."

Nick was now remembering that other Human Resources manager, Sarah Hayes, particularly the time she'd called Molly at her parents' cottage, hoping to dig up evidence of his sexual felonies, meeting her "duty of care." The anger he felt then came flooding back, too, as visceral as ever.

"In her mind I'm an employee," Haley went on. "I resist the freedom of 'horizontally organized workplaces.' I don't 'multiply connections' and 'proliferate links in the network.'"

"She doesn't seem like your other friends."

"That's another thing: she's jealous. She wants to be included in their circles more than she is."

Nick saw how that might be. He sensed rivalry in Margaux. She was an attractive woman but in the manicured, waxed, and toned manner of someone who worked on her appearance. Haley's beauty, by contrast, was unstudied and native. You might miss her in a crowd, but she could hold her own in the most elegant settings. Perhaps Margaux resented this. It came too easy for her.

He asked about Amir, and Haley admitted that she'd been avoiding him all this time. They'd gone out for a year before she started noticing just how traditional a man he was, with very set ideas about women that were never going to work for her. As she pulled away, he grew more possessive, and finally her patience ran out. That was why she didn't tell him about the pregnancy. It was also why she had no interest in taking up with him again. Margaux had nothing to worry about there.

"She thought you might not have a choice," Nick said.

"What does she know about my choices?"

"More than I do! Why didn't you tell me about the guy?"

"I don't know," she said cagily. "You're not an easy person to confide in."

"Why?!"

"You can be a little cold, Nick."

This ran through him like a knife quietly thrust.

"I'm sorry," she said, on seeing how much it upset him. "That didn't come out right." She frowned. "Nothing does anymore, dammit. I have no idea what I'm saying. The truth is I'm afraid to confide in you, and not only because I fear you judging me. Maybe it's because I respect your judgments that I fear them. I'm afraid to reveal how much a hash I've made of things. It hasn't been easy revealing what I have."

They faced each other as usual from opposite sofas, and for the first time in a while she came to sit beside him.

"Don't listen to me," she urged, putting an arm around him. "I didn't mean it. Margaux's gotten into my head."

"It's all right."

"No, it's not. It's the kind of lazy reproach people level at me all the time. It shows just how mixed up I am."

"How are you mixed up?"

She was quiet for a moment. He could see her searching for just the right words with which to answer him. "I feel my inner life is on display," she said. "Everybody's talking about it, everybody has an opinion about it, everybody wants to get into it. Meanwhile I don't have it anymore. There's no privacy. All I hear are other voices merging into mine."

He wanted to tell her he knew the feeling, but something in her tone made him think she meant it more literally than he ever could. As he saw no easy way of broaching the topic of audible hallucination, he asked instead if she was still experiencing coincidences when she went out.

"Not all the time," she said. "I'm sure it would be all the time if I looked hard enough, but I ignore them now. I distract myself. I pretend nothing's really happening."

He could hear in this how refractory to compromise she was still going to be. She might make a compromise, but she wouldn't like it, and she wouldn't mistake conformity for resistance either. If the price of truth was sanity, then insanity it would have to be.

"What can you do to get that privacy back?" he asked a little plaintively.

She shrugged. "I'll have to give that some more thought."

7

Around this time Nick received an email from Ozouf, who was in Paris with his wife Carolyn. It asked if he wanted to meet for dinner and made a point of inviting Haley, too. At first she begged off, not knowing Ozouf as well as Nick did. But he insisted. He said it would be good for her to talk not only with Ozouf but with his wife, a psychiatrist. The invitation had an element of serendipity in it. She should go "for the sake of coincidence," he said. In the end she agreed.

They met at a restaurant off the Place de la Bastille. From the outside it looked like just another brasserie, but passing through the revolving doors they found themselves in an interior of stunning belle epoque decor, with beveled mirrors infinitely reflecting tables, benched leather seats, tulip-shaped lampadaires, and a wisteria plant blooming in a ceramic vase under a stained glass cupola. As Nick and Haley sat spontaneously gushing with praise for the place, Ozouf told them it was one of the first brasseries opened in Paris and perfectly preserved in almost every detail going back to the 1860s. It reminded him of Marcel Proust. "Swann might have taken Odette here," he said, clearly relishing the thought.

He introduced Carolyn. Neither Nick nor Haley had met her before. A self-assured American in her late fifties, she was diffident at first, politely listening to Haley answer Ozouf's questions about her life since NYU and to Ozouf as he characterized a lecture he'd delivered the day before at the Sorbonne.

It focused, in fact, on Proust's *In Search of Lost Time*, teasing from the novel's famous moments of epiphany—Marcel dipping the madeleine in the tea, hearing the *petite phrase* of Vinteuil's sonata, seeing the uneven paving stones in Venice—a critique of "truth" understood in the Platonic sense as a nostalgic return to some higher metaphysical realm. At issue in these intense synesthetic experiences, Ozouf had argued, wasn't either an ultimate reality behind appearances or a self coming into contact with its essential nature. As much as the character Marcel might read them in these ways, he said, the writer Proust understood that "appearance as such" undid the "spell of pure autonomy" Marcel was under. Proust revealed, that is, both self and world as "empty forms," without the fullness or promise hoped for in them. Rather than a difference between truth and illusion, Proust dramatized the "illusion of something outside illusions."

The lecture was an unofficial job talk. Ozouf had been encouraged to think a position might open up in the French department there, if he could convince the right people. He feared, however, that he hadn't succeeded. "I don't know yet, but I expect the worst. Sadly, I remain too much of a deconstructionist—too interested in the practice, I should say. There's no such thing as a deconstruction*ist*."

"Why would that be a problem?" Nick asked.

"Intellectual fashions have changed, I'm afraid. No one's much persuaded anymore that internal analysis of texts, paying attention to their anomalies, their marginal details, exemplifies the dissident act or cultural politics it did when I was young. What people want now isn't the linguistic mediation that Derrida trained us to see in consciousness, in the voice, in speech. They want transcendental subjects, absolute truths, and radical breaks from a status quo that bogs them down in interpretive scruple. I understand this. I'm even convinced we need a reconstruction of philosophy at present—against the sort of 'truth' I see in Proust, it may be. But I can't shake old habits either, and this makes me a conservative in some people's eyes. Or an anachronism. I'm not sure."

"What would you say is wrong with deconstruction?" Haley ventured to ask.

Carolyn cracked a smile, shifting in her chair, warming to the conversation for the first time. Ozouf paused long enough to weigh his response against the patience it was likely to test in his listeners.

"Perhaps the most serious criticism of Derrida," he began, "is that he didn't adequately account for what academics call 'canon formation.' He taught us, for example, how to read a writer like Rousseau against the grain, but he didn't tell us why we read Rousseau, in what contexts for philosophy and literature as disciplines or for the university as a whole. He always saw himself as—he was, really—something of an outsider. But without that broader account, or that effective history of reading, the method can't fully acknowledge its place in professional-managerial fields. It risks becoming another strategy in the competitive games that organize those fields."

"An orthodoxy," said Haley.

Ozouf nodded. "Expressed in the person as a practical sense or a 'feel,' reducing criticism to something more like an aesthetic contemplation. Especially when the mistrust of effective history or totalizing assertion is taken as axiomatic, critics detect a spurious disinterestedness at work."

He paused, unsure of the key in which this précis sounded. "Perhaps 'universalism' would be the better word here," he decided. "That brings out the political objection. To think, or act, in a deconstructive manner limits us to a defensive ethics based on negative liberties and human rights. The operative principle is Kantian: 'respect' for life in its indemnity from harm, or 'evil,' which this ethics allegedly shares with a neoliberal order that is hostile to the state—at least to the welfare state. In such an order, markets are the proper medium of social provision and consent. 'Respect' is enforced in a security paradigm that trumps the state's regulatory powers, turning democratic norms into tactics—when it bothers with them at all."

This mouthful took everyone a while to digest. It put Nick once more back in Auckland, under threat of prosecution for human rights violations, in virtual lockdown—"indefinite detention" might have been the more resonant phrase—for three months. He saw better now what he'd been up against there: call it a spurious universalism. It was less clear to him, however, why the school's enforcement of an antidemocratic "respect" would have been ethical in any deconstructive sense, even with the school claiming his own moral ground against him. Protecting people from "evil" might have been what Sarah Hayes thought she was doing, but it hardly followed that any actual authority was being called out or undone, "deconstructed," his own included, since *he* was the only one concerned about that in his humble opinion. He wanted to ask Ozouf what he thought of all this but realized it might mean revealing to Carolyn what he knew of his extramarital affair, and he guessed she wouldn't appreciate that. He therefore held his tongue, listening while Ozouf extended his analysis of neoliberal order a little further.

There an answer to Nick's question did slowly emerge. Ozouf was attempting to characterize with more precision the "life" for which he'd alleged power became arbitrary in that order. Its principal feature, he said, was a fear or vulnerability in people sufficiently crippling to make self-preservation an exclusive focus. This attitude not only mattered more than law, right, justice, or a politically negotiated public interest; it converted the very idea of a public interest into a lie, even a dangerous lie. "It reminds me of the rationality at work in game theory," he said, "with both the selfishness it demands of each player and the hostility it shows toward unselfish behavior. The worst thing a player in the game can do, in fact, is to act from an altruistic motive, since that ensures no one gets the limited outcomes the game guarantees. For equilibrium to happen, everyone has to adopt what the schizophrenic mathematician John Nash bluntly called the 'fuck you, buddy' principle—as apt a maxim for 'life' in a neoliberal society as one is liable to find these days, I daresay."

"So mutual fear between paranoid people becomes all there is," Haley inferred.

"With the twist that rational egoism becomes both desirable and good. We love the buddy we hate, the friend-enemy, and we need the 'evil' that, as threat, quite literally animates us. In fact it defines and individualizes us."

"It makes us fear*some*," Haley quipped.

"Also detached," Ozouf added. "It indicates a power that is justified yet unavowed, even unconscious. It can't be questioned or even attested. With it, indeed, the adversarial quality in the game practically disappears, and what remains is a sentimentalized capitalism—sustained, once again, in 'respect' of a life determined by the right to be free from harm."

"And a deconstructive ethics accords with this capitalism," Haley said, "because it 'respects' life in that Kantian sense?"

"Oh well," said Ozouf, unable to hide his disdain for the judgment he'd just invited them to make. "Let's not be *too* uncharitable! No one traced this antisocial turning of life against itself more deftly than

Derrida in my view. It's not on thematic grounds that his detractors could possibly see him as its proponent. They worry more about a schizoid affinity in the practice, suspecting somewhere in it the mad genius of a person like Nash, who sees only the threat that torments him. The common premise would be an 'evil' so radical it determines everything else, even—maybe even especially—its determination as true or present, as there in the world."

"Evil is believing that evil exists," Haley echoed, trying without much success to parse this paradox.

"Or not believing it," Ozouf said. "It works both ways, which is to say in the world no less than in our subjective perceptions of the world. Radical evil forms a horizon for all thought and action. That is why one might say of a deconstruction, when it becomes methodical at least, that it assumes power in circular fashion, finding it wherever it looks. It's also why 'greed is good' and 'terror' a foundational premise for neoliberals."

A waiter came to the table, dressed in a black-and-white uniform, and smartly topped off their wine, intuiting they were still unready to order. He pulled a tea towel off his arm and gave the table a brisk wipe on one corner, stepping away again without either a word or a caught eye.

"Isn't it funny," Carolyn interposed then, "how different French waiters are from their Americans counterparts? They multiply and exaggerate formalities to remind us of their subordinate status. It's cold, aggressive even, but a shred of dignity is retained it seems to me. In America, by contrast, we force them to be our friends, to ingratiate themselves as if we're all cozily settled in at home and no one's really working. It's aggressive, too, in its way, but not very dignified, is it?"

This drily elaborated comparison had everyone thinking about power on a much more practical level. It also made Carolyn immensely likable. She came across all at once as a canny woman who knew how to grasp the essential. She had Nick thinking again about Ozouf's infidelity, about how it had affected their relationship. Nothing in her demeanor suggested it remained an issue. They seemed completely at ease with each other. Maybe Nick caught in the corrective pressure of her remark some skepticism toward Ozouf's oddly sideways effort at self-criticism. He imagined she might not have much patience with its vaguely masochistic overtones. But he didn't get the feeling Ozouf's deconstructive style had lost its credibility for her. She could laugh along with everyone else, for instance, when Ozouf went on to mention once having seen Derrida in that very restaurant dining with François Mitterand—a principal architect of neoliberal policy in France—even though the laughter that came strangely at Ozouf's expense still signaled his control over the irony he liked to cultivate. She felt the nuance here as much as Nick did, and recognized as well a potential in it for equivocation; but she didn't dismiss it simply because of that potential either. The irony was unstable, as Ozouf had long ago put it to Nick in his office at Brown. No one was exactly in control of the meaning.

In any case conversation held through the evening on the note of candid disclosure Ozouf had first struck. Haley rose to the occasion more than anyone. As the wine flowed and they partook of the excellent Alsatian cuisine, she loosened up enough to broach her own troubles. Before long it became clear to Ozouf and Carolyn that she was telling them of a serious crisis. To their credit, they listened to her accounts of strange coincidence right where they were most "real" and without the slightest condescension. All they cared about was what those coincidences meant to her.

"What are they trying to tell you?" Ozouf asked.

"That evil is radical," she said. "That I might resemble John Nash in more than just a figurative sense."

"Do you feel rational when the coincidences present themselves to you?"

"I'm not imagining them, if that's what you mean. I'm more prone to say the hallucination is there in the world, like an open secret. All I do is see that."

"But you don't conclude that your perceptions are the same as the evil you see," Ozouf guessed. "You don't identify with the hostility it implies."

"No."

"It's not the only world no matter how much it surrounds or confines you."

"I don't know what other world there is," Haley said, "but I guess I do think there has to be another world."

"Then you're nothing like John Nash," Ozouf assured her. "By his own admission he relied too much on rationality as a means of coping with his madness. He set about fortifying himself against the world by reducing it to simplified machinelike forms that anyone could analyze and predict."

"But it still might be schizophrenia," Haley pressed. "I've read that the symptoms can appear at my age just as easily as they can in your teens."

Nick took this divulgence in with as much freshness as anyone.

"I don't see why you need the label," Carolyn said. "Unless you don't trust your perceptions as much as you say you do."

"I'm not sure I can live with that trust."

"But without it there's nothing except the evil you see."

"Carolyn," Ozouf said. "You know it's not so simple. We have to make our compromises with things as they are."

"Of course," she said, riled by her husband's faintly admonishing tone. "But things as they are can be treacherous if we cede too much ground—particularly in this area of medicalized human behavior. Have the courage of your convictions, Haley. You aren't schizophrenic, the world is. And the evidence lies in the word itself, which is a perfect instance of the rationality Pierre-Yves was just speaking about."

"How so?"

"'Schizophrenia' doesn't explain anything," Carolyn said. "It's just a shorthand for symptoms that have no clear causes. To use it any other way is to give up on understanding the human mind. It's to acquiesce in that idea of life as an abstract competitive game, played by robots."

"Think of it this way," Ozouf added helpfully. "The diagnosis of schizophrenia entails another reduction in complexity to simplified machinelike forms. Context is excluded as causes are ignored in the checklists psychiatrists use to ascertain symptoms—"

"Often inputting the data on a computer for the diagnosis," Carolyn said.

"They then project that reduced complexity back into the world as, say, 'natural algorithms,' confirming the idea of people as machines without depth, isolated and anomic. The consensus that forms around this idea is then as 'natural' as those algorithms. It discloses itself not as a belief but as the spontaneous truth of one's being."

"Or it would," said Carolyn, "from the moment you understand yourself as a schizophrenic."

"I'd stop being able to see the madness *of* that consensus," Haley said.

"It would become the very measure of success in the treatment."

"Right."

Silence settled over the table. Nick felt Haley trying to fix the difference between resisting schizophrenia and the schizophrenia she was supposed to resist. It might have been harder to do than Carolyn imagined. In a world of mutual fear, or radical evil, where schizophrenia became general, as present in the diagnosis as in the thing diagnosed, an "open secret" of everyday life, resistance went well beyond simply trusting in one's convictions. It required resources Carolyn and Ozouf had that both of them lacked: careers, affiliations, affective family life, habits and dispositions cemented in success and recognized by others. Without such advantages serving as shields, if nothing else, against the power of that consensus to pathologize or hystericize, Carolyn's exhortations might sound a little hollow.

Ozouf, sensing a change of mood in Nick, took the opportunity to ask how he was faring after his father's death.

"I haven't had time to think about it," Nick said. "There's been so much else going on."

"You must feel at sea. Or 'in the blue,' as Henry James might have put it."

Nick smiled. "I don't know where I stand anyway. I have no context—unless you count that game life becomes for everyone in a neoliberal society."

"Where the excluded context is the context."

"Maybe I should say I'm finally touching ground," Nick said. "I'm finally growing up."

Ozouf gave this remark the consideration he thought it deserved by ignoring it altogether. "One thing you could do, it seems to me, is ground yourself," he said. "Give yourself a context."

"How?"

"Get involved in a research project. Write an essay or a book. Something focused, or for that matter more comprehensive, more holistic, that answers to why you feel so ungrounded."

"I'm not sure I have any answers."

"That's okay. It could be a starting point—the difficulty in being a subject of your own experiences and actions, in directing your own life."

The prospect held little appeal for Nick. That difficulty overwhelmed him more than anything. "All I seem up to these days," he said, hoping it didn't sound too much like an excuse, "is a rather desperate triage of facts, circumstances, episodes."

"I suspect you see more of a plot there than that."

"Then let's say I wouldn't know how to write it and still make a living."

Nick feared this was too abrupt. It did force a shift in Ozouf's thinking. "I take it you've given up on academia."

"I can't go on believing a career is still possible, no. I have to figure out what else to do, and it isn't clear how a research project would help with that."

Ozouf took this in with a sober expression, registering the dilemma where it touched on the kind of research they both preferred, one that not only required time and scholarship but mistrusted the whole idea of unitary subjects directing their own lives. In this regard deconstruction, with its stress on ambivalence, uncertainty, and paradox, really did court a kind of madness—all the more reason, to Nick's mind, why there had to be some structure on which to rely, some framework of identity (a job, say) in which its aporias could be lived out. There may be no such thing as a deconstruction*ist* on always shifting grounds, but neither was there a waiter with the head of a philosopher—except in the imagination of those who took the necessary advantages for granted. Their waiter, in his ongoing ministrations of the table, may well have wanted them to understand this. To Nick, anyway, it seemed his formal demeanor edged closer to contempt as the night progressed.

"I've grown confused myself lately," Ozouf admitted, "in my own work. I wonder if I haven't become too lax in my orthodoxies, too willing to mix up the way an academic sees the world with the way everyone sees. I do tend to turn historically contingent experience into formal puzzles."

"An aesthetic contemplation?"

"More or less."

"Are Derrida's critics right then?"

Ozouf let his frustration with the question show. "He wasn't prone to mystify social differences in the name of some innate refinement, if that's what we take the objection to be," he said. "Nothing unified his corpus from beginning to end more than a mistrust of intuition. But that didn't have to mean he played no part in mystifying social differences. The last thing he felt should be true of anyone, he said often enough, was a good conscience. The question is whether it's sufficient to know this, or to assert it as an ethical position in an academic field, or anywhere for that matter. Perhaps it's not. Perhaps it only leads to specialized language games played by insiders, by members of a club."

"I don't think that's true."

Now Ozouf smiled. "Well, perhaps it's fairer to say Derrida's concern with a necessary complicity, a necessary betrayal of one's autonomy—a necessary *hetero*nomy—strands us in a melancholic fatalism that is what his more careful critics see him offering. I'm not sure I have more to offer these days, I confess."

"I guess we have to cut the knot and take a stand anyway, like you were saying in New York."

"Indeed," Ozouf concurred. "If only the ground for taking that stand wasn't so treacherous."

"Or the stigma so personal?"

"Yes."

A raised brow warned Nick off topics he was right to suspect it would be awkward to bring up. Both men grew quiet, and in the interlude they became aware of Carolyn and Haley deep in their own conversation. Haley, all her inhibitions gone, was relating the ordeal of her miscarriage. Carolyn, sensing the problem was more serious than she even thought, offered practical advice, in particular about a place called the La Borde clinic.

"If you think you need professional help," she said, "it might be worth trying. It operates on principles of 'antipsychiatry' articulated by Jean Oury and, later, Félix Guattari. I believe it's close to Paris." She turned to her husband. "Isn't that so, Pierre-Yves?"

"In the Loire Valley, not far from Tours."

"There's no institution quite so progressive anywhere," Carolyn told her. "I admire it very much. You can be sure they won't push any normalizing agenda or treatment."

"That would mean drugs, wouldn't it?"

"A diagnosis of schizophrenia would entail invasive psychotropic medication."

"I don't want that."

Carolyn gave Haley's forearm a squeeze. "I'm glad to hear it."

8

Haley did some research on the La Borde clinic. What she found seemed promising. It did, indeed, push no agenda, offering, in the words of its mission statement, only a "shelter" and "sanctuary" for people who were for whatever reason no longer able to cope with their lives. Patients had considerable leeway over how to proceed with a rehabilitation program. They could work with or even without doctors if that proved the better approach. The only condition was hands on participation; patients were free to move about and manage their own time, but they had to engage in the actual administration of the clinic, carrying out various menial as well as medical tasks.

More intriguingly still, Haley said, it encouraged reading, discussion, and imaginative expression. The latter included theatrical productions—one of the most recent was Racine's *Athalie*. There would be no stigmatizing of thought, no demand to accept cognitivist dogmas or reduce desire to the level of simple biological need. The therapeutic emphasis wasn't on adjustment, happiness, fulfillment, or even comfort so much as the meaning of human suffering.

Nick still had to be persuaded. He wanted her to resist thinking of herself as crazy. He wanted that resistance to be enough of a resource to rely on in this world and still remain one's own master. But he couldn't much say why anyone should credit either wish in him, given his record. All it seemed he could do was hope for Haley the life of value and conviction he had not managed to find or make for himself, and that suggested, more than just hypocrisy, something abstract in the respect he gave others in that hope. He wouldn't call it mean, or cold; the function of abstraction for him was more self-protective than anything. But it may have kept him from seeing just how "in the blue" Haley was.

Slowly, then, he came around to the idea of her going to La Borde. What she needed, she told him, was, in short, relief from

Ozouf's neoliberal society. She could no longer be the neutral, controlled, self-monitoring paranoiac it demanded. No account she gave of herself made a difference either. It didn't matter whether her aversions were sound or unsound, whether her perceptions were true or mere private alterations of reality. The limits of her tolerance had been reached. She'd long felt them, suppressing tendencies to panic and obsession, but somehow she'd always been able to manage. Now she wasn't sure. That neoliberal society closed in on her like the walls of a maze, and the effort to come out again often took more energy than she had in her.

"Could you reach a point where you can't come out again?" Nick asked.

"I'll put it this way: there are times when I've had to spend the night."

"In panic and obsession?"

"In the maze," she said cryptically. "I wander in the dark, lost, cold, afraid of minotaurs and goblin kings."

He rolled his eyes. "Come on, Haley. Say what you mean!"

She looked steadfastly at him, wondering if he really wanted that. She decided nonetheless to be direct. "I can't filter anything. Sensations all come at once. I can't even filter my own thoughts. There's no cohesion. My mind is shot."

"I don't see that."

"It shows when I write. Then it's clear I can't give anything a logical structure. Words and metaphors just accumulate. My 'screenplay' is nothing but a mass of notes."

"That's writer's block," he assured her. "It's not a rational assessment of your abilities or your state of mind. You've probably never been more lucid than you are right now. It seems that way to me from our conversations."

"I suppose it wouldn't be so bad," she said, "if I could function normally."

"You can."

"No, Nick." Again she fixed him in her gaze. "I don't have the strength anymore. Nothing refreshes. I wake up tired. I can't face people. I can't keep up my image in their eyes. I can't be what they want me to be."

This last sentence visibly jarred him.

"What's wrong?" she asked.

"Nothing." He didn't want to tell her that his father had said almost the same thing to him, the last time they spoke.

ᚷ

Haley had years before taken steps to secure French citizenship, which ensured her full access to the national health system. This meant the cost of the clinic, if she did go, would be minimal. What she needed for admission was a referral, and she managed to procure that a few days later from a sympathetic doctor. Unfortunately, she then learned that she'd have to add her name to a list and wait an unspecified length of time, perhaps as long as six months. Since this jeopardized the whole plan, she appealed to Carolyn and Ozouf, who made some inquiries on her behalf. It turned out they knew one of the clinic's psychiatrists, who promised to see what could be done for her. Not long after a space opened up, and she was told she could come in a week's time. Before that, though, she was advised to visit and get a feel for the place. They offered prospective patients one night's room and board for this purpose.

Nick offered to accompany her. Julie was still with her mother in Tours, and they could take her up on the invitation to visit. Or he could drop Haley off and meet her again when she was through. But Haley preferred to go alone. It was a private decision, she told him, and it required as much presence of mind as she could muster. Him being there would only make that harder. She wouldn't even let him go with her to the train station when the day of the visit came. Nick assured her he understood, but it hurt his feelings nonetheless. She seemed to include him in the neoliberal society she no longer knew how to handle.

It didn't help that Margaux came over that same afternoon. A space had been found for some of Haley's things in her mother's apartment building, and they had agreed on a time to make the transfer. He gathered the boxes on the sidewalk ahead of her arrival so they could be loaded quickly into her car. Once that was done, the two of them drove to the eighth arrondissement, where her mother lived.

As they went, Nick noticed Margaux looking especially attractive. She wore a dress rather shorter and tighter than usual, along with shoes perceptibly higher in the heel. Her brown hair fell in layers around her shoulders. Nick remarked on the change, and she explained with a smile that she'd just come from work.

"You know, what most of us have to do during the day," she added, with a touch of sarcasm.

Her mother lived near the Place de Clichy on a street lined with more gray stone and mansard-roofed apartments. Nick followed Margaux through an entranceway to an inner courtyard, carrying the first box of books. There he met her mother, who spoke with a Polish accent. As they chatted, he realized the woman lived in the building as its concierge, not as a proper resident.

Margaux was very much aware of this discovery as he made it. He could feel her gauging the changes it wrought in his attitude toward her. And he had to say, sheepishly, that it changed a lot. The neighborhood had an overt bourgeois character, and Nick had come assuming for Margaux a background of similar affluence. But this fact, which he knew said a lot about class differences in French society, forced a revision. It threw an unexpected wrench into the disdain he felt with the other discovery of Margaux's resemblance to Sarah Hayes.

Unhappily, the storage space for the books lay up six flights of stairs, in one of the *chambres de bonnes* on the top floor. Nick had to lug each box up a cramped side stairwell. Midway between floors, the feeble light on its timer would switch off, and he had to put the box down to search for the button that would turn it on again. In those moments he felt trapped in a musty past—in those days of the city's modernization under Haussmann, when the building had most likely been constructed. He imagined the cars on the street outside were carriages. The men wore frock coats and top hats, the women voluminous crinolines. They were flaneurs and *courtisanes*, sensing the world come unglued in Manet's discrepancies or Pissarro's random brushstrokes. They tried to catch around corners and down alleys, with Baudelaire, the "memory of the present."

The sense of déjà vu was almost too penetrating. Nick wasn't only back in the past; the past was also present. What was he, after all, if not a latter day flaneur, wandering this city, as he had many cities the world over now, without ever settling in any of them? It seemed his lot to be perpetually displaced, in transit, adrift frankly, and if he were honest he'd have to say this aleatory condition wasn't altogether foisted on him. He wouldn't exactly say he'd chosen it; but he'd preferred it over what else was on offer. The terms of belonging had just never seemed that good. They required accommodations that were always more than he could make, even when he tried. In this, he supposed, he had a new way of understanding the odd oblivion of character that had kept him so often surprised by the mean spirit of the world. There may have been something of the flaneur's same conceit behind that, too.

When he emerged from the stairwell for the last time, exhausted and sweaty in the courtyard, Margaux had a glass of water ready. It was rare for him to need something as much as he did that right then. Margaux stood guessing this as he drank.

"You've done a man's job," she drily observed.

"It was more than I'd bargained for!"

They went into the office adjoining her mother's modest living quarters to say goodbye and headed back to Margaux's car, where she asked if he wanted to stop at her place for a glass of wine. It happened to be on the way back to Belleville. She spiced up the offer with dinner on her balcony, which sported a partial view of the Buttes-Chaumont Park. She caught the rising tide of his sympathy here. He could see it was hard for her to reveal her past as she'd done. He hated that he came across as someone whose social opinion she would have to worry about. He wanted to put her at ease on this score.

"I'd love to," he said.

She lived, it turned out, off the rue Petit, which Nick remembered as the place where Haley had witnessed the child hit by a car; in fact, they made the same jag by the corner where it must have happened, and he saw the blue placard set into the *pierre de taille* with the word *meaux* altered to *maux*. Haley must have been staying with Margaux when it happened. He almost mentioned this, but then thought better of it. She might not have found the alliterations amusing.

She warmed up leftover food—a chicken cordon bleu and lentil soup—to serve on the balcony. It was enclosed by a stone balustrade and nicely extended the space in her top-floor studio flat when the weather was mild and the glass doors could be left open. They sat at a table as night fell and the light from inside intensified to a warm glow. Over rooftops Nick could just make out the Corinthian-style belvedere on the top of a rocky crag in the Buttes-Chaumont.

"What an inviting spot," he said. "I feel lucky."

"Good." She poured him a glass of wine. "You've been through a lot yourself recently, I understand."

"Yes."

Margaux had lost her father, too, when she was fifteen. As they spoke of that, Nick felt how long it was since he'd been able to feel so easy with a woman. The last time he remembered was really with Bojena in LA. Both had a talent for the little companionable rituals that made for greater ease and lightness of spirit between people, no matter how much trouble there might be in the background. He missed the will for that in his life now.

Not that Margaux reminded him of Bojena in any other respect—beyond the fact that both were Polish. She had no developed interest in literature or art. Indeed, Nick had the impression she disliked those who did, or at least those who quoted from literature and art as though everyone understood what they meant, or should. Her associations with this habit were colored by her immigrant experience. Nick could feel it in the segues she made from her family life—she'd grown up in one or another ground-floor *logement* like the one where her mother lived—to the sense of superiority she'd encountered in people who were more secure in their right of belonging. Although she'd lived in France all her life, she criticized the culture as if she hadn't. The French were too intellectual. "They live so much in their heads," she said, "that, when it comes time for the heart, the food is cold."

Nick sensed in this a dig at Haley, who might not have been French but courted the same vices. The talk of supernatural events taking place around her was only a case in point. For Margaux it savored of pretensions she didn't much respect. When combined with a tacit desire for the prestige one measured in accumulated cultural capital, it pointed to an ambition that Margaux saw not only isolating Haley but leading to something like class prejudice. As the conversation shifted to Haley, Nick began to see—through a filter, to be sure, of concern for her friend—that Margaux considered her a snob.

That confused him as he sat enjoying the balcony, the food, the wine, the unexpected reprieve. On one level he could agree that too much introspection separated people from the trust and consolation that came with those companionable rituals. It broke indispensable social bonds, perhaps even generated the sort of comparison that led to social hierarchy, no matter how critically minded one happened to be. Perhaps what it meant for Nick to let go of the academic career, or any career, was to stop trying to be critically minded, to allow himself the comfort of ceasing to be a snob. The effort only hurt him now, after all: it widened a division between the head and the heart that was becoming more than he could bear.

On another level, though, he didn't much like how Margaux made sense of things. She defined herself against elitism but in the grain of a neoliberal society, where combining head and heart could have other applications of the kind Sarah Hayes would understand all too well. He felt this bias in her as he defended Haley, trying to make Margaux see the roots of her crisis in the pressures of femininity rather than in thwarted ambitions for status. He told her of Haley's film friends pushing her to sleep with a producer and the connection she made to the prostitution going on in the faubourg Saint-Denis.

Margaux dismissed Haley's response. "She's a bit of a prude, if you ask me. Prostitution is stupid and degrading, but it's a necessary evil all the same."

"Why do you say that?"

"It's a price we pay for other liberties," she said with a touch of annoyance at the question. "The only condition should be that the transactions are private and regulated, without pimps or brothels."

"For Haley those transactions stand for all relationships. They suggest a kind of generalized prostitution."

"Why is that such a surprise?!" Margaux cried. "What planet has she been living on?!" She shook her head in frank exasperation. "Haley can be so naive sometimes."

"Don't you think it's difficult having to cope all the time with a highly sexualized exchange?"

"Not so difficult you can't cope with it like an adult. It's not the end of the world. Chances for intimacy still exist between people.

I'd even argue there are more and better chances now than ever because relationships are transactional."

"Would you have slept with that producer?" he asked, bristling at that word "adult." Behind the standard it evoked lay the true naivete in his opinion.

"Probably not," she replied. "But it's a personal choice. I wouldn't judge someone else if she did. We're naturally networking creatures, Nick."

"That sounds a little cynical."

"Not at all! It proves how much better off women are now. Look at me. I make my own money. I have a career. I decide who I see or don't see, and I have the right not to worry about discrimination, harassment, or rape. Ask my mother what it's like to have none of that going for you."

"You're pretty sure of yourself there," he observed. "Is your life really so good and so free?"

"I'm saying the market works for women more now than at any time in history. Not only that: it takes its cues from women. It honors and integrates the communicative skills of the private sphere. I see it in my job every day. To succeed, you have to be empathetic, open, obliging, interpersonal."

"But the bottom line remains the same!" he cried. "We still have to be entrepreneurial selves."

"So?"

He saw the question form behind her eyes of just how adult he was, and in the spirit of a dare. He would've dismissed this as another sign of her conventionality, if he hadn't also caught himself out in his own at the same time. As they finished eating and sat facing each other at one corner of the table, he noticed her, still in the dress she wore to work, lean forward in a manner that showed her rather plunging neckline to advantage. He also stole occasional glances at her crossed legs, smooth and tanned, propped up on those heels and exposed through a part—the dress was buttoned down the front. He wondered about the shapes of her hips in the tightly hugging fabric. She saw this effect she had on him, too. Its hint of hypocrisy amused her.

"I'm not arguing prostitution isn't here to stay," he said more gingerly now, "or even that it isn't necessary in some sense. What do

I know?! But it bothers me that, in your picture, women no longer have a way to see what's wrong with their own objectification. Freedom of choice, made into an alibi for self-interest, turns the pursuit of self-interest into the only freedom there is."

"That's convoluted!"

"Well, exactly, because when it's the case, everything collapses into its opposite. There's no difference between sexual objects and social subjects."

"When aren't we both?"

"Never, I suppose. But accepting this condition as fabulous is no less a pretense because of that. One feels it every time self-presentation becomes the same putting out, the same feminine masquerade."

She heard, in this last remark, that he considered the game they were now playing no less of a game because she aroused him. The idea that he was deceiving himself, and diminishing himself as a man, if he failed to take typical libidinal urges as natural made no sense. They might be his urges without being natural or even defining him all that well. To think otherwise was only to rationalize the sexual violence that was, as Haley rightly sensed, structural in the world. This tacit stand left Margaux reflective enough to concede that she might have been too cavalier in her attitude.

"I do temporize when intimacy turns into negotiation," she said. "At heart I'm more comfortable if these things are separated. Nonetheless, it seems men and women alike have to keep up certain appearances, for the sake of that separation. Sex requires a bit of theater, don't you think?"

A smile creased her lips. The gleam in her eyes perceptibly brightened. She was flirting with him.

"It does," was all he could say.

"We have to be good actors, if we want to bring out something true."

He reached for a cigarette from his pack on the table. "You have me there," he said, lighting it. "I've spent most of my life angry at good actors. Maybe it's made me too bent on demystifying illusions."

"That can be cruel, too, can't it?"

"It can."

His regard for Margaux grew at this point. She managed to touch in him on a contradiction he'd never quite felt the same way before. It turned, in a word, on the question of sexual difference. Was it biological or socially constructed, absolute or relative, fixed or contingent? Usually he fell out on the latter side of such debates, asserting as ethical a tolerance toward identit*ies* that were compound, complex, and volatile; but when the occasion demanded, he did insist, privately at least, on arresting that volatility, that infinite divisibility, in some bedrock truth. Without it, everything dissolved, even tolerance, leaving a permissiveness that blent with the arbitrary power he wanted to demystify, to strike at in his father, in the world where he'd been so successful.

This contradiction was familiar to him. But Margaux had disconcerted him on another front, because she didn't mean by that word "theater" exactly this permissiveness; she meant a performance from the bedrock truth, and across the gap, *chacun à sa place*, of a fixed sexual difference. He could have said in response that she only confused a contingent with a natural fact, a relative with an absolute truth, but how really did he know that? From what ground could he know it, if not that of a truth he would have to concede was more than relative for him? Was Margaux right to find this ground in a theater that took its cues from conventions that were more necessary than he had thought? Maybe eroticism happened no other way than through the sort of flattery Margaux offered, putting out for him so that he could feel, if not more of a man in the contrast, then at least more sexually at risk as a man. Maybe missing this other stake in feminine masquerade had been the reason some women in his life had mistrusted his wariness of objectification, his sensitivity to sexual aggression, even his sympathy for the challenges they had coping with these vices in men.

Margaux surprised him once more by acknowledging her frustrations with that masquerade. It turned out her life wasn't working as well as she'd like, for all its advantages, not least where the chances for lasting relationships were concerned. The men she met—mostly at work—were either terrified or robots, and the reason in both cases seemed to be the standard everyone was expected to meet for the "sensitivity" in which she was charged to instruct them as a member of her sustainability team. Enforcing that standard could feel at times like a bad joke—never more, she told him, than when, recently, a man had filed a "hostile environment" complaint against her, simply for behavior that she would've thought perfectly innocent anywhere else. After that she had to admit the blend of calculation and emotion in the networking she liked to extol relied too much on euphemism to work. It didn't provide a stage on which a robust sexual theater could take place.

This sounded both true and ethical to Nick. There was even something incandescent about her because of it, something singularly capable of illumination. The wine they were drinking might have colored his admiration here, but he didn't consider it altogether unwarranted, particularly when amplified by the gratitude he felt for her feminine corroboration of that mean spirit at King's University. It had him hoping there might be other kinds of exorcism in his future, other kinds of settlement with conventions that, as hollow as they might feel in private and public life alike, still allowed for some measure of dignity. All he'd have to do was stop fighting against himself, yield to the flattery, and go with impulses that were fast becoming irresistible anyway, like leaning in to kiss Margaux, or running his hand up her thigh and under that dress, or taking her to the bed behind them to show her just how much of a man he could be. Perhaps love was simple after all. *Tellement simple.*

She didn't end up giving him the chance to find out. In what came as a disappointment, she cut the evening short by announcing she had to work again in the morning and he'd have to take the metro home. She gathered up plates and took them to the kitchen, and before Nick knew it they were standing by the bed saying their goodbyes. He felt foolish in the sudden contraction of his desires to this polite but firm rebuff, even as he figured it was for the best. The wine had gone too much to his head for him to remember that he still didn't like Margaux all that much. She knew it as well as he did. She even liked him better for having forgotten it as much as he had. It proved he could let loose.

"You and Haley are so serious."

"Things have been pretty intense."

"It's not fair to you."

"No?"

"I don't think she treats you well," she said, brushing past him to open the door. "You deserve better."

As she turned they looked rather more deeply into each other's eyes. "Thanks, Margaux," he said, wondering if he might be welcome back at some future point.

"My pleasure, Nick."

She reached up to kiss him on either cheek, with one hand on his shoulder for balance. He took in her heady scent, thinking a last wistful time of missed opportunities, and stepped into the hallway. She watched him retreat as far as a newel post by the stairwell and pushed the door gently shut, leaving him to the silence and the solitude. As he started his descent, he found another reason to be sad: what awaited him now was his first night sleeping alone in his dead father's home, a fate he'd so far managed to avoid. He couldn't imagine a more cheerless end to so arousing a night.

He entertained the idea of staying away, holing up in a bar or just vagabonding through the city as he'd often done in his student days. He could go down to the Seine and visit places he hadn't seen in a while, like the Pont des Arts or the crooked streets, squares, and *hotels particuliers* toward the Place des Vosges. Maybe the Café de l'Industrie would be open late.

He was interrupted in these deliberations when he reached the vestibule and opened the front door for a man just about to buzz an apartment. The man murmured his thanks and strode past him. But he hesitated an instant on catching an American accent in Nick's "*je vous en prie*," resisting an impulse to look back. The curiosity was mutual. The man was tall, handsome, with arresting sea-green eyes that were unusual for someone of North African origin. It took Nick a moment as he exited the building to begin putting this fact together with others, but he soon found himself in the grip of a strange suspicion: the man was Haley's Tunisian boyfriend, and, for whatever reason, he was headed to see Margaux. Standing dumbly on the rue Petit afterward, he didn't know whether to laugh or cry at the thought.

X

He decided against staying away, remembering the last time he'd given in to an insecurity similar to the one this discovery—if that's what it was—stirred in him. It turned out to be the right choice. Haley came back the next morning utterly distraught. She had trouble arranging for him her scattered impressions of the clinic, but he gathered that, while it had lived up to expectations well enough, it was still a hospital. The significance of having herself committed there had come rushing in on her.

"Everyone's crazy!" she cried as if that were a surprise. "People wander around in a daze, they mutter into corners, they strike at the air. I talked to one man who told me his name was Blaise Pascal. He kept calling me a 'thinking reed.'"

Nick held back what he believed, again that she shouldn't give any ground to the diagnosis of insanity. Workable compromises were still possible. She had only to understand the world's insanity without giving up on some minimal freedom to respond, to choose how it would affect her. Nothing could take that at least away from a person.

"I'd have to be one of them!" she said, her eyes now brimming with tears.

They sat together on the sofa that faced into the living room, fear getting the better of her enough to let him draw close and hold her. They hadn't been this tender with each other since he arrived there. Perhaps they'd never been.

"All I could think was 'I'm not here, this isn't real, I'm somewhere else,'" she said with her cheek resting on his shoulder. "I kept repeating that to myself, over and over."

At this she gave herself up to a grief Nick sensed ran back in her a lifetime. "I'm not here," she sobbed, and the note of pure bewilderment in her voice brought tears to his eyes, too. "I'm not here, I'm not here, I'm not here. . ."

9

Haley did some serious soul-searching over the next several days, under a pressure made worse when Nick learned by email of Dylan's imminent return to New York from Korea, where his teaching contract hadn't been renewed. He'd need his apartment again by the end of the month, and Nick would have to make another arrangement. Haley would shortly have nowhere to stay in Paris, making yet starker her other choice, to return home to Atlanta.

In the end she decided on the clinic. No one said she had to stick it out if it didn't provide the help she needed, and, indeed, little indicated that it wouldn't. The high caliber of the doctors she met was indisputable. She liked one in particular, a woman who offered psychoanalytic treatment in a Lacanian vein.

This time she wanted Nick to accompany her, and on the appointed morning they made their way to the Gare d'Austerlitz. On the train she sat for the most part in silence beside him, looking blankly out the window as Paris gave way to countryside. The gorgeous summer day wasn't enough to relax her. Nick could tell by a slight tremble in the hand she laid lightly on her thigh. He thought to comfort her but could tell she didn't want to be touched. He let occasional bumps of the shoulder as the train carriage swayed over the rails be connection enough.

They disembarked at a station in Blois, near Orléans, more than an hour before their ride to La Borde. They had espressos at a sidewalk café and walked through the town center to a terraced rose garden. From there they could see the Loire River, so still its waters perfectly reflected the light-fringed clouds in the sky.

Back at the station they boarded a van that took them out of town along a country road. Not long after they saw the clinic, situated in a parklike setting. The chateau was unexceptional by comparison with its illustrious brethren in the region, simple in style, with limestone cladding, glazed pitched roofs, and two modest turrets. The atmosphere on the grounds was informal. People of all ages were sitting and talking on a central lawn. Their soft voices mingled with frequent bursts of birdsong. No one seemed all that conspicuously crazy. When they met, on the way to an outlying administrative building, a silver-haired man Haley greeted as a doctor, Nick wouldn't have picked him out from others he presumed to be patients. No one was wearing a uniform.

He waited outside while a secretary checked Haley in. An orderly then took them to a dormitory. The room she'd been assigned was small, with a single bed and a desk, and no bathroom or kitchenette. It did have a casement window that opened onto trees and let in a nice dappled light. Haley said she was lucky to get it.

"It means they don't think I'm psychotic. Otherwise, I'd have to share a room."

They left without her unpacking and went to the chateau proper, where most of the social activity and therapy took place. There again, the patients didn't seem at all out of the ordinary to Nick: like any cross section of people one might observe waiting on the platform of a metro station. The sole exception was an old man with a scar down the side of his face. Sitting alone on a bench in the main hall, with his hand propped on a spread knee and his elbow defiantly pointed up, he looked angry enough to explode. Of course, he wouldn't have been out of place on that metro platform either.

They explored the grounds, passing what was once a carriage barn and entering a chapel that had been converted into a library. People were seated at the tables. Some of them appeared to be involved in their own projects, surrounded by open books and tapping away on laptop computers. It seemed to Nick a good place to work on a screenplay, a novel, or even just an essay on the difficulty of directing one's own life.

On returning to the chateau they found that a crowd had gathered near the entrance for some sort of art performance. An eerie atonal music spread across the lawn. Everyone's attention was on an Asian man, dressed in ragged clothes and a peaked hat. He stood in the doorway and seemed to be making his way at a snail's pace down the four limestone stairs. At first it was hard to tell if it was a performance at all, as people stood on either side watching without much respect accorded the man's presence. A woman holding a clipboard even appeared behind him at one point and called out to someone standing on the road that intervened between the chateau and the lawn, as if the man wasn't there. But he didn't let it bother him. He just concentrated on those stairs.

As the man at last gained the road, Nick realized what he was up to. He'd seen it before: the Butoh style of dance that his friend Carson practiced. He recognized the effort to make separate parts of the body move at the same time but in different registers or frequencies, as if the nervous system had been scrambled, signals crossed, and motor control over the body lost. Nick recalled the frustration he felt, back in LA, at the lack of conceptual clarity in Carson's performance. He didn't have the same feeling now. There was a sharp point to how the dancer was expressing the style. He meant to show just how unbearable the demands of self-care could be in the sort of administered world the building itself represented. For that reason the claim on Nick's attention was more compelling, and more unsettling, too.

Indeed, as the man inched forward across the road, striving for an impossible balance, Nick took the drama very much to heart despite its air of anticlimax. Or maybe because of it. In fact the hint of banality now seemed central to the intention—a sign of the social indifference that formed a medium in which everyone had to make their way whether they liked it or not.

Haley, noticing the effect the performance had on him, slipped her arm through his. Her sympathy made him still more emotional. He tried to push back through the shock that had for so long been tensing his character, looking for its sources. Nothing much came to mind, though. All he could recall for some reason was the remark from Stendhal that he'd quoted to his students in that aborted seminar at King's University, on the disorientation his friend Salviati's beloved Léonore made him feel: whenever he gave her his arm, the friend said, he "had to think how to walk."

That might have been an epigraph for the performance itself, only, of course, there was no lover. The dancer was alone in his disorientation. This became all too plain as he began to founder, lose momentum by the grassy verge of the road and fall to the ground. He went into a kind of seizure then—his eyes fixed on a void, his lips curled, his bared teeth opened on a silent mummified scream. At the conclusion of the performance, when he rolled up into a ball and stopped moving altogether, it seemed like an animal had crept there to die.

They went to sit at a bench on one edge of the lawn, talking over cigarettes about the performance, its revelation of a body bearing up, or not, in that medium of social indifference, until it was time for Nick to depart for the Blois station. Because of the performance, and because they were about to say goodbye, both felt a deeper ice break between them. They spoke more plainly about their feelings, their fears, their personal failings. It was evident how much they'd been circling around these things for a while now, unable to find the right register of trust, hiding in language. Life had made them both too defensive, too barricaded in private pain. Again like the man in the performance, they'd lost a lot of the attunement they once had in themselves and with others.

Sadly, the van appeared in front of the chateau before they could get very far in this new acknowledgement. Just when it seemed they were ready, it was too late. They'd have to miss each other as they had in that other circling sense, or as it seemed people often went missing in the usual run of time. And this failure might have more serious consequences now. The changes in front of them were more drastic than the past could quite stretch to accommodate. It may even be that they needed that past to break apart, to have less of a hold over them. As they headed across the lawn to meet the van, both wrestled with a suspicion that they wouldn't be as close as they had been.

"When will I see you again?" she asked as they came to a halt.

His flight to New York fell on the day after next.

"It might be a while," he said. "I'll have to earn the money for another plane ticket."

"I can still call, right? Your number will stay the same?"

"Absolutely."

She cast an apprehensive eye back over the lawn. "I have no idea what I'm doing, Nick."

"Yes, you do. I can't imagine a more considered choice."

"Everything feels so foreign."

"It won't always."

"I suppose that's how it should be, though," she said, upon reflection. "There should be the weight of a fear I can't escape."

"People are going to help. You can trust in that."

She nodded, drew a firm breath, and turned to face him again. She seemed a little cheered. "Thanks, Nick. For everything. You've been a good friend. I haven't said enough how much I appreciate that."

"You don't have to."

"I want to," she said. "You give a lot of yourself, and you don't expect something in return. You allow for room. You let me be myself."

"That's all I've ever wanted, Haley. Maybe I haven't always made it very clear, but it's true."

"Maybe I'm so used to conditions I can't tell when it's clear."

The driver started the engine.

"I think it's time to change that."

"Yes."

They embraced, communicating some part of that hold, that bond, felt between them.

He climbed into the van and slid the side door shut. As it took off he watched her recede in the rear window, growing smaller and more indistinct against the bulk of the chateau. He hoped that wasn't the same as it swallowing her up. Now that he was leaving, he admitted to something creepy about the place. No matter how organic it might feel, no matter how warm the people or sociable the philosophy, it was still an institution.

That might have been just what was needed, of course. This caught him short. Nothing would really be confronted in this world if not its structures, its invisible architectures, and how else did one do that except by grappling with them directly and from the inside? Maybe his discomfort was only a reluctance to engage, to concede a dependence on social institutions that he'd been running from for too long, like Proust's narrator in Ozouf's construction—or one of those flaneurs—under a "spell of pure autonomy." Maybe he should turn around and have himself admitted, too.

☧

As he had also arranged to spend a night with Julie and her family, he continued on from Blois to Tours. She met him at the train station and afterward treated him to a glass of Vouvray at a busy pedestrian plaza in the center of the city. Cafés and restaurants spilled out from the *rez-de-chaussées* of tall half-timbered houses. People sat at open-air tables in pleasant anticipation of a temperate evening. Nick felt revived in its atmosphere and grateful for Julie's company.

Her mother, Jeanne, lived down a narrow cobblestone street lined with contiguous three-story homes. The one Nick entered a while later had the same cut stone façade and tall shuttered windows as the others. Emmanuele greeted him in the foyer with a big hug, and a moment later he shook hands with a man in his sixties, Bernard, Jeanne's husband, who led him off to the guest room, up one floor and at the back. It was large and airy, with a private terrace that overlooked a walled garden.

He met Jeanne as they sat down for dinner. Julie had insinuated over that glass of Vouvray that she could be difficult, so Nick was surprised to find as personable a woman as he did. She spoke with a firmness that suggested authority, but she didn't much care if others saw it or not. Her standing in the world wasn't at issue in ways it might have been for her daughter, and that, he supposed, made her intimidating. Tall and thin, she also hinted in her bearing at an elegance that might have once mattered enough to demand it of others. In this she differed from Julie, who was unpretentious, if anything, to a fault.

The dinner progressed through its ritual courses—soup, entrée, salad, cheese at the end. Nick asked about Jeanne's work as an archeologist, which he surmised, from the numerous art books he saw around the house, had a connection to art history. The books, it turned out, belonged mostly to Bernard, who was a retired lawyer, but he was right. Her research focused, in Paleolithic culture but also, more broadly, on the impulse to represent, to convert the world into likenesses, pictures, Weltanschauungen. This allowed for an impressive range of associated interests. She spoke as effortlessly about thirty-thousand-year-old Venus figurines as about Jackson

Pollock's all-over line painting, and always with the confidence of serious thought behind her. It also explained the books Julie had at the apartment in Paris. Nick could see she'd grown up with her mother's interests—not always comfortably perhaps, but with an obvious respect.

Bernard excused himself first from the table, keen to catch a tennis match on television. Jeanne started to tell Nick about her current research project on Paleolithic art, but Emmanuele, having on him designs of her own, soon scuttled this brief. She led him into the living room and produced a stack of children's books for him to read to her. They sat in the corner of a sofa, as far as possible from the easy chair where Bernard had settled, and Nick began his recital over the sounds of tennis. Several times Emmanuele took it upon herself to correct his accent.

At length Julie, who'd been tidying up in the kitchen, took Emmanuele off his hands and to bed, leaving Nick by himself in the room, as Bernard had by then fallen asleep in his chair. Jeanne came to the rescue a few minutes later, gesturing for him to come with her. They went upstairs to an office dominated by two large computer monitors. She needed them for her work. It involved precise archeometric analysis of objects taken from various sites and digs.

She guessed he might be interested in the images. They included cave paintings drawn in black lines and glowing yellow ochre, bronze, and umber. They depicted animals in various postures: charging bison, blurred herds of gazelles, a lioness with raised lips and bared teeth—ready, Jeanne said with a dry humor, to mate. She noted how the uneven rock surfaces were exploited to suggest volume.

"Motion, too," Nick added. "A friend once told me torchlight was a reason for them working in caves."

"The proto-cinematic effect can be striking, yes."

Her focus, however, was not on motion so much as transformation. She showed him images of sculpted objects that blended human and animal characteristics: a tiger standing upright, carved out of a mammoth tusk, a clay wolf with bulging biceps and clasped hands. In such examples, a deeper figurative axis could be inferred as fluidity or malleability, the merging and crossing of boundaries that were spatial as well as corporeal. They ran not only between elements of the world but also between the world and something else.

She then showed him the object of her current research. In the inmost chamber of the Chauvet Cave in the Ardèche, she said, there was a hanging outcrop, or what she called a pendant, on which the lower portion of a female body had been drawn. To one side the line of her thigh petered out into the haunch of a lioness, which peered serenely toward two other feline creatures a short distance off. On the woman's other flank, a man with a bison's head seemed to be engulfing her with his body.

"It's a minotaur," Jeanne told him, pointing to the way the woman's other leg doubled as his. "The man embraces the sex of the woman, and together they designate an original bisexuality. At least that's my hypothesis."

Julie had entered the room by this point, Emmanuele put down for the night. She sat on one edge of the table, listening to her mother explain how the three figures had been drawn hundreds of years apart. This made the overall impression of hermaphroditism an oddly collaborative affair of Paleolithic man.

"So you don't see a fixed sexual difference there?" Nick ventured to ask. "More a relative simultaneity or overlapping?"

"Not if you mean by that some sort of androgynous fusion," Jeanne said. "I don't have much use for the mysticism of source goddesses and eternal oneness. If there is an innate bisexual disposition, it indicates a division, a gap, and a struggle. The idea is to account for how we move from it to become men and women, through the crucibles of language and culture. It's not to refrain from becoming men and women, to hold back in some fantasy of plenitude or self-possession, as if that was our nature."

"Sex isn't 'always already' gender then?" he asked, dusting off an old mantra from his graduate student days.

"Not if you understand gender merely as discursive form," she said, adjusting instantly to the new scope he gave the topic. "Sexual difference is a biological zero degree for whatever we are or might want to be. Without it social construction makes no social sense. Nothing is made from nothing, after all."

"But you don't prefer, in saying that, one identity or sexual order as more natural than another?"

"Not at all. Sex deflates the fantasy. It reveals the bad faith in believing our freedom means we don't have to give anything up, run any risk, or suffer any distortion of character on the way to becoming ourselves. Sooner or later we have to take responsibility for our drives."

Nick had the impression from a smirk on Julie's face that these remarks were directed at her and formed part of a larger conversation between them. But he took the implied criticism to heart as well. He did feel now as if he was standing on the edge of a social and sexual identity grown too costly to own. This had much to do with the attractions of the life in which he now found himself an envious visitor, but experience had made him hesitant, too.

He wondered, though, if Jeanne saw a difference between holding back and being held back on that way to becoming ourselves. He still couldn't accept there was *no* difference, even if he understood that it hardly mattered from a practical point of view. Constraints became inhibitions, and that's how one had to deal with them. Nevertheless, the fantasy was "real," its empty, or imaginary, freedom a requirement of participation in a world that turned the ethical criteria upside down. One had to adopt the habits of belief and deferral that Jeanne so disliked not just to get along with people but to survive among them at all, and not least as a sexual being. Why, then, if having an identity in this world was already to equivocate about that biological zero degree, was it equivocal not to *be* in the mandated fashion? Just what did it mean, when sex, rather than deflating the fantasy, *was* the fantasy in need of deflation, to "take responsibility" for one's drives?

Curious to know what both women might have to say about this, he nonetheless couldn't see how to bring it up without seeming too personal, like he was prying into that other conversation. So he said nothing and ended up taking the questions with him upstairs to his room. Not feeling tired, he sat on the terrace for a long time into the night, gazing out over the interior garden to more slate roofs and brick chimneys, smoking cigarettes and getting nowhere on his own except deeper into the muddle of his feelings about autonomy and compromise, alienation and resistance, men and women.

Ϫ

The next morning he went down to find Julie alone in the kitchen. The others had gone out. As they sat for coffee at the table, sunlight streaming through windows, Nick sensed they'd been left together deliberately. He presumed it had to do with his father's will, and indeed Julie soon pushed an envelope across the table with a check for the money left to him, including the $5,000. She insisted he have it. He argued with her, but sadly he was in straits too dire for much resolve. He would need it when he returned to New York.

With that settled, a lull in the conversation had Nick wondering about other unfinished business. Julie asked about his future plans and listened as half-heartedly as he laid them out. Then she cast around for other topics, conspicuous in their neutrality. Small talk wasn't coming easily to her. He helped by declaring how much he liked Jeanne. This brought that smirk back to her face.

"I take it she can be critical," he inferred.

Julie weighed her answer. "She's been a perfectly supportive mother, even when she hasn't agreed with my choices. She's taken very seriously the obligation to help a child become her own person. But that hasn't always meant being popular or even sympathetic. She tells me what she thinks, whether I want to hear it or not."

He asked how long Bernard had been in the picture.

"They married about ten years ago, after she moved here from Paris."

"He's never been a father to you then."

"No," she laughed. "My father's still very much alive. I rarely see him."

"Why not?"

The question posed fresh difficulties for her. "My father is something of a rogue. As I understand it, he's on the run from the authorities of several African countries, where he has a habit of cheating locals in business deals. I don't even know where he lives at the moment. Every so often I receive an email."

"You never mentioned him before."

"He's not someone I like to talk about. He's an awful man. He treated my mother abominably. As far as she's concerned, he doesn't exist."

"I see."

"Bernard couldn't be more different. He's very decent."

There was another uncomfortable silence. It stretched too long for either to ignore.

"I'm sorry," she said.

"Is there a problem?"

"No. I did, though, want to bring up something that's, well, delicate. My mother doesn't think I should. She says it's none of your business. But I feel you have a right to know that I haven't been entirely truthful with you."

"No?"

"Before Evan died, I told him I wanted a divorce."

"Ah."

"It wasn't an idle threat," she said, determined to be truthful now. "I'd talked to Bernard about it, and I'd made plans to send Emmanuele here, while the legal process worked itself out. Evan understood I was going to leave him."

Nick saw by her choking up where this was heading. He reached across the table and squeezed her hand. "It *is* none of my business."

"His death wasn't an accident," she said. "He killed himself."

"It doesn't matter."

"He wanted to punish me."

"You're not to blame."

She broke down, revealing the turmoil into which Evan had thrown her. Nick came to her side, putting an arm around her tense, muscular shoulders.

"I couldn't bear it anymore. He'd become impossible to live with. Aside from the distraction and the forgetfulness, he was so unpredictable, so petty and cruel, even to Emmanuele. I can't begin to tell you–"

"You don't have to. I know how difficult he could be."

"I told myself it was the disease that made him that way. I just needed to be more understanding. It was my fault if I overreacted. I wasn't trying hard enough. But in the end it all started to sound like words an abused woman would say to herself."

"You did nothing wrong."

"I was trapped in my own idea of care." This thought, uttered more to herself than anything, had her recovering some composure. "That's the worst part. It wasn't his fault. He never pretended to be someone he wasn't. I walked into his life with open eyes. I set the trap for myself."

"You couldn't have anticipated how hard it would get."

"It doesn't matter. From the start I presented myself as his caretaker. I made myself into his servant."

"You *were* his caretaker," Nick reminded her. "Besides, you know as well as I do how easily Evan made other people into servants."

The truth of that couldn't be denied. She went back over her life in the new light it cast. "He didn't respect me for it either," she said presently. "Even less as the Parkinson's got worse. In a sense he pushed me away."

"He made it impossible to stay."

"Yes."

"Then you have no reason to reproach yourself. He set his own trap."

This calmed her down still more. Both grew pensive, fitting themselves into Evan's trap, feeling it work into their sympathies and their scruples, too. If it hurt Evan to make the price of intimacy the loss of his respect, if his fear trapped him in an isolation that pushed him over that rail, the price in those he hurt could only be a certain coolness of spirit.

"A part of me hates him," she confessed.

"Me, too."

"But I also hate myself for hating him. It makes me feel so heartless."

"I think we both have to hate him more honestly."

She met his eye. "That's what my mother said."

"Then she's right again."

"But she doesn't say how love survives that."

"Maybe only by surviving it?"

"Was it never love then?" she asked, taking up the thread of another question he could see had been bothering her: why she'd been drawn to Evan in the first place.

"Of course not. I didn't mean to suggest so much. I don't really know what I mean." He paused. "I haven't had much luck with love, I'll say that. I might not be making very good choices, but there doesn't seem to be a lot of room for error either. Sometimes I wonder if there are good choices."

"What's left then?" she said, sounding a little desperate. "Heartlessness? Resignation? Are we just supposed to accept that love is nothing but narcissism and self-deception?"

In this he caught the tone of her mother. "Unless we take responsibility for our drives?"

She laughed. "She's not clear about how do we do that either!"

"I suspect we just do it," he said. "We start from where we're at or when we can't do otherwise, and go from there."

"There's no program."

"No."

As she considered whether she, or anyone, could ever be ready for that, a wan smile played into her face. "Well," she said with a shrug. "*Nous voici enfin.*"

⅄

The others soon returned, and they all went for brunch at a nearby restaurant. Later, Julie and he took Emmanuele for a bicycle ride through fields and vineyards outside of town. They arrived back just before dinner, which Nick regretted having to miss for the train to Paris. As he said his goodbyes, he wished he'd planned for a longer stay. In fact, he wished he could just stay.

He also didn't relish returning alone to the apartment in Paris. With Haley gone, no one stood between him and a reckoning with himself that events had long been helping him to postpone. Clearly it meant a confrontation with that ghost of his father. Its tomb was the upstairs closet where Julie had left his last remaining things. She had mentioned they included some photographs from Nick's childhood. He thought he might look through them, but when he arrived that night, he changed his mind. There seemed nothing more than sadness to be gained from it.

He went to the balcony and stood by the wrought-iron rail, thinking it might be another way to that reckoning. He picked out the scent of some night-blooming flower in the air, maybe from the black masses of trees that loomed over the roofs opposite. Then he looked down the sheer face of the building to the sidewalk below and imagined his father falling. He wondered about his state of mind in those last moments before he went over the edge, what he might have been thinking or whether he was thinking anything at all. It seemed reasonable to suppose that suicide proceeded no other way than in a trance, in a state of final disintegration and fear. It might not have been all that distant from his mood now, he thought. The comparison stretched only so far, of course, but he, too, was at the end of his tether. There was no way around it. Life had overmastered him. The next step could only be into some kind of abyss.

Right then the light for the adjacent balcony snapped on. The door opened, and François emerged holding a book in his hand.

"Excuse me!" he said. "I didn't know—"

"It's all right."

"I couldn't sleep."

"I was just going back inside."

In the owlish look François' round glasses gave him, Nick could see the pretense in what he'd just said. The man knew he was out there. It worried him. He feared Nick was about to do something rash. His solicitude had Nick wishing he'd made more of an effort to befriend him. Haley's antipathy, coupled with the claims his father had made of his metempsychotic trespasses, had put him on guard. They'd hardly spoken the whole time he'd been there.

"What are you reading?" he asked.

François held the book into the light. "*La nuit des prolétaires*," he said, drawing out the last rhotic consonant for effect. "By Jacques Rancière."

"Philosophy?"

"Well, yes and no. It's more a history of work in the nineteenth-century—especially the 1830s and '40s." He paused to make sure Nick's silence meant interest. "There's a theory behind it, about the nature of resistance and the right way for the intellectual to approach the realities of exploitation. But what drew me most were the similarities it alleges between that era and our own."

"Like what?"

"Precarity, in short," François said. "People in those days were temporary workers, dealing with decentralized forms of subcontracting, flexible specialization, the illusory value of qualifications and skills. Rancière focuses a lot on divided time, on dead seasons with no employment, on blurred lines between work and leisure. Nowadays we talk about the labor market collapsing and the 'pressure to innovate,' but it comes to the same thing. Not exactly the same," he added with a smile. "We have computers, emails, and apps. Work is 'immaterial' and 'affective.' But still. . ."

"Maybe I should read it. I'll need all the help I can get. I have to find a job when I return to New York."

"You're leaving?"

"Tomorrow morning."

"So soon?" François let his disappointment show. "It seems you've only just arrived."

"I'm sorry we haven't had more time to talk."

François heard in this a tacit admission that the distance hadn't been accidental. "It's all right," he said with a self-deprecating wave. "I can be a bother if I'm not checked."

"You haven't been a bother."

"You haven't let me!" he said jovially. "But I understand. I'm used to it. Your father was the same. He avoided me as a rule. He didn't like me much."

"No?"

"I think he saw me as a fan. I was a fan. He was such a good actor. I saw all his films. He brought out something true."

"What, do you think?"

He reflected for a moment. "A kind of inner turmoil," he decided. "An outrage at having to be the person you are, and no other. I sensed, in his roles anyway, that he knew that more honestly than most people. He made you feel how class is in the body."

"The body?"

"As habits, dispositions, relative degrees of confidence, savoir faire. It seemed to me that your father had a feeling for the way history lives in us, or through us."

"I hadn't thought of him that way before," Nick said, guessing François was more generous in his assessment than his father deserved. "In fact I'd always thought the opposite: that he blocked class consciousness, or distorted it in the social presence he had for other people. That's made it difficult for me, as his son, to know where I stand in any definite class structure."

"You float in spectacle society."

"Rather stupidly, I'm afraid," Nick said, struck by the precise weight François gave that phrase: it meant social relations mediated by images. "But one reason for the difficulty, oddly enough, was that my father didn't come from any particular advantage. He was born on a farm in the Midwest, and at some level he never stopped being that person. It was part of his appeal, but also part of the way he obscured class consciousness."

François nodded. "I did wonder if I was right in my hunches—or wrong in my projections! It puzzled me, how little interest he showed in his own art. I could tell by how curt he grew, when I did manage to corner him in a conversation, that I was violating some kind of taboo in analyzing it as I did."

Nick offered no reply. They both knew the real reason for his father's rudeness, beyond any other explanation, even illness. Some people simply weren't people to Evan. What they thought or felt didn't matter. They were beneath contempt. This attitude might not have been entirely his fault; it was a structural feature of fame itself and, as such, difficult to avoid no matter who you were or where you started. But it also came from deep layers of his father's personality. He *was* famous, through and through. He took to it. He had a talent for it. He was hard and pitiless like an icon.

They spoke around this cruelty in his father a while longer, unable quite to lay bare the wound it suggested for both of them, but touching on its edges enough to assure each other of sympathy. Nick may not have known where he stood as Evan's son, but Evan had always made it clear where he ranked as a man. Hierarchy mattered to his father even if it went for the most part unspoken. François understood how this might be the case, even as a fan. That taboo formed the limit of a popular culture that functioned to block possibilities of collective life and solidarity.

Later Nick tried to push past the hard, total object his father was to him, hoping to find on some hither side a man of flesh and blood he could properly mourn. That man was there, in specific indices of breath, mood, memory, but not, Nick had to say, affection. He wouldn't miss him as he did his mother. His father had for too long fought him to that affection, and not just by standing in the way but by permeating it, by coloring it with his dismissive attitudes and judgments. Nick would never be able to forgive him for that. It might be better if he didn't. The need now was to break that hard, total object in him. Better to let it plunge over the rail, along with the love it made so difficult.

He wasn't sure he could hate quite that honestly. The break would never be clean. He saw no way it could be, when the sense of inadequacy, with its demand to be something other or better, wasn't just a personal problem—when it was more or less exactly as impersonal as his father's presence in François's mind. That sense of inadequacy would therefore continue no matter how well Nick understood it. Indeed, the more he understood it, the more refined he suspected its demand would grow, the more fastidiously it would press in the recesses of his heart, on the most intimate impulses and desires, reminding him of life's zero-sum games. But that he saw this calculus as well as he did also seemed a good sign. It meant, at least, that he might resist in the right places. He might sort out what he could help from what he couldn't, firmer in the knowledge that a change would come only with another world than the one in which he had to plot his course now. He sensed a kind of change already in the thought. *There had to be another world.* If it brought no increase of hope or solace to put it in the imperative mood like this, it did at least offer a direction nothing else had. What it required of him was a commitment.

Coda

He found an apartment in Washington Heights. The corner brownstone was in disrepair, but the third-story flat was relatively cheap and roomier than anything he'd seen downtown. It had light from two sides and one window looked over a cherry tree.

The immediate neighborhood had no particular character. Except for his block, all the buildings were tenements or warehouses, some of them derelict. No one sat on stoops wiling away the summer nights in aimless talk. No kids played ball in the streets or bought ices from vendors, as he used to do. His chief pleasure would be taking walks on nearby Riverside Drive.

Dylan returned just before he could move in, and they overlapped in Hell's Kitchen for a night. Over drinks at a bar on Ninth Avenue, Nick heard a mouthful about the university in Korea, which had proven a nightmare. The atmosphere in Dylan's department was paranoid, power was arbitrary, and guilt by association was the rule. At one point a female professor had insisted Dylan's female teaching assistant—a graduate student—give her copies of all their email correspondence, for no reason except personal suspicion of their relationship; after the teaching assistant refused, everyone on the faculty turned on her, sabotaging her academic career.

Nick listened without surprise, resigned to a social logic that was all too apparent now. His only question was whether King's University took the disregard for people's rights from places like Korea or vice versa. He came no closer to an answer when Dylan went on to describe a "leadership training" seminar that he was forced to attend. It involved, unbelievably, both teachers and students. It took place in a hotel where he and his colleagues had to share rooms for a night. Everyone drank themselves just shy of a coma, he said, and events included not only games that had students sitting on their teachers' laps or even tied to their hips with rope but dancing and strip poker as well. Nothing would've been more natural than to move into the hotel rooms for wild sex, except that even a hint of this happening would have been enough to get you fired. The aim seemed to be to test the self-control of everyone involved, to see if the will could survive temptation even at the furthest limits of its destruction.

It became clear to Dylan that he would never survive in so perverse an environment. He left even before his contract expired. They'd stopped paying him by then anyway. They claimed he hadn't been in Korea much of the time and so hadn't earned it, even though he'd been showing up to work every day. They still owed him a month's salary.

"Relief doesn't begin to describe how I feel," Dylan said, fiddling nervously with a napkin on the bar, still in a state of shock Nick could tell. "When I left it was exactly like Walter Neff in *Double Indemnity*, after he killed the husband: I couldn't hear my own footsteps on the sidewalk."

The analogy didn't seem entirely apt. "You didn't kill anybody, Dylan."

"It's still the 'walk of a dead man!'" he cried, citing what else Walter Neff had to say about it. "I'm in the same position I was when I left. Nothing's changed. As backward and alien as Pusan fucking South Korea might be, it's only a variation of here. That's why I was there! It's all one horrible global hallucination."

Nick wished he had more to offer than his own variations on this theme. It suggested an almost transcendental homelessness to him, extended without limit and so deep into the soul that there was nothing outside it. His whole life seemed little more now than a gradual revelation of this dispiriting fact. Limbo was a human condition.

ϗ

He began to look for a job, quickly discovering just how difficult it was going to be. He called the contacts Haley had given him at technical writing companies, and they told him to forget about a full-time position. Firms were downsizing and the numbers of qualified people in search of even occasional work was distressingly high. He went to an employment agency and heard the same things said about copy writing, marketing, and public relations. In addition, he had the disadvantages of scant experience, few computer skills, and gaps in his employment record suggesting an inconsistent work ethic. It would be impossible for him to gain a foothold in these fields even at the entry level, since there his age was all but a disqualification.

The employment agency did think he could work as a grant writer for museums and nonprofit research organizations or as an editorial assistant at publishing companies. He went on a few interviews. The jobs interested him even though they paid absurdly low salaries—half what he was making at King's University. They were meant for young people just out of college: the reason, he guessed, why he didn't end up getting them.

He applied as well to be a proofreader in law firms, although they hardly paid much better and the work didn't interest him at all. It did spark the idea of going to law school. He had no idea how he would pay for it, unless he took on gargantuan debts that would weigh him down, in all likelihood, forever. But it made sense if the alternative was to correct the grammar of lawyers for hardly more than minimum wage.

Dylan offered to introduce him to the English department chair at City Tech, confident he could pick up classes there. The prospect of teaching part-time composition, however, held zero appeal, and Nick declined even knowing he could at least earn a little money while he looked for something else. He would've thought he'd regret this decision once he started temping, typically at midtown banks where he took orders from underwriters, managers, and traders, but even their casual indignities weren't enough to overcome his revulsion to the academic profession.

He did apply to be a French teacher at a private high school on the Upper East Side, and they found him sufficiently attractive to grant an interview. He'd be teaching language but also literature classes to bright students headed for Ivy League schools. But the competition was fierce because, as his interviewers were frank enough to tell him, it consisted entirely of native French speakers. He wouldn't hold his breath. And besides, there, too, the salary was close to half what he'd made in Auckland.

Gelacio tried to help him out in the academic publishing world. But while his recommendation seemed to matter with the people

Nick met, no jobs were forthcoming there either, at least in the short term. Gelacio also pointed him in the direction of bookstores like The Strand, where he used to be a buyer, as a stopgap measure. They *did* pay minimum wage.

Feeling desperate, he started going into restaurants and asking for work as a waiter, something he'd done before in his graduate student days. Even there too many people vied for the few available jobs and, especially at high-end establishments, he'd have to know someone before he got a break. He did start picking up occasional shifts at a small French restaurant in a cellar not far from Columbia University, with vague promises that it would become regular over time.

He thought of driving a taxi. He even applied, took the test for a hack license, and got hired at Yellow Cab. But they could only offer him a night shift to start, and that conflicted with the restaurant. He might have made the sacrifice if the average annual income of the New York cabbie wasn't around $25,000. He put it off for the time being. It remained an option if he needed it.

⅄

Shortly upon arriving in New York he received an email from Molly, announcing her enrollment that fall at NYU. It came as a surprise. They'd been in intermittent contact over the previous months, and though the tone between them was warm, neither said much about what was going on in the background. He understood by her silence on the subject that she'd decided against coming. He was glad to be wrong.

She'd arranged to live her first year in the Stuyvesant Town residence hall for graduate students off East Fourteenth Street, and she wanted to see him once she got there a few weeks later. He took this to mean she preferred he not pick her up at the airport or help her settle in to her new digs. Sean would be on hand for that, he imagined, as she lived quite close by. They'd be neighbors in the East Village.

Molly called Nick a day or so after her return. All she could talk about was the heat, bad even for August and a complete shock to her. Although Auckland could get pretty muggy in the summer, she had no point of reference whatsoever for nights that stayed as hot as days or a heat as trapped by broiling brick, concrete, and steel as she experienced it now.

He told her to get a cab and meet him at an outdoor café he knew by the Hudson River, under the West End Highway. A couple of hours later she found him, just before sunset, seated at a table on the edge of a crowded terrace, shaded by one of a gaggle of umbrellas and in view, across the promenade, of a pedestrian pier. He had a beer waiting for her, and to her immense relief there was a breeze coming off the glassy expanse of the river. The flush in her face subsided as she took a long draught, her gray eyes shining over the rim of her plastic cup. Nick noticed her copper red hair perceptibly more metallic from the application of some dye, and she seemed leaner through the arms and torso than he remembered her. The rose tattoo was unusually livid against the skin. Sweaty in her white T-shirt, she'd never looked more beautiful to him.

He couldn't say how he looked to her: sweaty in his T-shirt, and also leaner through the body after those abstinent months in Paris, but hardly full of vitality. That was not surprising after weeks spent scrounging for a livelihood. He wondered how anyone could possibly open up in the midst of so much false effusion, pushiness, and monotony. He might conclude no one could, if Molly didn't present a reason to think there were compensations on the other end. They depended, of course, on whether or not commitment to "another world" meant giving up altogether on love as one of the lures offered in this world, drawing him back into double binds of castration and fantasy.

He kept this worry to himself conspicuously enough for Molly to say he seemed "subdued." He tried to explain it in terms of what happened in Paris. She listened to the details of Haley's breakdown with a somber interest. The effect was to modulate their conversation into more sympathetic registers, on which connections could be made that recalled them not just to the intimacy they'd once shared but to a more general crisis of intimacy he could tell she'd been thinking about on many of the same levels he had—not least where it was a question of love itself, of its possibility in this world. Her reflective mood cheered him because it implied she might forgive his reserve. He'd be able to broach with her his uncertain feelings as a man, even as a lover, without them necessarily disqualifying him as both.

New York still felt hostile to her. She wouldn't have come back if not for Sean, who persuaded her that she needed to confront her fear at its source. Nick guessed Sean over-pushed the postfeminist line, segueing from the notion that no power should act on you to the belief that no power does act on you and life was a walk in the park. But that didn't make confronting fear less of a need for Molly.

"I think she's right," he said. "You can help each other to do it."

"Mm-hmm." She watched people moving fitfully past on the promenade, various thoughts on the subject, or the prospect, churning behind her eyes.

Presently she said, "Do you know what one of those guys told me that night we were sitting in Sean's apartment? I haven't been able to get it out of my mind. He was talking about his experience as a soldier, in the Middle East somewhere, and he confessed that he'd killed people, some innocent civilians. When I asked him how he could do that, he didn't say it was easy or hard. He didn't say it was wrong or right. He said it was 'necessary' so that 'girls like me' could enjoy the freedom we have here."

Nick groaned.

"I reckon he'd already put the drug in our drinks by then."

He placed his hands over his face and closed his eyes. In the darkness he saw the negation to which "freedom" had been reduced for that man. When he opened his eyes again, he also understood it was still there, in the commotion around them. That negation was present, or actualized, positive, in the world as in the will. It was a kind of global hallucination.

"I don't suppose it helps to tell you the guy's full of shit," he said. "He's just repeating cynical justifications given for him to hide his stupidity from himself."

"No," Molly smiled, "that does help."

"He isn't saying anything at all, even if that's what he's saying, or showing: that life for him is nothing but brute compulsion, dumb drive without desire."

She sensed in this remark, once again, the "purist" side of Nick she mistrusted, but with a better appreciation, he suspected, for what he sought to repel and what might be violated. At stake was just as much her resistance as his rationalism. Or, put another way, at stake was the assumption of a difference between them, and so her "purist" preference for sitting alone in dark rooms with the TV on. She had to wrestle now with the possibility, not only that she might be just as controlled as Nick in the fierceness with which she sealed herself off from her surroundings, but that true decision required a sacrifice she had always instinctively rejected. She didn't want to be responsible, to be "adult," if it meant having to feel guilty all the time.

"Is it bad to live without shame?" she asked, grasping the essential problem.

He answered slowly. "It depends on what you mean by 'without shame.' If it means not caring, maybe so. Then it would only be going along with things as they are, in that unsublimated drive, in that empty freedom—in a kind of hatred, finally. But I see no reason why it can't also mean the opposite: care without that hatred when it's turned around upon the self, when it's *self*-hatred. In that case it might be the only good there is."

She seemed unconvinced, and he knew why. He lacked credibility when it came to saying whether the latter kind of care was possible or not. He'd been hating himself for too long. To be convincing, that care had to be demonstrated more than rehearsed. It had to be a way of living more than a hope or an attitude. That's what she wanted from him. Indeed, she seemed to be telegraphing now that anything was possible between them if he could just cast off his shame. Did he have the wherewithal for that? Could he? Could anyone in this unforgiving age?

The sun had slipped behind the red sandstone cliffs of West New York in the meantime, and they'd finished their beers. Nick glanced over the crowded terrace at the long line of people that had formed by the bar where he'd purchased them. At that moment he recalled an idea he'd had on the way over for something they might do together. He decided to act on it.

"What do you say we get going?"

"Okay."

"We can find a place to eat later," he said, rising. "But I want to show you something first."

"What?"

"Just something. It's a surprise. We should leave now though."

"Why now?"

"Because what I want to show you is in Central Park, and we don't want to be in there too long after dark."

They vacated the table and walked up the embankment behind them to Riverside Drive, skirting the ghastly Trump apartment towers on the curve into Seventy-Second Street, which they followed into the city.

"How far is the park?" she asked.

"Not far."

"Is it some kind of monument?"

"No."

"A fountain?"

"No."

"A statue?"

"No."

"What else could it be?!"

"You'll see," he said, moving on.

She halted. "Fucking hell," she shouted at his departing back. "You're so irritating!"

They passed down long crosstown blocks punctuated by the canopied entrances of midsize apartment buildings. Approaching Central Park West, they saw the porte cochère of the Dakota, where, Nick thought with a jolt, the movie *Rosemary's Baby* had long ago been filmed.

They entered the park at dusk. Molly hesitated when Nick turned down an especially solitary and unlit path. "I don't know, Nick."

"It's all right."

"It's dark in there."

"I know where I'm going."

"That doesn't make it less dark."

"Come on," he urged, holding out his hand. "Trust me."

She looked steadily at that hand where it floated in the space between them, only with reluctance deciding to take it. They continued on. Soon another road appeared and, on its far side, an open expanse, the Sheep Meadow, backed by the midtown skyline. Molly relaxed on seeing people pack up their picnics and head slowly for the exits. No one seemed to feel in any danger.

"So where's this 'thing'?" she less charily asked as they struck out over the lawn, breathing in the earthy fragrance.

"Right here."

"Here?"

"All around us."

She craned her neck both left and right.

"And you're not going to tell me what it is?"

"You have to discover it for yourself."

"Like 'I spy.'"

"Sort of."

"Do I know what it is?"

"I'm not sure," he said. "Maybe."

"Can you see it?"

"I've been seeing it since we entered the park."

She let go of his hand and drifted off, intrigued now. He stayed quiet until they came to the edge of the meadow.

"It's easier in the trees," he advised her. "Look hard enough in the darkest places, and you'll find it."

She stopped before the eaves and peered under the canopy. The moment was still and calm. The only sound, aside from the hum of traffic on the Sixty-Fifth Street traverse, was a hubbub of cicadas all around them.

"This is ridiculous," she complained. "I don't see anything."

"Nothing at all?"

"Nothing."

"But all that is you see," he told her.

She frowned, not sure she liked his cryptic remark. But she kept her eyes on those darkest places until it dawned on her that winks of light weren't floaters in her mind or traces of her more subliminal thoughts. They were actually there.

"Whoa!" she said, stepping all the way under the canopy, where more bioluminescent pulses streaked the air.

"Fireflies."

"Yeah."

"They don't exist in New Zealand?"

"They do," she said. "They're not that common though. I've only ever seen them in these caves outside Auckland."

"They're everywhere here in summertime."

"I can't believe I haven't noticed them until now."

"They're easy to miss."

He came to her side. The interior fairly teemed with them. They almost forced you to shy away.

"They're marvelous, Nick."

"I used to collect them in jars when I was a kid," he told her, hearing as he did the ringtone from his phone alert him to a text message. "I'd come to the park with my father right around this time, and we'd catch them in a net. It was one of the few things I remember doing with him that he didn't fuck up in some way."

He glanced at the text—from Gelacio, with information about a reading group he'd been hoping Nick would join. Molly, meanwhile, reached out a hand, perturbing the candescent lines and arcs. They seemed, indeed, part of a supernatural fabric, revolving fitfully in another order of implication and exchange. Nick found himself combining them with the voices, words, and signs of the electronic communication that was happening still more invisibly around them. People really did live in a convergence of nature and dream, fact and fiction, chance and pattern. From magic to reason, man had come full circle, in data streaming from satellites to smartphones, back to cunning sprites and sorcerers' spells.

He wouldn't go so far as to say there'd been no such thing as "progress" in the meantime. As illusory as it might be, he suspected it was still the kind of illusion that manifested itself somewhere on the side of truth. It warranted a certain skepticism, for instance, about the modern faith in endless expansion and the ideal of domination driving it. Of course, this didn't make "progress" less of a bad metaphysics either. Reason *was* magic, or myth, reducing the unknown to settled formulas, uncertainty to abstraction, freedom to the strange necessity of a deadened and soulless consensus. Even the self-transcendence that, to Nick's mind, provided that skepticism with its best dynamic seemed little more at this point than the strategy of a personal survival, centered on the will to hallucinate one's satisfactions, to be deprived of something real. People only had to look honestly at their aversions to understand this. Truth was visceral, if it was anything at all.

Molly expressed a desire for dinner at a Szechuan restaurant she knew in the East Village. As they headed for the bottom of the park to catch the subway, he tried to convey something of these intuitions, sensing they didn't have the same force for her that they did for him. She listened with the impatience people feel hearing someone belabor the obvious. From this he could tell she was going to be all right in her new life. Things would come easily to her as long as she trusted herself. That might not be easy, but he guessed unsuspected capacities would emerge even on this front. The only question now was how he would fit in the struggle to take her self-awareness seriously. Neither had the answer, but again he felt, in the pleasure they took in each other's company, that the door was open for him to try. He had only to risk an intimacy that would never be pure but might just be true.

About the Author

STEFAN MATTESSICH has written three novels: *Point Guard*, a coming-of-age story set on the Northern California coast of Mendocino; *East Brother,* a satire about gentrification in a fictional California beach town; and most recently *The Riverbed*, about intelligent young people coming to learn about the darker sides of the suburban dream they call home. He went to Yale College and has a PhD in literature from the University of California, Santa Cruz, where he wrote a monograph on the fiction of Thomas Pynchon entitled *Lines of Flight*, published by Duke University Press. He has also written a wide variety of literary criticism and cultural theory. He teaches English at Santa Monica College and lives in Los Angeles.

www.ingramcontent.com/pod-product-compliance
Lightning Source LLC
Chambersburg PA
CBHW020248030826
48979CB00030B/2658/J

* 9 7 9 8 9 8 6 2 1 0 4 6 9 *